P9-CEA-746

PRAIRIE HILLS

SUSAN MAY WARREN
PAIGE WINSHIP DOOLY
LINDA FORD

BARBOUR
PUBLISHING

Treasure in the Hills © 2007 by Paige Winship Dooly
The Dreams of Hannah Williams © 2007 by Linda Ford
Letters from the Enemy © 2004 by Susan May Warren

ISBN 978-1-60260-409-4

All rights reserved. No part of this publication may be reproduced or transmitted in any form or by any means without written permission of the publisher.

All scripture quotations are taken from the King James Version of the Bible.

This book is a work of fiction. Names, characters, places, and incidents are either products of the author's imagination or used fictitiously. Any similarity to actual people, organizations, and/or events is purely coincidental.

Cover model photography: Jim Celuch, Celuch Creative Imaging

Published by Barbour Publishing, Inc., P.O. Box 719, Uhrichsville, Ohio 44683, www.barbourbooks.com

Our mission is to publish and distribute inspirational products offering exceptional value and biblical encouragement to the masses.

 Member of the
Evangelical Christian
Publishers Association

Printed in the United States of America.

TREASURE IN THE HILLS

by Paige Winship Dooley

Dedication

To my family: You are all so precious to me! Thank you for the support and the blessings and joy you've brought into my life. I love you all and am so proud of each of you. Thanks also to my husband, Troy, my mother, Sharon, and my good friend Rhonda for your critiques of this story.

Chapter 1

Deadwood, Dakota Territory, 1876

Babe's incessant chatter would be enough to send old Ben Parson into an early grave. The dignified man seemed to enjoy the entertainment, but he probably needed a break. His white hair stood on end where he'd run wet hands through it a few too many times, but his crinkle lines of laughter were at full depth as he listened to Babe talk. He did appear to enjoy the little girl's stories.

Emma Delaney sat back on her heels and watched as her five-year-old daughter took a quick breath before resuming her continuous speech. Too far away to hear what the tiny blond spoke of, Emma knew it would have something to do with her imaginary life and pretend friends. Babe lived in a fantasy world almost as much as she lived in reality. Emma decided now might be a good time to back off on the fairy tales they'd been reading.

"Don't you be bothering Mr. Parson too much, Babe. Come on over by me and give the man a moment of peace." Emma put a hand to her forehead to shade her eyes and watched for her precocious daughter to do as she'd been bidden.

"But, Ma, I'm in the middle of a story! I can't stop right here and leave Mr. Parson wondering what's gonna happen next!" Babe looked aghast over the thought that her captive audience would be left hanging. "Can I have a few more minutes, please?"

"She ain't a bother to me, Mrs. Delaney. The day passes a mite bit faster for me with her and her stories." Ben shifted his stiff body but didn't miss a beat of working his gold pan. "It'll be a sad day when this girl grows up and I won't have her by my side. She keeps my mind young."

Emma felt a pang of regret. "If you're sure. But you send her on over this way if your mind needs a break."

"Will do." Ben nodded at Babe to continue, and the sound of her sweet childish voice resumed. It carried along the stream before disappearing into the trees.

If only Ben knew that his dreaded day already hovers at his doorstep.

Emma pushed the melancholy thought aside and shrugged her shoulders, trying to ease the tautness that built up in them throughout the day. No matter how many breaks she took, the tension always remained and pulled her muscles tight as if they were hooked to a pulley. If she continued to pan for gold as she did now, her shoulders would be so tight they'd hitch up and settle permanently somewhere near her ears. Her body told her to hand over the claim to Mack and move on.

She'd realized of late that the fog of grief caused by the death of her husband, Matthew, two years earlier had lifted, and she felt ready to live again. In the time in between, she'd done well to lift one foot and put it in front of the other. The days had passed in a blur. She didn't know when things had changed—or when she'd begun to see the world more brightly again—but they had.

Her rediscovered joy in her young daughter led to a deeply buried desire to spend longer periods of time with her. Babe, no longer the complacent toddler who stayed at her feet, now wandered off farther and farther, and the day would come when Emma looked up from her work to find that her little girl had disappeared. It wasn't safe to have her around the stream and woods with little supervision.

The miners Emma worked near were safe, watching over both females and stepping in the few times someone got out of line, but others weren't so trustworthy. Most of the men at the stream had rented sleeping space in the Delaneys' barn and continued to do so, an arrangement that had allowed her to feel safe enough to continue work on the claim after Matthew had passed away. Already familiar with the boarders, she felt it prudent to keep the arrangement for her and Babe's security and protection.

One particular miner, Mack, had gone so far as to insist she hand the running of her claim over to him. He assured her that any find would profit her first and that he'd take nothing more than a small share to provide for his own needs. Emma knew she wanted to keep Matthew's dream alive and that work was the best thing to prevent her from breaking down from the devastation after her loss. But it was time for a change.

"Mama!" Babe's excited voice announced her arrival moments before she appeared. "We found gold! Mr. Ben said I could keep it! See?"

The tiny girl thrust the miniscule nugget in front of Emma's eyes, nearly blinding her in the process.

Emma laughed as she pushed the small hand a bit farther back from her face. "I won't see if you poke me in the eye with it. Let me take a peek."

The "nugget," not much more than a grain of dust in Emma's opinion, lay treasured in the palm of Babe's sweaty hand. "Oh, it's beautiful, baby! Shall we place it with the others in our bag?"

Babe nodded, and Emma pulled the small fabric bag from a hidden pocket of her dress. The worn bag matched everything else they owned, but it served its purpose. The tiny weave of the fabric kept even the smallest of nuggets safe.

"That's a pretty special find. If it were any bigger, I'd have to insist that Mr. Parson keep it for himself."

"Oh, he's found plenty bigger than this! He said he's having a right good day today, and this one's my reward for keeping him okipied."

"Occupied," Emma corrected. "You're a good girl to keep him company. Run and tell him thanks for the nugget and tell him we'll see him in the morning."

Babe ran off to do as she was told. Emma took advantage of the last few moments of quiet to gather up her supplies and wash up a bit. She wished she'd had what she could call a good day. The few dusty nuggets in her bag wouldn't add up to any value. But she plodded along because she knew they showed there was more than met the eye, if only she could find the treasure that evaded her. In time, the tiny finds would grow to be enough.

The family had moved to the outskirts of Deadwood when the rush first started and had a choice claim in the hills. Matthew had worked long days, and Emma accompanied him on most of them. As long as infant Babe stayed in a good mood, Emma worked right alongside her husband. Their cabin, rustic but secure, didn't take much maintenance, and Emma realized early on that she grew bored without a purpose to occupy her mind. She couldn't think of anything better than to be at the side of the man she loved, her best friend, as they worked to reach their dream.

Babe trotted over, and Emma rose stiffly to her feet. "Your mama's poor old body can't take this much longer, baby girl."

"You're not as old as Mr. Parson, Mama, and I'm *not* a baby girl!" A huff accompanied the statement.

"I stand corrected." Emma ruffled her daughter's unruly hair. The tidy braids that had been in place early that morning when they left their house were now more fluffs of curl than anything else. She plucked a leaf from the top of Babe's head. "Did you tell your stories while balanced on your head today?"

"Of course not!" Babe giggled. "But I did do some rolls down the hill by the fallen tree. Head over heel, all the way down to the stream. At the bottom I crashed into Mr. Duggin and knocked him into the water. But he wasn't mad. He said he needed to cool off anyway."

Oh my. Nothing but a lady, my daughter. Emma hid a grin. She'd make a stop by Phil Duggin's claim to apologize. Anyone else and she'd be mortified, but Phil was a trickster and would take the unexpected bath in stride. Men all along the stream whiled away the hours planning their strategies to get even with Phil's continuous pranks.

They began the trek home, and she glanced over at her daughter as she skipped along at Emma's side. Maybe it was time to switch the little girl over to pants like the men and boys wore. At least her pantaloons wouldn't be flashing as she raced down the hill. Emma knew the other miners loved Babe's childish antics, but she didn't need to put on a show. Or maybe it was confirmation that their time on the hill had come to its end, confirmation that Babe would wander and get into danger or situations that weren't best for a five-year-old. "Well, I think from the looks of your hair you brought part of that hill back with you."

She slowed her steps to match her daughter's and weighed her next words. "Babe, what would you think about spending our days at the cabin instead of up here on the hill?"

Babe's face, full of trust, tilted up so she could peer at Emma's. "Like on the Sabbath?"

"Like on the Sabbath, yes, but every day in between, too."

"I think that would not be fun. I like coming up to the hills. Jimmy Jacobs says he hates being home all the time with his ma. He says I'm lucky we get to go to the claims every day like his pa. His big brothers get to go, but he has to stay home. I don't want to be mad like Jimmy Jacobs while you go to the hills without me."

"I'd be at the cabin with you, sweetheart. I didn't mean I'd leave you behind." Emma suppressed her smile. Jimmy, Babe's closest friend, always longed to be like his older brothers. She didn't realize the five-year-old boy talked so much with her daughter. Where were the days when the two had sat on a blanket on the floor and screamed over a mutually desired block or spoon at Emma's and Katie's feet?

"Oh, that's different. . .a little bit. But what would we do all day?"

"We can explore around our house, so you'd still be in the hills every day. And we can start your lessons. I think you're more than ready. We can sew some pretty dresses. You grow like a weed, and I can barely button the tops of your bodices around you." She quieted as they reached Phil's claim. "Good evening, Mr. Duggin. I understand my daughter caused you some excitement this afternoon."

"Hello, Mrs. Delaney." Phil Duggin jumped to his feet, pulled his cap off, and worried it with his hands. His already ruddy face burned bright red. "It was nothing, ma'am, just a child having fun. I think we all know it's high time a prank turned my way."

"Long past due," a male voice called from downstream.

Phil ignored him. "If anyone were to get me, I'd love for it to be your daughter every time. That child can put a smile on the surliest man's face."

Another voice called their way through the twilight. "But we *will* get you, Duggin. When you least expect it." Laughter drifted up and down the stream. Phil had a lot of buddies who were anxious for their moments to get back at him. All in the name of friendship.

Phil flashed Emma a smile. "Anything to pass the time, ya know?"

"I do," she agreed. The days grew long, especially in the rougher weather. "Well, we'll be on our way, then. I wanted to make sure you were well after your tumble."

"I'm no worse for wear. You all have a good evening, now."

"We sure will. Thank you for your patience with my daughter."

They continued on, and Mack stood as they neared his partner's claim. "Hold on a minute and I'll walk you home."

She watched him as he worked. A man who took pride in his appearance, he had nondescript brown hair, long though trimmed, and pale blue eyes that were constantly watching her. The notion unnerved her at times, but she knew he felt it his duty to watch out for them now that Matthew was gone. Mack didn't like Emma and Babe to walk the short distance home alone, and he never failed to remind her. Emma knew her chance to discuss Mack's work with the claim had come.

"I'm all packed up and ready to go. Let's hit the trail." He ruffled Babe's hair, but she ignored him.

Emma found it odd that Babe warmed up to every other man on the mountain, but Mack, sweet as he could be, couldn't break through the icy shell that encased her daughter when he came around. She glanced over to see how he took the latest rejection. He didn't seem bothered in the least.

"Mack. . ." Now that the time had come, the words stuck in her throat. She cleared it and tried again. It was best to get it over with. "Mack, I think it's time for me to hand over the reins of the claim to you. That is, if you're still interested."

Mack's eyes lit up. "Are you serious? I've waited a long time for you to make that decision. About two years, as a matter of fact. You and the baby need to be at home, not working up here on a dirty claim."

"I'm not a baby! Don't call me that. My name is Babe." Babe stared up at him, hands clenched into fists at her sides.

Emma jumped at the vehemence in Babe's voice. She knew she'd made the right decision. Her daughter needed more of her time and training. No longer would the small child be allowed to run wild to intermingle with the ruffians who worked the mountain. She dropped to her knee and took Babe by the arms. "Babe, you apologize to Mr. Mack at once. You know better than to talk to adults that way."

Babe sent her a glare before turning to face Mack. "I'm *sorry*, Mr. Mack, but in the future you may now only call me Miss Delaney."

Emma gasped at Babe's outright defiance. Where had her sweet little girl gone? Had she waited too long to leave the claim? She needed to talk to Katie Jacobs.

"Mack, I don't know what's gotten into Babe, but I need to deal with her alone. If you don't mind, I'm going to stop off at Katie's before we head for home."

Mack's reluctance showed. "I don't like you walking alone, even for this short distance." They'd reached the clearing around her friends' place.

"I'll make sure one of Katie's boys accompanies us the rest of the way to the cabin. We'll be fine."

"If you're sure. I looked forward to the rest of the walk so we could discuss how to handle the change of hands with the claim. When do you want me to start? Tomorrow?"

"I hadn't thought that through. I've only just made the decision." She paused for a moment. "How about I finish out the week, and then we can start fresh with the changes on Monday. I need to prepare the men around us. Losing Babe's company will hit hard for some of them." She glanced over at her sober daughter. "But we can visit. We'll make sure to stop by often."

"That will be good. I need to make arrangements with my partner for the other claim, too."

Mack peered at Babe, and Emma couldn't discern his expression. Exasperation? Disappointment? No, it was a look of anger and resentment. She knew her daughter had been rude, but as an adult, Mack should know that children weren't always the most angelic beings. For that matter, most adults didn't know to hold their tongues when they should. She didn't want to excuse Babe's poor behavior, but Mack's facial expression took her by surprise.

She herded Babe ahead of her down the path that led to the Jacobses'. Mack didn't hide his intentions to court Emma, but so far Emma wasn't at a place where she could face a future with another man. She might be coming out of her haze of grief, but that was a far cry from wanting another man in her life.

If she were honest with herself, she knew deep down inside she had her own reservations about Mack. Something held her back, but she couldn't put her finger on what it was. She felt secure with him running her claim, but for now that was the extent of her trust. His response moments earlier had only increased that catch in her spirit. A shiver of apprehension passed through her.

Chapter 2

Katie, a strikingly beautiful woman even as she headed into middle age, stood in her yard and gathered laundry from the lines her husband had hung for her. Emma felt a pang of longing. An identical set hung in her yard, placed there by Matthew. Would the reminders never quit? Maybe she should consider moving on, away from the place where her memories lingered. If she were to make a change, why not change everything? She and Babe could move to a real city and get far away from Deadwood.

She shuddered at the thought. No way. She wasn't that far along yet. She couldn't leave and give up all she'd shared with her husband. Letting loose of the claim would be enough for now. She'd take one day at a time and figure out her future later.

"Do my eyes deceive me, or did my good friend Emma Delaney finally show up for a visit?" Katie called out. She stood with her hand shading her eyes. Her black hair was upswept, and she looked cool and fresh, even in the late afternoon heat.

Emma felt like a clod next to her. She swept back the blond strands of hair that had escaped the twist at the back of her neck to hang in front of her face. She knew her own brown eyes were etched with exhaustion. "Are we intruding? If so, we can come back on a different day." Emma now questioned her decision to stop by Katie's. The men would be home soon, and Katie had to be knee-deep in dinner preparations. She followed her friend onto the front porch.

"You know you never intrude when you visit. C'mon in here and get off your feet." They entered the cabin. "I'll get you something cool to drink. Babe, Jimmy's out in the barn. Why don't you go tell him you're here?" Katie bustled around the room while Babe scurried off to find Jimmy.

Emma watched out the window to make sure her daughter arrived at the rugged building in one piece. "Can I help? I've been sitting all day."

"No, you relax, and I'll sit with you in a moment."

Emma grabbed up some towels and bedding from the basket Katie had set beside the table. She began to fold while Katie threw a snack together. "Will the men be home soon? I don't want to interfere with your dinner."

Katie waved her words away. "They plan to work as late as daylight will allow. The days are growing shorter, and Hank's worried that we don't have much time left before winter hits with all its fury." She pointed a thin finger toward the wood-framed fireplace, where a kettle hung over kindling that crackled and popped with heat. "I have stew in the pot ready to go when they walk through the door. I can visit. What's on your mind?"

"I'm about to make some changes, and I need your encouragement. . .and prayers. I really need your prayers more than anything." Emma continued to fold as she spoke. "I'm going to leave the claim. Mack will take over, and I know it's silly, but I feel like I'd be a disappointment to Matthew. But I have to think of Babe, and she's starting to wander and her attitude is changing. I feel she needs more of my time and attention."

"First of all, you know you always have my prayers, even when we go weeks without seeing each other. You're on my list every day."

Emma felt some of the pressure let up at her friend's sweet words. Of course Katie prayed for them. She always had. Emma knew that.

"Second of all, I doubt Matthew would have expected you to keep up the claim in the first place, so you sure aren't failing him now. I think it's a great idea to let Mack take over. He's cared for you for a long time, and I'm sure he has your best interests at heart. In my busybody opinion, you need to take that next step."

Emma glanced up. "And that step would be?"

Katie leaned forward and took Emma's hand in hers. "Darling, you've been alone a long while now. It's time you found a man for yourself, and a pa for Babe. We worry about your being alone all the time way out here. Mack seems like a nice enough man. Maybe you should give him a chance, show him some interest."

Emma jerked her hand away and stood to pace across the floor. "I'm not at that place yet. I'm getting there, Katie, and I appreciate your concern, but I'm not ready." Her gaze took in the large room.

A sheet separated the sleeping quarters from the cooking area. Katie had her treasured rocking chair that Hank had crafted for her pulled up near the fire. Though sparse, the room felt warm through Katie's creative use of fabric and flowers. Little treasures and collectibles that she'd accumulated through the years sat on small shelves that Hank had placed on the various walls. Emma knew there was a doorway on the sleeping side that led to a newer room Hank had built on so that Katie would have some space and privacy from her four noisy sons.

"I'm not saying chase the man to the altar, Emma." Katie's humor softened her words. "I'm just saying you might want to give him a chance. See what he's about."

"I'll see what happens with all that in time. Right now I know Babe needs me. That will be my primary focus." Emma walked back to the table and sank down into a chair. "You know, it's odd. I know Mack is interested, but my heart isn't saying the same on my end. And on the way over here, Babe reacted to Mack in a way I've never seen her behave before. He tried to draw her into our conversation, but she lashed out at him instead. I don't understand why she doesn't warm up to him." She shrugged. "But then, I don't know why I don't warm up to him, either."

Katie laughed. "Keep your eyes open, pray, and see what happens. This break from the claim is exactly what you need to see what else God has for you and your future. I think great things are about to happen for you."

A ruckus in the yard interrupted their discussion, much to Emma's relief. She knew Katie meant well, but Emma didn't feel comfortable moving any further with the topic of Mack.

"Looks like the men have arrived! Why don't you stay for dinner? You know Hank will want you to join us. I know Jimmy would like it, too. He'll enjoy having Babe around to play with. And you know I'll love to have my coffee partner back. Stay and let us get reacquainted."

"I don't know. I look a mess." Emma gestured at the soiled hem of her blue dress where it had dragged in the mud at the side of the stream. "And my hair. . ."

"Nonsense. Sit there by the window, and I'll do your hair. Your dress is fine. How long has it been since you've been pampered, anyway?"

"About forever," Emma admitted. "But you don't need to cater to me. I'm sure you've worked hard today, too."

"Well, it's been about forever since I've had the pleasure of doing someone else's hair, you know? Let me play. I don't have the luxury of a daughter to doll up. The men won't be in for a while. They have to take care of the stock and clean up themselves. So sit and let me see what I can do."

Emma sat. Her friend kept up a steady stream of chatter without much input from Emma. Emma had to smile at the mental picture she had of a grown-up Babe doing much the same thing. She had no doubt Katie had been lonely of late. "It'll be fun to get together like we used to back when Jimmy and Babe were toddlers."

Katie grunted her answer, her mouth now full of hairpins. She worked in silence for a few minutes, then declared Emma beautiful and pointed her in the direction of the mirror.

Emma instead crossed over to the window and peered out in time to watch Jimmy catapult himself into his father's outstretched arms. Babe stood to the side, a sad smile of longing on her lips as she watched her best friend with his pa. Emma's heart cracked a bit at the wistful expression on her daughter's precious face. Maybe it was time to consider finding a father for Babe. She knew she'd never love anyone else like she'd loved Matthew—or at least she couldn't imagine doing so at this time—so maybe she'd been looking at the whole situation in the wrong way. Maybe she needed to focus on a father for Babe, not a husband for herself.

Babe was subdued during dinner. Emma knew bedtime wouldn't come soon enough for the child, but she also knew something bothered her daughter.

"I'm not sure a change at the claim is a good idea. Not with Mack, anyway," Hank said as he passed a plate of potatoes. "There might be some better choices to consider."

"Oh now, Hank, that's not a fair comment to make when Mack's not here to defend himself. Why would you say such a thing?" Katie's appalled voice caught Emma's attention and took her thoughts off her daughter.

Emma forced herself to concentrate on the conversation. "Why would you think Mack is a bad idea? He's been partners in the other claim for years, and I've not heard of any problems. He's never been in trouble that I know of. In all due respect, is there something about him you know that I don't?"

Hank measured his words. "I can't put my finger on anything. But there's something, a gut feeling if you will, that makes me ill at ease around him."

"I've not ever had a problem," Emma said, then exchanged a glance with Katie. That wasn't true. She did have that check in her spirit when it came to Mack, but she could never figure out what caused it, so it didn't seem fair to go by that alone when everything else about him added up fine. "Well, maybe I do have reservations. But I have no grounds to base my feelings on. I really don't have any other choice, either."

Hank wiped at his mouth. "I'd love to say I could loan you one of the boys, but I need them to work our area. Winter's almost here, and things will be hard. We need to be ready." His voice tapered off. "I'm sorry. I know life has been hard for you, too. Take one of the boys if you need to. We'll get along."

"I appreciate the offer, but for now I'll let Mack run things. I can always change my mind later. I've already offered him the job."

"I can work your claim, Miss Emma!" Jimmy about bounced off his seat with excitement. "I'm big and strong. I can work."

"I know you'd do a great job, Jimmy. But as I said, I already offered the job to Mack. Let's see how he does, and if he needs help, I'll bring up your name. Deal?"

Babe slammed her fist down on the table. "We don't need help from anybody other than my pa."

Silence bounced off the corners of the room. The adults exchanged startled glances, while Jimmy looked confused.

"You ain't got a pa." He finally broke the silence. "Your pa died a long time ago, and a dead man can't run a claim."

"Jimmy!" Hank's angry voice made everyone jump. "You hush right now."

"But it's true." Jimmy sulked.

Emma felt relief that her child didn't have an exclusive run on attitude. Apparently both children were in a period of testing to see what they could get by with. It must be the age.

Babe surveyed them all with an angelic smile. "I'm not talking about that pa. I'm talking about my new one."

Emma felt her face flame to a bright red. What was she going to do with the child? "You don't have a new pa, Babe. You're talking silly. You need to eat your dinner now so we can get on our way home."

And we can't head home a moment too soon. Surely her daughter didn't mean a reference to Mack. She'd shown him nothing but contempt. No, she couldn't mean him, since when his name was mentioned she'd said they didn't need his help. She'd probably made up a new pa as one of her imaginary friends. "Do you boys mind escorting us part of the way home? I promised Mack we wouldn't walk the trail in the dark alone."

"We'll do better than that. I can hitch up the horses to the wagon, and I'll run you home in that." Hank seemed as anxious to get the talkative Babe on her way as Emma was.

"Mama"—Babe's exasperated breath lifted her hair from her forehead—"I prayed for a new pa. He'll be just like Mr. Jacobs. He'll grab me up and swing me around and call me special names and buy me special treats."

Emma sent up a prayer herself—for a sudden hole to appear, large enough to fall into. The entire Jacobs family stared at her with ill-concealed amusement, waiting for her to clear a way out of this mess. "Finding a pa isn't that easy, Babe. A new pa doesn't just walk up to your front door."

"You told me God could make anything happen." Babe's face contorted into a pout. "Isn't that true anymore?"

"Well, yes, of course it's still true. But we live in the middle of nowhere—"

"Then it will be easier for my pa to know which cabin is ours! He won't have too many places to choose from."

How to explain this to her young daughter? The little girl had no idea of the expectations she had and what they meant. There was no way God would drop a perfect husband on her doorstep. . .now or ever.

15

Chapter 3

"Watch, Mama. My papa will do this."

Emma watched as Babe tossed her doll high into the air and missed catching her on the down side. The doll landed with a splat on the grassy dirt in front of the porch.

Babe hurried down to retrieve her baby, holding her close with words of comfort. "Oops." She glanced up at Emma with a regretful sigh. "My papa won't do it that way. Let me try again."

Emma blanched at her daughter's constant chatter about her papa. The little girl, more convinced than ever that her prayer would be answered by a father's appearance on their doorstep, about plowed down anyone who got in her way when a knock sounded at the entry. It didn't even have to be their cabin. It could be Katie's or Liza's, their other neighbor.

But it didn't stop there. She would also run up to other men when they were out and about, looking for her "pa." It could be a complete stranger walking into the general store. Each time, Babe's face would light up and then fall as she surveyed the newest prospect—or victim as he might be called. Not once had she declared she'd found her papa, much to Emma's relief.

The townspeople and their friends found the situation quite amusing. Word had passed around that Babe was in the market for a new papa, and everyone began to offer up suggestions to Emma. Matchmaking attempts had peaked higher than ever. Her nerves were wearing thin.

"Em, can I talk to you for a moment?" Mack walked up the path from the barn. He stood politely on the porch, waiting for an invitation to sit.

Not in the mood for company, especially Mack's company, which would probably start tongues wagging across all of Dakota Territory, she hesitated. She contemplated telling him no, but in the end politeness won out and she motioned for him to take a seat.

"The claim's doing well."

Emma nodded. She supposed his report was necessary, but she wanted him to get to the point.

"We've begun to dig a mine in the hill behind the claim. I've taken a look at the locale, and I think it has huge potential. The men around our claim have offered to get it up and going."

His use of the word "our" raised her hackles. She raised an eyebrow at him, and he quickly caught his mistake. "*Your* claim, of course. Sorry. But while I'm working it every day, I feel a certain ownership. I always keep in mind that if I do a good job, it benefits us all. I only referred to my stake in this, along with yours."

Emma motioned for him to go on. She felt a loss knowing that her claim now had a gaping hole in the hillside behind it. The area that once lay untouched by human hands was being destroyed for man's desire to get rich. She wondered how that could be the right thing to do.

"The mine will allow us to keep working even after the cold weather comes. We'll be partially protected from the elements." He paused as her mind drifted. "Em."

"Emma," she corrected without thinking.

His flat blue eyes narrowed. He corrected himself. "Emma. I think we need to talk."

I'm too tired to talk. I'm worn out through and through. Emma had thought letting go of the claim would refresh her, but instead, with Babe's constant badgering for a father and Mack's frequent hints at wanting marriage, she wanted to curl up and sleep for the next ten years.

"Talk about what?" Her voice was weary, even to her own ears. She knew what was coming and wanted to be anywhere but here. Where had chattering Babe gone when she needed her? Of course, the child still made it clear she had no use for Mack and disappeared as soon as she could when he came around.

"Us." He reached over and took her hand. Emma tried to hide her shudder. "I want you to marry me."

His clammy skin repulsed her. *Lord, if it's in Your will that I marry Mack, please change my heart about him. If it isn't in Your will, show me a sign that I'm on the right track, because I feel very confused.*

She did know that the more Mack was around and the more he immersed himself into her life at the cabin and the claim, the more she resented his presence. She didn't really need a sign from God to know her feelings weren't growing for the man. But she did long for a sign to show her the way out of this mess.

"There is no *us*, Mack." She pulled her hand away and stood to put distance between them. She paced for a moment, trying to gather her thoughts, then perched on the edge of her chair, as far from Mack as physically possible. Though she was tired of putting the man off and fighting his advances, she forced her voice to be gentle. "I'm not ready to have a man in my life, and you know Babe isn't ready, either. I have to think of her. I'm sorry, but I don't want to marry you."

Mack's dull eyes bored into hers. He obviously didn't like to hear that she didn't want to marry him. He made that clearer with each rejection. "Your daughter isn't ready for you to marry because you haven't told her that's how things will be. You need to discipline her and tell her she's a little girl and has no say in things such as this. You give the child too much latitude, and she's spoiled."

Emma's gasp showed her disbelief at the way he'd talked about her daughter. "I'll ask you to please never make a comment like that about my child again." *The audacity!*

"It's true. If she were mine, I'd take a stick to her backside. She has no respect, and I'm tired of her ruining my plans."

"Then it's a sure thing the child will never be yours. *Your* plans are about to crash down around you. How dare you speak of my daughter in that way—or speak to me with such disrespect, for that matter? I'd be best off to send you packing." Emma had again jumped to her feet and now continued to pace across the covered porch's floor. "You work for me, Mack, like it or not. If you can't abide by my standards, you're free to move on to work for someone else."

Mack stood and towered above her, his stance threatening.

Emma had never been so angry in her life. A brief moment of fear flashed through her, but she knew she was only a yell away from a whole barn full of loyal miners who would rush to her side if needed. She watched as he deflated before her eyes. Either he'd realized the same thing, or he could read her face well enough to know she wasn't going to back down.

"I'm sorry." Though his voice sounded dejected, she felt it was an act. "The comments I just made were out of line. It's just. . .I get lonely, and I think we'd make a great partnership. Babe would come around in time."

"I won't marry you, Mack. You need to understand that. I'm not going to change my mind." During the course of their conversation, that fact had come through free and clear. She felt a burden lift from her chest. Her prayer had been answered. "I'd like you to stay on and run the claim, but only if you can live with that fact."

Mack met her gaze and held it steadily before nodding and walking back to the barn without further comment.

❧

Josiah Andrews urged his horse forward, every bit as tired of the journey as was his magnificent stallion, Rocky. The rough terrain made for slow going, and they'd had to wind their way among the rocks, boulders, creeks, and streams that blocked their passage at every turn. If he'd had a straight route through, he'd have arrived in Deadwood weeks ago.

The hot September sun beat down, and Josiah wondered if the temperature always reached such warm extremes this far north or if the adverse weather had been put into place just for him. It seemed that if anything could go wrong on this trek, it had.

He'd been on the trail for years, and though he was on a mission to find a wanted man and to bring him back in, the official visit coincided with a need Josiah had for revenge against a man who had wronged him. He would avenge his brother's death if it was the last thing he did. And what better place to bring his enemy down than Deadwood? One of the most lawless towns around, rumor had it that a man was murdered there almost every day. One more body wouldn't make much of a difference.

A fleeting twinge of guilt passed through him, but Josiah shook it off. Though his motive for capturing the wanted man contradicted his plan for revenge, he felt he had no choice.

"C'mon, ole boy. I see some oats and a comfortable place to sleep in your near future, and in mine, too. Well, maybe not oats for me, but a good hot meal." They'd been riding for weeks, and the trail had warmed considerably as they'd neared Deadwood.

The vegetation grew sparser as they approached the outskirts of town, a sure sign they were close to their destination. Everything would be perfect as long as no one recognized who he was. At least before he caught his quarry. He'd analyze the sins of his plan after the fact. Until then, anything could go as far as he was concerned.

The town bustled with activity as Josiah rode in. He took his time, perusing it from one end to the other. He needed to be familiar with the layout. It seemed mostly filled with men, and several of the women he could see were definitely not the type he'd ever bring home to his mother. Though no church could be seen, plenty of gambling, drinking, and dancing establishments lined the rough dirt road.

Josiah urged his horse forward to a small hotel and tied him to the post out front. He removed his satchel from the saddle and mounted the rickety stairs that led to the hotel porch. A woman leaned against the doorway of a nearby saloon and propositioned him, but he ignored her and pushed into the stuffy interior.

Rooms opened off both sides of the foyer—one obviously a sitting room of sorts and the other, based on the clink and clatter of dishes, the dining room. A central staircase led up the right wall, and a counter wrapped along the wall to the left.

While Josiah stood and took in the hotel's floor plan, a bored man sat behind the counter and watched the action taking place outside, a bonus for a man who wanted to remain unrecognized. "Can I help you?"

"I need a room." Josiah plunked a few bills down on the counter. This would be the perfect place to lay low. "And I'll want a hot bath."

The man consulted a ledger, picked up a key from behind him, and handed it over to Josiah. "Top of the stairs and to the left. Your room is the second door, again on the left. Stable's out back."

Good, a room at the front of the building with a view of the street. Josiah wondered if his luck had finally changed. He could watch for his quarry, and no one would be the wiser.

❧

The bath and clean clothes did a lot for Josiah's disposition as he headed down to eat a late lunch. The room clanged with noise, and he wished for the dinner companions of the civilized towns he'd visited previously.

Here the tables were packed with miners, most with no manners at all. Local girls swarmed the room, talking to the men while they ate. Josiah picked a small table in the corner and put on his surliest face, hoping everyone would leave him alone.

A middle-aged woman hurried to his table. "Hi, I'm Sarah. I'm sorry if you've been waiting long. I didn't notice you slip in over here." She was out of breath from rushing around.

"I haven't been here but a few moments," Josiah reassured her. This woman would be perfect for his questioning. He placed his order, relieved to see that the room had begun to clear of most guests. They meandered outside and went about their daily business. Josiah had a feeling that he hadn't picked the quietest place in town for his stay. But from the looks of it, there wouldn't be any other place less populated. He'd have to use a pillow over his head to get a good night of sleep, if the number of saloons was an indication.

Sarah returned with his pork chop and potatoes. The town might be rough and rugged, but if the aroma of the meal held its promise, the food would be well worth the stay.

"Sarah, I'm looking for an old friend. I'm thinking maybe you can help me out with locating him." Josiah held his breath in anticipation after giving her the name. His effort finally, after all these months, had paid off. After Sarah spouted off directions on where to find the man he'd hunted, he couldn't hide his smile. Not even a miner, and he'd struck the mother lode.

Though his appetite hadn't diminished, he hurried through the meal, ready to get back on his horse and track his brother's killer.

❧

Emma placed the last clean dish onto the shelf and wiped her damp hands on a towel. Upon hearing a noise from out front, she hesitated, trying to place the sound. She hurried across the cabin's floor at the approach of a horse. She hadn't expected anyone at this time of day, and her friends Katie and Liza always walked when they came to visit. The men would eventually be back from the claims, but not for hours.

Babe slept on her small bed behind Emma as she peeked out the window to see a stranger approach. Hefting her rifle from its resting place on the mantel, Emma quietly lifted the latch and went out to meet the stranger.

He stopped the horse a safe distance away.

"Who are you, and what do you want?" she called out to him, hoping her voice wouldn't carry inside to wake Babe. "State your business or leave."

The stranger raised his hands. "I don't mean you any harm. I just have a few questions about the men who board here."

Emma moved down the stairs but kept her rifle aimed at his chest. From where she stood, she could see he had a gun in a holster by his side. She couldn't tell the make from this distance. But it wouldn't matter if he was a sharpshooter. Her rifle would never be a match for his gun, especially if he was a quick draw. "What kind of questions? The boarders here don't look for trouble, and they don't find any, either. They're all good men."

"I'm sure they are. I don't mean to make trouble, either." He forced his mount a few steps closer, then swung down from the saddle.

She couldn't help but notice the strong muscles of his legs as they rippled from the movement. Her heart skipped a few beats. Now that he'd come closer, she saw that he had to be the handsomest man she'd ever laid eyes on. Wide shoulders filled out his off-white shirt and complemented his slim hips and long, lean legs. Black hair tumbled over his forehead in disarray. But his good looks were marred by the underlying current of anger that simmered deep within his dark brown eyes.

"Don't come any closer." The rifle had drooped in her hold as she openly perused the appealing stranger. Catching herself, she swung it back up against her shoulder. She started to say she had a small child inside whom she needed to protect, but then thought better than to offer him the information if he had ill reasons for being there. "I won't hesitate to shoot."

The man had the audacity to chuckle. "I don't doubt that you will. I know you have a child, and I'd feel the same caution if I were in your place."

So much for keeping Babe a secret. "Who are you?"

"Forgive my lack of manners. The name is Josiah. Josiah Andrews. I'm new in town."

"You and every other man on the street." Newcomers poured into the town every day and had ever since the first nugget of gold was found. Emma had been there longer than most. They'd settled into the area before the first gold was discovered, which accounted for their great location and claim.

"I'd like to know the names of the men you have staying here."

"And I'd still like to know a good reason for me to tell you."

The man stepped closer and measured her with his glance. She wondered if he liked what he saw. Did he find her as appealing as she found him? Mentally shaking her head at her silliness, she warned herself not to fall into a ridiculous fantasy like Babe's.

"I'm looking for an old friend."

"What's his name? If he's here, I'll have him look you up. . .back in town." She hoped her meaning came through clearly—she didn't want the stranger lingering around.

"Mack Jeffries. Do you know of him?"

Just then the front door of the cabin burst open Babe-style, and the little girl hurtled out onto the porch.

"This must be Babe."

Emma's attention was torn. "Babe, stay back. Don't come off the porch."

Josiah took advantage of her attention moving away from him and stepped several feet closer.

"Stop! Both of you." Emma turned her focus back to Josiah even as she heard Babe's dainty footsteps bouncing down the stairs. Neither person listened to her admonition to stop.

"Hello, sweetheart." Josiah greeted Babe with a soft voice. His entire countenance changed, as if he were viewing an angel in the flesh.

"Hello, Papa," Babe responded, racing past Emma before she could stop her.

Emma watched in disbelief as her daughter flew into the surprised man's arms. The little girl buried her face in his shoulder before peeking up at her mother. "See? I told you God would send my papa to our doorstep."

Emma felt herself beginning to panic. Whatever the man's purpose, her most valuable treasure now rested in his arms.

Chapter 4

Unhand my daughter and you might ride out of here with your life." Emma motioned with the rifle, though she knew the movement had lost its effect with Babe's arrival on the scene. She'd lowered it to point at the ground and held it loosely in one hand. So far, in all honesty, the man had given her no reason to think he'd come to cause them harm. But she couldn't take any chances.

"Me unhand her?" Josiah looked down at the child who was clinging to him. "And how will you manage to shoot me with your daughter between your gun and my chest?"

Babe raised her head in horror. "You can't shoot my papa when he's only just arrived!"

Tired, out of patience, and wanting the man gone and Babe safely tucked away in the cabin, Emma pinned her daughter with a glare. "He's not your papa, Babe. He's a stranger. Now hop down like a good girl and get up here on the porch by your mama where I can keep you safe."

Babe ignored her and buried her face against his. "He smells good, Mama. Come over and sniff his neck."

"I will not!" Emma could feel the multiple shades of color as they flew up her cheeks. "Babe Delaney, get off that man right now."

"Are you sure? I have another side just for you." The stranger had the nerve to stand there and grin.

Emma's rebellious thoughts noted that it was a very charming grin.

"And I can't say I've ever heard words quite like that come out of a mother's mouth while her daughter is in her arms."

And what was that supposed to mean? Did he have a lot of females caught in his clutches by their mothers? Emma gasped, and her hand flew to her heart. She couldn't believe the man would toy with her like this. First he rode up looking dangerous—*and extremely handsome,* her traitorous thoughts added—and now he stood there gently clasping her wayward daughter in his arms like some kind of pink-clad porcelain doll. And his teasing words added fuel to Babe's papa dreams.

"Well, we obviously have some more work to do in the decorum and how-to-act-around-men area of life."

"Please smell his neck, Mama. You might like him and want him to stay."

"As I was saying. . ." This whole situation had become utterly ridiculous, and Emma had lost all control—of her daughter, the man who stood before her, and her life. "Babe, he's not a sweet little puppy you just decide to invite into your home." That didn't sound right. She sighed. "Please put my daughter down."

Josiah raised both arms in mock surrender. Babe remained where she was, hanging from his neck, hugging him for all she was worth. "With all due respect, ma'am. It's a long way down to the ground, and she might fall."

"Then bring her up on the porch. I give up." She watched as he secured the child in his arms.

The man tipped his wide-brimmed hat and sauntered past her onto the porch, where he dropped gratefully into a chair.

Babe repositioned herself and snuggled against his chest. Her brown eyes were huge as she stared up at him, and her fluffy blond hair framed her face in a most adorable way. Emma watched, entranced, as the anger disappeared from the stranger's eyes when he smiled down at the impish child in his arms.

He glanced up at Emma, and his mouth quirked up on one side. He had a dimple. "I hate to impose, but it's a long ride out here. Do you think you could fetch me a drink? I'd get it myself, but. . ." He motioned to Babe, who now appeared to be asleep.

"I'm not leaving you alone out here with my daughter."

"If I meant you harm, I'd have injured you already. It would have been nothing to hop on my horse and take off with her when she first jumped into my arms. And to further put your mind at ease, I came out here looking for Mack at the recommendation of Sarah over at the hotel. She knows I've headed this way, and if there's any foul play, I'm the first person they'd be after."

Emma had to admit that what he said made sense. "Let me get your water, and then you can tell me what you want with Mack."

She grabbed a mug and dipped it in the water pail before hurrying back out the open door. Josiah hadn't moved from his place in the chair, but with his head tipped back against the wood of the front wall of the cabin, he appeared to be asleep.

Emma stood staring and felt a tug in her heart. Babe looked so sweet cuddled in the man's strong arms. She also looked incredibly tiny. She wanted a papa so badly. It wasn't fair hers had been taken from her at such a young age. Emma didn't know how they'd get through this afternoon without breaking Babe's heart.

The man opened one eye and peeked out at her. "That my water?"

"Oh, I'm sorry, yes. Here." She handed it over, embarrassed to have been caught staring. She settled in a chair across from him. "Now, about your reasons for asking to see Mack. . ."

"It's personal."

"That's it? I'm supposed to hand over a man with no questions asked? Is he a friend?"

"At one time."

"But not anymore?"

"Nope. Not anymore."

They were getting nowhere fast. "He runs my claim."

Josiah sat up so quickly, Emma thought he'd drop Babe. But instead his arms gripped her protectively. "He's running your claim? For how long? Is that where I'll find him now?"

"I don't see how any of this is business of yours. You don't want to tell me the least little bit of reason why you're here, but you expect me to spill my life story to you?"

"That pretty much sums it up. There are things you don't need to know. But you shouldn't trust Mack so easily."

Emma grew tired of the man and his puzzling comments. "You have no idea how easy or hard it was for me to trust him. He's been a family friend for years—first to my husband, and after his passing, to my daughter and myself."

Emma wasn't sure why she defended Mack with such intensity when she'd been having her own doubts of late, but it probably had more to do with defending her choices. If the man questioned her choice in trusting Mack, he questioned her ability to reason in general, and for some silly reason, it was important to Emma to have Josiah's respect. It also seemed to be important because if she'd been wrong to trust Mack, her entire future stood at risk.

❧

Josiah studied the woman before him and wondered what thoughts were passing through her mind. She looked torn, as if she wanted to help but didn't know the best way.

"If you tell me where to find Mack, I'll take it from there," he said. "You don't need to be involved. I'll take care of my business with him, and you can go on your way."

"He's at the claim. It's quite a walk up that path over near the barn, and it will be dark before you arrive. It would be best if you waited until tomorrow to do your business with him. I'll tell him you came by."

"Right, and by tomorrow he'll be long gone. I can't—won't—take that chance. I've searched for him way too long to lose him now." He saw a shudder pass through Emma and felt bad for scaring her. "Look, I don't mean to bring you an added burden. I'll do my best to make sure our business doesn't interfere with you here at the cabin or in any way harm your little girl. But I have to confront Mack, and it has to be today. You have my word that I won't hurt him."

He still couldn't read the emotions that passed across her face. His previous words startled him as much as they appeared to startle her. How could he have promised not to hurt Mack? His whole intent upon coming here was to collect the ultimate price from the man. Mack had caused Josiah's brother's death, and he fully planned to exact the same payment from Mack. He felt a scowl cross his face and fought to control his emotions. It wouldn't do to frighten Emma.

"If you've searched for him for years and he's no longer a friend, I have to assume you have a vendetta against him. Am I correct?" Her brown eyes, identical to her daughter's, bored into him. "I rely on Mack heavily. If something happens to him, I don't know what I'll do."

"There are other men by the dozens who'd love to take over your claim. You said so yourself. New men come to town every day."

"Yes, but I don't want to give my claim away. I want someone to partner with me in running it. I took care of the claim myself up until a few weeks ago. It's become too hard with Babe along. She's at a very precocious age, and I was worried about her safety."

"So I can see." Josiah's warm laugh drifted over to Emma, and she looked surprised.

She motioned at the child in his arms. "You seem comfortable with her. Do you have a child of your own?"

Josiah felt the surprise register on his face at her question. "No. I've not been around children much at all. This one took me by surprise."

Emma appeared startled, then contemplative. "Hmm."

He wondered what the reaction meant. He then shook off the thought. He had one goal to follow—not counting his capture of the wanted man in town— and he needed to focus on that goal, not the two unexpected women who were taking his heart captive as he watched.

The guilt reared its ugly head again. If he succeeded in his plans with Mack, these two would be left high and dry. There would be no one to run the claim. He pushed the thought away. That wasn't his problem. She wasn't safe with Mack running the claim anyway. Ultimately, he'd do her a favor by ridding them of the man. His plan for Mack would be a blessing to the woman and child in the long run; they just might not ever know it. He felt sorrow that they'd not see it that way, but he knew his plan was definitely for the best.

❧

"I need to be on my way. Do you want me to lay her down inside or hand her off to you?"

Emma stood and reached for her daughter. Babe had napped long enough that there was no way she'd sleep through his laying her down. Emma didn't feel comfortable with the man entering her private quarters, either. She braced herself for the wrath of Babe.

"No! I want to stay with you, Papa!"

Emma smirked. She'd been right. Let the man deal with the little girl, since he'd been so smug earlier when her daughter had catapulted into his arms. He threw Emma a look begging for help, but she merely shrugged. She watched as he lowered himself to one knee and placed Babe on her feet.

"I have to go now, but I enjoyed meeting you."

"Papas don't just leave their children. I want you to stay here."

He again looked up at Emma, confusion apparent on his face.

"She's been praying for a papa, and she's sure one will be sent to her. You arrived, and. . ." Emma waved her hand as if that explained it all. She didn't want to go into the whole sordid mess.

"Oh." He stared at the little girl. "I'm sure you'll find that papa someday soon. If I see him, I'll tell him to head this way, all right?"

Babe's face screwed up, and tears gathered in her eyes. "But you're the one He sent."

"I'm here to finish a plan put into place long ago, not to be a pa, Babe. I enjoyed meeting you, and you're a daughter that would make any father proud. I'm sorry it won't be me." He stood.

Babe clutched his leg. "But I don't want *any* father; I want you!"

Emma decided she'd let the man go through enough torture to get even for his interrupting her afternoon. She peeled a crying Babe from his thigh. "Come along, Babe. Let the man be on his way."

Josiah sent her a grateful look and started down the stairs. "I appreciate the water and the information."

"You're welcome." Emma stopped short of calling out that he was welcome back anytime. She also felt sad as the man walked out of their life. What a crazy thought!

He stopped near his horse and looked back at them with a strange expression. He shook his head as if to clear it and readied himself to ride.

"Papa!" Babe broke out of Emma's grasp and flew down the stairs.

Josiah turned around to see her barreling toward him and stepped forward to meet her, swinging her up into a circle and spinning her around. He set her back down on the ground and knelt down to her level again. "I tell you what, baby doll. If your mama says it's okay, I'll come back through here before I leave town. I'll stop off to say good-bye."

Babe couldn't speak but nodded.

Josiah glanced up at Emma, and she nodded, too. What else could she do?

She knew inside she wanted to see him again as much as her daughter did. And with that spin in the air and endearing name—which Babe would have railed at Mack for—he'd just firmly ensconced himself into Babe's heart as her pa.

Emma led Babe inside, so flustered at her daughter's enamored chatter and her belief that Jesus had indeed led the man to their doorstep to become her pa that it took her precious minutes to realize Josiah had left by way of the trail that led to the claim.

She flew into action, knowing that his intentions weren't the best when it came to Mack and that she'd unwillingly—or willingly, led by Josiah's charm—directly placed Mack into danger. "Come, Babe, we have to hurry and get up to the claim." She gathered up Babe's boots, dusted off her dirty stockings, and shoved the leather on the little girl's feet.

"Ouch, you're hurting me, Mama!" Babe fought her, and Emma forced herself to slow down and be gentler.

"Your feet are growing again. They barely fit into your boots. I'll have to buy you a bigger pair next time we're in town."

"Oh, new boots! Can we go now? I want my papa to see them."

"No, we need to get to the claim." Emma didn't even bother correcting her daughter. She contemplated dropping Babe off at Katie's on the way but knew she couldn't afford the wasted minutes it would take to do so. And Katie would be full of questions that Emma didn't have time to answer, or even have answers for! Babe would fuel the fire, too, when happily telling Katie and Jimmy that her father had sure enough arrived on their doorstep and had swung her around and called her baby doll. Emma would never get out from under their inquisition after that.

She grabbed Babe's hand, hustled out the door, and took off at a run. She slowed when she heard her daughter's labored breathing. Bending down, she took her daughter upon her back and moved as quickly as she could with the heavy load. She didn't believe Josiah had told her the truth about not hurting Mack. His life hung in the balance. She had to make it to the claim in time.

Chapter 5

Emma could hear the raised voices even as she neared the opening in the trail. Out of breath, she set Babe down and walked over to Ben Parson. "Could you take Babe over to your claim and distract her while I find out what this is all about?"

Ben shook his head even as he reached for the little girl. Emma knew the motion had to do with his frustration with the men, not with caring for Babe.

"I don't know what's gotten into them boys," he said. "It seems things usually stay pretty calm up here compared to the problems at the newer claims in other areas."

"Well, the tall one *is* a newcomer, and apparently he's bent on shaking things up over our way. Thanks for keeping Babe occupied. I appreciate it."

She watched as Babe skipped along at Ben's heels, already telling him her newest story. Emma cringed as she heard the words "my papa" in the conversation. Poor Ben was already getting an earful. Emma would have a lot of explaining to do when she returned to collect her daughter.

Ben handed Babe a lightweight gold pan he kept handy for her visits and hunkered down beside the towheaded waif. He glanced over at Emma with a smirk and eyebrows raised in question.

Emma rolled her eyes and turned to push herself through the crowd.

Mack stood at the side of the stream, and Josiah towered over him on the hill above. A gaping hole, the new mine entrance, loomed behind him. Emma couldn't make out their words. Though obviously angry, the men spoke in hushed voices.

Just as she broke through the last wall of men, Mack picked up a shovel and held it high over his head.

"Mack, no!" Her cry was lost in the scuffle.

She watched in shock and horror as Josiah glanced up, registered Mack's intent, and shoved the other man, hard. Mack went down. Josiah uttered more words, and Mack flew to his feet.

Josiah seemed to want a discussion, whereas Mack preferred a fistfight. Josiah's hands splayed out in front of him in a gesture of backing off, but Mack swung at him and connected with his right jaw.

"No." Emma's voice was but a whisper now. She didn't waste the effort of yelling when she knew the men wouldn't hear her even if she stood two inches from them.

Josiah's head snapped to the left. He stumbled but somehow managed to keep his footing. He bent and placed his hands on his knees as he fought the stars that had to be circling his head. Emma knew the effect because she'd experienced the same when hit in the jaw by an out-of-control horse a few years back.

A small trail of blood poured from his lip, and he swiped at it with his sleeve, oblivious to the bright red that stained his off-white shirt. He glanced over at Mack and said a few more words.

Emma looked at Mack for the first time. With his hair in disarray, he looked like he'd had his share of hits before Emma's arrival. But it was his eyes that sent a shiver of fear coursing through her body. They were wild, the eyes of a man who wasn't in his right mind. Had he always been this way and hidden it well? Or was this a side of Mack that came out when he was crossed? She well remembered his anger over her refusal of marriage. She didn't know how this day would end, but she was sure she didn't want Mack running her claim any longer, nor did she want him on her property.

She moved forward as the men stared at each other. Josiah dropped his head again, letting down his guard, and Mack took advantage and threw two more punches. Josiah dropped to his knees. Emma's hand flew up to cover her mouth. Bile rose in her throat, and she felt like she was about to be sick.

"I told you, I'm not going to fight, Mack. You need to come with me. A fight won't change the way things are. There're legal ways to deal with this."

"I'll die before I come with you. You just want to get me away from these witnesses so you can kill me." Mack's glazed eyes stared at the gathered crowd.

Josiah's voice was labored. "No, if I wanted to kill you, I'd do it now. Here in front of God and everyone. It's what you deserve, and it's what you'll get if I start with one swing."

Emma saw Mack's thought process in motion before Josiah had another chance to defend himself. Mack reached for the shovel, and everything slowed down in Emma's mind. She saw the shovel arc up. She saw Josiah reach for his gun. But before he could connect with the handle, the tool connected with the side of his head with a sickening *thud*.

The crowd stood motionless for a moment, and then all surged forward. Though Josiah was the stranger, he'd done nothing to instigate the violence against him. At least not that Emma could see. These were good men, her neighbors, and they didn't stand for an unfair fight. No one had expected to see the damage and anger Mack had just shown.

"Josiah!" Emma dropped to her knees beside his still body. She hoped Ben was keeping Babe from seeing this. "Josiah, can you hear me?"

Blood poured from the gash in the side of his head. Someone pressed a handkerchief into her hand, and she placed it against the flow.

"Josiah, you have to wake up. Stay with us. We'll get you help." She looked up at Phil Duggin.

"There's no way we can get him to town in this condition, ma'am. The ride would be too much for him. The best we could probably do is to get him down off this hill." He scratched his head as if the action would improve his thinking. "We need to get him stable."

"Take him to my place." Emma was as surprised as the men around her when the words popped out of her mouth. But the truth was, it was her claim and her worker who had caused him to get in this mess—even if Josiah had ignored her request to wait until another day—and she felt responsible for the man.

She looked around. "Where's Mack?"

The men glanced at each other, and finally a voice from the back of the crowd called out, "He took off through the far woods like he had a bear on his trail."

Emma didn't want to think the worst of Mack. He *had* been there for her during the past two years, but if he wasn't guilty of whatever Josiah had claimed, why had he reacted with such rage and then run off?

"Did any of you hear what the actual argument was about?"

Mutters of denial drifted around her.

"No, ma'am."

"Too far away."

"Stream too noisy."

"They talked in quiet voices until those last few exchanges at the end."

"Okay," she finally said. "We'll take him to my cabin. Someone needs to ride out for Doc." Emma gently pulled the handkerchief away, relieved to see the bleeding had slowed. "Let's get going."

"I'll go for Doc." Phil headed down the trail.

"Stop by my place and take one of the horses. You'll get there faster, even if it's a bit out of your way to town."

"Good idea. Will do." He hurried off down the trail with a few of her boarders following along to help.

Emma stepped back, and several men moved forward to take her place. They secured Josiah for the trek back to the cabin by placing him on a heavy blanket they could carry between them. She hurried over to snag Babe so they could be on their way.

Though in a hurry to keep up with Josiah, she started to update Ben on the situation, but he waved her away. "I'll catch the news from the menfolk. You go on ahead. But take good care of the man. According to Babe, he has an important place in your lives." His eyes twinkled with his teasing.

A small smile formed on her lips against her will. "He's a stranger, Mr. Parson. He has no place in our lives other than my trying to keep him alive until Doc can reach our cabin."

"I hear ya, ma'am. I hear ya." He tipped his hat at her and shooed her off toward home. "But I have to say I witnessed a good part of that confrontation, and the man was trying not to get into a physical altercation with Mack. It takes a good man to refuse to fight when fighting commences against him."

"Or a coward," young Bill Mercer jeered from across the stream.

Ben measured him with a glance, and his expression showed he found the younger man lacking. "That man is no coward. I wouldn't go up face-to-face with him for anything. His anger simmered under the show of patience, but I wouldn't want to be on the receiving end of a bad situation with him. He's one fierce man, and why he didn't give Mack more is beyond me."

"He promised me he wouldn't hurt Mack." Emma broke in on the conversation. "I don't know why, because his intent came across loud and clear even back at the cabin, but somewhere in the conversation he felt compelled to make me that promise. I guess he kept it, huh?"

"Well, little missy, maybe you ought to take your daughter's prayers and beliefs to heart. Looks to me like Someone bigger than all of us might have a plan here."

"Oh no. No way. This is not what Babe thinks. I'm sure Josiah, er, Mr. Andrews, had every intention of coming up here for no good, but for whatever reason, he decided not to make a public scene with his vendetta." She was glad Babe had wandered out of hearing range to pick wildflowers and missed the conversation.

Walking the few feet away to collect her daughter, she took Babe's hand and turned her toward the trail. "Now, if you don't mind, I'll be off to see to the man and prepare him to go with Doc as soon as he can get by to pick him up. I don't want him at my place a moment longer than he needs to be."

❧

"What do you mean he can't travel yet? He has to. He can't stay here!" Emma heard the dismay she felt as it flowed through her words. What did Doc think, telling her the man had to stay put where he was? He lay in her cabin. . . in her bed! He couldn't possibly stay.

"Emma, I know you heard me loud and clear when I explained his condition. He has a concussion. If we move him now, he'll never make it to town alive. And the noise there won't be conducive to his recovery, either. Out here he has you to care for him, the fresh air, and quiet."

Emma raised an eyebrow and glanced at Babe, who sat outside the front window singing at the top of her lungs about "a papa come to stay."

"Well, maybe not quiet, but it still beats the ruckus he'd deal with in town." Doc had the nerve to chuckle at Babe's choice of song. "She's excited over this, isn't she? You don't want to break the young girl's heart, do you?"

"I don't want to build her hopes, either, and this man isn't gonna be her papa. She needs to accept that. I can't take care of him." Emma smoothed the cover even as she said it. *Way to show my reluctance to help.*

Doc stared at her for a moment and sighed. "I see your situation and understand your reticence. If you want me to move him, if you feel in any way he's a threat to you, I'll take him along whatever the result may be. We can pack him on blankets and drive slow, but. . ."

"But if he dies, his blood's on my hands right along with Mack's?" Emma let her breath out in a huff. Doc knew she'd never send the man to his death. He knew exactly the words to use on her.

"I didn't say that." The glimmer in Doc's eyes matched Ben's earlier twinkle exactly. It seemed as if everyone had been let in on a secret that she alone didn't know. "I'm just telling you how it is. You've always wanted me to be direct with you."

"Yes, when it comes to Babe's health and well-being. I don't want you to mollycoddle me when she's sick just because you worry I can't take the truth. But this. . ." She waved a hand at the man in her bed. "How am I to care for him? I'm single and a widow. It isn't right."

"Sometimes life and death don't worry about propriety." He moved to pack his bag, then picked up his hat from the chair near the door. He stopped with his hand on the latch. "Seems you could get one of the men from the barn to help with any needs you might have with his care. I know a couple of them have right colorful pasts and are used to caring for gunshot wounds and the victims of those bullets."

"My men? How is it you know this and I don't? Most of them have been boarding here for two years. I didn't know any of them had that type of past!" Emma wondered now what she'd been subjecting her daughter—and herself—to by keeping these men around. "Maybe it would be best if I asked them all to leave. I sure had Mack pegged wrong."

"Sure, if you want to care for Josiah alone. Send 'em all packing."

Emma caught Doc's insinuation. If she sent them on their way, she'd have no one to help with Josiah's care. Not a good idea. At least not now. She'd keep them around until Josiah improved enough to care for himself. Meanwhile, she'd spend a bit more time with the men, asking about their lives, and see what they were about.

"Emma, if the men were a threat, you'd have known it by now. Those men would do anything for you. They're all patients of mine and rave about what a wonderful woman you are. You have nothing to worry about with any of them." He hesitated. "If there were to be concerns about any one of them, I'd have bet my money on Mack. There always seemed to be something simmering under the surface when it came to him."

So much for my discernment. She'd thought him the safest of them all. . .and the most trustworthy. But now that she thought about it, that was mostly because of her deceased husband's faith in him. "Thanks for sharing, Doc. I'll see you in the morning, then?"

"Yes, and don't worry. I've got him stabilized, and there isn't anything to do but keep an eye on him and follow the few instructions I left for you in case he comes to before my return." He pulled the door open, and Babe's happy squeal carried through the opening. "If you'd feel better, have the men sleep in shifts on the porch. That way someone will always be near if you need him."

"And what if a stray bullet comes for one of them while he's on my porch?" Emma's smile gave away her teasing. But truth be told, she couldn't tell Doc which man would possibly be used to bullets tearing around him, so she didn't feel very qualified to pick which ones should come to her rescue if needed. She'd rather stick it out by herself. She briefly considered asking Doc to escort Babe over to Katie's or Liza's but quickly brushed the thought away. Her daughter didn't need any more notions about Josiah's role in their lives put into her head, but if Babe left, Emma would be alone with Josiah. That wouldn't do at all.

Emma couldn't admit to herself whether she feared him or her feelings toward him more. She'd simply have to nurse the stranger back to health and send him on his way. She could handle this. He surely wouldn't be around for much more than a day.

Chapter 6

Josiah tried to open his eyes, but they wouldn't cooperate. He turned his head, and a shooting arrow of pain throbbed through his head. He forced back the darkness that tried to recapture him, but before he could register any information about where he was or what had happened to him, a warm cloak of unconsciousness embraced him and again wiped away the pain.

It seemed minutes, but Josiah could tell hours had passed when he next regained consciousness. Earlier, when he'd tried to peer out from between his lashes, bright light filled the room. Now semidarkness cloaked the area, allowing Josiah to briefly take in his surroundings. Nothing felt familiar.

A scuffling noise to his left had him turning his head in that direction. He moaned as a burst of pain shot across the side of his head. He squeezed his eyes shut to block it out. When the wave of accompanying nausea passed, he again forced his eyes partly open and met a brown-eyed gaze inches from his own.

"Mama, he's awake!" Babe's gleeful shout caused Josiah to squeeze his eyes shut.

"Shush, child," a voice chastised from across the room. "You'll scare him to death." The voice moved closer, its tone soft as velvet. "Now hurry off to bed as you were told. Mr. Andrews will still be here when you wake up."

Josiah waited a moment but didn't hear the little girl leave. He opened his eyes and peered out at her. She still nestled almost nose to nose with him, with both elbows against his pillow and her chin balanced upon folded hands. "Hello, Papa." She gave him an angelic smile.

A chuckle escaped Josiah's lips. He didn't have the energy to correct her. "Hello, baby doll." His raspy voice made him wonder how long he'd been unconscious.

So he was at Emma's place?

He heard a growl of frustration that had to have come from Emma. "Babe, he's *not* your papa. You have to stop this nonsense! Now scoot on over to bed."

Babe obeyed with a huff.

Josiah watched as Emma tucked her daughter snugly into bed. He could hear the soft prayers of mother and child before Emma dropped a kiss against Babe's forehead and patted the blanket that covered her. "Sweet dreams. See you in the morning." She stood watching her daughter for a moment then turned to hurry over to him.

His pulse picked up. He didn't know if it was from wariness over her feelings about his being there, excitement that a beautiful brown-eyed blond headed his way, or frustration that he lay helpless in her bed, weak as a baby. He never had been one to laze around, and he didn't take kindly to people coddling him. He tried to rise to a sitting position, but the blinding pain quickly put him flat on his back.

"Not ready to jump out of bed, I see." Emma's soft voice held a glimmer of humor. "You need to stay still and rest until morning."

Josiah didn't need to be told now that he'd tried to sit up. "How long have I been sick?" His scratchy throat caused him to cough. He went stiff to fight off the pain. He heard the sound of water being poured into a glass, and then Emma's soft fingers eased under his head, urging him to lean forward and take a sip.

The soothing water flowed down his parched throat, but he couldn't stop the awareness of her touch. He pulled back, motioning that he'd had enough. "So how long?" His voice sounded stronger, not so rough.

"Since yesterday afternoon." He felt his expression change from confusion to frustration. "Mack hit you with a shovel and knocked you out cold before taking off into the woods. No one's seen him since."

"Argh." Josiah tried to keep his voice down, but he couldn't believe he'd let Mack slip through his fingers again. Not this time, when he'd been so close. "He's not come back for his things?"

"No."

Josiah tried to rise from the bed again. Emma pushed him down. Her no-nonsense touch seared through his blanket, firm enough to make clear she'd have nothing to do with his trying to leave. She picked up a small glass bottle from beside the bed and measured out a dose. "Take this. Doc said it will help with the pain."

He turned his mouth away from the medicine. "I don't need anything. I need my wits about me."

"You can take that up with Doc in the morning, but for now, he said he wanted you to have it. If you don't take it, you'll toss and turn all night in pain and keep us all awake. Stop being difficult and do as the doctor ordered."

He glared at her, but her tone allowed no argument. Now he knew how Babe felt, with her little huff of frustration. He opened his mouth and took the bitter liquid. "There's nothing wrong with my arms, ya know. I could have done that myself."

"I'm sure you're perfectly capable. But we don't want to waste any, and I'm here to care for you. Let me do my job."

"So about Mack—would you know if he returned?"

"The men are watching and will detain him if he comes close again. But only if I give them good reason. They aren't going to hold him until you're better just so you can run over and start another altercation with him."

"I didn't. . ." His voice tapered off. He couldn't really deny he'd started the fight, if only by his presence. "I don't want trouble. I never intended to be a burden to you."

"So you're not going to tell me what this is all about?" Emma pulled a chair up close so their words wouldn't wake Babe.

He stared at the woman while trying to gather his thoughts. *Breathtaking.* The word popped up from nowhere but definitely described the beauty sitting before him. He understood why every bachelor in the surrounding Deadwood area seemed to board in her barn. Her brown eyes radiated warmth, and tendrils of blond hair curled in a beguiling way at each side of her cheeks before tapering down to tease her neck. The neck—along with her cheeks—that now flooded with color at his blatant perusal.

"Sorry." He moved his attention to the lamp behind her. "I'll tell you, but not now." He forced a yawn and hoped she'd believe the tired act and leave him alone until he could better focus on his explanation. In this state of half wakefulness, he didn't trust his words not to betray him. When she'd asked her question just now, he thought she referred to his staring. He'd almost blurted out that he found her attractive enough that he would consider staying if he thought he had a chance to win her heart. Instead, he caught himself at the last moment after realizing her question was aimed at his issue with Mack.

She laid her cool hand against his forehead, and he closed his eyes at the soothing sensation.

"You have no fever, so I'm hoping the risk of infection is going away. I'm sure you need more rest, though, so sleep and we'll talk in the morning." Her hand lingered.

He wanted to beg her to keep it there, tell her he'd be well before she knew it if she kept her healing touch against his skin. But she moved it moments later, and he opened his eyes to watch as she scooted her chair back away from the side of his bed.

"Doc stopped by yesterday afternoon and again this morning. He said the wound looked well and that he expects you to have a full recovery within a few days. As soon as you get up and around, you can move out to the barn with the other men. You're welcome to stay as long as you like out there."

Josiah suddenly decided he'd not wish for a fast recovery. He liked being in the homey warmth of Emma's place. "What wound do you refer to?"

"You have a gash where the shovel connected."

"Ah. Left side of my head." The reason for the shooting pain when he'd tried to look over at Babe.

"Yes. Doc stitched it up and said today that it's healing well. But it might bleed if you move around too much, so he wants you to stay in bed until he gives his approval for you to be up and around."

"If he insists."

Emma smiled as if she knew his intentions.

Josiah admitted he wasn't the type to languish in bed if not completely necessary, but if Doc said he had to stay. . .who was he to argue? He fought to hide his own grin.

"Somehow you don't strike me as the kind to take a doctor's orders that seriously."

"The company's good here, and service seems to be okay. I'll do my best to endure." He quirked his mouth up in the smirk women seemed to love and watched as Emma responded by rolling her eyes before pulling the curtain between his bed and Babe's.

He heard her walk around the room, her soft breath blowing out the lamp that burned on the mantel before finally settling into the far side of Babe's bed with a creak of the wood frame.

Tired though he was, Josiah had a feeling he'd be hard pressed to get a wink of sleep with the beautiful woman so close to his space. If he had to crawl out, it might be best if he moved to the barn. The two ladies in the cabin had him enchanted in a most endearing way.

⁓

Emma snuggled close to her young daughter on the small bed meant for one. She'd placed Babe between her and the stranger for her own sense of propriety.

Her job was to nurse the man back to health and set him on his way, nothing more. But her fingers still tingled from her touch against his sun-kissed skin. She realized as she lay in the dark that she held them against her lips. She dropped her arm to her side and clenched her hand tight, willing her mind to veer off to another topic.

She should be focusing on how to keep Babe safe from her papa dreams. Or she could figure out how she was going to take over the claim again with the newly excavated mine and Babe more at risk than ever. Now that the child had her papa notions, she'd also be interviewing each male she met along the stream, filling him in with her innocent way on how her mama needed a husband so she could have a papa. The child could humiliate her mother without even trying. Emma tossed onto her side, trying to escape the mental picture of every man in the area applying for the job of Babe's papa.

No, she'd not go there. She needed to find a replacement for Mack. That would solve her problem of keeping Babe at home until this silly phase wore off. More than likely, Emma's nerves would wear out before that ever happened, but she could dream. Her daughter didn't have the run on fantasies.

The thought made her glance over at the curtain that separated her from the attractive stranger. Maybe she should have kept it open. She could have watched in the moonlight to be sure he was okay.

Now she lied to herself! She only wanted the curtain open so she could stare at his handsome silhouette without his knowing. If truth be told, she suddenly wanted Babe's desire for a papa to come true as much as Babe did. She'd become smitten with the dark, mysterious man.

She huffed out a sigh at her ridiculous thoughts and flipped to face the opposite way. As if her thoughts would stop just because her back now faced the curtain. She could hear his steady breathing and resented that he could sleep when her overly tired brain ran wild with foolish emotions. After a good night's sleep, she would be able to face the error of her ways better. If only sleep would come and rescue her. She sighed again, the sound louder than she'd meant it to be.

"You might try counting sheep. It always works for me when I'm restless." Josiah's voice, full of laughter, carried across the room.

He'd heard her tossing and huffing and sighing! Her face flushed so deeply she opened her eyes to see if the red radiated throughout the cabin, lighting it for all to see. The intimacy of his being so near stifled her.

"I'm sorry. I didn't mean to keep you awake." Her voice sounded loud in the dark. It had been a long time since a man's presence had filled the tiny cabin. "I'm not used to sleeping in such tight quarters."

She flinched. Now she'd drawn his thoughts to her sleeping—or nonsleeping in this case—body. Simply scandalous!

"I mean by being cramped up in this tiny bed with Babe." Even worse! Now it sounded like she was fishing for a reason to move to a bigger, less crowded bed! Why hadn't she told the men to put Josiah in Babe's smaller bed, allowing the two of them to share the larger bed? Or better yet, put him in a bed out in the barn where he'd be at the mercy of the boarders instead of her?

She knew the answer to that one. The risk of infection out there far outweighed the discomfort of having him here in her cabin. He was a man. She was a woman. Those were the facts. But they were both adults. They needed to buck up to the situation and act like it. She had to figure out a way to divert their focus away from their sleeping situation and close proximity before they said or did something immoral. She had no intention of dishonoring God through her thoughts or desires.

"Mack's responsible for my brother's death."

All right, then. Maybe only her thoughts and actions needed to refocus. Apparently Josiah's thoughts were far, far away from her prone form lying on a bed mere feet away from his own. She interrupted her own musings as his words sank into her sleep-deprived brain. "Mack killed your brother?" Surely she'd misunderstood. Or the medicine had taken effect and caused the man to talk crazy.

"Inadvertently, yes." The words came with a hesitance, as if he'd rather blame Mack for outright murder than admit an indirect action.

"How?"

"Are we going to wake Babe up with our talking?"

Josiah's consideration for her daughter touched her heart. This man, stranger or not, didn't seem the type to harm a woman and her daughter. And he felt less a stranger the more time she spent in his company.

"No, once she's out, nothing will rouse her." Emma rolled back over to face Babe and the curtain. She pushed her daughter's hair off her face. The motion didn't change the rhythm of Babe's soft breathing. "Tell me about your brother."

"We were partners with Mack, had grown up with him through our childhood years. We had no reason not to trust him." He grew silent.

Emma let him gather his thoughts.

"We worked various jobs as we traveled, headed out West, and had amassed a small fortune. The plan was to earn enough to start a ranch that would be big enough for us all. We'd be able to buy everything we needed from the start and would work together to make it a success."

Again he paused.

"I'm listening." She didn't want him to worry that she'd finally nodded off during his painful narrative.

"One morning we woke up to find Mack gone, along with our money. We searched high and low for him over the next few months. My brother, Johnny, couldn't handle it and began drinking heavily. Next thing I knew, he'd gotten himself into a skirmish at a saloon and ended up with a bullet in his heart."

He stopped.

Emma waited, not knowing what to say. She prayed for the right words to come. "I'm so sorry." Maybe not the most profound words, but they were from the heart.

Josiah still didn't speak.

"I understand your animosity toward Mack, but why do you hold him responsible for the bullet another man used to send your brother to his death?"

"We both—my brother and I—were raised better. We both loved God and relied on our relationship with Jesus. He was a huge part of who we were."

Emma didn't miss the past-tense reference to his relationship with God.

"Johnny wasn't a drinker. Everyone loved him. His joy of life radiated out to all who knew him. He began to drink only after we'd lost our dreams, the dreams that Mack stole from us."

"Why would he do such a thing? Did you have a falling out? Did you see signs that Mack felt slighted or angry or left out?"

"We had no warning. One night Johnny and I headed off to bed, worn out from a heavy day of work. Mack said he'd join us later, that he had things to do. We didn't either one give it another thought. The next morning, we woke up and checked his room at the hotel, and though his stuff still filled the space, he'd not slept in his bed." Josiah shifted in his bed and groaned at the effort. "Ah, I've got to remember not to lie on my left side for a few more days."

"Do you need me to get you anything?"

"No, I'm fine. I forgot for a moment about my head."

Emma figured that was a good thing. If he could forget, the pain must be lessening. "So he hadn't slept in his bed. . . . He'd already skipped town?"

"We weren't sure what had happened. Mack, though brought up the same as us, had always tested the limits. He liked to have a drink or two at the saloon, and we figured he'd struck up with a woman. The thought upset us, but when he didn't come around for a couple more days, we became alarmed. No one seemed to know where he'd gone. He'd disappeared into thin air."

"Did you track him to a saloon?"

"One man said he'd seen Mack enter the saloon, but no one seemed to have a memory of what happened to him after that. We were in the process of rounding up a search party and stopped by the bank to pull some money to fund the trip. That's when we found out we'd been had, and Mack had taken the whole lot and run off days before."

"I don't know what to say." Mack had worked around Emma and Matthew for years. Had he robbed them right under their noses, too? Had the new mine or the claim produced gold that Mack had kept for himself? She hated to even entertain such thoughts, but now that she knew his character, the thoughts and doubts were there. "He's worked off and on with us for so long. . . . Why didn't I see it? Would he have harmed Babe and me in order to get our money if we found a fortune, too?"

Josiah released a pent-up breath. "I don't have an answer for that. I'm just glad I came along in time to prevent him from reaching his plan, whatever it might be. If that was my purpose in being here, it's a good start."

"What do you mean, 'start'? What's your plan?"

"Emma, I have to avenge my brother's death. The loss of his life can't be in vain." Josiah's flat words were cold, emotionless.

"You have to let the anger go, Josiah. If you hold on to it, you'll end up just like Mack, or worse. I saw an undercurrent of anger in him of late, enough to have me on edge before you arrived. I'd already decided I needed to let him go."

"I'm glad you didn't."

"Because you want him for yourself?"

"No, because I have no idea what he'd have done if you'd cut him off before he found his next treasure. He'd likely have harmed you or Babe."

Emma shuddered and pulled Babe into her arms. She needed to feel her daughter's heart beating against hers. Josiah's first thought had gone to her and Babe's safety. That was an improvement. A couple of days ago she'd have seen a different reaction from him, she was sure.

"My head's starting to pound again. I need to rest. But, Emma?" He stopped to make sure she still listened. His voice was starting to slur.

"Hmm?"

"Don't judge me for my actions until you've walked in my shoes."

"It's not my place to judge you, Josiah. That's between you and God. I only know that if you don't focus back on God, you might end up angry like Mack. . . or dead like your brother." The thought shouldn't bother her as much as it did. She hardly knew the man. "One more question. Where's the fortune now? Mack doesn't appear to have money. Wouldn't he have set up his ranch by now if that was his plan?"

"I'm not sure. That piece of the puzzle doesn't make sense, but I'll figure it out before this is all over."

"Do you need anything for your head? A cool cloth?"

"Nah. It's nothing a good night's sleep won't cure. I'm not sure what came over me and caused me to talk so much."

Emma's soft chuckle filled the air. The medicine had loosened his tongue. "Yes, what happened to the man too tired to speak a bit ago?"

She could hear the laughter in his responding words. "I needed that time to refocus my thoughts. I didn't think the direction they were heading was a good idea."

Again Emma felt her cheeks fill with red. But this time a certain joy accompanied her embarrassment. Josiah sounded more at peace than he had since his arrival. Maybe she'd be able to help him work through his anger toward Mack and let it go. And beside that important fact, she was relieved to know that apparently she wasn't the only one corralling her wayward thoughts after all. It would be interesting to see what the morning would bring.

Chapter 7

Emma woke early and dressed in the dark, taking extra care not to wake Babe. She'd slept in her dress from the day before, knowing she'd need to check on her patient during the night. She peeked around the curtain at Josiah, who still slept soundly, his rhythmic breathing a reassuring sound to her worried ears.

Josiah had had a rough night. Several times his thrashing had awakened her, and she'd gone to calm him, concerned that the medicine, while numbing the pain, would cause him to do damage to his stitches. The concoction apparently led to nightmares and hallucinations. Or maybe it was just Josiah's fighting his own demons that caused his lack of sleep and turmoil. Regardless, Emma hurried to his side each time and did her best to waken and calm the man, sitting by him until he fell back into another restless sleep. When he moaned in his slumber, she'd reluctantly measured out another dose of the laudanum, as the pain seemed too great for him. Now, at dawn, he finally slept in peace.

The morning light that slid through the window allowed her just enough brightness to heat the stove and prepare coffee. Quietly, she worked to make breakfast. She stirred up a pan of biscuits then set them aside. She'd heat the biscuits whenever she heard her housemates rouse and would fry up some ham and eggs to go along with them.

Pulling a warm wrap around herself, she stepped out onto the porch to drink her coffee while having quiet time with God. She loved to sit out there and pray, taking in the beauty of the sun as it rose over the hills. No one stirred over at the barn, though usually some of the men would be up and about and would wave as they headed to the mines for an early start. Though tired, she needed this time to gather her thoughts. Once Babe awakened, she'd not have a moment to form another cohesive thought.

She lifted her cup to her mouth and froze as she heard a sound in the trees. Half standing, she worried Mack had returned. He knew her early morning routine, and it would make sense he'd try to contact her at that time, when he knew no one else was around. She knew Josiah was in no condition to help her in a crisis, and she doubted any of the snoring men in the closed-up barn would come to her aid.

Having her coffee outdoors probably hadn't been the best idea for today.

She should have stayed within the safety of her home, with the door latched, until the situation with Mack was resolved.

Just as she stood to hurry inside, the trees parted and her friend Liza stepped through. Emma put a hand to her heart in relief. She hadn't realized how tense she'd been until that moment.

Maybe it would still be best to move Josiah into town. But then again, moving him wouldn't guarantee her and Babe's safety in the event Mack returned with a vendetta of his own. And she couldn't ask the boarders to give up days at their claims to watch over her. She'd feel safer with Josiah here and would have to take their situation one day at a time.

"Hi, Emma. Is it too early? I know you like your quiet time, but I took a chance you'd be up for a visit."

Her good friend must have caught wind of a stranger on the premises and had to come check out the situation.

"Come on up and have a seat. I'll get you some coffee."

Liza smiled with relief and sank into a chair.

Emma slipped inside and poured another cup of coffee for her friend, wondering over the visit. Maybe it had to do with Josiah, but Liza looked pale and didn't seem her normal bubbly self. Though how else would she look this early in the morning, before she'd even had a chance to make herself a cup of coffee? She exited the door and closed it gently behind her.

Liza stared into the distance, not appearing to notice the sunrise as it burst into color before her.

"Liza? Everything okay?" Emma spoke softly, but Liza still jumped at the sound of her voice.

"Oh. Yes. Well, to be honest, no." Her smile quivered, then failed. "Oh, Emma, I think Peter's going to leave." Her voice broke, and she fell silent.

"Leave? You mean, you all will pack up and move away?" Emma's heart fluttered at the thought. Though she probably had more in common with Katie and felt closer to her as a friend, Liza was the nearest neighbor, and Emma had come to rely on her nearby presence over the past two years. "What's caused this?"

Liza's eyes filled with unshed tears. "The claim isn't doing well, and we don't have the money to buy supplies. We've struggled for weeks, and Peter has grown more distant every day. I reassure him that things will be okay, but now I don't know. He came in late last night, this morning actually, and fell into bed without a word to me. I have no idea where he's been, but I could smell liquor on his breath." She set her coffee aside. "We have no money for basic food, and he manages to find himself some liquor."

Emma didn't miss the bitterness in her words. "I'm so sorry. We have plenty.

I'll put together some things for you before you go."

She cut off Liza's protest before she could voice it. "You were there for me when Matthew died. I don't know how I would have made it through that time without you and Peter. Now it's my turn to give back. Let me do this."

Liza nodded.

"Where will you go if you leave? Do you have family back East?" Emma pushed away the worry that crept up at the thought. It was late in the season to try to cross the prairies. It would be a tough trip even if they left right away.

"I don't think he intends to take Petey and me along. I have a feeling he's going to bolt on his own."

"Oh, Liza, surely not. Peter has been a rock ever since I've known him. I can't imagine his doing such a thing! He loves you both dearly."

Liza sipped her coffee and shook her head. "Not anymore. He's not said two words to me in weeks. He comes in late and leaves when I'm busy doing something else so he doesn't have to speak to me. Something's not right." She set the coffee down and walked to the porch rail, peering up at the sky. "I've prayed that God would send me an answer or allow Peter to find something, anything, at the claim to encourage him to go on. But there's been nothing. I feel so empty and alone."

"I've been right here. You know you can come to me whenever you need to. Why did you wait? You shouldn't carry this burden alone."

Liza glanced over at her with a sardonic smile. "Did you come to us when you were struggling after Matthew passed on?" She shook her head. "No. We didn't find out until we came to visit and found the place in complete disarray. If I remember right, one of your men had to come over to ask for our help in rousing you out of the cabin."

Emma blushed as she remembered the awful few weeks immediately after she'd lost Matthew. Babe was a mess, the cabin untouched, and she couldn't drag up the energy to do more than plunk a few morsels of food before her daughter. Liza had come and forced her to carry on. She'd then teamed up with Katie, and the two dear friends kept a constant vigilance on Emma and forced her to move forward.

"You're right. I didn't come to you. But you know better and have no excuse not to come to me. We've been through so much together. We'll get through this, if it even happens. I've learned that God always has a purpose. Let me pray for you."

The women sat close together and prayed. Liza sobbed at Emma's caring words. As Emma finished her prayer, she hugged Liza close, joining with God to protect her friend in any way she could.

"Thanks." Liza wiped at her tears. "Peter will be so angry if he finds out why

I've come. But I needed a friend, and after not sleeping all night, I figured I'd best get over here early so we could talk before you leave for the claim. How's that going for you, anyway?"

"I'm not—well, I haven't been—working the claim for the past few weeks. I turned it over to Mack. But now he's missing, and I suppose I'll have to go back to mining myself." She considered asking Liza to watch Babe. They could work out an arrangement where she could compensate her friend by supplying food to her and Petey. She had doubts about it being a good idea, though, if Peter's moods weren't steady. She didn't need to place Babe into a possibly unsafe situation. She pushed the idea away. "The claim is doing okay. We've made enough to get by. We have plenty to share."

"Mack's missing?" Liza ignored her offer to help, and instead Emma's words seemed to pick up Liza's drooping emotions. "What happened to him?"

"A stranger appeared a couple of days ago and said he needed to talk to Mack. I asked him to wait, but he went to the claim instead. By the time I'd gathered up Babe and placed her with Ben Parson, they'd gotten into an altercation and Mack hit the stranger, Josiah Andrews, on the head with a shovel."

"Oh my. Was he okay?"

"He's fine, but Mack took off into the woods and hasn't been seen since." She stopped to warm her hands with her own cooling coffee. "For a moment when I heard you in the trees, I thought he'd returned."

"I didn't mean to startle you. I knew my time would be limited, so I took the direct route through the woods instead of crisscrossing on the paths. Sorry if I caused you to worry."

Emma smiled and took Liza's hand in her own. "You caused me no grief. I'm glad you stopped by. I needed a break. Taking care of Josiah kept me up all night, and you've helped me refocus for the day."

Liza asked, "Taking care of Josiah?"

"Yes. Mack's blow knocked Josiah unconscious, and he had a concussion. The men brought him here while Phil went for Doc. We figured Doc would take him right back to town, but Doc worried that any move would kill Josiah. His medicine caused him nightmares, and I was up with him until he calmed."

Leaning forward with a teasing gleam in her eyes, Liza whispered, "Is he easy on the eyes? Tell me about him. Maybe God dropped him here on your doorstep for a purpose."

"Liza! What am I going to do with you? The man's injured. That's my only focus."

"Surely you've had a moment to notice his looks. Is he someone you could look at for the rest of your life? If not, I'd think you'd send him out to the barn with the other men."

Emma laughed out loud and had to quickly hide her mortified chortles in order to correct her friend's wayward thoughts. "I suppose he's pretty easy on the eyes, but I didn't keep him in the cabin because he's pleasant to look at. The things you come up with sometimes."

"So if he were ugly, you wouldn't send him to the barn?"

Her lighthearted friend was back for the moment.

"Of course I wouldn't send him to the barn. Even if he were ugly, he'd need my care. That's all this is about. I'm interested in only the man's well-being."

"Well, that's sure good news for an injured man to hear, ugly or easy on the eyes."

Both women yelped at the sight of Josiah standing in the open doorway of the cabin with a smirk on his face.

Emma's heart picked up a few beats. Even injured, Josiah looked heart-flutteringly handsome. A dark shadow covered his previously clean-shaven jaw. He'd need to take care of the stubble soon. Emma couldn't remember where she'd placed Matthew's shaving utensils, and then she couldn't believe she even considered finding them for this stranger. Besides, most likely he had his own supplies in his bag, wherever the boarders had placed it.

She tried to turn her thoughts in another direction. "How are you feeling this morning?"

Josiah shouldn't even be up on his feet yet. The fact that he leaned against the doorway for support showed his weakness.

"Better." He swayed in the doorway before resting against the wood frame once more. "I'll be up and out of your hair before you know it."

"So I see." Emma rolled her eyes. Why were men always so stubborn about admitting they weren't invincible? She glanced over at Liza, who still sat with her mouth gaping. "Liza? Liza!"

Her friend jumped. "Oh, sorry, you were saying?"

"I wasn't *saying* anything to you, but you're gaping." Emma glanced over at Josiah, who winked at her.

She realized her manners were sorely lacking. "Josiah, I'd like you to meet my friend Liza. She and her husband, Peter, live just over the other side of the hill, through the trees. They're our closest neighbors."

Stepping forward, Josiah reached for a chair and lowered himself gingerly to sit. "I'm right pleased to meet you. It's always good to meet one of *our* neighbors." He captured Emma's eyes and held them captive before releasing them with a teasing smile.

A warm current ran through Emma at the intimacy of the statement. Again she caught herself wishing the illusion that they were a family could last. She realized—or finally admitted to herself—that she was lonely.

"I'm glad to meet you, Josiah. Emma's needed a man in her life."

"Liza! This is only temporary." This time she refused even to look over at Josiah, but his resounding laugh flowed across her. He had a nice laugh, even if it was at her expense.

Relief flooded her when Josiah turned the tables on her overly talkative friend. "Speaking of needing a man in your life, I hated to eavesdrop, but you're just outside my window. I heard what you said about your husband. Peter, right?"

An expression of pain moved across Liza's face.

"Maybe I could talk to him?" Josiah pinned Liza with his stare. "Sometimes it helps a man to have another's input. I don't mind."

Emma thought that was the sweetest thing Josiah could have said. "You'd really do that? For someone you don't know?"

Josiah moved his attention to Emma. "Of course I would. What kind of ogre do you expect me to be? I know I rode in here with a chip on my shoulder—"

"A boulder would be more like it," Emma interrupted.

"A shoulder boulder, Mama? What's that?" A sleepy-eyed Babe walked through the doorway and crawled up on Emma's lap.

Emma laughed. "A rhyme is what that is, sweetheart. How'd you sleep?"

Babe snuggled close. "Fine. I love to cuddle with you."

"And I, you. But I think I have a black eye today from your wiggles." Emma looked up to see Josiah watching the verbal exchange with a tender expression on his face.

"I don't wiggle that much," Babe said adamantly, sitting up straight with a frown. "Do I?"

"No, honey. I'm only teasing. You're a great cuddle bear to sleep with, too."

Babe settled back. "I want to sleep like that every night. Then Papa can sleep in the other bed."

"Oh, Babe." She didn't even bother to correct the youngster's comment this time. It did no good. "Josiah—Mr. Andrews—won't be staying much longer. It isn't proper. He'll be on his way, or at least he'll move out to the barn with the other men."

"Until you get married?"

"Until he goes his own way."

Josiah cleared his throat, probably to hide his laughter. "I'll stick around awhile, baby doll, if it's okay with your mother."

Emma nodded.

"I still need to find Mack, and I want to help with the claim until we figure out another plan, since I ran your worker off. I'll move out to the barn today."

"Are you sure you're up to it? You need to keep those stitches clean."

"I'll be fine." He turned back to Liza, who'd sat silently ever since Babe came outside. "What do you say? Is there any way I can help?"

"I appreciate your offer to help, Josiah, but I can't accept it. Peter would be furious to find out I'd come over and talked about our situation." She stood. "As a matter of fact, I need to be heading back home right now. Petey will wake up soon, and I don't want him to be alone with Peter or wake him up sooner than necessary. Peter's too much of a bear lately."

"Mama? Can I go over to play with Petey today? I miss him."

"Not today. Another time."

"Soon," Liza added to the little girl. "Petey misses you, too."

"Okay."

"Scoot inside and get ready to eat. I'll be along shortly to finish breakfast." Emma shooed her daughter out of hearing.

Liza looked at Emma. "I'll let you know if we need anything. I promise."

Josiah forced himself to stand, too. "Let me get you some supplies. You can tell Peter that Emma had a surplus and blessed you with them."

Emma analyzed his words, wondering why she felt touched by his thoughtfulness in offering Liza her things instead of being offended as she had been when Mack referred to the claim as "ours."

"You sit, Josiah. I'll put something together." Emma hurried to collect a basket of food for her friend.

Liza followed her inside. They scooted aside as Babe barreled past, the child not wanting to miss a moment of Josiah's company.

Emma couldn't imagine the feeling of not being able to provide for her little girl. "Tell him this basket is a thank-you gift for you all helping me get on my feet two years ago." She had plenty of eggs to share. She'd gather them in a moment. She continued to add a selection of basic foods that would carry Liza through for days.

Liza laughed. "You don't think he'll wonder why now? After two years?"

"You can tell him I've found my footing and am just getting my act together. It's true."

"I can see why." Liza's voice turned wistful as she looked out at Josiah, who held Babe on his lap. "Peter doesn't even give that kind of attention to his own son. That man you have out there is one sweet fellow."

"Josiah has nothing to do with my feelings. And he's not *my* man." Emma wondered how many more times she'd have to say that phrase before he left her place. She tucked a towel-wrapped supply of muffins into the overflowing basket. She kept one out and handed it to her friend. "Eat this before you fall on your face in the middle of the woods." She led the way outside through the back door and went over to collect the eggs. "I realized weeks ago how much time had passed me by and that I'd just barely been surviving. It's time for me to live again. . .and you'll feel the same way as soon as you and Peter get through this rough spot."

Liza wrapped Emma in a fierce hug. "Thanks for being my friend."

They walked around the side of the house, and Liza said good-bye. Emma offered to help carry Liza's load, but her friend waved her away. "I've kept you from your breakfast long enough. You take good care of him now, ya hear?"

Emma sent her back a playful glare and headed in to finish their breakfast.

"She seems to be a sweet lady." Josiah must have followed her inside. He held Babe's chair as she sat down before settling at the table beside her. He looked exhausted.

"She is. I can't believe Peter's acting as she said. I mean, I'm sure he is. Liza wouldn't exaggerate about something that serious." She tucked the biscuits into the oven and added a bit more wood to the fire.

"Failing to take care of a loved one is a huge burden for a man to carry."

Emma wondered if he referred to himself with the words. In his mind he thought he'd failed his brother. "You were sweet to offer them food."

"At your expense?" His voice held amusement. "Do you often let others give away what is yours?"

"I'd already planned on preparing a basket."

"Let me pay you back for all that you gave her. I can replace what is needed next time we go to town."

There it was again, his use of "we." Though she was sure he didn't mean anything by it, she couldn't help the smile that took over her face. A trip to town had never sounded so inviting.

Chapter 8

Josiah collapsed as soon as breakfast was over and slept most of the day away. He woke up in time for dinner, ate ravenously, and then fell back into bed again.

Emma kept Babe entertained outdoors as long as possible then brought her in for bed.

"I don't wanna go to bed," Babe whined. "It's barely dark outside. I want to play with my papa."

"For the hundredth time, he isn't your papa." Emma didn't think her patience would last until Babe crawled under the covers. The child had been irritable all day, and Emma hadn't slept well the previous night. She wanted nothing more than to settle Babe in and to give in to the weariness that consumed her body. "Hold still while I get your gown over your head."

Babe continued to wiggle and whine.

Emma captured her with an arm and held her steady while slipping the white nightdress over the small child's body. Babe felt a bit warm. Emma hoped she wasn't coming down with something. It would be bad enough to care for Babe when low on sleep already, but even worse for Josiah to catch something in his weakened state.

Babe began to cry. Emma pulled her onto her lap and sang to her softly. The child lay stiff in her arms, but exhaustion soon won out, and she relaxed and fell into a deep sleep. Emma eased her onto the bed and pulled up the bedclothes to tuck her in.

She checked on Josiah, saw that he was sleeping soundly, and turned down the lantern before climbing into bed next to Babe. She said her prayers quietly but didn't get far before dropping off into a deep sleep herself within minutes.

～

The next morning, Josiah woke up before Emma and Babe did. He felt much better, so he crept out of bed, careful not to wake them. He eased the door open and slipped outside into the early morning air.

Everything felt fresh up here in the hills, and Josiah relished not having to breathe in the dust that had been his companion on the trail for far too long. The aroma of coffee brewing carried across the yard, and Josiah followed the enticing scent to the barn. He needed to check out his new quarters anyway. He felt good enough today that he might as well make the move. Now would be a good time to speak to the men and settle in. They'd be heading to their claims soon.

A booming voice carried through the pre-dawn dim. "Hey, it's the knock-out man. Come on in and get a cup of coffee."

Leaving the barn doors open as he'd found them, Josiah let his eyes adjust to the lack of light and followed the voice.

"Phil Duggin," a younger man greeted him. "Have a seat. We're glad to see you up and around. We weren't sure for a while there whether you'd come through or not. That was one nasty bump to the head."

Josiah nodded as he sipped the warm coffee Phil placed in his hands. "Josiah Andrews. Glad to meet you." He shook Phil's hand and looked around. The structure was sparse but more like a boardinghouse than a barn, from what he could see. He turned his attention back to Phil. "Were you there when the. . . accident happened?"

"Not much of an accident from what I saw, but yes, I was one of the men who helped. I went for Doc. I grabbed my stuff while in town and moved out here myself the other night. Emma said she had room, and I like the location."

"You have room for one more? I'd like to get out of Emma's hair now that I'm up and around. She's been good to me, but she and the little tyke seemed to be faring poorly last night and this morning. I'm thinking she isn't getting much sleep with me around."

Phil motioned for Josiah to follow him. "Most of the men went on up into the hills already, but I'll show you around. It's a nice arrangement. I took over Mack's area. We stored his things up front so he can pick them up whenever he returns." Phil motioned to a stack of belongings in the far corner by the door. "I know the men said they had another spot in the back here. Let me show you."

The area was clean, private, and welcoming. It had a cot, a small table and chair, and a shelf for clothes.

"The first men that boarded with the Delaneys took the liberty of closing the back area off into private rooms. The space above your room can be used as storage if you need it. Most of us live pretty sparsely, though, and are fine with just the room."

Josiah thanked him and decided to move in as soon as Emma woke up. His horse already occupied a stall at the front of the barn, and he walked over to check on him. "Pretty comfy there, eh, fella?" He greeted his stallion with a pat to the head. From the looks of things, he'd never get Rocky out of here again. His mount was so well fed and gleaming with attention, Josiah knew he needed to thank whoever had cared for the creature.

He headed back to see if Emma was awake. No sign of life came from the house, so he settled on the front porch, exhausted from the effort of exploring his new home.

Emma awakened, shocked to see the late hour. She and Babe never slept this late! But then, they'd never had a houseguest who needed such care, either. Josiah! She'd slept so hard she hadn't checked on him once. When she found his bed empty, she stepped outside to see him sleeping in a chair on the porch. She slipped back inside and made coffee, biscuits, and eggs. Babe slept through all the banging of pans and slamming of the stove door.

The food was ready before her daughter and houseguest roused enough to come to the table. As Josiah sat down, Emma noticed that he still looked exhausted. She knew Doc would be back soon to check on him. He'd first said he'd return today, but the miners had told her the previous night that Doc had been called out the other direction, and it would be another day or two before he returned to the cabin.

"Do you need anything? Something for the pain? You're pale." Emma stated the obvious, but Josiah might not know how rough he looked.

"No, I'm fine. I went out to explore the barn, though, and I think I'll move my things over today and stay there from now on." He poured Emma a cup of coffee before filling his own mug. "I'll be fine as soon as I'm settled. I'll rest a bit as soon as I have everything in place."

Emma eyed her food but didn't feel like eating. She picked at her biscuit while they talked. "Are you sure you're ready? Maybe it would be best to wait until Doc takes a peek at you."

"I've met Phil Duggin. He seems like a good man. He told me he'd help with anything I need, so I think I'll be fine. The men can always come for you if I need attention."

"Sounds like a good idea. But do send someone to call for me, no matter the hour, if there's anything at all that you need."

"Will do." He pushed back in his chair. "Baby doll? You want to help me carry my things outside?"

When Babe halfheartedly nodded her head yes, Emma knew something was up. She watched as her little girl slid off her seat, her food barely touched. "You feelin' all right, Babe?" She reached over to feel Babe's forehead.

"Yes, Mama. I'm just tired."

How she could be tired after sleeping so hard the night before and so late that morning was beyond Emma's understanding, but with Josiah's arrival, the little girl had been surrounded by excitement. Maybe with Josiah in the barn, they'd both catch up on sleep that night.

Emma had a lot of chores to do over the next two days. She washed their clothes and bedclothes, baked bread, tidied up the cabin, and fell into bed exhausted both nights.

Josiah kept insisting that he should go to the claim, but Emma assured him the claim would be fine for a few more days without their attention. She had wanted Doc to give Josiah a clean bill of health before he began his work. Instead, the stubborn man had worked around the cabin, clearing out weeds that had taken over during Emma's lack of attention while working the claim, shoring up the fence where it had sagged, and mucking out the stalls while the other men were gone. Though the miners did a lot around the place to show their appreciation to Emma for letting them stay there, knowing she didn't have a man around to keep the place up, there were still things that they never had time to do. It was nice to have Josiah taking over those chores, though Emma was sure he'd have been better rested at the claim when all was said and done.

On the fifth day after Josiah's arrival, Emma forced her way out of bed with a pounding headache. Relieved to have things clean and some food made in advance, she promised herself to take it easy. She'd overdone things while caring for Josiah and now would pay the price.

Babe continued to be cranky, and this morning she didn't budge when Emma tried to wake her up. She decided to let the little girl sleep, hoping the extra rest would improve her mood.

Emma went outside for her usual quiet time. After praying, she watched as Josiah approached from the barn. They'd gotten in the habit of sharing coffee and breakfast each day, her way of thanking him for the work he'd done around the place. "Doc should be here today to check you over. From the look of things, I'd say he'll declare you well enough to do whatever you want."

Josiah sent her a smile. "So you're saying I'm looking good? 'Pleasing to the eye,' as Liza would say?"

Emma's face heated at the comment. "You didn't miss a thing from that conversation, did you? How do you know you didn't imagine those words while you had your concussion?"

"If I had any doubt, your blush a moment ago proved otherwise." He settled in his chair and laughed. She'd placed his coffee on the rail, and he reached for it and took a sip. "Ah. This hits the spot. It's been a mite chilly the past few mornings."

"Do you have any blankets? The barn can get quite cold. We have extras if you want some."

Josiah surveyed the clouds. Gray and fluffy, they promised rain. "I might have to take you up on them until I can get to town. I still owe you a trip. Do you feel up to going soon?"

"I'm caught up on things around here, so we can go at any time. Maybe after Doc arrives, we can go the next day?"

He nodded and drank his coffee, quiet for a few moments, lost in thought.

He finally glanced around. "Where's Babe this morning? I thought she'd be up and ready to follow at my heels again today."

"She's not feeling well, but I guess I do need to rouse her. I can't let her sleep all day."

"You look a bit pale yourself. Let me get her, and you sit and relax. I'll bring her out here." He rose and walked into the cabin. Emma didn't have the energy to argue. She tipped her head back against the chair and let the cool breeze soothe her body.

She must have dozed, because when she opened her eyes, the sun had changed position. Babe and Josiah were nowhere to be seen. She stood to her feet and swayed, grabbing the porch rail for support. Leaning forward against it, she shaded her eyes and looked out toward the fenced area where they let the horses and cows roam—Babe's favorite spot for Josiah to take her. There was no sign of them.

Dizzy, she walked to lean against the front wall of the house, and a feeling of panic washed over her. Where was Babe? She'd trusted her with a stranger, had fallen asleep, and now her daughter was gone.

She stumbled into the house and saw Josiah sitting in the rocking chair, a sleeping Babe held safely in his arms. Relief swept through her until she noticed the look of concern on Josiah's face.

He stood, walked over, and eased Babe down onto her bed. He'd stripped her down to her last layer of clothes. "Emma, I don't want you to get overly concerned, but have you noticed Babe running a fever lately?"

Emma tried to gather her thoughts. Her woozy brain wouldn't work properly. What was wrong with her? "Um, yes. I think she's felt a bit warm a few times over the past day or two. Maybe longer. She's been irritable and not quite herself for the past three or four days." She stopped and ran her hand across her aching forehead. "I thought it might be excitement due to your arrival, but she might be taking sick. Why?"

"I don't want to alarm you, but she's burning up. I've been rubbing her down with a cool cloth, but it isn't helping much. I think I'd better ride for Doc." He closed the gap between them. "You don't look much better. I came out to get you when I couldn't rouse her, and I couldn't get you to wake up, either. I figured you were plumb worn out." He reached over to feel her forehead. His touch sent shivers through her, but her skin felt as if it were on fire.

"I'm fine. Let me check on Babe. I need to cover her up."

"No, she's burning up already. We need to cool her off, not trap the heat in. She can't afford to get any hotter."

A sob escaped Emma's throat. She couldn't lose Babe. Her little girl's flushed features and labored breathing informed her that she was very sick. She bent down and recoiled at the heat in Babe's skin. "I don't know what to do. I can't think. Yes, do go for Doc. He should be heading this way anyhow. Maybe you'll meet up with him on the way to town."

Josiah stared at her, concern written all over his face. "Emma?" His voice seemed to come from far away.

Emma tried to respond but couldn't. She turned to look at him and felt herself start to fall. Then everything went black.

Chapter 9

Josiah caught Emma mid-fall and carried her to the bed that had been his only a few days earlier. He laid her gently atop the covers and felt her fiery skin. Babe wasn't the only one sick. For the first time in his life, he felt overwhelmed. There'd never been a situation in which he didn't feel in total control, but suddenly these two females were sick and totally reliant on him. They'd been so good to take him in; he didn't want to let them down. He didn't dare leave them alone long enough to ride to town. Even Liza's or Katie's would be too far away.

He sent up a rusty prayer to God, begging for help. If someone would just stop by, Josiah could either send him on for Doc or have him stay while Josiah went himself. He was afraid if he left them now, Babe might get up and wander off in her delirium. Emma was too ill to care for her. She'd never even hear her daughter if she tried to go outside.

Babe cried out, and he hurried to her side. "Papa!"

"I'm here, baby doll. It's okay. You're going to be okay. I'll take good care of you." He pushed the damp blond hair back from her face.

She continued to sob. "I need you, Papa. I hurt. My mouth hurts."

Josiah's heart melted at her words. He carried her over to the window and angled her for a look into her mouth. He cringed at the sight of the open sores that coated the insides of her cheeks and throat. "Ah no. Not this." He pulled the little girl close against him, opened the front door to allow cooler air to filter in, and sank back down onto the rocking chair. He gently rocked, crooning sweet words to the helpless little girl in his arms. If his suspicions were correct, the little girl had smallpox. He reached over to the tepid water in the bowl beside him and resumed rubbing her down with the cool cloth. He prayed like he'd never prayed before.

Hours later, he heard the arrival of someone on horse-back. He tried to place Babe on her bed, but she whimpered and clung to him. He took her along to the door, relief spreading through him as he watched Doc ride up to the porch. "You're a sight for sore eyes, Doc."

Doc glanced up at him, then at Babe. "I thought I came to check on you, but it looks like I have a new patient." He tied the horse to the porch rail and grabbed his bag from the saddle.

Josiah put a hand up to stop the doctor. "If I'm correct, Doc, Babe and

57

Emma both have smallpox. You'd best stay where you are and tell me what to do from there."

Waving him away, Doc continued up the stairs. "I've spent the better part of each day since I've seen you caring for folks just like these two. After years of treating patients with the disease, I've never caught it. I'll be fine."

He entered the cabin and motioned for Josiah to lay Babe down on her bed. Josiah hovered, not wanting to stray too far from the little girl who'd stolen his heart. She looked so frail and helpless lying there. He'd do anything to get back the impish girl who talked incessantly, always full of intelligent questions.

Doc examined Babe's mouth, then lifted her gown and checked the rest of her body. "Yes. It's smallpox. I'm afraid there's not much I can recommend for you to do, other than keep her cool and calm." He looked over at Emma, who tossed and turned on her bed. "Looks like her mama is in the same boat."

He walked over and pulled the curtain closed while Josiah returned to the rocking chair with Babe. The skin on his arms burned from the heat coming off her tiny body. Doc's silence as he checked Emma made his heart beat faster. He wished he could go over and see for himself that she was okay. He knew it would be improper, but he'd come to care deeply for her in the short time he'd stayed at their place. Emma had no one else to watch over her. The thought worried and bothered him at the same time. It wasn't his place to worry, but for the first time in years, he wanted to settle down and care for someone. He couldn't think of anyone better than this sweet lady and her daughter. They had captured his heart.

"Emma's in the same condition. I've given her something to help her sleep. I'll leave it on the table over there, and you can give her more when needed." Doc rounded the curtain. "You're going to have your hands full. I don't know what to tell you." Pulling his glasses off, he held them while he stared at Josiah. Concern etched his features. "I'd send my wife over, but she's taking care of a family on the other side of town. They're all down with the pox and have no one to care for them. At least Emma and Babe have you. You realize I'll have to place you all under quarantine?"

Josiah nodded, familiar with the routine. He'd already been exposed and sailed through the last quarantine with only a light case of smallpox. "What about the men at the barn? They've all been around me and also Babe."

"Ben Parson came down with the virus the day you came to town. I'm sure he and Babe were exposed at the same time by whoever brought the disease in." He packed his bag. "But the men here have all been exposed already. They can go ahead and work the claim or hang out here, whatever they feel up to, but I don't want them anywhere near town."

He quieted, deep in thought. "I think Liza and her clan have already had the pox, too. I'll head over that way and see if she can't come over to help."

Josiah couldn't explain the depth of relief that he felt at Doc's words. He knew the last thing Emma would want was for him to care for her in a deeply personal way. He'd hold down the fort and do whatever needed doing, but if Liza could come over to do the daily personal care, he'd be forever in her debt. Otherwise, he'd eventually have to face up to a very put-out Emma.

"Let me take a peek at you before I go. Though you look fit as a fiddle, from what I can see."

Josiah started to stand, but Doc waved him back into the chair.

"I can do what needs doing right here." He poked and prodded at Josiah's stitches and bruised head. It wasn't near as sore as it had been days earlier. "You can send up a prayer of thanks that it's healed wonderfully."

"I'll do just that. I've not prayed in years, not until today. You are an answer to my prayers, showing up like you did."

"I'm glad it worked out. Keep the ladies as cool as you can, but there isn't much more you can do. The sores will start to break open, and it's important to keep them from being infected. If Liza can help with bathing the ladies, you might wash their sheets daily so they can keep as clean as possible. It won't help that they'll be sweating through this fever. Fortunately, the fever will lift about the time the sores break open. If they get to that point, they should heal just fine."

Josiah's heart sank with worry. He knew the doctor's words were meant to encourage, but he also knew smallpox was a deadly disease and played no favorites. The next few days would be critical to whether Babe and Emma pulled through. Only time would tell if they both would make it.

~

"I think she's coming around. Josiah, come over here and tell me what you think. The fever seems to have broken."

Emma struggled to place the familiar voice. The darkness dragged her back, but she fought it. Liza. The woman speaking had to be Liza. But why was she here, and why couldn't Emma open her eyes?

A strong hand covered her forehead. "Thank God. You're right." A laugh rang out over her head, causing Emma to jump.

"Josiah! Shhh. You startled her."

"Oops, sorry."

The hand moved away, and Emma felt a loss. A cool cloth replaced his touch.

"If you'll step outside and bring in those fresh sheets, I'll bathe her and she'll feel so much better. The worst is over. Now we just have to keep the sores clean so they don't get infected."

Josiah's voice murmured his agreement, and Emma heard a door open, then close.

"Em? Can you hear me?" Liza caressed her with the cloth. "You've been unconscious with a fever for days. Smallpox. Babe's here and doing fine. Josiah's taken excellent care of you both, not leaving your sides unless I shooed him out."

Emma struggled to wake up. "Babe." Her voice croaked, but Liza apparently understood.

"Oh, honey! Babe's here. I'm glad you're okay. We've been so worried!"

Emma heard the cloth being dipped in water, and then Liza wrung it out before wiping down her arms.

"Babe's right behind me in her bed, sleeping like the angel she is. We've already cleaned her up and changed her into a dry gown. She's fine. Her fever broke last night."

Emma opened her eyes and stared at her friend. The low level of light told her it was evening. Though a lantern burned on the mantel, Liza had pulled the curtain.

"Let's get this soiled nightdress off and get you into a fresh one. You've sweated through so many outfits during the past few days. Josiah has kept up the cleaning, cooking, and laundry. He's an amazing man."

Emma had no energy to help Liza remove the damp gown. It was all she could do to focus on her friend's words. Josiah had done all that for them?

"You just lie still. I can do this." Liza worked the garment up over Emma's torso and out from under her.

Emma heard the door open and Josiah's strong voice call into the room.

Liza called for him to wait. "I'm changing her now. Leave the bedclothes on the table, and I'll call for you when we're finished."

Emma flushed with embarrassment. She felt as helpless as a child. "Let me. . ."

No more words would come out. Too weak to talk, she knew she'd never be able to dress herself.

"Nonsense. I've done this for days." Liza stood, walked around the curtain, and crossed over to the table. Emma could hear her rustling the fresh sheets. "I've folded them just right. If we can ease you up, I'll peel away the dirty sheets and put the clean ones back in place all in one swoop."

Nodding, Emma tried to help. She felt as if all her muscles had locked up on her. Liza, small though she was, managed to do the job on her own. Emma rolled over onto the crisp, sun-dried sheet, inhaling the scent of fresh air.

"Josiah?" Emma's voiced cracked again. "Josiah cared for us?"

Liza hurried over to fill her glass with water. Emma had a vague recollection of Josiah doing the same thing throughout the past few days. She took a gulp and choked.

"Slow down now. You need to take it easy." Liza held Emma's weak neck and head up while she drank, then lowered her to the pillow. "Josiah has been a rock. We've both had smallpox already, but I couldn't leave Petey alone. I've come over each day to bathe you, but Josiah had the brunt of the work on his shoulders. You are very blessed to have his devotion. He's a special man, Emma."

Emma nodded her head. Sleep descended upon her, but she forced herself to acknowledge the thought that she'd been at Josiah's mercy for the last few days. She had no idea what she'd uttered in her fevered state or how her sick body had betrayed her.

Even while married to Matthew, she'd never been this sick. Yet a stranger ended up being around to care for her in this weakened condition. The man she'd rescued from near death and a concussion had taken over the care of her and Babe. Most likely, he'd saved their lives.

She only hoped she could look him in the eye when the illness passed. Who knew what liberties he'd taken when she was at her worst? She chastised herself for the thought. She'd never seen him act as anything but a gentleman. Liza was right. He had to be a special man to stay and care for two sick females. Females he barely knew.

Babe had also been right. Only God could have sent this man to their doorstep at a time when they'd needed his care the most.

Emma heard Josiah knock, and Liza called him in. Emma feigned sleep, not ready to face him. She heard him walk to her bedside and stop.

"How's she doing, Liza? Did she pull through the worst?" The level of concern in his voice surprised her.

Matthew had been a wonderful husband, but the few times she'd been ill— and when she was with child with Babe, when her mother helped her—he'd stayed as far away as possible.

She'd never known a man like Josiah, who would be so gentle at a bedside, especially when he barely knew her. It had to be his way of repaying the debt he felt he owed her for her kindness while he had the concussion. That would explain the devotion.

"She's going to be fine, Josiah. You can stop worrying now. Keep her calm and rested." She laughed. "If I know my friend, you'll have your hands full with that. She and Babe will keep you on your toes now that they're feeling better. They won't take to being stuck in bed while these sores heal, I can promise you that."

Josiah's voice sounded choked when he spoke his next words. "If I have to tie them down, I'll keep them calm. I'm just glad they pulled through. I never want to go through days like that again. Ever." His voice shuddered. "Whew. Those were some rough days they took us through, huh?"

"Yes."

Emma heard nothing but silence for a few moments. She fought sleep, knowing she shouldn't eavesdrop but wanting to learn more of Josiah's feelings toward her.

Liza spoke again. "You've come to care for them quite deeply, haven't you?"

"I have. Babe worked her way into my heart the day I rode onto their place. Emma came out, rifle in hand, and more than ready to use it. She has spunk. I like that."

"That spunk is what's carried her through the past few days. And her daughter's a miniature of her mama."

Emma heard her friend as she gathered up her things.

"I'm off to check on Petey. Katie took him for the day, but I don't want to wear out our welcome. You take good care of these two."

"You know I will, Liza. Thanks. For everything."

Emma heard him walk over to the stove.

"I have soup ready. Take some home with you, along with this corn bread."

Emma wiped at a tear. The man cooked, too? Of course, he'd lived alone, so it made sense, but most men would stick to the basics and would never think of cooking for a neighbor like Josiah just had.

She fought off the thought that he might be after her claim and gold, too. But really. . .how was she to know that he was any different than Mack? Just on his word, the word of a stranger? Granted, Mack had never taken care of her and Babe in this way. According to Liza, Josiah had gone beyond measure to make sure both women were provided for. And he'd never shown the anger Mack kept hidden away behind his eyes, ready to come out on a whim. The men were cut from different cloth, and it wasn't hard to see which one came out woven with the richest, most vibrant depths. Josiah had quality.

He closed the door behind Liza and headed Emma's way.

She closed her eyes again and forced herself to breathe evenly. She wasn't ready to face this man who continued to take her by surprise. She'd have to face him soon enough. In her present state, she'd probably do something crazy like throw herself into his arms and beg him to marry her. Babe's imagination and dreams were rubbing off on her. She needed to wait to face him with a clearer head. It was bad enough that she had very little recollection of the past few days. She refused to do anything to embarrass herself further.

Chapter 10

Ｉt's good to see you awake." Josiah's voice greeted Emma before she even realized she'd opened her eyes. He sat in a hard chair, which was tipped back against the wall. When their eyes met, he let the chair plop to the floor and leaned forward to appraise her, hands folded across his knees.

Emma didn't know what to do. She wanted the man to be anywhere but here. Her hair tumbled into her face in disarray, and she knew she looked a mess. Her next thought was one of wonder that she even cared what this man thought about her. But in her heart she knew she did. "What day is it?"

"Sunday." He stared but didn't say anything more.

Her befuddled mind tried to grasp the time passage. "So I've been asleep. . ."

"This fever hit four days ago."

"I've missed four days?"

She watched as Josiah winced. "Actually, that was the second phase of fever, when you broke out in the rash. See, the bumps are scabbing over now."

Emma raised her hand and saw the ugly red spots. "When did I talk to Liza?" She fought back a sob. She hated feeling out of control. "I thought I talked with her yesterday."

"Your fever broke that day, but then the rash started in full force, and you weren't yourself again all week."

The sob worked its way free. Josiah leaned forward and pulled her close. She fought to push him away. "Don't. I look awful. I'm such a mess."

He continued to hold her. "I've seen you in this condition for the past week and a half. Don't you think I'd have run by now if I were going to? There's nothing wrong with accepting help when you need it."

His arms felt wonderful around her, comforting and strong. She hadn't felt this safe and loved since Matthew died. She sobbed into his shirt until she gained control of her emotions. It wasn't right for him to hold her this way. She reluctantly pushed him away again, gently this time. "I'm okay now. Thank you."

"You aren't used to being taken care of, are you?" Josiah moved his chair back a bit, giving her space, but only a few inches. "It's time you let someone else help carry the load."

She wrapped her arms around herself and nodded, not sure which part she agreed with. She wanted a bath but felt too embarrassed to ask him to prepare it for her. "Will Liza come today?" If so, she could have her help with the bathing, and they could shoo Josiah out of the way. A sudden thought came to her. Where was her daughter? She jerked upright with a yell. "Babe!"

Josiah jumped at her raised voice. "She's fine, Emma. Relax. She's outside with Phil, feeding the animals. And yes, Liza will be over in a bit. She's come over every day to care for you." He put his hand up against his chest. "You just took two years off my life. I don't need that with the ones you already took with this illness. I've been worried sick about both you and Babe."

Emma lay back against her pillow, the sudden movement taking out of her what little strength she'd mustered. "Sorry. I just noticed she wasn't in her bed. How'd she bounce back so much quicker than I did?"

"You know how children are." Josiah's voice was teasing, but admiration filled his eyes. "And I know how Babe's mama is. I'd assume that you were already ill when you overdid it on the cleaning after caring for me. So you went into this already exhausted, where little Babe had all her energy to focus on getting well."

Chastised, Emma ignored his comment.

"Hit a nerve, did I?" Josiah wasn't giving up.

"I might have felt a bit under the weather, but I had no clue I was about to be hit with something so serious. Next time I have a deadly illness, I'll make sure to take a couple of days off to rest beforehand."

Josiah's warm laughter filled the room. "Ah, she's back with snappy attitude and all." He stood. "I'm glad you're feeling better. If you don't mind, I'll go rustle up your daughter and let her say hello. I've been fighting her off for two days. She's bound and determined to take over my duties as your caretaker."

Emma flushed, the sensation crawling up her neck. "I sure appreciate your caring for us. Most men wouldn't have stuck around, let alone taken over in this way."

"You were too sick to care for yourself, let alone your daughter. I did what I had to do." He wouldn't look her in the eye.

"So you're saying you did this because you had no choice. . .no one else could fill the shoes? You were stuck with the job?" Emma's words showed her hurt, though she knew she had no right to feel that way. At least he was honest about his intentions.

"No." Josiah's voice went soft. "I had no choice because my heart wouldn't let me walk away from you, either of you." He reached out to caress her cheek. "Your little girl isn't the only one that's holding my heart hostage." With that comment he walked out the door.

Emma didn't know what to say anyhow. It wasn't like her to be at a loss for words, and he'd stumped her twice in the past thirty minutes. She heard his bellowing voice call out that a certain someone had asked about Babe.

"Was it Petey?" Babe called back.

Josiah's chuckle carried through the window. "No. Petey's not here."

"Jimmy?"

Babe had to know neither friend was here at the cabin. She had to be toying with Josiah. Emma smiled at her daughter's precociousness.

"Then who?" Babe sounded genuinely at a loss, as if she had run out of choices.

"How about your mama? But maybe you're too busy playing to talk to her right now."

"Noooo!" Babe's happy squeal wound around Emma's heart. Her baby had missed her. And she missed her baby.

The door burst open, and Babe flew through the room and plastered herself against her mother. "They wouldn't let me hug you or anything, Mama! Josiah wanted you all for himself. I got mad at him."

"Angry."

"Yes, that. He wouldn't let me touch you. He did all the touching."

Josiah had rounded the door and stood frozen in place, his face burning red. "It wasn't quite like that, I assure you."

"Did you let me wipe her face down when her fever shot up?"

"Well, no. But I didn't want you to spill water on her gown and cause a chill."

"Did you let me feed her soup or sips of water?"

"No, Babe, you know I didn't. But you tried that one time—and you did a fantastic job—but remember the soup slopped, and we had to have Liza change her clothes and the whole bed."

Emma felt like a newborn babe. There she lay like a lump while her daughter and the man she loved coddled her like an infant. *The man I love?* Where had that thought come from?

"Hello, I'm right here." Emma interrupted her own thoughts, as she was uncomfortable with the direction they were heading. "Tell me what you've been doing."

Babe's eyes lit up. "I've been helping Mr. Duggin work outside. *He* lets me help." Her young eyes sent daggers at Josiah.

Emma tried unsuccessfully to hide a grin. The corner of Josiah's mouth rose into a smirk as he shrugged. Maybe the days of Babe's papa hunt were over.

"Mama?" Babe leaned against the bed. The tiny pink rosebuds on her powder blue dress accented her pink cheeks. "Do you really love my new papa? You told Josiah that while he cared for you."

Emma's blush turned to a full-fledged burn. *Scorch* might be more like it. "I didn't."

Josiah had the gall to laugh. "You did. But I knew you were delirious. It's okay."

"No, it's not okay! I can't believe I'd say something like that."

"You did, Mommy." Babe looked angelic with her chin propped upon her hands.

"Thanks," Emma muttered, wondering why on earth she'd had Josiah call her daughter inside.

"You're welcome."

Emma mentally rolled her eyes. She turned to Josiah, who was suddenly busy in the kitchen. "So what exactly did I say?"

Babe began to dance around the room, twirling her skirt, and called out in a singsong chant, "You said you *loved* him and that you'd *marry* him and that no one else has ever *cared* for you like *he* does."

Emma pulled the cover over her head.

Josiah's voice still held traces of laughter as he spoke to her daughter. "Babe, why don't you go outside and finish up with Mr. Duggin, then we'll see about getting your mama to the table to eat with us."

"Okay." Babe ran to Emma's side. She pulled at the cover, but Emma held it tightly in place. "Are you playing hide-and-seek?"

"Just the hiding part."

"Oh. That's not fun. You have to seek to make it work right. I guess I will go back outside. Maybe Mr. Duggin will play the game with me properly."

She scurried to the door after a random peck on Emma's head. The door slammed shut, and Emma thought about praying for the fever to return and take her away into oblivion. She lay quietly, hoping Josiah would stay outside after seeing Babe safely to Phil and give her some peace.

No such luck. Josiah entered and walked over to pull the quilt from her face. "You don't have to hide from me. Ever."

She blinked at the sudden onslaught of light. "Oh yes, I do."

"Look. People say all kinds of things when they're ill. I understand that. I didn't take offense. I actually kind of liked hearing it."

Emma groaned. "When did you say Liza would be here?"

"I think I hear her now." He walked to the door and called out, "You have a friend here who needs rescuing."

Never had Emma been so happy to hear Liza arrive. After Josiah excused himself to go out to the barn for the washtub, Emma sat up shakily to regard her friend. "So did I make any odd or offensive statements to you?"

"Babe told you that you declared your undying love to Josiah, huh?"

"My undying love?" Emma swayed. "No, she just said I told him I loved him and would marry him. How bad is it? You can tell me. What else did I say?"

Liza dropped down onto the bed to sit beside Emma. "He knew you were talking crazy. It's all right."

Josiah returned with the tub and began to fill it with the hot water he had boiling on the stove top. "You'll feel a lot better after a soak and fresh clothes. I'll take Babe off Phil's hands for a while and let you ladies catch up." He hesitated. "Do you mind if I take her up to the claim with me? Lunch can wait."

"No, I don't mind. Take your time."

"Good. I want to check things out. I ran up there once while Liza stayed with you both, and Phil's been watching things, but now that you're on the mend, I'd like to take a more thorough look myself." He brought over more water and placed the pan on the table. "Babe can use the change of scenery, but I'll carry her most of the way so she doesn't get too tired. We'll be back in time to eat."

Emma looked at Liza for confirmation of the plans. She hadn't considered her daughter's frailty and recent illness.

"They'll both be fine. You can trust Josiah fully with her, and she's fit as a fiddle and does need to get away for a bit. It will do her good."

"Are you still interested in helping with the claim? At least until I get back on my feet?" Emma couldn't imagine that Josiah didn't want to get on with his own life and be on his way.

"Absolutely. I told you I feel responsible for chasing Mack off. I intend to see this through."

"For how long?" Emma knew she couldn't count on him to run things indefinitely. He had a life. Somewhere. She still knew next to nothing about him. But she'd remedy that as soon as she recuperated. She couldn't trust the mine to another man who might be as untrustworthy as Mack had turned out to be. But evidence of Josiah's goodness surrounded her. Surely he wouldn't go through all this just to win her over so he could steal from her. Though it seemed clear Mack had.

"As long as it takes." He knelt down to look into her eyes. "I know things have been crazy ever since I rode up. I'm sorry for that. But I'm not sorry I ran Mack off. I'm still sure he planned to take the claim away from you. And if he couldn't, he'd just take what he found."

Emma shook her head. "I still can't believe—"

Josiah interrupted her. "Did he ask for your hand in marriage?"

"Well, yes. I told you that."

"If he married you, the claim would become his. Didn't you say he looked angry at your rejection? Why would he feel that way unless you were keeping him from what he wanted to take as his own? And I don't mean you as a wife."

His observation did nothing for her self-esteem. Emma realized he clutched her hand with his own. She liked the sensation.

"If he truly loved you and wanted to make you his wife, he would have looked hurt when you said no, not angry."

Emma had to admit he made sense. Again she shivered with foreboding. She didn't want any more run-ins with Mack, on Josiah's behalf or her own.

Chapter 11

A week later, Emma felt enough like herself to resume her full responsibilities. She noticed supplies were running low. They'd need to take that trip to town soon. She picked up where she'd left off with preparing Josiah's breakfast before he headed out to work each day.

"Smells wonderful in here as usual," he said as he entered the house and hung his hat near the door.

Babe sat in her chair at the table and grinned up at him. She'd made her peace with Josiah, forgetting her anger as soon as he handed her the small wooden doll he'd carved for her from a tree branch. Though it was primitive, she coddled the "baby" in small blankets Emma had sewn for her from scraps of fabric.

Emma hurried to finish breakfast preparations. "I only have to get the biscuits out and we can eat."

"I see Gabby's awake and ready for her breakfast." Josiah nodded at the doll that lay beside Babe's arm.

"Silly, Gabby doesn't eat here with us. She can only have bottles. She's taking a nap. She just likes to lie by me when she sleeps." The doll hadn't left Babe's side since she'd received it.

Emma heard Josiah's chair creak as he sat down. "We need to go into town. Would today be too soon? We can go tomorrow if you have other things to do. I don't want to leave you here alone, and I owe you some supplies."

"We can be ready today." Emma looked forward to the end of her quarantine and the change of scenery. She'd taken short walks since her illness, but Josiah always kept her close to the house, not wanting to see her back in bed with a relapse. She turned to her daughter. "Baby, we're going to town!"

Babe squealed and grabbed her doll. She swung her around and danced through the room in excitement.

Emma motioned her to sit and placed the final dish on the table. "But you don't owe me anything, Josiah. I'm indebted to you for our care and can't ever repay that."

Josiah ignored her and began to dish up their food.

Emma sat beside him. They felt like a family, but Emma knew she shouldn't get attached. Even with her best effort, she'd not been able to dig out any more information about her boarder. She hadn't felt lonely in a long time, but she certainly would after Josiah headed off to other parts. His comment about her staying alone intruded into her thoughts. "Are you still worried that Mack will return and cause a problem? I'd think he would be long gone by now."

"I don't want to take any chances. He put a lot of time into his plan of trying to get your claim, from what I've seen, and I'm not sure he'll give it up that easily. We've been lying low, too, so he hasn't had much chance to act. I'd rather you both come along with me to town, so I can have peace of mind."

Emma playfully said, "I never said I didn't plan to accompany you to town. Babe and I look forward to our visit too much. You couldn't shake us if you tried."

The trip into town was uneventful but beautiful. The crisp fall air filled Emma's lungs, refreshing her after the stale air in the cabin. Josiah said he had business at the general store and a few other places, so Emma and Babe decided to visit with friends before meeting up with him at a later time. They stopped by three different homes before heading over to the hotel to eat lunch.

"There's Petey and his mama!" Babe almost tore out of Emma's grip in her excitement at seeing her friend.

Emma tightened her grasp and held the child back from being run over by a fast-moving horse. "Babe! You have to be careful. That horse would have trampled you." She pressed a hand to her chest and felt her heart pound through her dress as she caught her breath.

Liza had heard the commotion and waited on the other side of the dirt road. Emma hurried across after the dust cleared. Petey and Babe grabbed each other and swung in circles.

"C'mon away from the road now," Liza prodded. "You already almost had one accident too many." She led the way up onto the boardwalk.

Though Liza's voice seemed light, her expression betrayed deeper emotions.

"Is everything all right?" Emma whispered as they reached the top of the stairs. No one else shared the area nearby. The children stood in front of the nearest window a few feet away and made faces at their reflections in the glass.

"I should be asking you the same. How are you feeling?" Liza neatly side-stepped Emma's question.

"I'm feeling fine. Great, as a matter of fact. Getting out of the house and coming to town is the best thing to happen to me lately."

Liza smirked. "Better than Josiah?"

"I'm not sure what you mean," Emma hedged. She knew her friend referred to their blooming relationship, but Emma refused to admit it. "If you mean the care he gave us, you're right. He's a very nice man."

"Right." Liza's chuckle sounded forced, maybe even a mite bitter. "He's wonderful, Emma, and you'll be crazy if you let him get away. You can't afford to let a good man like him go."

"I'm not sure I have any say in holding him or letting him go. He's his own man, and I have no idea of his plans or how long he'll be around. I know you have ideas about us, but really, there's nothing there to speak of."

"You're telling me you have no feelings for him?"

"I'd be lying if I said I didn't, and you know it. I just don't know where those feeling will lead. He's a very private man. I have no clue what he's thinking."

Liza appraised her. "I know he's as smitten with you as you are with him. I've watched over the past few weeks enough to know that. And he's not the type that would ever pick up the bottle or change on you, either. He's dependable and steadfast. Don't let him go, Emma. Promise me."

So Liza wasn't doing well after all. No wonder she'd changed the subject. "Things aren't any better with Pete?" Emma kept her voice low. She touched Liza's arm, but Liza pulled away, hugging her arms against her chest.

"Pete's left us."

Emma couldn't stop her gasp of surprise. "For how long?"

"For good. He packed his things and took off. I've not seen him in a week."

Emma's heart plunged. Some friend she was. Liza had suffered silently, alone, for a week, and Emma had been so caught up in her own world and recovery that she'd not taken a moment to wonder why Liza hadn't come around. But she knew that even if she'd analyzed Liza's absence, she'd have figured that after all the time Liza had spent at their place, she needed time to catch up on her own work. Liza's absence after her daily visits should have alerted her to the problem. Not once had Emma suggested they go over and help or check on them.

"I'm so sorry." The words were empty and inadequate, even to her own ears. "What can I do to help?"

"Nothing." Tears coursed down Liza's cheeks, and she swiped at them angrily. "I don't know what we're going to do, though. I can't make it here alone. I have no way to support us."

"Did Pete say anything when he left? Anything to help you make sense of this?"

"No. He'd been drinking more and more, and that last morning, he just got up out of bed, packed his things, and said he was done, he was leaving, and we'd better not try to follow or stop him."

Emma didn't know what to say. She couldn't imagine Matthew doing that to them. Even Josiah hadn't run out on them when they'd been sick, and he wasn't even officially responsible for their welfare. "We'll get you through this. You won't want for anything. You have my word."

Liza wiped her tears again. "You're sweet to say that."

"I mean it. I felt the same way when I lost Matthew. Babe and I have survived, and so will you." She glanced over at Babe and Petey when she said it. Liza followed her glance and looked over, too. Both children had their mouths plastered against the glass, making faces at the shopkeeper who worked within. The shopkeeper stood just opposite, leaning on his broom and smiling. "How can you not survive with that little guy to keep you going?"

"You're right." Liza laughed through her tears—a good sign. "The things that boy does to get a laugh out of me have held me together all week."

"Well, keep holding yourself together, because the worst is behind you." Emma motioned to Babe to move on along the boardwalk ahead of them and took Liza's arm in hers. "We're heading over to the hotel for lunch. Let us treat you two, and we'll come up with a plan."

Petey grabbed Babe's arm and mimicked the ladies, nearly tripping in the process. Babe fumbled for the upper hand, not wanting Petey to hold her arm. She wanted to hold his. They tussled until they almost walked into the rail outside the hotel. Petey finally knocked Gabby out of Babe's other arm, sending the little girl into tears.

Emma sent Liza on inside to get a table.

"Here, Gabby's fine," Emma consoled, dusting off the beloved doll before handing her back to Babe. She dropped to meet them both at eye level. "We're going to go inside to eat, and I want you both to be on your best behavior. Understand? No fidgeting or fighting."

They both nodded. Emma took one child in each hand and followed Liza. A lady from the saloon lounged in the hotel doorway.

"Look, Mama! That lady don't have all her clothes on, and she's outside where people can see her!" Babe's voice couldn't have blared out any louder if she'd tried.

"Don't be rude, Babe." Though it did cross her mind that if the woman had dressed herself fully, she wouldn't be confronted by a five-year-old who threw out her thoughts on a whim. Too embarrassed to meet the woman's gaze, she stepped inside the door.

"Emma! What a nice surprise!" Sarah met her at the entry to the diner and directed her over to where Liza sat beside the front window. They were at the late end of the lunch crowd, so the room only held a few other customers. Sarah followed her over to the table and helped the children sit down. "I sent a man over to your place looking for Mack a few weeks ago. Did he ever find his way out there? I've not seen him since."

"He found us."

Sarah leaned close as she filled Emma's glass with water. "He's quite an eyeful, don't you think? Did he head on out of town?"

"No, he's actually staying at Emma's now." Liza's eyes lost their sadness for a moment and twinkled as if she couldn't resist making the statement.

"In the barn. With the boarders. . ." Emma's voice trailed off. She didn't know why she sounded so defensive. Her character spoke for itself.

Babe's voice popped into the conversation. "You mean Josiah? My new papa?"

Sarah stood straight and waited expectantly, eyebrows raised.

Emma laughed. "Babe's on a papa quest. She decided God sent Josiah to be her new papa. We're still working on that." She took a sip of her water.

"Still working on making him her papa? I see." She winked at Babe before walking off as Emma sputtered. Sarah called back over her shoulder, "Let me know when you're ready to order."

"Babe! You simply have to learn to sit quietly and keep your thoughts to yourself," Emma hissed when her choking fit had passed.

"Don't be so hard on her, Emma," Liza said gently. "Maybe if I'd been more outspoken, I'd still have my husband around. Sometimes things just need to be said."

Emma ruffled Babe's hair with her hand. "But those things seem to send me into a fit of embarrassment each time she opens her mouth lately." She shook her head. "Well, let's get something ordered so we can get on with our lunch. I'm starved."

They chatted about Liza's situation as they waited for Sarah to bring their meals. Emma racked her brain trying to think of a way for her friend to raise funds. Matthew had made things easy for Emma as far as income after he passed away. They'd already had the boarders to bring in money, and Matthew had been careful with their spending and thoughtful when buying.

She took Liza's hand and bent in prayer, asking God to watch over her friend and to make a way for her to provide for herself and Petey.

Sarah returned with the food. Petey looked ready to pounce on it, while Liza again teared up. Emma wondered how long it had been since they'd had a decent meal. The aroma of roast and glazed carrots curled up to tickle Emma's nose, and she realized that for the first time since her illness, she was also famished.

Sarah leaned down to cut Babe's and Petey's food while encouraging the women to go ahead and eat. "I heard about your smallpox, Emma. How you feelin' now?"

"I'm much better, thank you. This is the first time I've been able to get out, and this town, rough though it might be, is a sight for sore eyes!" She peered out the window before turning back to her friends. The tender roast melted on her tongue. "Oh, this is so good."

Liza nodded her agreement but didn't speak. Petey and Babe chatted away in their own little world.

Sarah looked at the window, lost in thought. "The view could be better if I could find time to get new curtains up. The old ones faded to the point of looking raggedy. You know I pride myself in keeping a homey atmosphere. I couldn't stand their dreariness any longer."

Emma looked around and had to admit the room had looked much better with the windows framed by fabric. "So business must be good if you're too busy to sew."

"More than good. I can't even find time to think lately. I've hired a girl to help, but it still takes the two of us to keep things going."

A plan began to formulate in Emma's head. "Have you thought about hiring someone to make the curtains for you?"

Liza raised her head and showed interest in the conversation for the first time.

"You know how few women live in this town." Sarah scoffed. "Other than the saloon girls—and I'm not sure sewing is on their list of abilities—there aren't any seamstresses banging down my door. Even the few women that come into town lament the lack of a good dressmaker. Their husbands are striking gold, and now that they have money to spend, they don't have anyone to sew for them like they did back East."

Emma knew that one of Liza's treasures was a treadle sewing machine. "What if I said I knew someone who could fill that order and more?"

Sarah smiled. "I'd hire her in a moment and have a long line of women behind me waiting for their turns. Do you sew?"

"No, but Liza does."

Sarah pulled up a chair and sat down next to Liza. "Really? Would you be interested in making the curtains, and maybe some dresses, too?"

Liza nodded. "I'd love to. I'll take all the business you can send my way."

Sarah looked skeptical. "Are you sure? I'm telling you, you'll have more business than you'll know how to handle."

"I'm positive."

Emma took hold of her friend's hand. God had wasted no time in answering that prayer.

Sarah glanced toward the kitchen. "Do you have time right now to go over to the mercantile with me to pick up fabric? I don't want to rush you, but I'd love to get this room back in order as soon as I can. I only have a little time before I'm needed to help with dinner."

Liza glanced down at her empty plate and then over at Petey's. He'd all but licked his clean. "I'll be ready as soon as Emma's finished."

"No, go ahead now." Emma waved her away. "Babe and I will finish up and head that way in a few minutes. We'll be right behind you."

"If you're sure." Liza's eyes had new life as she stood and, leading Petey, followed Sarah out the door.

The quest for gold had caused so much heartache for so many families. While a few were striking gold and becoming rich, many more were struggling just to put food on the table and make it through each day. Emma wondered if the cost was worth it. Her own mine had already caused greed from Mack and problems she'd never thought about.

She shook off the heavy thought and forced her mind to stay on Liza and her blessing. Emma's heart swelled. She knew God answered prayers, and though she knew her friend had been praying for help for a long time, this answered prayer felt instantaneous.

She leaned back in her chair and watched out the window while waiting for Babe to eat her last few bites. As contentment settled over her, a commotion across the street caught her attention and chased away her happy thoughts. Her heart plummeted. If she'd thought Josiah was on the up-and-up, the event unfolding outside the window now said otherwise.

Chapter 12

The doors of the saloon across the street had burst open, and several men tumbled to the boardwalk before rolling over the edge and onto the road. Dust puffed into the air around them as the brawl continued. Josiah burst through the door with a drawn gun and aimed it toward one of the men.

Emma saw his lips move but couldn't tell what he'd said.

The fight stopped immediately, and the men stood to walk back to the saloon. They disappeared from sight.

Emma grabbed Babe's hand and dragged her out the front door. As she reached the steps outside, a gunshot fired from inside the saloon. Her heart skipped a beat as she wondered about Josiah's safety, but then she reminded herself he was the only one she'd seen with a gun.

The doors burst open again as a man hurried onto the wood planks out front. "Somebody get Doc! A man's bleeding inside."

Another man followed him outside. "Don't bother. It's too late for him. He'll need a coffin instead."

"Then I'll get the sheriff." The man pounded away down the boardwalk at a run in his haste to bring in the law.

Again Emma's heart pounded in fear. If something had happened to Josiah, she didn't know what she'd do. She'd come to depend on him, and Babe would be devastated beyond words.

The men disappeared inside and the excitement seemed to have died down, so Emma eased closer to the building, anxious to find out what had happened. Josiah hadn't reappeared, and though she wanted to trust him, she had to wonder what he'd been doing at the saloon and why he'd had a gun.

A man, his face pale—probably from the events that had occurred inside—stepped out in front of Emma.

She caught him by the arm as he passed. "Excuse me, but could you tell me who was shot just now?"

He jumped at her touch. "Two men were fighting after having too much to drink, and a stranger intervened. The fight went on, and the men took it outside. The stranger ordered them back inside and pulled a gun, which he held on the instigator. As they entered, the drunken man pulled a gun, and a shot was fired. The man dropped dead on the spot."

Emma was glad she'd pulled Babe close against her skirt and had covered the young girl's exposed ear with her hand. "The stranger shot him?" Josiah had killed in cold blood?

"Not sure who shot him, ma'am. I only saw the stranger with the gun, and it was pointed at the dead man. But most every man in there carries a gun. Could have been any of them." He wiped at the sheen of perspiration on his forehead. "Now iffen you'll excuse me, I need to be heading home. I don't often stop off in these types of places, and I think I just had a real eye-opener on why that is. I'll be goin' home to my missus and stay there from now on." He tipped his hat and was gone.

Emma hoped he meant it. That would be one less man likely to run out on his family. Though troubled about Josiah, Emma didn't dare enter the saloon, especially with Babe along. Surely the victim was the inebriated brawler, as the man had said, and not Josiah.

She moved up the boardwalk, stepping aside as the sheriff rushed past, her heart heavy with concern. Had Josiah just killed a man? The image of her rescuer and protector just didn't line up with the thought of Josiah as a killer.

She glanced down the alleyway between the saloon and store as she passed and caught sight of Josiah sneaking out the back door of the saloon before hurrying down the road that ran behind the buildings. Emma felt mixed emotions. Why would he sneak out just before the sheriff arrived unless he had something to hide?

❧

Emma stopped by the general store and hurried over to find Liza near the bolts of cloth for sewing, obviously so engrossed in the task that she hadn't heard the commotion down the street. She hesitated to interrupt after seeing the sparkle on Liza's face as she discussed ideas with Sarah. Her friend was excited about something for the first time in months. She didn't want to take that moment away by bringing in her doubts and concerns about Josiah.

She turned back toward the door to leave when she heard Clara, the shopkeeper, enter from her quarters in the back of the store.

"Emma Delaney! Don't you dare leave here without saying hello to me first."

With a smile planted in place, Emma turned to her friend. "I'm coming back, but I have an errand I need to run first. I'd stopped by to see if Liza could keep on eye on Babe for a moment, but she's so busy I don't want to impose. I'll just take her along and we'll be back shortly. I'll visit with you then."

"Nonsense! I have Petey in the back room with me, eating a stick of candy while I work. Liza had an awful time keeping the boy near her with all the enticing items in here, so I offered to visit with him while she shopped. Let me take

Babe back with me, too. I love the company of the young'uns, and you can do your errand in peace."

Emma felt relief wash over her. "If you're sure. What if you get a rush of customers?"

"John's ready to return to the front, and he can keep an eye on things out here. He just finished up his lunch. You run along now, and if it's okay with you, I'll let Babe pick out one of those peppermint sticks she's eyeing over there, and she can join us for a bit."

Emma laughed as she realized her young daughter had wandered to the candy display while they'd chatted. The child stood motionless, Gabby hanging precariously in her hand, as she perused the many glass jars of candy lined up on the counter before her. "One piece, baby doll. Clara's going to take you to the stockroom to play with Petey while you eat your candy, and I'm going to run an errand. I'll be back before you know it."

Babe nodded, her eyes never leaving the peppermint stick that Clara removed from the jar. She wrapped it in paper and passed it over to Babe. Babe waved, then turned to take Clara's offered hand, happily skipping alongside her through the connecting door of the back room.

Emma hurried to the front of the store. Liza hadn't even noticed her presence. She and Sarah were deep in discussion over the best color and fabric to hold up to the sunlight and daily wear of curtains. A couple of other customers had eased closer and now interrupted to ask about having dresses made.

Pushing the door open, Emma hurried from the shop, nearly bumping into Katie, who stood just outside. "Katie!" Emma moved forward to hug her best friend. "How are you? I've not seen you since we became sick."

Katie returned her hug. "We've been dealing with illness, too. I was so sorry not to have been more help than I was. I helped out with Petey when I could so Liza was free to focus on you. But now we're on the mend, and I hear you are, too?"

"We are. It feels so nice to be able to walk and get around. I never want to go through an illness like that again." Emma sent up another silent prayer of thanks that they'd all made it through with their lives. She knew others in the community hadn't been so blessed. She'd need to ask who else needed assistance so she could repay Josiah's and Liza's kindness by helping the others.

She took a step away. "I'd love to stay and chat, but I have to run a quick errand, and Clara's watching Babe until I return. I don't want to take advantage of her kindness."

"I understand." Katie looked disappointed. "Promise me you'll head out our way soon?"

"Most definitely. Babe and I both are hungry for a visit and to get out of the house for an afternoon. We'll see you soon."

She hurried away from the store, following Josiah's path. When he'd left the saloon, he'd been heading east.

After thirty minutes of searching, she'd had no luck finding him. Retracing her steps, she stepped hesitantly into the alley between the saloon and store. The air was cooler there, and she shivered, feeling as if unknown eyes watched her pick her way between the trash and debris that filled the space. It would have been smarter to walk around the block to the back side of the buildings, but that would take valuable time she didn't have.

She emerged onto the back road and looked both ways. Not many people traveled back here, mostly owners and men wanting to rest their horses in the shade. Several figures sat in clusters beneath the trees beyond the road, and Emma again wondered at the practicality of wandering alone back here with a killer on the loose.

She turned in the direction that Josiah had traveled and glanced around to see where he could have gone. The livery stood off to the side, apart from the other buildings, and she wondered if he'd gone there.

"Emma," Josiah's voice called out from the far side of the rough timber building. "Over here." He patted a wooden crate beside him.

Emma slowly walked over to join him. Her apprehension mounted as she studied his face. Though not a look of evil that she'd expect a man who'd just committed murder to wear, his expression seemed haunted.

"You heard about the murder in town?"

She sank to the box he'd offered her and nodded. "I'll ask right out. Did you kill that man?" She braced herself for the answer.

He shook his head no.

She couldn't begin to describe the relief she felt. She sensed that he told the truth. "Then why did you skulk out the back door just as the sheriff arrived? That's the act of a guilty man." She pushed her hair back out of her eyes, perplexed. "What do you have to hide, Josiah?"

"I have nothing to hide." Josiah stood and paced in front of her. "I've not been completely on the up-and-up with you, though. You know I'm here to find Mack, but I was officially sent here to find another man, the one in the saloon."

"As in a hired killer?" A shiver passed through her. Would Josiah have killed if someone else hadn't killed first?

"No. I'm a U.S. Marshal. I'm here on the side of the law. The man shot down back there was wanted on many charges, murder being only one of them. I didn't come to town today with the plan to arrest him, but as I left the general store and stashed my supplies with the wagon, I saw him through the swinging doors. I couldn't miss my chance to apprehend him." Josiah kicked at a rock in exasperation. "I wanted to capture him alive. I tried to take him quietly, but he reacted with violence. A few of the guys there jumped him. He'd been causing a ruckus with several of them it seems, so they took pleasure in helping me out. As they reentered the saloon on my command, another man pulled his gun and shot my man in cold blood. The men grabbed the killer and brought him to the floor and held him down while another went for the sheriff."

"They why the disappearing act and sneaking out the back door?" Emma wanted to believe him, but his actions didn't match up.

"I have to assume the man who shot him did so to keep him quiet. Though I didn't make it public who I was or what I wanted, the victim—or criminal, to be more accurate—knew exactly who and what I represented. He was running scared. He pulled his gun on me, and that must have been enough to make his sidekick realize he posed a risk to the operation. Before I could get a shot out in self-defense, the other man shot his buddy down before the victim had a chance to think about pulling the trigger on his own gun."

Josiah's story began to make sense.

"The sheriff knows why I'm here. I wasn't skulking around to avoid him. But with part of the gang still on the loose, and at least one member in the saloon at the time of the gunfight, I couldn't take a chance on my cover being blown. Though the gunslinger knows I had a bone to pick with his friend, he doesn't know if I was there as a lawman or as an outlaw."

"So you're free to leave? Or do we have to wait until you can speak to the sheriff about all this?" Emma's enjoyment at being in town suddenly dissipated, and she wanted to get Babe and return to their cozy cabin.

"The sheriff will stop by your place later, when he has things under control over here."

Another thought occurred to Emma. It disturbed her more than she cared to admit. "You were really here as a marshal? So now that your job is done, do you have to go back to get a new assignment?"

"I'm here to see through this situation with Mack. The man I chased here was an annoyance, and now that he's out of the way, I can fully focus on protecting you and Babe. The authorities know I have other reasons for sticking around and are supportive of my capturing Mack. At least, I need to bring him in for questioning on the theft of our money."

He stared at Emma, his gaze drilling deep into her soul. "Is there anything else you need to ask? Or can we pick up where we left off and continue this conversation after we get out of here?"

Emma licked her lips, suddenly speechless. Josiah's eyes searched for understanding, and she felt her heart tug in his direction. She stood and moved closer without consciously realizing she wanted to close the gap between them.

Josiah reached for her and pulled her close.

She leaned against him for support, her cheek resting upon his chest, the stress of the day catching up with her.

His work-roughened hand reached back to grasp her head. He twisted his fingers through her hair before gently tugging on it to tip her head back, forcing her to look up at him. Lowering his head—and much to Emma's surprise—he caught her mouth with his in a gentle but very persistent kiss.

Chapter 13

The dizziness that swept over Emma after Josiah's kiss caused her knees to give out.

Josiah chuckled as he grasped her tightly around the waist, preventing her from sinking to the ground. Once she was steady, he pulled back, still holding her arms, and smiled. "Now that made every bit of the day's stress go away."

Emma felt dazed. She'd come out here to see if Josiah had possibly killed a man and now stood in his arms in full sight of anyone who chose to walk around the corner of the livery. At the realization, she stepped backward and pulled out of his strong embrace. Her knees buckled again, and he touched her arm to steady her.

He gave her a crooked smile and took her arm in his, suddenly a proper gentleman for the benefit of anyone who looked on. "Let's go get Babe and head home."

Emma nodded, still too shaky and surprised to speak. She liked the way he'd said that. Home. Again, as during breakfast, he acted as though they were a family and ready to go back to their place together. She shook off the thought. Though Josiah had kissed her, he hadn't declared his undying love. She didn't want her mind—or heart—to jump to inaccurate conclusions based on one kiss.

Josiah guided her in the direction of the store, his touch gentle on her arm. "I bought the basics when we first arrived in town and stashed them in the wagon. I figured we'd pick up anything I missed after I met up with you."

He recited the list of supplies he'd bought, and she nodded, sure he'd bought everything needed for now. They stepped aside to let another couple pass as the boardwalk narrowed. The breeze picked up, and Emma shivered, the thin fabric of her seafoam green dress not much protection against the cool air. Gray clouds moved across the sun and blocked its warm rays.

"You're cold. C'mere." He pulled her against him.

Emma felt her face flame at the curious glances from some of her distant neighbors. She crossed her arms against her chest to ward off more of the chill air. Because she and Josiah weren't acting inappropriately, she ignored the stares and stayed in the warmth of his arm.

Josiah seemed unaware of the stares, or maybe he just didn't care. He smiled down at her. "I'd hoped to catch you for lunch, but obviously things didn't go as I'd planned."

"That's fine. I ran into Liza and invited her to eat with Babe and me." Emma was glad to find a safe topic to discuss. "Pete left her, Josiah. I hate what the rush for riches in the hills is doing to the families around us."

That stopped Josiah in his tracks. He turned so he could look into her eyes. "He's gone? For good?" At her nod, he continued. "I can't imagine how a man can do that to his own flesh and blood. Probably an inane question, but how's she doing?"

A couple of hours ago Emma would have given him the sad version, but now, with Liza finding hope through her sewing, she answered the question on a more positive note. Josiah cared, really cared, about people. He'd be happy for their friend. "She's holding on. I left her at the general store, where Sarah was picking out fabric so Liza could sew new curtains for the restaurant. As I walked out, I heard a couple of other ladies inquiring about her services as a dressmaker, so I think she's going to do all right."

Josiah grinned. "That's the best news I've heard all day."

"Yes, but Liza's situation has made me think. Pete came here after a dream. Then he let that dream take over him, and he made it more important than his wife and his son. . .everything. I don't want to end up like that. I want to let go of the claim. It's not worth it—all the trouble it's causing, the greed people will have for what is in these mines. No amount of gold or riches is worth the pain and danger this is bringing to Babe and me."

"What Pete did to his family is wrong, but that's not the claim's fault or anything other than a result of his own choices." He caressed her arm, his touch sending a jolt of warmth through her. "But that claim you speak of belongs to Babe and to you, and Matthew wanted you both to have it. It's his legacy. I've said it before and I'll say it again, I'm here for the duration, to see this thing through, and I'm staying until I know that you and the claim are safe."

Her heart dropped at his words. They didn't sound like the thoughts of a man planning to settle down with a wife and daughter. Though he hadn't ever said he would stay, his kiss had told her differently. But then, despite what the kiss had been to her, maybe it was only a passing fancy to him. The opportunity had been there and he took it.

Emma forced a smile to her face, though her heart felt as if it were cracking into a million tiny fragments. She pushed the thoughts away and continued, hoping her voice didn't show her pain. "I know, but riches and strife just aren't worth this to me. What else do I need? I have enough money to see Babe and me through. We have the homestead and raise a lot of our own food. We're happy."

A cloud passed across his face, but she couldn't tell what caused it. Maybe it bothered him that he hadn't entered into her equation, or more than likely, it bothered him that she would let the claim go so easily.

"I hope there's one thing more that you need."

His words confused her, but she hoped he meant he did want to be a part of their lives. He stared at her another moment, searching her eyes, then tugged her around, and they continued their stroll toward the store. She did need one more thing in life to make her happiness complete. She needed him, no doubt about it. But she couldn't yet voice the words or admit that she'd fallen in love with him somewhere along the way. If she'd read him wrong. . . Well, she'd be cautious and enjoy their time together then take what came up the road.

They were in no hurry as they walked to retrieve Babe, and Emma was content to bask in Josiah's company. She loved the feel of his arm around her waist and the feeling of safety his embrace brought her. She and Babe were blessed to have such a man in their lives at this difficult time.

It was no coincidence, in her opinion, that Josiah had arrived when he did. Mack had made his move, and she did not know how to stop him. She owed Josiah a great deal and hoped he stuck around long enough for her to show her appreciation. How she'd do that, she didn't know, but she would think of something.

The store loomed in front of them, and Josiah held the door for Emma to walk through.

Clara glanced up with a perplexed smile. "Did you forget something? I thought you'd long left town."

Emma's heart plummeted.

"We came to collect Babe." She forced a smile, but her heart beat a hard staccato against her chest. Surely Clara hadn't forgotten she was taking care of the little girl. Or maybe Liza had taken her along to find Emma when she left. That was surely the situation.

"But she was picked up not thirty minutes after you left her here." A sudden panic filled Clara's eyes. "Liza finished with Sarah minutes after you left the store and offered to take Babe to find you, but I insisted she stay here since we were having such a good time. By the time I returned to her in the storeroom, she'd fallen asleep on a pile of blankets. Mack walked in moments later and said you'd sent him to collect her. I didn't give it another thought since he'd been in here with you on previous trips, and he's a boarder at your place and all. . ."

As Clara's voice tapered off, Emma felt her knees weaken for the second time that day, but for a very different reason. She became aware of, and thankful for, Josiah's supportive arm holding her up, because otherwise she'd have dropped to the floor in despair. "I. . .but. . .I. . .oh no." A sob burst forth, stopping her words for a moment. "Clara, I never sent Mack over here to get Babe. I haven't even seen him in weeks!" Her words stopped again as she struggled for a breath, suddenly unable to get air into her lungs.

Josiah tightened his grip on her arm and turned her to face him. "Stay calm. Take some air in. Easy now, that's it."

She gasped and felt a rush of air flow into her lungs, and she inhaled deeply.

"It's going to be okay, Emma. Don't fall apart on me now. We've got to focus on getting our girl back. Take some more deep breaths."

He kept his gaze focused on her, and his steady demeanor and comforting words encouraged her to calm herself.

"Okay now?"

"Yes."

"We don't have any time to lose." He turned back to Clara. "When did you say Mack came by? Tell us exactly what happened."

"I'm so sorry." Clara worried her apron with her hands. "It's been nearly an hour, I suppose. He walked in all friendly-like, and after chatting a moment, he said he'd been sent to collect Babe. I told him she was asleep in the back, and he said that was perfect and headed right back there and gently picked her up, taking care not to wake her." She glanced up at her husband as he walked over to join them. "I thought it odd that he appeared relieved that she'd fallen asleep, but"—she shrugged—"it didn't strike me as out of the ordinary that you'd have him collect her. I saw your wagon out front and thought you'd all meet up out there. We got busy then, so I never noticed your wagon didn't leave. I'm so sorry."

Josiah waved her apology off. "No need to feel bad now. You didn't know. Mack's been on the run for weeks, but we haven't made it public knowledge. It's a private situation, or at least it was before he pulled this latest stunt."

Though he seemed calm, Emma could feel the tension and rigidity of his muscles through his shirt. His fingertips dug into her arm, and he only loosened his hold when she wiggled out of the tight grip.

"Sorry, Emma." He rubbed her arm where he'd clenched it then turned to the storekeepers. "We need to go after Mack. Will one of you go for the sheriff and let him know what's happened? Tell him to meet us up at Emma's claim."

He turned to her. "Will he know where it is?"

"He knows the spot. But why there?"

"I have a feeling in my gut. That's what this is all about. It makes sense to me that he'd take Babe up there as a hostage. I think he'll use her as leverage so he can take over the claim."

"But he has to know he won't get away with it!"

"He's not thinking right, so the less time he has with her the better. We need to get going."

Emma watched as his jaw set in a firm line.

He touched her cheek with the back of his hand, wiping away the lone tear. "We'll get her. Don't you worry." His hand dropped, and he hurried outside.

Emma followed. She prayed for her little girl's safety while Josiah made plans.

"We'll take the wagon as far as your place, and then I'll continue on by horse. I want you to stay inside, with the cabin locked, just in case I'm wrong. I don't want both of my ladies in Mack's clutches." The whole time Josiah talked, he worked on readying the horses for the ride. He lifted her up onto the seat of the wagon, then paused. "On second thought, you go ahead to the cabin, and I'll run over to the livery and borrow a horse. That saves time. Stop by the sheriff's office and tell him I said that you need an escort home, instead, and that someone needs to stay there with you in case Mack heads your way."

Emma shook her head in disagreement. "There's no way you're cutting me out of this, Josiah. My little girl is with that madman, and I'll not sit at my cabin, huddling in fear, while she's out there with the man she hates. Don't you see? Babe's the only one who saw through him from the start. That's why he said it was perfect that she was asleep when he picked her up. If she hadn't been, she'd have only gone kicking and screaming. He'd have never gotten out of town." Her anger turned into a sob, but she continued her rant. "But when she does wake up, she'll be madder than a wildcat, and who knows what Mack will do to silence her. I'll not be left behind when my baby girl needs me."

Josiah didn't argue. He jumped up beside her and raced the wagon down the street and over to the livery.

The harrowing ride took seconds, but to Emma it seemed an eternity. She dared not question Josiah about his plans, not wanting to distract him and possibly cause him to rethink her going along.

He jumped down before the wagon fully stopped, unfastened Rocky, and entered the structure at a run. Within seconds he returned, digging through the parcels he'd placed in the back.

Emma climbed down and stood at his heels, refusing to let him get far away in case he decided to give her the slip. Moments later Sam, the liveryman, led Rocky from the barn. Emma noticed that the horse was saddled and ready to go.

Josiah took his parcels from the wagon to the saddlebags and stowed them there before slipping a shotgun up over his shoulder. He pulled his handgun from the holster that had been hidden beneath his jacket, the fierce-looking weapon tucked against the left side of his chest. A revolver rested on a belt that he wrapped around his waist. It hung at a low-slung angle, where he'd be able to grab it quickly if needed. He pulled the revolver from its holster, flipped it open, and looked inside before snapping it shut and returning it to its place on his hip.

"Surely all those weapons won't be necessary." The words stuck in Emma's throat, and she had to force them out. "My baby girl is up there with an apparent madman. If you go in with guns blasting, she's likely to get hurt, and not necessarily by Mack."

"We have to be ready. I have no clue what we're riding into or what Mack has planned. Babe's safety—and yours, since you insist on going along—is my utmost concern. If you stay here, I'll be able to fully concentrate on getting your daughter safely back to you. If you don't, my attention will be split and it will be harder on all of us."

"I'm not staying," she insisted. "Now, when do we get this show on the road?"

He swung up onto the saddle and reached to grasp her outstretched hand. She clutched him like the lifeline that he was, and he swung her up behind him. Sam assured them he'd look after the wagon.

Emma hugged Josiah's waist tightly, her full skirt billowing out behind them as he urged Rocky into a fast clip. Burying her face against his back, she clung to him, trying to draw strength and optimism from him and into her fearful heart.

They headed out behind the buildings and rode toward the hills.

Emma tried to figure out how her wonderful day had gone so wrong. She took comfort in the fact that the sheriff had been notified and would meet them with his deputies, but for now they were on their own, and she had no idea what Mack had planned for her daughter. A horrible thought occurred to her, and she tightened her grip around Josiah, leaning in to be heard over the horse's hooves. "What if Mack intends to take Babe just to get even and feels the best way to hurt me is by hurting her?" Her shrill voice carried on the wind as they sped toward the mine and hopefully Babe.

"Don't be thinking like that," he called back.

"How can I not? He's angry, he's unpredictable, and he's vindictive. Babe's going to be out of control when she wakes up and sees who has her. She wasn't nice to him even at the best of times. If she fights him. . ." The wind swept her voice away.

"I said don't think like that!" Josiah's tone brooked no argument.

Emma stubbornly continued. "How would he quiet her? She's so tiny. It wouldn't take much to hurt her." Her voice broke as she pictured her trusting daughter, tears pouring down her face, blond braids in disarray, as she peered up at the scary man in terror. Babe wouldn't sit by quietly. She'd scream and hit and make such a ruckus, Mack would react in fear of being heard.

Josiah urged the horse to go faster. "Just pray, Emma. Right now your prayers will do more good than any suppositions. We don't know what awaits us up there, but we do know God is bigger than the situation. Have faith that Babe's safe and that Mack's not so far gone that he'd hurt her."

He was right. She again rested her cheek against his back and thanked God for the strong man who provided strength to her weary soul. She wrapped her arms more snugly around him, placing her hands over his chest. She could feel his heartbeat, strong and steady, and flattened her fingers over the reminder that this living, breathing champion had been sent to watch over them. She felt confident he'd do everything in his power to keep them both safe. "Babe's safety comes first."

"What?"

"Babe's safety, it has to come first. You said I'd be a distraction, an added concern, but I don't want you to worry about me. I just want you to get my daughter to a safe place."

She was surprised to hear a soft chuckle escape him. "You'd be a distraction even if you weren't here. You've been nothing but a distraction to me since we met, Emma Delaney. I can't ignore my concern for you, but I promise getting Babe out of Mack's possession and into ours will be the highest priority on my mind."

She smiled. Peace descended upon her. She had complete faith in Josiah and thanked the Lord for sending him to protect her and Babe. Though she could sense his anger at Mack through the tension that permeated every muscle in his body, she knew his focus and drive centered on keeping them safe. She figured even now Josiah's thoughts were back on the best plan of action to use when they neared the claim.

His next words were unexpected—his line of thought far from where she'd expected it to be. "Of course, if you weren't pressed so tightly against my back, I could probably think a lot more clearly."

Emma felt a blush flood her face, though she silently smirked, too. She had no intention of letting go or moving a fraction farther away from the man she loved. Even though he didn't know of her emotions toward him, and even though he possibly didn't return her feelings to the same depth, she intended to draw every bit of strength from him while she could. Deep down, she also feared for his safety but refused to add those fears to the ones that already pervaded her being. Instead, she focused on the fact that his words gave her a security that he wasn't as immune to her charms as she'd feared a bit earlier.

"I'm not moving an inch, so if you want your thoughts to be focused away from me, you'd better get us up the hillside and face up to the man who holds our most valuable treasure."

"Will do," he agreed, spurring the horse even faster. "Though only to free Babe, not from any desire to pull my thoughts away from you."

A bit later, he slowed the horse and dropped from the saddle, motioning with a finger to his lips for her to remain quiet as he lifted her down. Pulling Rocky into the shadows of the trees, he tied the horse securely. He made some motions with his hand, and the animal dropped to a resting position on the ground.

Emma looked at Josiah, curious. Stepping closer, she whispered, "I've not often seen a horse lie that way. Why is he doing that?"

"In my line of work, there's a lot of gunfire," Josiah replied in a low tone. "This minimizes the chance of his getting hit. It's for the safety of both of us—his to stay alive and mine so that he can get me out of any situation alive. Now hush before you get us both killed."

Emma shuddered at that reality, knowing it now stared them in the face.

Josiah took her hand while simultaneously pulling his revolver from its holster. Holding it steady in his hand, he urged her forward. Just before they broke through to the clearing that ran along the stream, he stopped, pulling Emma close into his embrace. His rough cheek brushed against her soft skin as he leaned in close to whisper, his breath dancing against her ear. "I want you to stay here. I'll get Babe back to you as soon as I have things under control."

Emma didn't want to stay—she wanted to find Mack and scratch his eyes out at the very least—but she reluctantly nodded her agreement. Josiah needed to work, and she had to trust him to do his job well. She had no reason to doubt his ability.

He held her tightly against his chest, whispered a quiet prayer for the situation, and then pulled back to drop his lips to hers, brushing softly against them with a promise to return. He slipped off into the trees so silently even she couldn't hear him, though she knew he had to be only a few feet away.

The sudden chill that overtook her had nothing to do with the bereft feeling she had now that Josiah's arms no longer surrounded her. Nor did it have to do with the cold breeze flowing through the treetops above her. Secure in her protected place, she'd lost track of the cold afternoon air. The chill that surrounded her held something more sinister. The air thickened, and she struggled to breathe just as she had at the store. Only this time she didn't have Josiah by her side to coax her back to a steady pace.

She rationalized that the eerie feeling had to do with only the fact that Josiah had been her rock, and now he was gone. They'd stopped running, and her focus was single-mindedly on Babe and the danger that enveloped her. But in her heart she knew her rationalization played her the fool.

She began to pray, but the feeling of oppression grew stronger by the moment. Wrapping her arms around her chest, she slowly spun in a circle and surveyed the area around her.

A grating yet familiar chuckle raised the hair at the base of her neck before she'd completed the turn. Mack stepped out of his hiding place behind a set of trees. "Well, well, well, what have we here? It appears your hero has delivered you right into my waiting arms. I have to say, the kiss was rather disheartening to watch, but the end result—your being left to my selfish devices—is surely worth the wait and tortuous display of affection."

His hair stood in disarray, his eyes darted around wildly, and—based on the foul stench of whiskey that carried over to her on the breeze—he'd had more than a little to drink. "I have to wonder what it would feel like to have you meet my kiss with such eager abandon, pressing your body close against mine, like so many times in my dreams. I'll experience that moment soon, even if I have to force the event with Babe as the dangling carrot."

Emma could only watch in fear as he stepped closer, holding his revolver with shaky hands while pointing it directly at her.

Chapter 14

Josiah watched from the nearby trees as Emma's expression changed from anger to revulsion, until finally, fear settled across her delicate features. Josiah had circled around as soon as he'd left Emma's side. The rustling in the trees was a dead giveaway that someone had stalked them. The unsteady drunken gait, and not-so-careful attention to noise, alerted Josiah that Mack was nearby. He hated that he'd had to use her as bait, but he was confident that he could turn things around. Only the man's reference to using Babe as bait brought him a small measure of peace. From the sound of it, Babe had been safely stashed away somewhere in case Mack needed her for bargaining power.

"You'll only know of Emma's sweet kisses over my dead body." Josiah forced his voice to sound steady, though the sight of Emma with a pistol pointed at her scared him to death. Relief passed over Emma's face. Josiah realized she'd finally noticed him standing a few feet to the left of Mack.

Josiah cringed as Mack swung the gun awkwardly from Emma to Josiah, then back to Emma again, apparently deciding he had a better chance to control the situation with the weapon focused on her. Unfortunately for Josiah, Mack was right. He wouldn't jump ahead with a gun of any type aimed at Emma, especially when the firepower was held by shaky, alcohol-directed hands.

"Lower the weapon, Mack, and we can talk this out."

"I ain't lowering anything." Mack staggered, nearly knocking Emma down as he bumped into her. He swung the gun toward Josiah, and Josiah ducked behind a tree, sure the weapon would go off in Mack's wobbly hold.

Emma reached out to steady herself against a tree, and Mack grabbed her around the waist, pulling her tight against him.

Josiah bit down an expletive. Old habits died hard. Emma now formed an effective shield for any shot Josiah could get against Mack. Since she was nearly as tall as the gaunt man, Josiah couldn't even get in a good head shot now. He silently prayed. Maybe the sheriff and his men would arrive and move in from the other direction.

He peered around the tree to see that Mack held Emma with one arm slung just under her ribs, and from the looks of it, his grip was tight enough to break them. Mack's attention was on the woman in his hold, giving Josiah a momentary advantage. He moved quietly back into the trees.

"Where's Babe? What have you done with her? I want to see my daughter." Emma's voice, now strong, carried through the greenery to where Josiah waited.

Josiah mentally applauded her. If she did it right, she'd keep Mack distracted enough for Josiah to make his move.

"Babe's fine," Mack slurred. He momentarily sounded confused. "I think. Well, if she listened to me, she'll be fine."

"Mack, where is she? She's five years old. You can't expect a child of that age to listen to much of anything, especially when she's in a situation like this. Did you leave her in an unsafe place? Take me to her, please. I'll do anything you want—just let me see my daughter."

"You'll do anything I want anyway." Mack's laugh circled around Josiah, the sound grating on his nerves.

"I'll sign the claim over to you. You don't need Babe or me. No amount of riches is worth this to me, Mack. Take me to my daughter. I'll sign the claim to you, no strings attached." The strength had drained away, and Emma's voice now held a desperate quality.

Josiah could tell she was reaching a breaking point in her panic to know where Babe was. Her next move would be to try to get away from the fiend on her own, a situation Josiah had to prevent. He had to do something, but he wasn't in place to do anything without jeopardizing Emma's safety. And Babe's unknown whereabouts complicated things. He couldn't take a chance that a wayward bullet would find its way to the small girl.

Mack laughed. "You think this is only about the claim? It's about you, *darling*. I've worked hard to prove my devotion and worthiness to you. I will have your hand in marriage before this is all done. I'll have the claim, too, but marriage to you is what I want. For years I had to watch you dote on Matthew, and now you're turning your affections toward Josiah. It's not right. I earned your love, not him."

Emma's strain carried through her attempt to calm her tone. "You don't earn someone's love, Mack. Sometimes love just happens when you least expect it."

Even through the stress, Josiah's heart leaped at her soft words, hoping they referred to him. He was nearly in place. He and Emma could hash out their relationship later. For now, he'd best focus on subduing Mack while keeping him lucid enough to tell them where Babe had been stashed.

"You'll marry me, or both Josiah and your daughter will die." Mack's comment ended in a grunt.

Emma elbowed the man at his harsh words.

Josiah got a quick glimpse of the action as he peered through the trees while moving silently around the perimeter of the clearing. His heart lunged before he ducked back out of sight. They couldn't afford to make Mack any angrier.

As Josiah stepped forward to cause a diversion, a soft sound carried across the stream from the other direction, stopping him in his tracks.

❧

Where is Josiah? Emma felt as if he'd abandoned her after he'd ducked into the trees. Was he still lurking somewhere nearby? Or had he taken this chance to go after Babe? She guessed if it was the latter, it would be for the best. Babe's safety mattered above all else, and she'd told him that. But she still couldn't help the feeling of abandonment caused by his disappearance.

Mack hadn't spoken to her since she'd elbowed him. He'd tightened his grip on her ribs and had caught her free arm in his tight clutch.

She finally spoke, wanting to keep his thoughts on her and off Babe and Josiah. "Surely you know that by hurting my daughter, you'd be hurting me. And Josiah—" She bit off the comment. She'd been about to say that he meant nothing to her, so Mack had no reason to cause the man any more pain. But she couldn't say the words that were not true. Josiah meant everything to her, and she couldn't voice the lie even to save their lives.

"What about Josiah?"

Mack's fetid breath made her gag. She tried to turn her head to the side to grab a gulp of fresh air. His hold tightened further, making Emma woozy. She couldn't catch her breath.

"Don't pull away from me. The more you fight, the tighter I'll hold you. I'll only release you when you come to your senses and agree to marry me. Let Josiah have your daughter, and we'll all live happily ever after."

"Unhand her or you'll not live at all, Mack. It's over. Give up."

Emma had never been so glad to hear a specific voice in all her life. Well, except maybe Babe's. She desperately needed to know her daughter was safe.

"In your dreams, Josiah. You'll not take another thing from me." Mack jerked her hard, turning in a circle, making them a moving target so Josiah couldn't risk a shot.

Josiah's voice carried through the trees. It was hard to figure out which direction the sound came from, even for Emma. "What have I ever taken from you, Mack? It was you who took our fortune, if you'll remember back a few years."

Mack jerked to the left. "You and Johnny always had everything going for you. You had the strong upbringing. You had the most beautiful women's attentions. You had your faith."

"We lost our parents at a young age, Mack. We never cared about the women's attentions. We had a goal to reach and worked hard to get there. We shared our faith with you and trusted you as a brother. And you stabbed us in the back for our trust and took away our dream of the ranch."

Josiah's words carried from a new direction. Emma knew he silently moved through the trees, an action that caused Mack confusion. Mack again tightened his grasp on her as he tried to pinpoint Josiah's location.

"Where is he? Where *is* he?" Mack softly mumbled. He gasped. "I know your game, Josiah! Johnny's here, too, isn't he? You're trying to confuse me, but it won't work. You're messing with my head, and I can't think real clearly right now."

He backed against a tree, dragging Emma along with him. "You're both out there, ready to shoot me. I ain't moving, and I ain't letting go of Emma. You'll have to kill us both before that happens."

Emma knew he meant it.

"Johnny's dead, Mack. I'm not playing any tricks on you with him. I never will again. You ruined him."

The pain in Josiah's voice must have struck a nerve with Mack. No one could fake the torture that filled his words. "Is he telling the truth? Tell me, Emma. You've never lied to anyone that I know of."

Emma nodded, his grip still too tight to allow her to speak. He'd moved his arm from her ribs to her neck, freeing his hand to hold his weapon toward the trees, but the act also cut off the air to Emma's throat. She pulled against his arm for all she was worth, but she couldn't budge him. His focus was single-mindedly on Josiah.

Josiah's voice, louder now, called out to them, telling Mack about Johnny's death and what had caused his demise.

"My fault? All my fault. . . I can't take any more. Enough." Mack seemed to wilt, lowering his gun, and again sobbed the word, "Enough."

Emma, aware that Mack's focus had drifted, grabbed her moment to take action.

"Can't—breathe—" She feigned a faint and went limp.

The movement caught Mack off guard as he tried to keep his hold on her, and they both toppled forward. A gunshot rang through the trees, and Emma heard a scream.

Quickly realizing the scream was her own, she clamped her mouth shut, her terror paralyzing her. She couldn't move.

A few moments later, her world went black.

❧

"There you go, easy now. Breathe deeply, that's it."

Josiah's steady voice reached through Emma's fog, pulling her out of the darkness.

"Babe."

"She's fine. I have her in a safe place. Just relax for a moment while I check you over."

Emma felt Josiah's warm hands on her head as they explored for cuts or bumps. She tried to push his hands away. "I'm fine. My baby. . ."

Josiah ignored her and continued his exploration. She liked the feel of his strong hands. They made her feel secure, as if nothing could ever hurt her again. She had to think for a moment to remember what she feared and why she needed to feel safe. . . Mack! If Josiah was with her, Mack could be sneaking off to recapture Babe!

"Mack will get her!" Emma pushed to a sitting position, her head exploding with pain as she tried to open her eyes.

Josiah gently forced her head back down onto his lap. "Shh, I'd not tell you to rest if Babe was in jeopardy. She's fine, and Mack's right here."

Emma forced her eyes open.

Mack leaned forlornly against a tree, his posture defeated, his gun missing from his hand. He seemed to have shrunk in the past weeks, now just a shell of the strong man he'd been. "I can't stand the pain anymore." Mack's voice carried across the clearing. "The guilt. . ."

Emma noticed Josiah kept an eye on the man while finishing up his examination of her. "How do you feel now? Can you tell me what hurts? Do you feel pain anywhere?"

Gingerly shaking her head, Emma eased to a sitting position. "I feel fine now. Mack held me so tightly, I couldn't catch my breath. And. . .he didn't smell very clean. Sorry." She glanced over at the hurting man. "I feel bad saying it. But between the lack of air getting to my lungs and the rancid air I did get, I guess it was a bad combination."

She took a deep breath, filling her lungs with much-appreciated air. "I felt like I was going to pass out, and I thought if I could cause a diversion, you'd have a chance to intervene. As I fell, I heard the gunshot, then felt pain, and everything went black."

"Mack went down with you. I'm not sure if you hit his pistol or if you hit that tree nearby or if you both knocked heads on the way down, but you have a nasty bump on the side of your temple. The gun went off, but the bullet went straight up in the air, so no one was hurt. If you're sure you're okay, I'll go get Babe. She's pretty shook up and scared. I don't want to leave her alone any longer than necessary."

Emma grabbed his arm, determined to go to her child and unwilling to be left behind with Mack.

Josiah didn't even bother to argue. He sent her a grin and stabilized her against the tree, holding up a finger in a motion for her to wait a moment. Walking over to Mack, Josiah ignored the troubled man's griping and tied him securely to the tree that supported him.

Mack glanced up at them with pain-filled eyes. "Enough."

Chapter 15

Emma waited, fidgeting, as Josiah stared down at Mack. "We'll be back in a minute. The sheriff and his men are on their way and will be here soon. Don't make things worse on yourself."

Mack nodded, dropping his head in shame. "I'm ready to make things right. I want to tell you what happened."

"Not right now. We have to get Babe. But when we return, I'll be more than happy to hear your story. Though I can't imagine what was bad enough that you felt you had to take our fortune and run."

Josiah turned and gently took Emma by the arm, turning her toward a slight path between the trees. They entered the chilly shade, and Josiah's arm circled her waist, his body heat keeping her warm. "She's just ahead." Emma hadn't missed Mack's bloody lip or black eye. She realized Josiah had wanted to kill the man for what he'd put them all through. His need to take care of her and Babe must have overruled his need to pummel the man into unconsciousness.

He hurried her through the underbrush, apparently as eager as Emma was to be assured of her daughter's safety. She had a hard time keeping up but refused to ask him to slow, and he kept his pace.

They broke through the trees, and the most beautiful sight in the world met her eyes. Rocky still lay where Josiah had instructed him to wait, with Babe curled against him on the far side. She slept like an angel without a care in the world, her chest rising and falling with each breath. A small smile tilted the corner of her mouth, as if she dreamed pleasant thoughts. Josiah had positioned her so that any stray bullet would hit his beloved horse before it hit Emma's treasure.

This was Emma's treasure in the hills, her beautiful little girl. No claim, gold, or fortune could ever replace the perfection of her daughter or her daughter's presence in her life. A sob escaped at the sight of her daughter, safe and secure while snuggled up against the horse's warmth.

"Babe."

Babe stirred. "Mama!" She jumped to her feet and ran to Emma's waiting arms. Tears spilled down their cheeks. "Mama!"

"Shh, you're safe now. It's all right." Emma held her close, buried her face in Babe's soft hair, and drank in her scent. "I'm here."

"That bad man tooked me, Mama. I woke up and he told me to stay quiet. I screamed and tried to bite him and he said he'd hurt you if I didn't do as he said." She reached up and caressed her mother's face, her expression full of fear at the memory. "I got quiet and he brought me here and tied me up. I told him I hated him and he stuffed his nasty handkerchief in my mouth."

Emma rocked her daughter as her tiny body shuddered with the force of her sobs. She found it odd that Babe didn't even recall Mack by name. A lot had happened since he'd been at their place, and Mack did look different with a beard and his loss of weight. It might be possible Babe really didn't recognize him. Tears ran down her own face as she imagined her daughter's terror, knowing she'd been helpless to rescue her at the time. "We're safe now. Josiah made everything safe."

Babe continued on as if Emma hadn't spoken. "I wiggled and wiggled until I got the hanky out of my mouth. I screamed as loud as I could, and my papa came to get me."

Emma looked around for Josiah and saw him standing nearby, tears streaming down his face as he wrestled with his own memories of the moment and his emotions. His jaw again clenched in anger.

After a moment, he cleared his throat. "He'd left her in the mine. It was dark inside there, and she was terrified." He looked away, clearly battling his desire to take Mack out for the pain he'd caused them.

"We're all safe now. Let it go, Josiah."

"I brought her back here, not knowing if you were dead or alive. I had to make a choice, and you said Babe came first. I'd been sneaking around to corner Mack from another direction when I heard Babe's faint cry. I secured her with Rocky and promised her I'd be back as soon as it was safe."

"God was watching out for her, Josiah. He used you to save her. I'll never be able to thank you enough."

He shook his head. "I had to leave you with a madman to find her. You'll never know the anguish that went through me knowing I had to make that choice. When I think of what could have happened. . ."

"But it didn't happen! You were able to find Babe and then come back to save me. You did it, Josiah. You kept us both safe, and in the process, you stopped Mack from hurting anyone else."

Josiah dropped to his knees and pulled both Emma and Babe into his arms.

Emma had never felt safer. "We're going to be all right, Josiah."

"Only if you promise never to leave my side," Josiah said, peering intently into her eyes. "I want you to marry me, and I want to be Papa to Babe. Please say yes."

Emma didn't take the time to answer. Her kiss said it all.

Babe interrupted, clapping her hands in glee. "I *told* you he would be my papa!"

Emma reluctantly pulled away from Josiah, and they both laughed. "That you did, Babe. That you did."

Josiah rose and tugged Emma to her feet, then picked up Babe, and in unspoken agreement they headed through the bushes toward Mack. Words tinged with guilt flowed from Josiah as they walked. "I lost control when his gun went off and I saw you fall. I hit him for all I was worth. I couldn't stop the blind rage I felt, knowing he'd almost succeeded in ruining me again. I realized the shot had gone high and that you were fine, but I pounded him anyway. I assured myself that you hadn't been shot, and then I ran to make sure Babe was still safe with Rocky."

"Thank you, Josiah. You did the right thing with Babe." She knew he'd feel guilt over his loss of restraint with Mack, but what man wouldn't have blown up at that point? "I love you."

Josiah stopped and pulled her into his arms again, holding her tightly against him. "I love you, too."

Mack was exactly as they'd left him, sagging against the tree.

Babe made a strangled sound at the sight, and Josiah pulled her close against him, reassuring her that she was safe and that he'd not let Mack ever hurt her again. She melted into his arms and buried her face in his neck.

Mack glanced up at the trio, his face contorting into pain at the sight. "I'm so sorry. So very, very sorry." His eyes had cleared, and he seemed sober. "I need to explain."

Josiah motioned for him to continue.

"I know you trusted me like a brother, but you never knew my true thoughts. As the years passed, I grew to resent how naturally everything came to you and to Johnny. The women flocked to you each time we'd enter a new town, and you both seemed oblivious. I wanted that kind of attention from them, but you had it and didn't even care. You had a single focus—to earn your money and get your ranch."

Josiah interrupted. "Our ranch, Mack. You'd always been an equal partner, and I thought you knew that."

Mack shook his head. "I'd never be a part of what you two shared. I know you meant it when you said you'd cut me in, but I never broke through that bond the two of you had. I could never be as good as the two of you. You'd work hard and go to bed early. I never could settle down that way. I'd have to go out for a drink. . ."

"And we never judged you for it. It wasn't our place."

"No, but I judged myself. I knew I wasn't good enough to be a partner with you. I fought the urge to drink but always failed. I knew you had to be disappointed in me."

"Your guilt is your own, Mack. We prayed for you and loved you as a brother, nothing more, nothing less."

"I know. But one night—that last night—I decided I'd had enough. I wanted to see respect and pride in your eyes, not frustration and confusion when it came to me. I'd taken to gambling a bit, but that night things got out of hand. I couldn't seem to stop, so I went to the bank and ended up losing it all, our entire fortune. The one you'd cut me in on and we'd all worked hard for. We were so close to getting our ranch, and I was sure I could get that last bit of money and things would be great between us. But instead"—he shrugged—"I lost it all. Even what wasn't mine to lose. I couldn't face the two of you, so I skipped town. I figured I'd make the fortune somewhere else, and when I did, I'd return what I'd taken tenfold. Instead, I made my life more of a mess, ruined things for Emma, panicked, and here we all are." He looked at them all with pleading eyes. "I don't deserve your forgiveness, but I ask for it anyway. I want to make things right. I want to face up to what I've done."

Josiah measured him with his eyes but didn't say a word.

"Babe?" Mack's voice softened. "I'm so, so very sorry that I scared you. I'll never hurt you or scare you again. All right?"

Babe laid her head on Josiah's shoulder and stared at Mack for a few moments while they all waited. Finally, she raised her eyes to Josiah. "Mack's nice now?"

Josiah hesitated for a moment before answering. "It appears so."

Babe wiggled from his arms and stepped forward a few feet toward Mack. Her blond curls tumbled in disarray, making her appear younger than she was. "I forgive you. But stay nice now."

Emma thought her heart would break at her daughter's brave words. They could all take a lesson in forgiveness from her.

Mack nodded his agreement. "I'll stay nice, Babe."

They heard a rustling behind them. Help had finally arrived. Late, but at least they now had assistance. The sheriff and his men burst from the trees, surrounded Mack, untied him, and threw him on the ground.

Babe screamed, and Josiah dashed to grab her in his arms. She again buried her face in his neck, crying, "Papa, Papa."

Emma hurried forward to say that Mack had already been subdued. The sheriff handcuffed him and pulled him to his feet.

Josiah walked over and pulled Emma close.

"With all that's gone on, Josiah, what do you plan to do with Mack now?" She caressed his back then reached up to rub Babe's arm that stayed clenched around his neck.

Josiah stood silently, emotions warring on his features, before turning to face her. "Your love has shown me I can be redeemed and has given me a new hope. You've helped me find my way back to God, something I never thought I'd see happen. I'd pulled away too far. But you've shown me His love again and have allowed me to find love with you. With your agreement, I'd like to give the same chance to Mack." He paused. "He's a broken man, and I'd like to forgive him and help him find his way."

Emma threw her arms around him and pulled him close for a kiss. Josiah met her lips with his own.

Babe voiced her complaint at being squished between them, and Emma pulled slightly away, her laugh muffled against Josiah's shirt. "You're a good man, Josiah Andrews. I knew it from the start."

"Oh, the day you met me on your porch with a rifle pointed my way?"

"Well, maybe just after that." Emma felt her face flush at the memory. "More like when Babe threw herself into your arms and declared you her papa, and you stayed around anyway."

She looked up at the brave man who had done so much for her and Babe. His change of heart toward God was a joy to behold, and she relished watching him let go of his desire for revenge, opting instead for forgiveness.

Josiah's brown eyes searched hers. "You never gave me a formal answer to my question. Must you make me wait?"

"Question?" Emma was perplexed. He'd asked her many questions. She'd already shown her approval of his decision to forgive Mack.

"Babe, what are we gonna do with your mama?" Josiah's voice came across so tortured that even Babe had to giggle.

"He asked you to marry him, Mama. You didn't answer. You just kissed him. Say yes! Please!" Babe tilted her blond head and smiled in an endearing plea. Josiah had to adjust his grip to prevent her from tumbling out of his arms.

"Yes, say yes, please?" Josiah echoed, his grin just as irresistible. He had a wild look about him, dirt smudged across his face from his tumble with Mack, dark hair blowing around his shoulders, and his dark brown eyes sparkling with mischief. He looked more like a savage outlaw than a civilized lawman. "Let me be your husband and be a proper papa to this little girl here."

"I thought my kiss said yes for me," Emma hedged, shrieking as Josiah used the arm that held her close to tickle her with no mercy. "All right, yes, I'll marry you!"

Cheers broke loose behind them, and Emma turned mortified eyes to the sheriff and his men.

" 'Bout time you tied the knot again, Emma," one called out.

"Yes, we thought you were gonna let this perfect papa for Babe get away," another added. "We even had a small bet going. . ." He glanced quickly over at the sheriff. "Er. . .uh. . .I mean, we all had an opinion on how things would turn out."

Sheriff Bates shook his head and brought Mack over to where the happy couple stood. "Best wishes to you both. Why don't you all get squared away, then come by my office in the morning. Until then, we'll make sure Mack has everything he needs, and you can decide how you want to handle things at that time."

"I appreciate it, Sheriff. We'll see you in the mornin', then."

Emma watched as Josiah and Mack exchanged glances, and her heart melted at the peace that filled Mack's face as he took in the forgiveness in Josiah's.

Josiah led them back to Rocky, where the horse now stood in wait. He set Babe gently on the ground and walked over to dig around in his saddlebags. "I had a special surprise to give my little girl, but I seem to have misplaced it."

Babe frowned and moved closer. Emma held her back, catching Josiah's eye and noting the twinkle in it.

"What was it, Papa?"

"Well, give me a minute. I'm sure it's here somewhere." He fumbled around a bit more, though there was no way the object he sought could be lost in the bag. "Ah, here it is!" He turned with an exuberant grin, hiding the item behind his back.

Babe literally jumped with excitement. "What is it? Show me! Please!" The latter comment was added only after Emma's nudge to her back.

Josiah dropped to his knee and pulled a brown package from behind him with a flourish. Babe pouted her dismay as the surprise still lay hidden.

He held it out, and Babe glanced up at Emma. Emma nodded, and Babe tenderly peeled back the wrapper.

Even Emma gasped at the beauty of the exquisite porcelain doll that lay before them. "Oh, Josiah. . ."

Babe squealed with glee as Josiah handed her the doll and then carefully swung his daughter-to-be through the air with his strong arms. Babe cradled the doll in her arms and looked at Josiah with pure adoration.

Emma blinked back tears of joy. A papa to swing her daughter into the air, just like in Babe's dreams. And even more important, a man to share Emma's life, one who would also cherish her greatest treasure.

Emma watched her daughter's dream unfold at the same time her heart's desire for a loving husband was met.

Epilogue

Emma stood before the large looking glass and studied her appearance. Her face glowed in the mirror's reflection. Her eyes were bright with joy. It was hard to believe the happy bride who peered back was her. She brought her hands up to her face, trying to cool her hot cheeks.

Katie and Liza stood beside her.

"Stop fretting," Katie admonished. "You'll splotch your cheeks."

"I'm not fretting. I'm trying to see if this is real or a dream."

"It's no dream, dear. Your handsome prince awaits you on the other side of that door."

"Oh my." Emma dropped to sit in a nearby chair. "What am I doing? I'm really marrying him. I hardly know him! Is this the right thing for Babe? For me? Help!" It was a fake plea. She knew Josiah was the man for her.

Both women laughed.

Katie placed her hands firmly on Emma's shoulders. "Josiah is the best thing to happen to both of you in a long, long time. He's smitten, not only by you, but by your daughter, as well. I think if you refused to marry him at this point, she'd go ahead and make him her papa without you. You no longer have a choice."

Emma grinned. Her friend was right. Babe had known the man would be her papa from the moment he rode into their yard. Emma was the one who took some time, though in her heart she'd known he was special at that first glimpse, too.

Liza pulled her to her feet. "We need to stuff you into some more layers. Your groom won't want to wait forever."

"That's such a flattering thought. Thank you." Emma turned sideways and perused her side profile. Whew, as slender as ever.

"My comment didn't refer to your size. I merely stated that we need more than petticoats on you before you make your appearance."

Katie lifted the gorgeous wedding gown, and Liza took the other side. They raised it over Emma's head and carefully lowered it over her finished hair. The two women had worked her long tresses into a vision of beauty. Her hair was upswept from her neck, and tendrils of curls hung loosely to frame her face, just the way Josiah liked it.

"Mama, I'm a fairy princess," Babe called from across the room.

Liza had created both of their dresses. While Emma's was an elegant work that hugged close to her body before gradually widening at the hem where it touched the floor, Babe's was a concoction of pink and white. She now twirled about the room so quickly that Emma was afraid the little girl would fall and hit her head or get sick.

"Slow down, baby doll. You don't want to miss the ceremony. Your new papa will be sad if you can't make our family day."

Babe froze and swayed as her eyes struggled with the sudden loss of motion. She plopped down on her bottom and balanced herself with a hand on each side of her legs. "I don't want to make my papa sad."

The ladies behind her muttered and tugged as they forced the multitude of tiny buttons at the back of her dress to close.

Babe rose slowly to her feet. She smoothed the dress. "Is it okay?"

"Your dress is fine, and you look gorgeous." The dress had puffy white sleeves and a high waist, pulled in with a shiny pink sash. The full skirt featured layers of white and pink, so when Babe spun, the different colors parted like the petals of a flower. The effect was stunning, and Babe couldn't resist spinning in circles to watch it flow.

Emma felt so proud of her friend's skill and the intricacy of her work. Liza now had more work than she could handle, and women were lining up to get her to make their next dresses for each and every occasion. She knew Liza and Petey were going to be fine.

Katie had fixed Babe's hair in a miniature version of Emma's own. She looked precious.

"There," Katie said to Emma. "I think we have it. Step back and let us look at you."

Emma did as she was told.

The women stared at her until she felt like a horse on the auction block. "Well?"

"You're breathtaking."

"Josiah's going down in a dead faint when he sees you."

"Mama, you look like a princess, too!"

Strangely enough, the odd conglomeration of comments calmed her pounding heart. "Thank you. I think I'm ready to marry my future husband now." As a matter of fact, she couldn't become Mrs. Josiah Andrews a moment too soon. Her heart fully embraced the idea. He completed her in a way she'd not realized since losing Matthew.

Instead of feeling sad at the thought of her late husband, she felt peace. She knew Matthew would be happy that she'd married again and had found someone to love her and Babe. She also knew he'd be relieved to know Babe had a papa looking out for her. As stunning as the young child was, Josiah would have his hands full chasing off suitors before they knew it. Already he complained about the "attentions" of Jimmy and Petey.

The door banged open against the wall as Petey burst through. "Mother! They're ready for you. Hurry!"

Liza laughed and took her son's hand and steered him back out the door.

Katie took both of Emma's hands in her own. "Are you okay? I can wait and walk with you if you need me to."

Emma leaned over to kiss her dear friend's cheek. "I'm finer than I've been in a long, long time. Thanks for caring."

"I'll always care, and I'm always here for you. I'm happy you've found Josiah. He's a great man."

Katie left and closed the door behind her.

"Well, Babe, this is it."

"You mean we're *finally* going to marry Josiah, Mama?"

Emma laughed. "Yes, we're finally going to marry Josiah."

Babe dropped her voice to a whisper. "Thanks for saying yes."

"You're welcome," Emma whispered back. She reached for her daughter's hand and clasped it in her own. "Let's go get our man."

Mack waited for them on the porch. "You look a vision. Both of you."

"Thank you, Mack. That means a lot." Emma was thrilled that he'd made a full turnabout in personality and now worked to make amends with Josiah. She quietly thanked God for the progress he'd made.

"I mean it. Your example of forgiveness and love, not to mention lack of concern about riches, made me realize there was more to life than I'd realized. I thought money brought happiness. Then I found out it caused grief like I'd never known before. I lost the two most important things in my life—Josiah and Johnny." He paused. "I can't get Johnny back, but I can work to make things right with Josiah."

"You know money isn't important to Josiah, either. You can't pay him back financially."

"I know. But if I can get my life right with my Lord, I think that will please your husband and my best friend. What do you think?"

"I think you'd do him proud if you follow through on that plan."

Mack moved forward and crooked his arm. "Now, let's get going and marry you off to that man before he—or your bouncing daughter over there—passes out from the pressure."

Emma called for Babe, and the little girl ran over to stare up at Mack. He offered her his other arm, and Emma held her breath in anticipation. Mack had come a long way, but would he suffer a setback if Babe rejected him again?

She needn't have worried. Babe sent Mack her most charming grin and happily attempted to copy her mother's hold on his arm. "Take us to our wedding, Mr. Mack. Please."

"Don't mind if I do," Mack spouted back playfully. "Oh, wait. I have something for both of you." He dug a small bag out of his pocket and withdrew two delicate necklaces. Each held a small nugget of gold. "These are for you both, matching necklaces that I had made from the first nuggets I ever pulled from the claim."

Emma reached for hers while Mack bent down to fasten the other around Babe's neck. "It's perfect! Oh, Mack, we gave you these nuggets for you to keep. You shouldn't have done this."

"I did, and I wanted to. The gold belongs to you, and I want you to see that I'm giving back the firstfruits of my labor. I wanted to give you a gift, and this felt like the right one to give."

"We'll both treasure the necklaces, won't we, baby doll?"

Babe still stood in awe at wearing her first piece of jewelry ever. "Yes, ma'am, we will."

Mack looked embarrassed at their appreciation and urged them on to meet Josiah. But a happy grin filled his face as they went.

The trio walked around the corner of the house into the crowded side yard. The flowers had burst into bloom the day before, as if wanting to add their beauty to the celebration of love.

Josiah stood next to the pastor, and his face filled with such adoration as their eyes met that Emma began to cry. He took a step forward as she watched, and the pastor put an arm out to stop him from moving up the aisle to his bride.

"Now don't shed too many tears and miss seeing your own wedding, Emma." Mack's whisper brought her to her senses.

She was on her way to her new life with the man of her dreams, with Babe by her side. There was no way she'd blur that vision with tears. She held her head high and moved forward to meet the man she loved.

PAIGE WINSHIP DOOLY

Paige enjoys living in the South with her family, after having grown up in the sometimes extremely cold Midwest. She is happily married to her high school sweetheart, and they have six homeschooled children. Paige has always loved to write. She feels her love of writing is a blessing from God, and she hopes that readers will walk away with a spiritual impact on their life and a smile on their face.

THE DREAMS OF HANNAH WILLIAMS

by Linda Ford

Dedication

To my special, dear friend Brenda who has encouraged me, prayed for me, and shared coffee with me for more years than either of us cares to admit. May God continue to bless you in every way.

Chapter 1

Quinten, South Dakota, 1893

Hannah Williams felt the ground shake, then heard noise like thunder off the hills, followed by the pungent odor of hundreds of overheated bovine bodies. By the time the air filled with dust, she stood with her nose pressed to the window, watching cows stream down the street toward the holding pens at the rail yard. She shivered at the sheer number of them, their bulk. If they happened to decide to crash to the sidewalk and push into her premises. . .

She glimpsed cowboys astride horses. Some rode beside the herd; several more brought up the rear. They seemed to know how to control the animals, though she couldn't imagine how anyone could contain that tide of flesh.

As soon as the melee passed, she hurried outside. She didn't intend to miss the thrill of watching the cowboys corral this wild herd.

A group of excited boys jostled her as she hesitated several yards from the penning area. An exciting tension trickled across her spine at the noise of the cows pushing and bawling a protest against these strange surroundings, almost drowning out the sounds of men calling to each other and to the animals.

Nearby, a man on a big bay horse waved his arm in a circle, and several cowboys rode around the edge of the herd, turning them steadily toward the open pens at the end of the street. The cows hesitated. The man jerked his hand upward, and one of the cowboys edged toward the lead cows balking at the gate.

Suddenly, several animals bolted and the whole herd stampeded toward her. She pressed back against the wall of the nearest building, sucked in her breath to make herself smaller, and prayed the animals would miss her.

The big cowboy bellowed at the others then galloped toward her. He waved his hat at the animals and turned them toward the pens. The lead cows again hesitated at the gate then burst through, and like a flood, the rest followed.

The man who'd saved her from certain destruction rode to the gate, pushed it shut, then called to the others who gathered round him. He sat tall and big in the saddle, he and his horse moving as one body. He wore a black leather vest over a dusty gray work shirt. Like the other cowboys, he wore a red bandanna knotted around his neck. He said a few words to the other men. The way a couple of them hung their heads, Hannah guessed they'd been scolded. Two cowboys reined around and circled the pens. The others headed down the street. Hannah expected they would be looking for a bath, a hot meal, and a cold drink, not necessarily in that order. As they cantered by, she couldn't help thinking many of them looked more like boys than men.

"Ma'am?"

She jerked around to see the big man at her side. He doffed his hat. His dark brown eyes twinkled. "First time you've seen cattle moved through town?"

"First time I've seen cows so close. I thought I would be trampled. Thank you for saving me."

He swung his leg over the saddle horn and landed neatly on both feet, then banged his black cowboy hat on his thigh, dislodging a cloud of gray dust. "You were never in any real danger. I made sure of that."

This was the closest she'd been to a cowboy, and she studied him. "You're the head cowboy?"

"You could say that. I own all these steers. Jake Sperling." He nodded almost formally.

She'd heard the Sperling name. Biggest landowners in the area. A powerful family who controlled much of the business around the cattle industry. And this was Jake, the owner. She'd heard rumors indicating he carried his power and authority like a badge, expecting others to honor them as much as he did. In fact, she'd heard he acted like he was the cream on the milk.

"I'm Hannah Williams." If she had to venture a guess, she would say he was not yet thirty, young to be in such a position. But then what did she know about when men in the West learned to control others? Maybe some were born to it. She only knew she intended to stay as far away as humanly possible from men who had such aspirations and ability. And opportunity. Living with her stepfather had taught her that lesson well.

But her curiosity overcame her caution. "What happens to all these animals now? Where do they go?"

He jerked to his full height. "Allow me to show you." He turned back toward the pens, the horse clopping on his heels.

Hannah hesitated a fraction of a second, considering the need to get back to work, even more briefly reminding herself she wanted nothing to do with men who exuded authority. But she did want to see how the cattle were handled, and he'd offered. No harm in that. It's not like she intended to give him any right to order her about. She fell into step beside him, hurrying a little to keep up with his long strides as she picked her way across the dusty street, carefully avoiding the steaming odorous piles left by the cows.

In the three weeks since her arrival in this cow town at the end of the railway, she'd glimpsed a way of life that appealed to her. Men were men. But women were given rights not expected back East. A single woman could even file a homestead claim.

Hannah smiled. She could imagine what Otto, her stepfather, would have to say about that. Her smile flattened. How could Mother have married a man so diametrically opposite to Hannah's father? Her father had been dead almost four years, but even though she was twenty-one and all grown up, Hannah still missed him so much. He would be happy to see Hannah finally had a way to be independent. He'd always encouraged her in that direction.

Jake went right to the wooden rails of the fence and leaned over, not a bit intimidated by the press of animals. Of course he wasn't. He worked with them daily.

But this was the first time she'd been close enough to a cow to touch it—if she had such an inclination, which she most certainly did not. The animals were even larger and more frightening close up. One animal tossed its head, rolling red, wild eyes and spraying slobber. Hannah gasped and backed several feet from the fence.

Jake laughed. "They can't hurt you. See." He reached over and patted one on the rump. The animal snorted and pushed away, causing even more commotion in the herd.

"I can see well enough from here." *And smell too well.* But determined not to show any weakness, she forced herself to the fence and leaned her arms on the rails as if feeling not a bit of trepidation.

The man grinned at her. "You should see it when a couple more herds arrive and all the pens are full."

"I can't imagine the noise." She grimaced. "Or the odor. How long do you keep them here?"

"As soon as the buyers see them, we cut a deal, load them on the railcars, and ship them east." He pushed away from the fence and stared hard at the station as if the building itself had done something to offend him. "I expected the buyers to be Johnny-on-the-spot. They better show up on the next train or they'll have some hard explaining to do. I can't afford to keep these steers standing around any longer than necessary."

She chose to ignore his dire comments. "I can't imagine how you get these wild things to march into railcars."

"No problem. We chase 'em up the ramp. You just have to know what you're doing."

Three boys ran past, screaming like banshees. The cows crashed into each other in their attempt to escape this frightening racket. The far fence creaked a protest.

Jake clambered up the rails. "Look out, boys," he called. "Hold 'em back."

The two patrolling cowboys raced to the troubled spot and drove the cattle back.

Jake slammed his hat on his head. "Keep your mind on business. I don't want to have to round up this bunch again. If they get out, you can bet it'll mean your jobs."

The two sketched salutes and looked scared half to death.

Hannah wanted to protest. They could hardly be blamed for some noisy children.

"Thank you for explaining it to me," she said, her words much softer than her heart. She had a distinct dislike for people holding power over others. In her mind, each person—male or female, young or old—should make his or her own decisions in life. And under God's control only. Not under the whims of another person who was stronger or had more power.

As she turned to walk away, Jake wrapped the reins of his horse around the top rail and followed. "Would you care to join me for dinner this evening?"

His grin invited her even more than his words, but she'd had her share of men with power—real or imagined. Otto had been more than enough. "I'm sorry. I'm a working girl. I seldom have time to get away." She increased her pace. "In fact, I'd better get back."

Jake slowed, let her hurry on, and then called, "Where do you work? When are you done for the day?"

She paused, turned to face him, saw his wide smile, and almost wished she didn't have to work. If only he were a regular cowboy and not the powerful owner, she might consider taking a few hours away from the demands of her job. "I really have very little time off right now. I'm just trying to get my business operating." She wouldn't tell him where she actually worked—in the burned-out hotel two doors from the general store, next to a law office on one side, a vacant lot on the other. Not that she thought he'd bother looking her up, but she couldn't take the chance. The last thing she needed was someone who might be a prospective guest showing up before she was ready to reopen.

"I'll see you around," he said.

As she hurried back to the hotel, she wasn't sure if his words were a promise or an order. Nor why it mattered.

She paused outside the Sunshine Hotel. What had her grandparents been thinking to name it that? The eternal optimists, always expecting sunshine and roses on their pathway. She hoped they were finding exactly that in California where they'd gone in search of more adventure.

When her grandparents had given her this hotel in Quinten, Dakota Territory, it had been an answer to prayer. A way to escape her controlling stepfather and establish her independence. She paused to silently thank God. But between her grandparents' departure and her arrival, the hotel had suffered a fire in the dining room, leaving the room with a hole in the middle of the floor and most of the rooms smoke damaged. Without money to hire a crew to do the cleaning and repairing, Hannah had little choice but to do the job herself.

She'd scrubbed the front windows until they gleamed, scoured the mud and water stains off the sidewalk, and managed to clean the door. But only a new coat of paint would successfully hide the water damage.

She pushed her way inside and adjusted the CLOSED FOR REPAIRS sign so it could be read from the outside. After much elbow grease on her part, the lobby was almost presentable. She'd managed to remove most of the water and smoke damage, but again, only paint would fix the wall next to the dining room. "Mort," she called. "Are you here?"

The long, cadaverous man who seemed to be part of the gift from her grandparents slouched into the room. "Where you been, miss?"

"I was watching the cattle being driven to the rail yards."

"Now you'll have to dust everything again." He nodded toward the walnut table in the lobby she'd spent hours cleaning.

"Did you get the drapes down?" She'd given him instructions to remove the drapes in the back room where she slept. The smell was almost overpowering. She couldn't afford to have them professionally cleaned or replaced, but perhaps hanging them outside for a few days would air them out. In the meantime, she'd tack a sheet over the window for privacy.

"Took 'em down. Hung 'em outside like you said. But if you ask me, the best you can do is burn 'em and buy new ones."

"Yes, that would be nice, but I can't afford it. Is there lots of hot water?" If she scrubbed the wall next to the dining room one more time, perhaps she'd get rid of the smoke stains.

"Boilers are full. Still got to clean the chairs like you asked."

"Fine." It was like moving mountains to get Mort to go faster than a crawl, but grateful for his help with hauling water and moving the heavier stuff, she wasn't about to complain.

A little while later, she perched atop a ladder, scrubbing at the wall, her nostrils protesting at the smell. For the most part, the overpowering odor had disappeared from the room except when she got the walls wet.

As she scrubbed, she tried to plan when she could open. The work took much longer than she expected. So far she'd managed to do the lobby and the big suite of rooms in the corner upstairs, hoping, she supposed, at some point she could have guests and start to get a little money. Enough to pay Mort and buy paint would be a nice start. But somehow she had to first get enough to fix the huge hole in the middle of the dining room floor and replace the drapes in there. Nothing could be done to salvage them. And the sooner she got them all down and burned, the sooner she'd get rid of that acrid smell. But Mort moved at his own pace. If they weren't so heavy, she'd do it herself.

She didn't look up when the door opened. Mort must have gone out for something and decided to use the front door rather than go around outside again.

When someone smacked the bell on the desk, she practically fell off her ladder. A woman cleared her throat.

"I'm sorry," Hannah said, righting herself. "We're not open for business at this point."

The woman tugged at her gloves. "Surely you can't be serious."

Hannah climbed off the ladder and headed for the desk. "We've had a fire. I'm still trying to clean up." She waved her hand around to indicate the work in progress.

The woman gave a dismissive glance. "But I always stay here." She drummed her fingers on the desk as if to let Hannah know she might as well quit stalling.

"I'm really very sorry, but I'm not prepared for guests."

"You? Maude and Harvey own this establishment. Where are they?"

"My grandparents. They've gone to California and left me the hotel."

"They left?" She looked about. "Well, I will miss them, but I wish them all the best."

"You knew my grandparents?" Well, of course she knew who they were. That wasn't what Hannah meant. It sounded like this woman knew them as more than businesspeople.

"Maude was always so good to visit with when I came to town." The woman marched toward the dining room. "We would sit in here for—oh my. Seems you've had a disaster."

"A fire," Hannah repeated.

The woman stared for another moment then returned to the desk. "Well never mind. We can get along without the dining room. But I can't imagine staying anywhere else. All the other hotels will be crowded with noisy cowboys coming and going at all hours." She placed her gloves beside Hannah's clasped hands and leaned toward her. "I'm sure you can find something suitable for a few nights. Can't you, my dear?"

Hannah looked into brown eyes and sensed the gentleness hid a steely determination. She admired the woman's perseverance, but she really wasn't ready for guests. Didn't know when she would be, in fact. But she was tempted. After all, there was the little problem of finances.

The door flung open again. Could no one read the sign? Closed for repairs meant closed.

She blinked as Jake strode across the room, his boots thudding on the floor. She'd been forced to throw out most of the carpeting, destroyed by mud, water, and smoke, but the boards had polished up nicely if somewhat reluctantly. How had he located her? And why?

He nodded at her before he turned to the other woman. "Mother, what are you doing here? Didn't you see the sign?" He turned to Hannah. "I'm sorry."

Hannah nodded, not knowing if he meant sorry his mother had ignored the sign or sorry she owned this damaged hotel. But before she could respond, Mrs. Sperling pressed her hand to her forehead and moaned. Her legs crumpled under her.

Jake swept her into his arms and looked around for a place to lay her. Hannah hurried over and put a cushion at the end of the sofa she'd cleaned and prayed it didn't still smell like smoke.

Mrs. Sperling's eyelids fluttered. "I'm sorry," she whispered.

Jake rubbed her hands and looked worried. "Mother, I told you to take it easy. You didn't have to come to town. I can conduct the business on my own."

Hannah watched the broad hands gentle the smaller, paler ones and remembered her father encouraging her in much the same way. He'd warmed her hands many times when she'd stayed outside too long or sat up too late trying to memorize her schoolwork. But more than his touch, she remembered his words, "Hannah, my daughter, you can do anything you put your mind to."

The picture inside her head changed. She and her father had been in his store, helping customers. A young man had come in with his mother, speaking so rudely to the woman he'd brought tears to her eyes. Her father waited until they left then said, "Hannah, you can tell a lot about a man by the way he treats his mother. Pay attention to that. It's the same way he'll treat his wife."

Hannah was certain Jake expected complete compliance from the men who worked for him. She remembered the way he'd spoken of the buyers and knew he'd accept no nonsense from men he did business with, either. But if her father was correct, Jake had a tenderness toward his family.

His mother spoke. "You can handle the business. I only came to help spend the money once the business is complete." She pushed up on her elbow. "I need a new dress and some material for new curtains and. . ."

Jake straightened and frowned at his mother.

The older woman fell back against the cushion and draped her arm over her forehead. "Though I don't know how I'll manage it all. I should have insisted Audrey accompany me." Her voice was as thin as thread.

Jake groaned. "No doubt she'd bring the boys."

"Of course. Why should you mind? They're sweet and well behaved."

Jake sputtered.

Ignoring him, his mother explained to Hannah. "Audrey is my daughter, and she has two little boys."

"Mother, pull yourself together. We have to find rooms."

Hannah stared as the woman pressed her palm to her chest. "I'm feeling a little breathless. I'm just too exhausted to find someplace else." She waited until her son turned away then winked at Hannah.

Hannah almost choked holding back her laughter. Jake might be powerful, obeyed as the boss, but his mother played by her own rules, something Hannah admired.

Jake strode to the dining room door. "This isn't going to be fixed anytime soon."

"I'm sure Miss. . ." Mrs. Sperling smiled gently. "I'm sorry, dear, I don't believe you told me your name."

"Hannah Williams."

"Well, Miss Williams, I'm sure you can find us something, can't you?"

"The dining room—" Jake protested.

"We can eat anywhere we want. But I want to stay here." The older woman's voice began strong and then, as if she'd remembered her fragile condition, grew weaker. "I've always stayed here, and it just wouldn't feel right if I didn't."

"Mother, you'll just have to accept—"

Hannah decided then and there a woman so determined to exert her independence should be accommodated. "The suite in the corner upstairs is ready for occupancy. I could let you have it, but, as you can see, there will be no dining available."

The woman sighed. "Thank you. I'm sure we'll be very comfortable."

Jake's expression darkened. He shot Hannah a look of accusation then faced his mother. "Mother, this is absurd. There are plenty of rooms available in town."

"But Miss Williams has just offered us rooms here."

Jake glowered at his mother. Hannah felt the familiar and unwelcome tightening in the pit of her stomach—the same feeling she got when she'd somehow challenged Otto's authority. Often she didn't even know what she'd done. Her father had encouraged the very things that brought on Otto's disapproval, so Hannah was left inadvertently crossing him on many occasions. His anger frightened her. She feared she would drive him to violence. But his sullen silence was even more frightening. It left her wondering when he'd finally punish her and how.

How would Jake deal with being challenged? He exuded power and control in a way that made Otto look insipid. Was Jake the same? Would he demand obedience from his mother? Insist on it? Send her silent messages promising to deal with this matter later—in private?

Mother and son confronted each other. Pressing her advantage, Mrs. Sperling patted her cheeks and managed to look weak and helpless. Something—Hannah was convinced—completely fabricated. Jake continued to look ready to grab his mother and stalk out the door.

Hannah stepped aside, realizing she'd unconsciously moved out of his way, expecting him to mow down anything and anyone in his path.

She jumped when Jake let out an explosion of air. "Very well, but it's going to be inconvenient to say the least." He stalked to the door.

Hannah blinked at his departing back.

Mrs. Sperling bounced to her feet. "My bags are at the livery," she called to her son.

Hannah pulled her thoughts together as best she could, still barely believing Jake had given in so easily. Or had he? Was it just for show? "Aren't you afraid of making him angry?" She gasped. "I'm sorry. That was inappropriate of me."

But Mrs. Sperling laughed. "He takes himself seriously enough for the both of us. Now tell me, dear, how long have you been in town? How do you like it? Where have you come from? Do you have an address for your grandparents? I'd like to write them."

Hannah laughed. Obviously Jake's mother didn't fear him, but then being his mother would most certainly affect the dynamics.

"I don't have the rooms ready. If you'll excuse me, I'd better take care of them."

Mrs. Sperling trotted after Hannah. "I'll help you."

Hannah stopped and faced the woman, her expression suitably serious even though her insides bubbled with amusement. "But I thought you were exhausted."

The older woman chuckled. "I've just experienced a miraculous recovery."

Hannah laughed with her. "I don't imagine anyone but you could get away with that."

Mrs. Sperling's brown eyes twinkled. "Get away with what?" Side by side, they climbed the stairs.

"I'd guess Jake expects his orders to be followed."

"He prefers it, I'm sure."

Hannah understood what wasn't said. Jake liked to be obeyed. Only his mother got away with defying him.

Chapter 2

Jake reined his horse into the street, automatically touching the brim of his hat at several ladies, his thoughts still on his mother. He should have insisted she remain on the ranch. These trips to town were too strenuous for her. Miss Williams failed to realize it or she wouldn't have allowed his mother to talk her into offering them rooms in her damaged hotel. He should take his mother home immediately, but first he had to find the cattle buyers and negotiate a fair price for his steers. He and the other ranchers had discussed this, decided on what they considered a reasonable price, and agreed to hold out together for it. If they stood unified, no buyer could persuade one of them to undersell the others.

He stopped in front of one of the hotels and thudded across the sidewalk and into the quiet, clean-smelling interior to ask for the buyers and was informed that none of them had registered. He spun out and rode to the next hotel to receive the same response as he did at the third and last hotel in town. He paused to look around the lobby. Muted red carpet patterned with medallions, heavy maroon drapes—a calm, restful atmosphere. If they had to stay in town, why couldn't his mother have chosen one of these hotels?

Jake suddenly remembered his mother's request and headed for the livery. At the same time, he'd go by the station to see if the buyers had sent a telegram.

"Silas," he called as he stepped into the cool interior. "Is there a telegram for me?"

"No, sir. I'd've found you if there was."

"You're sure Mr. Arnold hasn't sent a message?" Mr. Arnold was the one buyer Jake could count on. He'd been eager to do business with Jake and the others.

"Nothin'. Nothin' at all."

"Then they must be on their way." He'd have to cool his heels until they showed up. Easier said than done. He needed to finish his business and get back to the ranch. Even with Frank in charge, he couldn't neglect his responsibilities for long and expect things to hang together.

He then went to the livery. He spoke to one of the men working there. "Have my mother's things sent to the Sunshine Hotel." He tossed the man a handful of coins.

The worker gaped. "The Sunshine? But it's—"

Jake didn't allow him to finish. "Right away. She's waiting for them." He returned to his horse and rode to the pens to check on his herd.

Shorty patrolled on the left. On the other side, Jimbo's horse stood at the fence, but there was no sign of the boy. He'd been warned about keeping his mind on business.

Jake reined his horse to the right and edged around the fence. Jimbo sat on the edge of the wooden trough, his arm around a young girl. "Jimbo," Jake roared, "I don't pay you to socialize."

The boy jerked to his feet, his mouth working. The girl ducked behind him, her eyes wide as a cornered deer's.

"I've warned you—"

"Mr. Sperling, I ain't been visiting more'n a minute." The boy's Adam's apple bobbled as he swallowed hard. "This here's my sister, May." He swallowed noisily again. "I ain't seen her in three months. She's been telling me about Ma and Pa and the young ones."

Jake hesitated. By rights the boy had used up all his chances. It seemed a lifetime ago, but Jake remembered what it was like to be so young and uncertain, trying to deal with adult responsibilities and wondering if he could handle them successfully. "Find Con to take your place; then go visit your folks."

Jimbo threw himself on the back of his horse, pulled his sister after him, and headed for the road. "Thank you, Mr. Sperling," he called over his shoulder.

Jake watched the herd as he waited for Con to arrive. His thoughts turned toward the business he hoped to conduct. This delay was costly, as Mr. Arnold should know. Jake lounged on his horse, watching the animals shuffle about and settle into the new place. They'd be fine as long as nothing spooked them. But if Arnold didn't show up soon, he'd have the task of feeding and watering the bunch. He sighed. He wanted nothing more than to get back to the ranch where things were more predictable, more under his control. He did not like the feeling that he held on to the whole affair by a slippery rope.

Trying to keep his mother safe was more than enough challenge. He knew what she would do in town—shop until she exhausted herself. And without a dining room, she'd be forced to go out after a tiring day in order to eat. He would have to watch her carefully to ensure she didn't jeopardize her health before he got her back home.

As he often did when he was alone with his thoughts, he turned to prayer. It seemed more natural to talk to God on the back of a good horse than in church. *God, You know how I need to get these animals sold so I can get back to the ranch.* It was up to him to see the ranch and the family properly taken care of, but he couldn't manage without God's help. He let the peace of knowing God's care sift through his tense thoughts then ended as he always did. *Help me fulfill my responsibilities.*

He shifted in the saddle as Con rode up to him. Jake gave him instructions on watching the herd but didn't hurry away. This was about the only place in the whole town where he felt comfortable. Finally, with a belly-cleansing sigh, he turned away. Time to deal with his mother and her needs.

He tied his horse in front of the hotel, crossed the sidewalk, and flicked a finger at the closed sign. Trust his mother to ignore the sign and the impracticality of staying here. But he feared if he insisted on moving, she'd upset herself and end up in bed. He sighed. Somehow they'd manage, inconvenient as it was.

He threw open the door and wrinkled his nose at the odor of smoke and lye. He'd sooner sleep with the cows. He heard angry muttering and followed the sound to the dining room. Hannah teetered on the top of a ladder struggling with blackened drapes. What was the woman thinking? Someone should tell her how dangerous ladders were.

"Miss, get down before you fall." His voice rang with the same tone he used with his hired hands, expecting them to jump and obey.

She jumped all right, and put herself completely off balance.

He leaped forward. "Stay right there," he ordered, shifting course to avoid the hole in the middle of the floor.

She pawed at the curtains, trying to right herself. A tear started at the edge where the material had burned. The sound began slow, like a beginning thought, then picked up speed. Her fragile balance shifted as the drapes parted company with the rod. Caught in the drape, she tumbled off the ladder.

In his haste to stop her descent, he stumbled over a chair and caught one foot between the rungs. He reached for her. In a tangle of charred drapes and a now broken wooden chair, they hit the floor. Whoofs of air exploded from two sets of lungs.

Jake couldn't move. His feet were snarled in chairs and fabric. The ladder had fallen across his legs. He'd have matching bruises to prove it.

Miss Williams sprawled across his chest, trying to fight her way out of the drapes encasing her. Her struggles landed elbows in his chest and face.

"Stop it," he muttered, and when she grew more frantic, he wrapped his arms around her, making it impossible for her to move.

"Let me up. I can't breathe." Her voice was muffled.

"Take it easy. I'll get you out." He kicked away the ladder and chair and rolled to his knees, then set to work untangling the fabric until she emerged.

She inhaled sharply and pushed hair out of her face, smearing charcoal over her cheeks, and shuddered. "That was dreadful. They stink."

He sucked in air filthy with the odor of the burned drapes as he pushed to his feet, feeling a pain in his shins from the encounter with the ladder. He dusted himself off. "You had no business up there. Who's in charge around here? How can he be so irresponsible as to allow you to do such a dangerous job? Where is he? I'll speak to him."

She scrambled from the drapes and stood up to face him, her eyes boring into him. Very pretty hazel eyes, he noticed. "I am in charge. I am responsible for me. I don't need someone to take care of me."

"You can't be in charge."

"And why is that, Mr. Sperling?" Her voice was low, gentle. But her flashing eyes told the truth. She did not welcome his opinion.

Not that he cared what she thought. Someone had to see that she didn't do such foolish things in the future. And when had he gone from being "Jake" to "Mr. Sperling"? "This is not a job for a woman."

She pulled herself as tall as she could. Her eyes turned almost green; her cheeks flushed. "Really? And what do you propose to do about the fact that I own this place and intend to fix it up so I can open for guests?"

He struggled between anger at her stubbornness in refusing to give in to his hard stare and amusement at her attempt to be fierce. She'd find out soon enough there were things a woman had best leave for a man to do. It scraped his nerves to think she'd probably get hurt trying. His father had drilled into Jake that women were the weaker sex and men were responsible for protecting them. "You would have been injured if I hadn't caught you."

She flicked the idea away with a dismissive wave of her hand. "I was perfectly safe until you scared me. Don't you know you shouldn't sneak up on people like that?"

He narrowed his eyes. "Don't you know you shouldn't stand on the top of a ladder?" What was wrong with her? Didn't she care she might be injured? "In the future, stay on the ground."

"I don't see that my future is any of your business." She spat the words out. Suddenly, her mouth rounded. "Oh, you're hurt." She reached for his cheek then pulled her hand back and pointed.

He touched the spot she indicated and saw blood on his fingers. "It's nothing."

"It needs to be tended to." She waved him toward a chair, saw it was charred, and waved him toward another. "I'll get something to clean it with." Without giving him a chance to protest, she hurried into the back room, which appeared to be the kitchen.

He chuckled when he heard her startled exclamation. She must have seen her reflection.

When she returned, her face and hair had been fixed. She approached him with a white cloth and a small basin of water. She put the basin on the table then hesitated.

"I can do it myself," he said.

She nodded and handed him the cloth.

He sponged at the area.

"A little more this way," she indicated. "It's still bleeding some."

The outer door opened. They both turned toward the sound.

His mother called.

"In here," he said.

His mother appeared in the doorway, took one look at him, and pressed her hand to her chest. "What happened?" She swayed.

"Mrs. Sperling." Hannah raced to his mother's side, but he tossed chairs out of his way and got there first. He swept his mother into his arms and headed for the sofa, Hannah hot on his heels.

"She should be at home," he muttered. "These trips to town are too strenuous for her."

As he laid her down, her eyes fluttered. She let out a little squeak. "You're bleeding."

"It's just a scratch." He rubbed her wrists and felt her pulse. It seemed strong enough.

"What were you doing?" his mother demanded.

Hannah spoke. "I'm afraid I'm responsible for any damage he's incurred. I decided I couldn't wait any longer for Mort to take down the burned drapes. But they decided to take me down instead. Your son broke my fall."

Mrs. Sperling pulled herself into a sitting position and glanced past her son to Hannah. "You aren't injured, too, are you?"

The girl moved closer. "Of course not. I'm pretty hardy." She glanced at Jake.

Jake was about to say he was hardy, too, when his mother answered for him. "He wrestles cows. I doubt you could hurt him much." She took Hannah's hand. "Rose's Ladies' Wear has the prettiest selection of bonnets. They've just arrived, Miss Rose said. You'll have to come with me to see them."

Feeling dismissed, Jake sat on one of the narrowed-backed, fancy-cushioned chairs.

"Mrs. Sperling, I couldn't possibly. I have to get this place ready for guests."

"But we are guests."

"Yes, my very first."

Jake's stomach growled loudly, announcing to everyone in the room he hadn't eaten since breakfast many hours ago.

Mother swung her feet to the floor. "I'm hungry, too. Shall we find supper?"

Jake eyed her. She seemed just a little pale and in no hurry to stand. He guessed she was still a little weak from her faint, though she'd probably deny it. "Mother, I don't think you're up to going out again."

His mother shot him an annoyed look. "I'm fine."

"You stay here, and I'll bring back something."

"I'd worry about you." She rubbed her chest as if it hurt.

Jake's stomach growled again. Louder. More persistent. He really needed to find food soon. But Mother looked so worried he didn't dare leave her. She leaned her head back, her eyelids fluttering.

"Hannah, perhaps you would be so kind as to prepare us something," Mother said.

The girl stared. "The dining room isn't open."

Mother lifted a weary hand. "I know that, my dear. But surely you eat. Wouldn't it be possible for us to share your meal?"

"B–but—," Hannah sputtered.

Jake knew he should have put his foot down from the first. This was not a safe place for his mother. The dining room was in shambles. Hannah seemed bent on risking life and limb to prove she could do a job beyond her capabilities. "Mother, you can't be serious. You knew when you insisted on staying here that we'd have to go out to eat."

She pressed her hand to her left shoulder. "I know, but it's not like we need anything special."

She spoke for herself. Jake was about ready to butcher one of his own steers and roast it in the alley. He got to his feet and headed for the door. "Anything in particular you'd like me to bring back?"

His mother moaned and fell back on the cushion. He halted. Dare he leave her?

"I don't mind sharing my supper with you." Hannah spoke softly, sending Jake a look that dared him to argue.

"That would be lovely," Mother whispered without opening her eyes.

Jake ached to reject Hannah's offer. His mouth flooded at the promise of a thick steak. But his mother's fragile state swayed him against his personal wants. With a sigh, he mentally kissed the steak good-bye. He jerked a chair to his mother's side and plunked down on it. "That will be fine," he told Hannah.

"I'll get right at it." She spun on her heels and headed for the kitchen.

Jake watched his mother, worried she was so quiet. He made up his mind. "In the morning I'll hire someone to take you home."

Her eyes opened quickly, and she fixed him with a determined look. "You'll do no such thing. I have shopping to do."

"You'll exhaust yourself."

"How can you think of sending me home as though I've been naughty?"

Jake felt caught between wanting to obey his mother and being the one responsible for her health.

His mother draped her arm over her forehead. She looked so exhausted, he decided he would personally take her home as soon as it was light out.

"Don't deprive me of this little pleasure," she pleaded.

He wanted to say no. But he couldn't. After all, she must get lonely at the ranch. "Very well, if you promise to be careful."

"I promise." She smiled gratefully. "Now why don't you go see if you can help that sweet girl?"

"Me?" Give him a fire and a slab of beef, and he could cook up a meal to satisfy the largest appetite, but he turned all feet and thumbs when he tried to do things indoors.

"I'd help, but—," his mother began.

"You stay here and rest." He reluctantly planted his feet under him and made for the dining room door, certain the last thing Hannah needed was his assistance. He stuck his nose into the room where she worked. "How can I help?" Should he warn her of his ineptitude in the kitchen?

She stopped chopping something into a bowl of flour and considered him. "Help?" She sounded so surprised, he stepped into the room.

"I'm sure there's something I can do."

She looked about ready to refuse.

"I insist." Mother would have a fit if he didn't do something.

Hannah didn't look very happy about it, but she nodded. "Very well. You can slice the chicken." She wiped her hands on her apron and pulled a glass platter from the cupboard. "Arrange it on this."

He held the platter gingerly. It shone in the light and looked like it would break if he held it too hard. Or worse, slip from his fingers and shatter on the floor if he didn't trap it firmly. Not daring to breathe, he marched around to the opposite end of the long wooden table. Very carefully, he put the platter next to the jar of canned chicken. He tested the lid, found she'd already loosened it, and grabbed a fork she shoved toward him.

Now he had to get the pieces of chicken out of the tightly packed jar. How hard could it be? Nothing compared to dropping a lasso over a racing cow. He clenched the jar firmly in one hand, stabbed the fork into the contents, and yanked hard. He practically jerked the jar out of his fist but didn't remove any meat. He put the jar squarely back on the table. He thought of wrestling it to the ground, using brute force and ignorance on it.

"Wiggle the meat out of the top," Hannah said.

He stole a glance at her, suspecting she found this amusing. But she seemed engrossed in rolling out some dough on the tabletop. If he didn't miss his guess, they were having biscuits—with chicken, if he could manage the simple task.

He tightened his grip on the jar and sawed the meat back and forth until it slipped through the top and promptly flew across the table to plop in front of Hannah.

"Whoops," she said and waited for him to retrieve it.

He grabbed it with the fork and pinned it to the platter, where he butchered it with a knife. Slices. . .she wouldn't be getting. Chunks would have to do.

He managed to get the rest of the chicken from the jar to the platter without any disaster. Then he backed away, hoping to escape.

"The biscuits will be a few minutes. Where do you want to eat?"

"Obviously the dining room is out."

"Obviously."

He glanced around the kitchen, guessing Hannah ate alone here most nights. It was a cozy place with the range at one end, a big window at the other, and well-stocked cupboards in between. He was about to suggest this would be a nice place to eat when she spoke.

"Perhaps I should move one of the tables into the lobby." She headed for the dining room.

"Table in the lobby would be fine." She didn't need his consent, but it would be nice to be consulted. After all it was he and his mother who were being served.

She chose a table in the far corner, one hardly affected by the fire, and started to push it toward the door.

He grabbed it.

"Thank you," she said, all prim and formal.

"You're welcome," he replied, equally formal.

"I'll get some hot water and scrub it."

"I'll get some chairs," he said.

"I can manage on my own."

"So you've said, but what kind of man would I be if I sat and watched you lug furniture around?"

They hurried to the doorway. Arrived at the same time.

He stood back and nodded for her to go first. "Please."

She nodded and preceded him. "Thank you."

"You're welcome."

His mother groaned. "Can we manage without the stiff politeness? It's a little tiresome."

"I'd be glad to," Jake said, "if Hannah will stop saying thank you every time I move."

Hannah opened her mouth as if to argue then shrugged. "I wouldn't want to be tiresome." She hurried to the kitchen for hot water.

He sighed. She'd been so warm and friendly down at the rail yards. But now she acted like he was personally responsible for the fire in her hotel. Why the big switch? He'd done nothing to make her so disagreeable. Unless. . . He thought of her reaction when he'd told her to stay off the ladder. Maybe she blamed him for the torn drapes. But that didn't make sense. She only planned to dispose of them. Slowly a thought surfaced. Had he offended her by telling her she couldn't run this place on her own? But she couldn't. Didn't take a Philadelphia education to realize that. He grabbed two chairs and placed them next to the table.

Hannah returned, scrubbed the chairs and table, spread a snow-white table-cloth, and then set the table.

His mother sat up. "Where's the other chair?"

"What other chair?" Jake demanded.

"Do you expect Hannah to serve us after she's offered to share her meal? Get another chair so she can eat with us."

Hannah backed away. "Oh no, Mrs. Sperling. Really. I prefer to take care of you first." She fled to the kitchen.

"Jake, how could you?" his mother whispered. "Persuade her to join us."

He snagged a chair and put it at the table, then went to find Hannah. She didn't look up when he entered the room. "Please join us for supper."

She glanced up then, staring at him long and hard.

"I insist," he added for good measure.

"Very well. You're the boss. Please make yourself comfortable. I'll bring in the food."

He wanted to explain it wasn't because he was the boss. Nor even because his mother had wanted it. He had unnecessarily offended her by setting out only two chairs. He hadn't meant to. But he didn't know how to make up for it. It seemed everything he did only made matters worse. He returned to the other room. "She'll be joining us in a few minutes," he informed his mother as he assisted her to the table.

Hannah arrived with a huge tray balanced on one hand. He might have offered to help but decided it was safer for everyone if he sat tight. Hot biscuits, a platter of chicken that looked nothing like the mess he'd created, a tray of cheese, and a pot of blackberry jam made his stomach lurch in expectation.

"This is lovely, dear," his mother said. "How did you manage it in such a short time?"

Hannah smiled. "My grandmother left a well-stocked pantry."

At least she got along with his mother. He wondered who would ask the blessing.

Mother solved the problem. "Hannah, would you like Jake to pray over the food?"

Hannah looked hard at Jake. Did he see surprise? Guardedness? As if she expected him to be a pagan just because he'd inadvertently offended her? Though, in fact, he'd been nothing but kind and accommodating. He'd even agreed to stay in her derelict hotel. How was that for kind? And he'd been helpful. He glanced at the platter of chicken that she'd rearranged. Well, he'd tried.

"Please, Mr. Sperling, would you?"

He pulled his attention back to her request. "Jake. It's Jake. Remember?" She'd been a lot less formal when he'd shown her around the cattle. He corralled his wandering thoughts and bowed his head to murmur a quick prayer.

After the prayer, Hannah passed the food. "I hope the next time you're in town I'll be officially reopened."

Jake slathered butter on the biscuit and took a bite. "The repairs seem like an extraordinarily big task for a woman on her own. Seems they'd best be dealt with by a man. Or better yet, a crew of hardy men."

Hannah ducked her head, contemplated her food for a moment, and then shot him a look flashing with annoyance. She obviously did not like him pointing out the impossibility of a woman dealing with this job. "I'm quite capable of handling it. My father raised me to take care of myself, and I would never disappoint him by backing out of a challenge."

"Does he know the hotel has been gutted by fire?"

"He's gone."

"Gone?"

His mother sighed. "Jake, don't be so thick. She means he's passed away. I'm sorry, dear. I can see how much you miss him. Now, let's talk about something else." She pinned Jake with a glance. "Jake, another topic, please."

"Like what, Mother? The cows?"

"Really, Jake, that isn't all you know."

She was wrong. What did he know besides cows, ranching, and work? But his mother persisted. "You could ask her about herself."

Jake studied his mother. She smiled.

"Very well." Jake turned to Hannah. "Tell me about yourself."

Sweetly, she said, "What would you like to know?"

"I think you are enjoying my discomfort."

"But no, sir. Why would you think such a thing?"

"Maybe because of that little smile teasing the corners of your mouth."

Her smile widened. Her eyes sparkled with mischief. Something inside him jerked like a cow reaching the end of a rope. It left him breathless and dizzy.

Suddenly he was curious about her. What did she like to do? How did she spend her free time? Did she have free time? He had his doubts. This hotel needed a ton of work. "Is your mother alive?"

"Yes. Alive and well and living with her new husband back East." She ducked her head, ate a bite, and then looked at him. "What about you? Where's your father?"

"My father is also dead." He heard his mother's indrawn breath and patted her hand.

"Things have never been the same since he passed on," his mother said.

"I've tried to continue his work." It seemed he could never live up to his father's ideals.

"That's not what I mean. You've done a very good job, my dear. I just never expected to have to grow old alone."

He laughed. "Alone? You have a cook who is also a dear friend. Audrey and the boys are in and out so often I'm surprised they don't claim bedrooms. And then there's me. We share the same house. When are you ever alone?"

"It's not the same."

He relented. "I understand what you mean."

Hannah watched the exchange and smiled. "Tell me about the ranch."

He settled back, comfortable with this topic. He talked about how his father had decided money was in cows, not gold, and picked a spot with lots of water and grass and protection. "He had a dream for Quinten to become the cattle capital of the West. And when the railway came, he was ready." He realized how long he'd been talking about the ranch and skidded to a halt.

She smiled. "It sounds fascinating. I've always lived in the city. Father owned a successful mercantile store until his death. I always think of him smelling like old cheese and kerosene." Her smile faltered for a moment. "My stepfather is a banker. My grandparents are the only adventuresome members of the family."

"Until now," Jake said. "Seems to me you've acquired a man-sized adventure here. It looks like a ton of work."

"I'd say it appears considerably easier than trying to corral a herd of wild cows."

They all laughed, though Jake's amusement was tempered by annoyance. Chasing cows was men doing men's work. Hannah's trying to fix up this place on her own didn't make a lick of sense.

⁂

Hannah toyed with her napkin. She would have enjoyed company—a pleasant change from eating alone or trying to converse with Mort—if it had been only Mrs. Sperling. But Jake robbed her of that enjoyment. He didn't approve of her independence. Like Otto, he wanted her to conform to "acceptable" behavior, which meant being a docile woman who knew her place. No managing without a man's input and help.

She ducked her head so no one would see her smile. Jake's help in the kitchen was laughable. Of course, like Otto, he'd probably willingly admit the kitchen was a woman's domain. Hannah had no wish to become a man. Certainly no hankering to chase cows just to prove she could do a man's work. She wanted only the freedom to make choices, express her opinions, and follow her dreams.

She knew not all people longed for independence the way she did, but God had given her the desire and now the opportunity. She'd not let criticism or adversity deter her.

The door opened and two men strode in. She sighed. Either the whole town was illiterate or thought closed signs didn't apply to them. The men wore big cowboy hats they quickly took off. "Mrs. Sperling," each said.

"Mr. Riggs and Mr. Martin," Mrs. Sperling said. "Meet Miss Williams, new owner of the Sunshine Hotel."

"Miss." They nodded toward her then turned their attention to Jake. "Our herds are a mile from town. Thought the buyers could come out there and see them."

Jake pushed back from the table and rose to his feet. "None of them has showed yet."

"They ain't here?" The shorter one, Mr. Martin, looked angry.

"There's a train due in twenty minutes," Jake said. "Let's go meet them." He tossed some coins on the table. "Mother, while I'm out, try to get your rest."

Hannah's cheeks burned. She hadn't expected to be paid for sharing her meager meal with them. It had been a courtesy, but he'd effectively put her in her place. Or rather, the place he expected of her—a willing servant to his demands.

She grabbed the coins and hurried after him. "I don't want—" But the door closed behind him, and by the time she threw it open, he was riding away. She stared after him, her insides coiling like the fire-damaged curls of wallpaper. She sucked in several deep breaths before she returned to the table.

"My dear." The older woman patted her hand. "He didn't mean to insult you. He's just very single-minded about business. He takes his responsibilities so seriously." She sighed. "He was only fifteen when my husband was injured in an accident. Seth barely survived. He never walked again. Never got out of bed even. Although I miss him so much, it was a mercy when he went. No more pain and suffering. I picture him in heaven, enjoying the use of his legs again." She sniffled into a hankie.

Hannah murmured her condolences, but when she began to clear the table, Mrs. Sperling caught her hand.

"Do you mind listening to an old woman's prattle?"

Hannah laughed. "You aren't old nor do you prattle." She sensed the woman longed for someone to converse with. Hannah wasn't opposed to the idea. It had been lonely with only Mort or passersby to talk to. Work could wait. "I'd love to sit and chat."

Mrs. Sperling picked up where she left off. "Seth couldn't move about, but he still ran the place. Jake became his legs and hands. He expected a lot from the boy. And now Jake expects even more from himself."

Hannah didn't want to hear about Jake. She especially did not want to listen to his mother excuse his behavior. "You have a daughter?"

The woman smiled with pride. "Audrey. She's the opposite of Jake in many ways. Never worries about responsibility. She knows how to enjoy life. She married Harvey, who owns the neighboring ranch."

"You're very proud of her."

"I'm proud of both of them."

Hannah knew Mrs. Sperling believed her words, but when she spoke about Audrey, her voice held a whole different sound than when she spoke of Jake—as if Audrey pleased her and Jake served her. Hannah dismissed the idea. She was reading more into it than she had any right. She knew nothing about the family.

She let Mrs. Sperling talk for a long time and served her tea and cookies as they visited. But after the woman tried several times to unsuccessfully hide her yawns, Hannah stood. "I think I'd better take care of these dishes."

"And I'd better go to my room. Thank you again for sharing your meal with us."

Hannah cleaned up the meal, tidied the kitchen, and hauled the drapes out to the alley where Mort could finish burning them in the morning. She yawned and stretched. She would like to go to bed, but until Jake returned, she couldn't lock the front door. She had no choice but to wait up.

She went to her room, picked up her Bible, and returned to the lobby to settle herself behind the desk and wait. She opened the scriptures where she had placed the bookmark last night—Deuteronomy, one of her favorite books. She began to read, enjoying the retelling of the desert journey and how God had worked among people. It encouraged her to know He still did.

Her head jerked as sleep overcame her. How long did Jake intend to stay out? She pushed to her weary feet, shivering as someone thudded past on the street. She'd never stayed open so late. She felt alone and vulnerable. If one of the cowboys with too much drink in him came through the door. . .

She made up her mind then and there and hurried out to the small building in the back to knock on Mort's door. A light shone from inside, so she guessed she wouldn't be waking him.

He opened up. "Yes, miss."

"I need you to watch the desk. Mr. Sperling is still out."

He nodded. "I'll be right there."

She hurried back inside. Thankfully, Mort had not grumbled.

At the station the next morning, Jake climbed off his horse and momentarily leaned against its warm flank. No cattle buyers had come in on last night's train. Jake managed to snag a few hours of restless sleep; then he, Riggs, and Martin met the first train this morning. Still no buyers.

Riggs stared at the train as it pulled from the station. "Where are they?"

Jake's gut convulsed. "Let's find out."

The men strode three abreast into the depot.

The stationmaster glanced up at their approach and looked worried. Jake spoke for them all. "Silas, is there a telegram for me?"

"No sir, Mr. Sperling." He glanced at the telegraph key. "Nothin' at all."

"Then I want to send a message," Jake said, his voice as hard as the knot in his stomach. "Mr. Arnold. Stop. Where are you? Stop. Why the delay? Stop."

Riggs nudged him. "Forget 'where are you.' We just want to know why he's not here."

Jake nodded. "Take out that part."

Silas glanced at the three of them, waiting for them to nod. "Send it," Jake said. "And the man better have a good reason for being so late. I'll accept nothing short of a death in his family."

Martin smacked his fist into his palm. "Or serious injury."

Jake knew what he meant. Martin was known to have a short fuse. He wouldn't be opposed to using his fists if Mr. Arnold was simply dangling them at the end of a rope hoping to force them to sell at a lower price. "Best wait and hear what he has to say for himself. Could be he's on his way right now."

They turned and strode toward the door. The men parted ways outside. Riggs and Martin headed back to their herds.

Jake returned to the hotel, where he lingered a moment at his horse's side. Things just couldn't get any worse. As he thumped up the wooden steps, he thought he heard a familiar sound and shuddered. He was tired. His mind played tricks. At least he hoped so.

But as he opened the door, he realized things were about to get a whole lot worse.

Chapter 3

Uncle Jake. Uncle Jake." Two bodies launched themselves at him. They were small. Together they weighed less than a hardy calf, but he knew from experience that they had the ability to cut him down at the knees if he didn't brace himself. He backed up until he hit a solid wall and prepared for the attack. And just in time. One small body hit him at knee level. The other grabbed Jake's hands and crawled up his body like some kind of monkey.

"Hey, boys. Where did you come from?" Guess it was too much to expect Audrey would keep them at home and out of his hair.

The smallest one, the four-year-old knee nipper named Sammy, screamed, "We get to stay with Gamma."

Luke, a year older but only a few pounds heavier, continued to pull himself up Jake's body until he planted his face directly in front of Jake's. "Momma said we could have fun in town."

"She did, did she?" He shuddered, picturing just what sort of fun the pair would have.

"Where's your mother? Where's Grandma?" He edged his face past Luke's and located his mother sitting next to the window in the lobby. "Where's Audrey?"

"She wanted to go with Harvey on his business trip. She asked if I would mind keeping the boys. Of course I agreed."

"You can't keep them here."

"Why not? They'll enjoy a few days in town."

"A few days?" He sputtered and stopped to rope in his thoughts. "We can't keep them out of trouble on the ranch. On two ranches. How do you expect to corral them in town?"

He looked around the lobby, seeing it for the first time. The prissy furniture. The breakable knickknacks. The polished wooden floor—beautiful and just perfect for two little boys to slide on, leaving scratches he guessed Hannah wouldn't appreciate.

His mother answered his question. "You can herd two hundred head of cows by yourself. Surely you can keep an eye on two little boys."

"Me?" When had he volunteered for the job? "Can't you keep them here?" As he finished studying his surroundings, his doubts multiplied.

Hannah came to the door of the dining room, an adoring expression on her face as she watched the boys.

"Don't let their innocent appearance fool you," he warned her. "This pair can be deadly."

She tore her gaze from Sammy, her smile receding as she met Jake's eyes. "They're sweet."

He glanced past her to the dining room, visions of one of the youngsters falling into the hole, and saw she'd erected a barrier with lengths of wood. He knew it wouldn't keep the boys out. Nothing but a solid wall would.

Luke squirmed out of his arm, and as Jake tried to snag him, Sammy escaped. The pair circled the room, screaming at the top of their lungs. His mother closed her eyes and pressed her lips together so hard they disappeared. He could hardly blame her. The racket was worse than weaning time at the ranch. *Ahh*, for the peace of his cows. . . He could think of nothing he'd sooner do than get on his horse and head out of town.

"Have they eaten?" He was forced to raise his voice to make himself heard.

Hannah chuckled. "Steadily since they came."

He groaned, remembering their bottomless appetites. He grabbed Sammy as he roared past. "How would you like to go get something to eat?"

Jake winced as the boy roared his approval. "You don't have to yell. I'm not deaf." Though he would be if Sammy kept screaming in his ear.

"I like yelling," the boy said.

"Yeah, I noticed." He turned to the other screaming child. "Luke, if you stop running and yelling, I'll take you to the restaurant."

Luke skidded to a halt. "Can I have anything I want?"

"I suppose so."

Luke screamed his approval and raced for the door. Sammy slipped from Jake's grasp and galloped after him, doubling the noise.

"Halt!" Jake yelled. But neither boy slowed down. Jake almost fell as he skidded to the door in time to stop Sammy but too late to corral Luke who stood on the sidewalk still screaming. Jake's horse reared, and a rider on the street struggled to keep from being thrown into the dirt.

Jake grabbed Luke and yanked him inside. "Stop that racket right now."

"What?" the boy yelled.

"Stop yelling!" Jake realized he was yelling now and pressed the heel of his hand to his forehead. "Please, be quiet." Blessed silence filled the room. "That's better. Mother, shall we go to the restaurant now?"

His mother fluttered her fingers. "I have a headache. You go without me."

He stared at her. "Me? Take these two out by myself?" He shook his head hard.

"Jake, there are only two of them."

"And one of me." He shifted his gaze to Hannah. If she came along there would be two for two.

She must have read his thoughts. She held up a cloth. "I'm working."

"But you have to eat, don't you?"

She crossed her arms and looked disinterested in his plight. He tried to think of a way to convince her. If she were one of his outfit, how would he handle it? Ask nicely? And then insist. She wasn't one of the hired hands, but surely the same process would work for her.

"Hannah, I would appreciate it if you would accompany us to lunch."

She glanced over her shoulder as if measuring the work she had.

"You aren't going to finish up anytime soon, so why not take a break?"

She shifted her gaze from the dining room to the two boys.

He wasn't above using the pair as bait. "Boys, wouldn't you like Miss Hannah to come with us?"

He grimaced as they yelled, "Yes!" Why did his sister let them be so loud?

Hannah smiled at their eagerness. "Very well. I'll come along. Give me a minute to clean up."

Jake had been about to say she didn't need to bother. They weren't going anyplace fancy. Not with his two nephews. Where he planned to go there would be working men and cowboys. Besides, she looked perfectly presentable in her pretty little blue cotton dress, but she hurried away before he could get the words into shape to speak.

He tried to keep the boys at his side while they waited, but even though she was only gone a few minutes, by the time she returned, they were circling the room at full gallop, their voices about to shatter the windows. Jake captured Sammy as he raced by and wondered if he would have to hog-tie the pair to get them to the restaurant in one piece.

Hannah held out her hand. "Luke, walk with me." The boy trotted over and took her hand as simple as that. She glanced at each boy. "Now let's see who can be the quietest."

"For how long?" Sammy asked.

"Until we get back. I think I might have some cookies for anyone who is quiet the whole time we're gone. You can talk, but quietly. Like gentlemen."

Sammy squirmed to his feet and took Jake's hand.

Jake gave Hannah a hard look. "How did you do that?"

She shrugged. "I just asked them." She'd pulled her hair into a soft roll that made him notice her pretty features. A wide, smiling mouth, a pert little nose with just a hint of freckles, and hazel eyes that he already knew could turn cold one minute and fiery the next.

"I asked them, too. It didn't work as you might have noticed."

"You ordered them."

He blinked. "I—"

She smiled sweetly. "There's a difference."

"Of course. I know that." Except he couldn't remember ordering the boys about. And if she thought he had, then maybe he didn't know.

They strode down the street. The boys were so quiet, Jake shuddered, wondering when they would explode. He glanced at Hannah. She smiled as if she enjoyed a secret. Suddenly he relaxed. This wasn't going to be so bad after all.

They reached the restaurant. Several of his outfit nodded greetings and watched, as curious as newborn calves, as Jake found a table for his group next to the window. He and Luke sat across from Hannah and Sammy. Hannah fussed about Sammy for a moment then left him to down the glass of water the waitress brought. Beside him, Luke did the same. Jake tensed, ready to rescue a glass should either boy upset his.

They drained their water and sat on the edge of their chairs swinging their feet. Sammy screamed as they kicked each other.

Jake thumped the tabletop. "Boys, keep the noise down."

Hannah shot him a look that made him squirm more than his words had made either boy squirm. She touched Sammy's shoulder. "Remember, speak quietly if you want cookies when we get back."

Sammy stopped pumping his legs. "What kind?"

"What's your favorite?" she asked.

He glanced at Luke. "What is?" he whispered.

Luke whispered back, "Molasses."

Sammy turned toward Hannah, serious as a judge. "Molasses."

"Then it's a good thing that's what I baked this morning, isn't it?"

Jake studied Sammy. Light brown hair and blue eyes, like his father, and a rash of freckles. Luke, darker than Sammy, didn't have quite the innocent look Sammy managed to fool strangers with but was just as capable of mischief. Jake couldn't imagine how the pair got into so much trouble. It seemed to stick to them like a bad smell to a pair of boots.

Audrey had dressed them to come to town in dark brown trousers and matching pale brown shirts that made them look like innocent young children. In fact, if he didn't know them so well he might have been as fooled as Hannah, her eyes all warm as she watched them.

She looked healthy enough. Good bones. Good conformity. Good gait—though he supposed it was called something different in a woman. The sort of woman a man wanted to take home and care for. Why did she want to do a man's job? What would it prove except her foolishness at trying? And it would bring only disappointment—or worse, if she fell off a ladder with no one around to catch her.

The murmur of conversation and the clinking of china in the kitchen filled the silence as Sammy pressed his lips together so he would pass the quiet test.

The serving girl placed heaping plates before them. Jake grabbed Luke's hands before he could dig in. "Grace first." He murmured a quick prayer with one eye not quite shut so he could watch Sammy. He almost relaxed as Hannah covered the boy's hands with hers.

The food was robust, just like a man needed. For the first time he realized how few women were in the room. Probably most of them preferred one of the fancier places. Would Hannah? He'd seen her scrubbing walls and dragging down old drapes. She'd had flour dusting her nose as she bent over a table rolling out biscuits. He tried to imagine her in the finest restaurant in town and found not only could he, but he liked it. Right then and there, he promised himself he'd take her one day. For his enjoyment as much as hers. Though she had probably been to all of them already. Maybe accompanied by someone else. He was startled to realize how much he didn't like that idea.

"Have you been to the other restaurants in town?" he asked.

"Not yet. I've been rather preoccupied with the hotel."

"What made you think you—" He paused. Better not suggest she couldn't run the hotel. He'd already noticed she seemed a little sensitive about that. "What made you think you wanted to run a hotel?"

She laughed softly, a sound like the wind racing through the trees. "Actually I never thought of it until my grandparents asked me if I'd like to, and then I jumped at the opportunity."

"So this is a sudden decision?" If he intended to ask her to the fanciest restaurant in town, he'd better do it before she changed her mind about the hotel business and headed back East.

She reached over and cut Sammy's meat into little pieces. "Sudden? I suppose. Though I'd been praying for such an opportunity for a long time. I just hadn't known what shape it would take."

He worked that about in his head as he devoted some attention to his meal. He just couldn't see it the way she did. "How is it an opportunity for a young woman alone?"

She paused with a forkful of mashed potatoes halfway to her mouth. Her eyes flashed like sun off rocks lying below the surface of a mountain stream. All shiny and bright. "Perhaps it depends on the young woman."

Their gazes clashed. Locked. He read determination, stubbornness even, in her eyes. He sought the right words to express his feelings, not willing to concede to her opinion, wanting to save her from disappointment when she found she just couldn't do it on her own. Not wishing to say again what he really thought—that it was man's work she aimed to do—he settled on saying, "Everyone has his limit."

Her eyes held a glittering challenge. "What's yours, Jake Sperling?"

Jake's thoughts tangled like old rope, caught in things her eyes seemed to promise—knowing, sharing, longing, and hundreds of butterfly ideas he couldn't name. His mouth opened, but no words formed in his brain.

Luke's grunt pulled his attention away from her probing look to the child struggling with his meat. Jake reached over with his knife. "I'll cut it."

Luke shook his head. "I do it myself." He dug his fork in harder. The meat skidded away and landed in Jake's lap. He grabbed it and wiped in on the napkin before putting it back on Luke's plate and, ignoring the child's stubborn glower, cut it into pieces. Only then did he turn back to Hannah and answer her question. "Maybe my limit is little boys."

She laughed, and the sound sank into his senses like a breath of spring. "Little boys are becoming men. I'd think you, of all people, would encourage their independence."

"Independence means responsibility, and these two aren't ready for that." He felt the heat of her look—like being branded. He wondered what she thought. He waited for her to say it.

Someone jostled his elbow. "Hey, Jake. When are we heading back to the ranch?"

He turned to Zeke and saw several others hovering behind him. "Waiting for the buyers."

Zeke looked surprised. "Thought they was supposed to be here when we arrived."

Jake tried to shrug it off. "I expected them." He pushed back from the table. "Boys, I'll be in touch real soon." Luke and Sammy had cleaned their plates down to the pattern on the china. "Are you done?" he asked Hannah.

She nodded.

"Then let's be on our way." He had to take care of the herd.

❧

Hannah fell into step beside him, liking the sound of his boots striking the wooden sidewalk. A good, solid sound that she hoped would force her thoughts back to a firm base.

Her reactions to this man were sharp and sometimes unexpected. Why should she care if he thought she couldn't run the hotel on her own? It didn't matter, except his attitude, so like Otto's, annoyed her half to death. And just when she'd decided the sooner he returned to his ranch the better as far as she was concerned, her opinion of him shifted. Watching him cut Luke's meat and seeing the way the little guys adored him made her insides feel like warm cream. Why it should be, she couldn't say. But she didn't like it. It made it hard for her to remember the importance of her independence.

She increased the length of her stride, trying to keep up with him.

The boys' voices rang out clear and strong as they galloped ahead like wild colts.

"Luke, Sammy, slow down," Jake ordered. The pair hesitated half a step then roared forward. Jake groaned. "Trouble just waiting to happen."

Hannah chuckled at his consternation. "You're proud of them, and I don't blame you. Sammy is almost pretty but definitely a boy full of sweet, innocent mischief. Luke is already learning to temper his natural bent for finding trouble."

Jake snorted. "I don't see the innocent part, but trouble is their middle name."

Hannah laughed breathlessly as she tried to keep up with Jake's long strides.

"I need to get back to my responsibilities," he said.

"Me, too. I've noticed nothing gets done when I'm away."

"What about Mort?"

"Yes, Mort." Did he think Mort made up for her trying to do a "man's work"? She would soon change his mind about that. And about her needing a man. She could manage on her own. "Mort has one speed—slightly faster than a crawl. In his mind, he also has one job—night clerk. I haven't much call for such a position right now. I've tried to get him to do a few other things. Mind you, I'm not complaining. I appreciate his help with the water and fires."

"He should do more. I'll speak to him."

"Our arrangement works just fine."

"I can't believe your stepfather allowed you to come out here alone."

She stopped and gave him a look full of hot displeasure. "My stepfather tried to make me reconsider. He tried to force me to become an obedient young woman who'd let him make all her decisions. But he has no right. Neither do you. My father encouraged me to be independent. I will not disappoint him." Ignoring the way his mouth dropped open then shut with a click, she steamed forward.

In three quick strides he caught up. "Hannah, no need to get angry."

She slowed her steps. "I'm not angry. No. That's not true. I am angry. I'm tired of you suggesting I should give up my hotel because I'm not a man."

"Well, you're not." He chuckled.

She was not amused. "I'm not trying to be. But that doesn't mean I can't manage without one." She stopped and faced him. "Now, does it?" Her words were soft, yet he'd better not make the mistake of thinking she'd given in.

She watched emotions shift across his face—stubbornness as if he intended to argue, confusion as if the whole idea surprised him so much he didn't know how to tame it, and then quiet resignation. But if she thought he'd accepted her stand, he quickly corrected her.

"You'll find out soon enough that you can't manage on your own."

She clamped her mouth shut to keep from telling him exactly what she thought of his attitude. *Lord, forgive me for being so angry.* She took a deep breath and allowed peace to return to her heart. "Sorry, but I intend to prove you wrong."

He shook his head. His mouth pulled down at the corners.

Hannah couldn't tell if he was resigned to her decision or sad because he expected her to fail.

"If you change your mind and want some help—"

She cut him off. "I won't." She headed after the boys again.

"Boys, slow down," Jake called. Then quieter, for her benefit, he added, "They're getting awfully loud."

She saw Sammy's boot catch on a board and gasped as he sprawled headfirst into a display of buckets outside Johnson's Hardware Store. The buckets tipped over with a crash that rattled the air. She and Jake rushed forward together.

A horse whinnied. Hannah caught a glimpse of a rider trying to control his mount and noticed a flash as a wagon roared by with the driver sawing on the reins. But her attention centered on Sammy. Several buckets bounced off various parts of his body. She feared he'd be injured. She reached for the child. "Sammy."

He looked past her to his uncle. "Uncle Jake," he cried.

Jake swept the boy into his arms and sat down on the sidewalk to hold him close. Sammy wrapped his small arms around Jake's neck and hung on, sobbing loudly. For a minute, Jake hugged the boy so tight Hannah feared he'd do further damage, and then Jake eased him back and looked into his face. "Are you hurt?"

The boy screamed.

"Where?" Without waiting for an answer, Jake scrubbed his hands through the child's hair searching for damage. He pulled up the boy's shirt and checked for injuries. Satisfied he wasn't seriously hurt, Jake pulled Sammy back into his arms and held him tight. "You'll be fine, little guy."

Hannah's eyes stung with tears. Not from sympathy for Sammy's pain, even though she felt sorry for the boy. She wasn't even sure she could say exactly why she felt so close to crying except she envied the child that certainty of love and approval and acceptance from Jake. Her father had given her the same thing, and she missed it almost as much as she missed him.

Luke hung back, concern written all over his face. As soon as he saw his little brother was uninjured, he threw himself at Jake.

As Jake's arms opened, Hannah's heart unfurled around the edges like a springtime leaf opening to the warmth of the season.

Jake pushed to his feet and clasped a boy in each hand. "Time to get back to your grandmother."

Sammy practically beat the door down as they arrived at the hotel and screamed for his "Gamma."

"Nothing wrong with his lungs," Jake murmured.

Hannah grinned as Mrs. Sperling captured Sammy in a hug and tried to piece together the story spilling from the two boys. "I'm just glad he wasn't hurt."

Hannah left the family to fill in the details and headed for the kitchen. She really did have to get to work. Before she reached the dining room, the outer door burst open and a young man skidded to a stop and glanced around. "Mr. Sperling," he shouted, "got a telegram for you."

Jake took the yellow paper and glanced at the message. With a muffled complaint, he crumpled it in his fist. "Someone had better have a good explanation for this."

"You need me for anything else?" the boy asked.

Jake gave him some coins and dismissed him.

"What is it?" Mrs. Sperling demanded.

Jake hesitated. "Nothing for you to worry about, Mother."

"If it's to do with the ranch, it concerns me." She held out her hand. "I want to see it."

Hannah grinned at Jake's helpless expression. Mrs. Sperling certainly bounced from fluttering, helpless female to strong woman when it suited her.

But Jake didn't relinquish the telegram. "It's from Mr. Arnold saying the buyers aren't coming."

"Does he say why?" the older woman asked.

Again Jake hesitated, and Hannah sensed the message said more than he cared to share with his mother.

"Jake, you might as well tell me. I can deal with the facts better than whatever my imagination dredges up."

"He says he's received information our animals are diseased." He bunched his hands into fists. "I'll find out who started this rumor, and when I do. . ."

A shiver raced across Hannah's shoulders. She felt pity for the person causing his anger. Jake would deal with him severely. Jake was not a man to thwart. He expected compliance with his orders. She wondered if that extended to young women who challenged him about running a hotel.

The two ranchers she'd met the day before stomped into the lobby. "Saw Silas's boy over here. Did you hear something from the buyers?" Riggs demanded.

Jake handed him the telegram.

Martin read it over his shoulder. "It's Murphy. No doubt about it."

Hannah watched Sammy's eyes grow wide as Martin swung his fist as if pummeling the man named Murphy.

Jake held up his hand to silence the other two. "Mother, would you take the boys upstairs or outside?"

Mrs. Sperling had already risen. "I think we'll go see if we can find some penny candy."

Hannah squatted to the boys' level as they passed. "I haven't forgotten the cookies. I'll save them for when you come back."

"We was quiet, wasn't we?" Luke asked.

"You were very quiet." She met Jake's gaze past Luke's head and exchanged a small smile with him. They both knew the boys had been as quiet as could be expected.

The ranchers waited until the door closed behind Mrs. Sperling then resumed their conversation.

Hannah ducked into the kitchen, but even there, she could hear every word.

"Should've known Murphy'd do something like this when he refused to join us in settling a price and said he intended to ship his cattle further up the line rather than pen them with us. Murphy stands to turn a nice profit if he's the only supplier." Hannah knew Martin said the words. He struck her as an angry man. "We ought to get together an outfit and take care of this the old-fashioned way."

"Knowing and proving aren't the same," Jake said, his voice hard.

"I suggest we drive our cattle to where Murphy has his and provide him some stiff competition," Riggs said.

"It's a waste of time and money," Jake said. "What we need to do is prove to Mr. Arnold the animals are healthy."

"And how do you propose to do that?" Martin demanded.

Hannah knew the continual thudding sound was Martin pounding his fist into his palm. "I could send a couple of my hands to persuade him."

"I'll send him a telegram informing him he's been misinformed," Jake said.

The other two laughed.

"Mr. Arnold always struck me as a reasonable man," Jake added.

There were some grunts, and then Riggs said. "Let's do it, then."

Boots clattered across her polished wooden floor. There came the thud of the door swinging shut, and then blessed quiet.

Hannah returned to the lobby and looked around. If she stripped the smoke-stained wallpaper from behind the desk, she could replace it after the Sperlings paid her. She tried to concentrate on how their leaving would give her cash to buy new wallpaper. But she kept thinking how quiet it would be without Mrs. Sperling to visit with, the little boys to amuse her, and Jake to—what? Annoy her? Make her wish for something she once had? She tossed the idea away. Nothing about Jake and his life even vaguely resembled what she'd had.

Overcome with homesickness, she hurried to her room. She opened the top drawer of the chiffonier and dug under her stockings until she found a small case.

Chapter 4

Hannah sat on the edge of the bed and opened the black case. Her vision blurred as she ran her fingertip over the pocket watch her father had left her. It had two tiny diamonds mounted on it. Everything else of value had been sold to pay bills after his death. Even the house had to go to the bank. Her father had gone heavily into debt providing Hannah and her mother with nice things. Things they didn't need. Or at least she didn't. She wasn't so sure of her mother. It seemed she couldn't deal with the harsh realities of fending for herself even though Hannah had promised she could manage for the both of them. No doubt it explained why her mother accepted Otto's offer of marriage as soon as her mourning period ended. But for Hannah, security at the cost of her independence constituted too high a price. She'd never told her mother how demanding Otto had been. *Thank You, God, for giving me a way out.*

She blinked away the tears. She had only to pick up the watch to see her father, hear his voice as he told her he was proud of her, and smell again his unique scent of oil and produce from working in his store. She could still hear him praise her independent spirit.

She closed the case and shoved it back out of sight. She would fix up this hotel and return it to the profitable business it had been for her grandparents. Her father would be proud of her.

She marched back to the kitchen, armed herself with hot water and a scraper, and headed for the lobby to tackle removing the wallpaper.

It proved to be a messy, sticky job. She had half the wall left to do when Mrs. Sperling returned.

As Hannah started to climb off the ladder, the older lady stopped her. "We've already eaten, and I think we're ready for an early night."

Hannah knew the boys were tired when they accompanied their grandmother up the stairs without protest. The cookies would have to wait until tomorrow.

She returned to her task, attacking the sooty paper with a vengeance. She'd show Jake she could do this. She had to prove herself equal to her father's expectations.

"Seems every time I turn my back, you climb a ladder."

Hannah, startled at the sound of Jake's voice, steadied herself, relaxed her tense grip on the scraper, and turned to see him leaning against the desk, grinning. "It's part of the job."

"At least you aren't perched on the top."

Hannah glanced at the remaining corner and decided not to finish it while she had an audience. She climbed down, wiped her hands on a rag, and used her arm to brush her hair out of her face. She wouldn't look at her reflection in the windows to see how mussed she had become. But she felt a bit of paper in her hair and flicked it away.

He grinned and picked out a few pieces. "How long have you been at this?"

"Since you left." A big clock hung next to the stairs, and she looked at it and gasped. It was long past suppertime and almost dark out.

"It doesn't all have to be done tonight, does it?"

She brought her gaze back to him, surprised at how weary he sounded. "Seeing I'm my own boss, I can do it whenever I want." She said it airily, but until she got the place ready to open, she had no income.

He grimaced. "Being the boss means you never get to relax. Mother and the boys?"

"They went upstairs hours ago. Haven't heard a sound since."

"Then I don't have to worry about feeding them." He stretched.

"Did you get your business taken care of?"

"We sent a telegram asking the buyers to come see for themselves. Don't expect we'll hear back until morning."

"What happens if they won't come?"

He rolled his head back and forth and rubbed at the back of his neck. "I suppose we go find them ourselves. Riggs and Martin are all for dragging Mr. Arnold out by the scruff of his neck."

"And what do you think?"

"It took me hours to round up some feed for the animals. And it's only enough for one day. I just want it over with so I can get home and take care of things." His stomach rumbled loudly. "Sorry about that."

"Haven't you eaten?"

"Had to check on Mother and the boys first. I'll go find something now."

Hannah checked the time. "I doubt anything will still be open."

"I'll have to wait for breakfast, then."

"I haven't eaten, either. There's enough for two—" She hesitated. Would he be willing to share her meager fare again?

"You're sure?"

"I wouldn't ask if I wasn't." She headed for the kitchen then turned back, realizing Jake hadn't moved. "Come on. You're welcome to join me."

He tossed his hat on the desk, brushed his hair back with his palms, and followed, hesitating in the doorway. "Remember, I'm not real good in a kitchen," he murmured.

She laughed. "Not to worry. I can manage on my own."

He nodded and sat at the far end of the table.

She stirred the fire to life and put the kettle on the hottest part of the stove and tried to decide what she could make for him. In the end, she fried eggs and potatoes and served biscuits left from the day before.

He reached for her hands as he bowed to pray.

She wanted to pull back, not wanting to get even remotely close to him. He objected to her independence as strongly as Otto had. But it seemed childish to refuse to hold his hands as he prayed, so she turned her palms into his, noticing the roughness of them, the way they seemed to overpower her and yet still feel so gentle.

When he said, "Amen," he didn't immediately release her.

But Hannah couldn't keep her head down forever and slowly brought her gaze up to his. She saw warmth in his brown eyes and wondered what he felt.

Then he smiled. "Thank you for this."

She nodded, ducked her head, and concentrated on her food.

Jake savored the potatoes, crispy and salted to perfection, and the eggs with runny yolks just the way he liked.

Maybe if he itemized the merits of the food, he'd stop thinking about how her hands had felt—small, yet firm and strong. Not unlike the woman herself, he guessed.

Hannah puzzled him. Why did she insist she could fix this place by herself? The smell of smoke persisted in every corner. He swung off his chair and closed the pocket doors to the dining room.

She questioned him with her eyes.

"Thought it might keep out some of the smoke smell."

"I guess I'm used to it."

He wanted to protest she shouldn't have to get used to such a thing but knew she'd take objection to his interference. Still, why should she? What was she trying to prove? He stuffed half a biscuit in his mouth to keep from asking.

She'd said something about her father. As if he would approve. He couldn't imagine any man would willingly allowing his daughter to take on such a task. "What happened to your father?" At her startled expression, he added, "I know he died. I'm wondering how."

"Pneumonia."

"Oh." His mind flooded with questions, but a man could hardly blurt out things like, "How long did it take? Did he suffer?"

"It was mercifully quick," she said, answering his unspoken questions.

"That's a blessing."

"I suppose you're right, though it didn't seem like it at the time. I thought my world had ended. In some ways it did. My father had gone into debt to build a big house. I guess he thought that's what Mother wanted."

"Did she?"

She shrugged. "I shouldn't speak poorly of her, but it does seem she prefers comfort to independence. It's the only reason I can think of for her marriage to Otto."

Jake tried to digest that. His father had made him promise he would always see that his sister and mother were kept comfortable. He assumed that's what a man did for a woman. But Hannah made it sound less than second best.

She chuckled. "I'm afraid Otto bit off more than he could chew when he got me in the bargain. I'd sooner be less comfortable and more independent."

"Independence carries a price—responsibility."

In the dim light her eyes looked dark and bottomless. He could feel her thoughts reach out to him and dig deep into his heart as if trying to fathom his meaning. For a moment, he thought she would acknowledge the truth in his words, but she only chuckled. "Comfort can carry a price, too. Especially if it means being controlled by another's desires. I'll take the alternative."

Disappointed by her stubbornness, Jake swiped his plate clean and leaned back. All sorts of arguments crowded his mind, proofs she was wrong, but at the set of her mouth he guessed she didn't care much about proof.

She went to the cupboard and pulled some cookies from a tin, placed them on a plate, and put them on the table. "The boys were so tired tonight they didn't even stop for cookies. I'll have to be sure they get some before they go out tomorrow."

He jerked forward. "I suppose Mother wore herself out, too?"

Hannah smiled. Her eyes twinkled. "She seemed glad enough to go to her room."

He glanced at the ceiling, wondering if he should check on her.

"I'm sure she's sound asleep by now," Hannah said.

He pulled his attention back to her. Why did she grin so widely? Just looking at her made him smile in response. He liked the way her eyes crinkled at the corners. He wanted to pick out the remaining flecks of wallpaper peppering her hair but guessed she might object to such a bold move.

She blinked before his stare. "Tell me about your father." Her voice sounded husky. "Your mother said he had an accident."

"Yeah. Gored by a bull."

Her eyes widened. She sucked in her breath in a quick little motion then didn't seem to be able to let it out. She scrubbed her lips together two, three times, and then air escaped her lungs like a hot wind off the dry plains. "How awful."

"It wasn't pretty."

"I'm sorry. And you were still young."

"I don't remember being young." He had grown up really fast after his father's accident. "My father died inch by inch in agony, but he never stopped being in charge. And in the months he lived, he taught me everything I'd need to know to take over." He'd learned long ago to speak of it without feeing anything, to think of his father's death with emotional detachment. A man had to move on from such things, concentrate on his responsibilities. There wasn't room for weakness. His father had taught him well.

"Does it seem strange to you that your father's death gave you more independence and responsibility than you wanted and my father's death deprived me of mine?"

"It's not more'n I can handle."

"Of course not." Her eyes carried unspoken disagreement.

He wanted to prove her wrong. It had never been more than he could handle. He would never falter in his responsibilities. "And you've bitten off more than you can chew." He circled his head, indicating the hotel.

She fiddled with her napkin a moment then fixed him with a solid stare. "As you said, it's not more than I can handle."

He didn't want to agree. In fact, the more he got to know Hannah, the more he wanted to protest. But somewhere between the fried potatoes and the last crumb of cookie, things between them had shifted. And he didn't want to spoil this new feeling—like the moment a horse stops bucking and realizes it can either fight or cooperate. Bad example. Yet somehow it fit. He and Hannah had somehow, somewhere in the discussion, silently, mutually, he hoped, agreed they could be friends. Not wanting to spoil that flush of understanding or whatever he decided to call it, he refrained from saying anything about the hotel.

He pushed his plate aside. "That was good. Thank you." He rubbed his hands over his thighs.

She narrowed her eyes. "Aren't you going to toss me some more coins?" She breathed hard.

"Why would I do that?"

"You did last night."

He tried to remember. Riggs and Martin had stormed in, ready to do business. He'd gone with them to meet the train, expecting the buyers. Had he unthinkingly dropped some money on the table as he normally would when eating out?

He had. "I wasn't thinking."

"I suggest you do so in the future."

"I apologize."

She considered him for a moment then nodded.

He thought she meant to say something more, but a bell clattered somewhere in the distance.

Hannah bolted from her chair. "Someone's in the lobby. Can't anyone read the closed sign?" She pushed the doors open and headed across the dining room.

Jake quickly stood. "Watch the hole in the floor." Someone was going to get hurt. He followed her, skirting the hole.

The lobby, lit only by the light from the kitchen, lay in shadows. A cowboy clung to the desk, swaying as he leered at Hannah crossing the room. "I's here for a room," he slurred.

Hannah took her place behind the desk. "I'm sorry. We're closed."

The cowboy swung his head around to stare at Jake, the movement almost tipping him over. He grabbed the desk, pulled himself upright, and turned back to Hannah. "Aw, lady. Bet ya can find me a room somewhere." He leaned over the desk, leering again.

Hannah stepped back. "No, sir, I can't. But I'm sure the Regal will have a room for you."

"Wizened-up old guy runs the place. Not like here." He grabbed for Hannah, but she ducked out of his reach.

Jake had seen enough. He crossed the room in three strides. "Cowboy, you're done here." He kept his voice low, but the young man jerked up, not missing the sound of an order. Jake squeezed the man's elbow and accompanied him to the door. He fought the temptation to shove him into the street.

Even so, the cowboy stumbled and almost fell.

Jake watched, knowing his wish to see the boy flat on his face in muck was not very Christian. He slammed the door and turned the lock. He faced Hannah.

She hugged her arms around herself, her eyes wide and dark.

"Did he scare you?" he asked.

She shook her head. "Not at all."

His insides burned at her denial. "He was drunk. He might have hurt you."

"I don't think so. I'm not completely helpless."

"You're alone here. How did you think you'd stop him?"

"Just because I'm not a man doesn't mean I can't take care of myself."

This helpless feeling when he thought about her situation—wanting to protect her, knowing she resented his suggestion that she needed it—had been simmering since he'd seen her on the ladder and caught her as she fell. It reached the boiling point as the drunk threatened her. It now seared through his insides and spilled over. "He's bigger, stronger than you."

She reached under the desk and pulled out a bat, brandishing it like a sword. "I'm not entirely unprepared."

He pulled up straight and stared at her. His hot, humorless surprise made him laugh. "A bat? Do you think he was going to throw a ball?"

"I'd pretend his head was a ball."

With two steps, he quickly closed the distance between them.

She must have seen the anger in his eyes or guessed at it. She started to back away.

He shot his arm out and snatched the bat from her hand. "Now how would you stop him?"

Even in the poor light he could see he'd made her angry. "I wouldn't try. I wouldn't have to. Because"—she stalked to the desk and leaned over, pushing her face so close he eased back six inches before he could stop himself—"I wouldn't be here. If I was open—and I'm not—Mort would be at the night desk."

"Your fine-sounding argument didn't keep that cowboy out."

"I normally keep the door locked after dark." She leaned forward another inch. "It's only unlocked tonight because I had to wait for you to come in."

He pushed his face closer. "Don't be so stubborn. This is not a safe place. The work is too much, the risks too great, the—" He forgot his third reason as he breathed in the scent of wallpaper paste from her hair and a whisper of something so sweet he thought of fields of wildflowers so full of nectar a thousand bees danced in joy. His gaze dropped to her mouth. His thoughts skittered so wildly he couldn't begin to capture them.

Hannah pulled back. "You are gravely mistaken, Jake Sperling, if you think I can't do this. I can and I will."

He reined in his thoughts. He had never before in his life felt the desire to shake a woman until her teeth rattled. He stuffed his hands in his pockets. "When you find you can't, I'll help you pick up the pieces."

She snorted. "I suggest you don't hold your breath waiting."

He smacked the bat onto the desk and stalked up the stairs.

Hannah waited until she heard his door shut. Only then did she sag against the desk. The drunk had frightened her. But it wouldn't happen again. In the future she'd be sure the door was locked or Mort was at his job as night clerk.

She went to her room and sank to her bed. Shivers ran up and down her spine. She opened her Bible and read for a few minutes. Finally, admitting the words weren't making any sense, she closed her eyes and prayed. *Thank You, God, for keeping me safe.* She just wished it hadn't been at Jake's hands. Why was he so determined to see her fail? Didn't he have enough to worry about with his own family and his ranch to run?

She went to the chiffonier again and pulled out the case containing her father's pocket watch. She pressed it to her chest, forcing her thoughts away from the drunk, and with a little more effort, away from Jake. She focused on what her father would have said. "My independent little girl, you know your mind. I like that. Don't let anyone tell you you can't do it."

He'd encouraged her independence. He admired the quality in her. It had become her defining characteristic.

She returned the case to its place and prepared for bed. Under the covers, she whispered another prayer. "God, please help me not fail."

Hannah woke the next morning, her determination solidly in place. She quickly went to work on the hotel.

Mrs. Sperling and the boys came down as Hannah mopped the lobby floor.

"Do you have our cookies?" Luke yelled.

Hannah was beginning to wonder if one of their parents had difficulty hearing. That would explain why they felt the need to talk at the top of their voices. "I promised them cookies yesterday for being so good," she told Mrs. Sperling.

"Why don't we go find breakfast then come back for tea and cookies?" their grandmother asked.

The boys screamed their delight at the idea.

"Do you mind?" Mrs. Sperling asked Hannah.

"That would be fine." She glanced up the stairs.

"Jake left to see if the buyers had come on the early train. He's worried about the cows." The older woman shook her head. "I can't understand why the buyers haven't come. I'm sure Seth could have persuaded them."

Hannah wanted to protest. Jake had surely done his best. But it wasn't any of her business, and she turned back to her work as Mrs. Sperling left with the boys.

The lobby cleaned, she headed upstairs to tidy the rooms the Sperling family used. She finished that task and returned to the main floor.

The door opened and three men in suits entered.

"I'm closed," she called.

"We're not wanting rooms," one said, "but we are here on business. Are you Miss Williams?"

"I am." She hurried over to the desk, feeling the need to look official. "How can I help you?"

"Allow me to introduce myself." The first man stepped forward. "Mayor Stokes." He bowed slightly, his bowler hat pressed to his chest. "These two gentlemen are Mr. Wass and Mr. Bertch, members of the town council. Mr. Bertch is also the safety inspector."

They nodded, shifted from foot to foot, and avoided her gaze.

Hannah told herself she had nothing to be concerned about, but still every nerve in her body went into quivering attention. "To what do I owe this honor?" Maybe it was a welcoming committee.

Mayor Stokes, apparently the official spokesman, pulled a paper from his pocket. "It's about the fire. Or should I say the water bill from the fire."

She blinked. "What do you mean?"

The mayor harrumphed. "As you know, or being new in town perhaps you don't, the town is dependent on well water for its supply, and we have instituted a policy that if people exceed reasonable use, they should pay for it."

"Really. Who determines what is 'reasonable use' and when it is exceeded?"

"Why the town council, of course. It's part of our job."

The other two men nodded vigorous agreement.

The mayor continued. "We almost pumped the well dry dowsing your fire. Here's your bill." He shoved the piece of paper toward her.

At first she didn't take it, but he shook it demandingly. She opened it and read the amount and gasped. "This is outrageous."

Mayor Stokes looked as if she'd personally called him a blackguard. She hadn't, but she began to think she'd be correct if she did. The other men found something very interesting to study on the wall behind her.

She pressed her lips together to keep from sputtering. "Could you be so good as to tell me when this water rationing policy came into effect?"

The mayor ignored her question. The other two continued to study the wall. Their silence was answer enough.

"Is that all?" she demanded.

"There's one more matter. I told you Mr. Bertch is the safety inspector. He's here to inspect the hotel."

Hannah's cheeks grew hot. Her stomach tensed. "My hotel is not open for business yet. When it is, it will pass any sort of inspection."

Mayor Stokes blinked several times. "I understood you have guests here right now."

The Sperlings. She could hardly deny it, though they'd practically forced her to allow them to stay. "Temporarily," she muttered.

"Then Mr. Bertch is obligated to conduct his inspection."

The three of them marched toward the dining room. Mr. Bertch pulled out a pad of paper and pencil and began to make notes. Hannah knew he had no need. The damage was plain, as they must know. Everyone in town knew.

He circled the room, Mayor Stokes and Mr. Wass treading on his heels. He barely glanced into the kitchen, returned to the lobby, and pretended to inspect it. Only his gaze went up the stairs.

"Miss Williams, this place is not safe for habitation."

Chapter 5

I t will be," she protested. "I need time to fix it." Time, money, and supplies.

The three men put their heads together and muttered, and then Mayor Stokes faced her. "We'll give you three weeks to pay the water use fine and complete the repairs. If they aren't complete then we'll be forced to impose further fines." He cleared his throat. "We're being more than generous. We could condemn the place today and board up the door."

Mr. Bertch dropped a paper on the desk; then the three marched toward the door.

Hannah read the notice they left:

This is to inform Miss Hannah Williams that the Sunshine Hotel must pass a safety inspection in three weeks' time or be fined a hundred dollars.

Her cry of outrage brought Mort from the backyard. "Problems, miss?"

She waved at the paper on the desk as she hurried to her room to think this through in private.

She sank to the edge of her bed. It seemed obvious the mayor and his associates had targeted her, but why? Was it the money, or did they want her out of town? Maybe like Jake, they thought it wasn't a job for a woman.

She looked at the drawer holding the little black case. Her father would expect her to handle this. But how? She considered her choices. Quit? Not an option. Ask for help? Briefly she let her mind swerve toward Jake. Would he help her if she asked, or side with the town fathers? Probably the latter. That left her with one alternative. She had three weeks. In that time, she had to get the hotel ready for occupancy and earn enough to pay the water bill.

She headed back to the lobby and stood looking around. With a little bit of wallpaper, it would be presentable. Why couldn't she take in guests with the same arrangement she had with the Sperlings? Reduced rates because the dining room wasn't available. If she had the dining room door closed off, surely Mr. Bertch couldn't condemn it as unsafe? It would be inconvenient for her to have to go outside to get to the kitchen, but if it meant having paying guests, she would do it.

She marched up the stairs to study the eight unoccupied rooms, all with considerable smoke damage. She knew much of it could be scrubbed away with soap and water—and lots of elbow grease. Well, she'd better get at it.

She persuaded Mort to take down the drapes from the first three rooms and hang them outside to air. She'd try sponging them later in the day. She carried the ladder upstairs then, armed with hot water, soap, and lots of rags, headed for the first room.

"Miss Hannah. Miss Hannah." The siren sound of two little boys rang out.

She dropped her cloth in the water and went down to serve the promised tea and cookies.

❧

The next day was more of the same. Mrs. Sperling took the boys out for breakfast then returned for tea and cookies. Other than that, Hannah spent every spare moment scrubbing and cleaning. She caught glimpses of Jake as he hurried in and out. According to Mrs. Sperling, he hadn't been able to persuade any of the buyers to come and spent his day trying to find feed for the cows.

She had three rooms scrubbed and their bedding stripped down to the mattresses. She didn't have to bury her face in the ticking to realize they'd need a good airing. She wondered if Mort would do it, but he'd been at the desk until late last night waiting for Jake to return. She'd promised him she wouldn't disturb him. That left her to do the task on her own. She tugged a mattress off the bed. It was unwieldy but not heavy. Surely she could get it down the stairs.

She pushed, pulled, and dragged it to the hallway, got it to the top of the stairs, and then paused to catch her breath and consider her next step. She could drag the mattress, but if it got away on her she'd be pushed down the stairs. Nope. Better to push it down than have it push her. She got behind and shoved. It clung to the carpeting. She pushed harder and managed to get it to the top step. Somehow she'd figured it would dip down the stairs. Instead it merely stuck out. She pushed some more. It still stuck out. She kept pushing but couldn't believe how the mattress continued to defiantly stick out over the steps.

Hannah gave one more hearty shove, and the mattress flipped flat, dropping its full length to the steps. She bent to grab the sides, hoping to control its descent, but it took off. She fell to the padding as the mattress gained speed. She clung to the edges. *Bump, bump, bump.* She felt every step in her chest, then her stomach, knees, and toes. As she realized the trip down the steps was going to be slow but bumpy, her initial alarm gave way to amusement.

The mattress reached the polished wooden floor and picked up speed. Hannah giggled. This was fun. She laughed harder. If anyone saw her now, they'd think she'd gone crazy. Maybe she had, but she hadn't laughed like this in a long time. And it felt good.

At that moment the door opened and Jake strode in. She barely had time to holler, "Look out," before the mattress struck his ankles and ground to a halt.

He teetered a minute like a tree cut down at its roots, waved his arms madly, and then toppled, landing beside her.

Laughing so hard tears filled her eyes, Hannah rolled away.

"What are you doing?" He was obviously not amused.

She tried to stop laughing, but the harder she tried the harder she laughed.

He grunted and sat up. "Don't tell me Luke and Sammy are up to mischief."

She shook her head. "Just me," she managed to gasp as she sat up and faced him. Seeing the look of disbelief on his face, she again laughed.

He looked from her to the top of the stairs then shook his head. "Why are you riding mattresses down the stairs?"

She stifled her laughter. "It was unintentional, believe me. But fun." She got to her feet and brushed her hands over her hair. She must look like a wild hooligan. But she didn't care. For the past three days, she'd done nothing but work and worry about this hotel. In fact, in the month since she'd arrived, it had been nothing but work. Like Jake once said, being the boss meant never having time off.

"Care to tell me what you were trying to do?" Jake asked.

"I wanted to get this mattress downstairs so I could take it outside and air it." She chuckled.

He scowled, obviously still not amused.

She tried again. "If I'd known it was so much fun, I'd have done it sooner."

Nothing but a frown. "Where's Mort? Why haven't you asked him to help you? Are you so set on proving how independent you can be that you're willing to risk life and limb?"

"Oh, come on, Jake. I didn't get so much as a scratch. See." She held out her arms and turned them over for his inspection. Ignoring his grunt, she chuckled. "I think God knew I needed to remember life is supposed to be fun. I was getting all caught up in work."

"How many mattresses are you planning to bring downstairs?"

"Eventually all of them, but right now I'm concentrating on three rooms."

He headed for the stairs. "Show me which ones."

"No need. I can do it myself."

"You might not be so fortunate next time." He continued up the stairs with Hannah at his heels.

"Which rooms?" he demanded at the top of the steps.

She indicated the ones. "I need to get the rooms ready to let out as soon as possible. Sooner, even."

He hoisted a mattress to his shoulders and edged his way out the door. "Seems you have a lot bigger problem than the mattresses."

"What do you mean?"

"The hole in the middle of the dining room floor."

"I plan to close the room temporarily. Surely there will be those who would take the rooms at a reduced rate." She counted heavily on it.

"I suppose so." He carried the mattress through the dining room and out the back door and propped it against the shed wall then headed back for the third mattress. She followed him.

When he paused at the top of the stairs with the mattress balanced on his shoulders, she asked, "Sure you don't want to try riding it down?"

He shot her a look. "Not in this lifetime."

She followed him again. "It was awfully fun."

"I'll take your word for it." He propped the mattress beside the first, retrieved the one from the lobby floor, and then stood back and dusted his hands. "You didn't say where Mort is."

"Doing his own thing, I suppose. I can't expect him to work day and night."

"Either get him to take these back upstairs when you're ready or wait for me."

She'd never planned to carry them up on her own, but his bossiness irked her, and she couldn't resist letting him know she didn't need him to run her life or her business. "And if you or Mort aren't here? Do you expect me to drink tea and twiddle my thumbs until one of you returns? You're sadly mistaken if you think I'm going to pretend to be a helpless female who flutters her fan and waits for a man to pick up her hankie."

They'd reached the dining room. He jolted to a halt and studied her long and hard.

She tore her gaze away. She'd been rude, and she tried mentally to justify her behavior. "What you don't understand is I haven't time to waste. The town council paid me a visit. I have no choice but to get this place up and running before—" She bit off the rest of her explanation. She hadn't planned to tell anyone about the visit. She found it humiliating to confess just how close she felt to desperation.

"Mayor Stokes and his cronies were here? What did they want?"

"Nothing." She headed for the lobby, leaving him to stare after her or follow—whatever his inclination.

He followed, grabbed her arm, and turned her to face him. "What did they want?"

She set her mouth. It was none of his business.

"Has it anything to do with us being here?"

She stared at him, reluctant to reveal anything.

"I could persuade Mother to move."

"Don't do that." She needed the money for paint, paper, and a hundred other things.

"Then tell me what's wrong."

She pulled away and sat at the little table where she'd served them. "I've been fined."

"You broke the law?"

She laughed. At least he sounded suitably disbelieving. "Apparently there is a penalty for the overuse of water, which this fire caused."

"I didn't think you were even here at the time."

"I wasn't, but as owner of the hotel I have the dubious pleasure of qualifying for the fine."

He snorted. "How wonderful. So you plan to reopen soon? What about that hole?" He nodded toward the dining room.

She explained her plans. "Only one thing bothers me. The safety inspector could choose to say it isn't good enough." She ducked away from his study of her. Hannah knew before he spoke what his solution would be. Still it annoyed her when he gave it.

"Hannah, why are you doing this to yourself? You could sell the place or at least hire a manager or—"

"You mean admit I can't manage on my own? I'd never do that."

"What are you trying to prove? Everyone has limitations. It's not weak to admit them."

"I think it bothers you to think a woman can get along without a man."

"Why would you want to?" His voice was low. His eyes bored into hers.

She realized they weren't talking about the hotel anymore but something more basic. Something involving only the two of them.

Did she want to be without a man? A man who loved her and cherished her, even maybe took care of her? Somehow her father had been able to do both yet still encourage her independence.

She had only to let her thoughts drift a breath away from the present to remember his returning home in the evening, smelling of the store. She could see him backlit against the open door then coming into focus as the door closed behind him. She felt again the anticipation of watching him hang his hat and shrug out of his jacket. Only then did he turn to her and Mother. He kissed his wife and hugged Hannah. She could hear his words in her memories: *And what worlds did you conquer today, Hannah?* He loved to hear of her adventures.

"I'd like to marry someday. Have someone to share my life." She missed having someone be as pleased to see her, as proud of her accomplishments as her father had been. Her missing took on solid shape that sank, heavy and cold, to the bottom of her stomach. She would welcome the same acceptance from a man she could love and spend her life with. Could she ever hope to find the same thing with a man her own age? Certainly not with Jake. He ruled his world. And she did not want to be ruled.

Jake glanced at the clock and jumped to his feet. "I'm going to miss the train. Tell Mother I've gone to find the buyers and convince them to come here. I'll be back day after tomorrow." He dashed up the stairs, returned with a carpetbag, and with a hurried good-bye headed out the door.

❧

Two days later, Hannah was scrubbing yet another room, wondering why she had the feeling she was waiting for something. Her mind pictured Jake. It wasn't as if she missed him. She'd known him only a few days. Hardly long enough to have given her cause to hurry to the window when she heard the late afternoon train yesterday. Even knowing he didn't plan to return until today, she had waited long enough to be sure he hadn't changed his mind before she'd returned to her work.

She was still cleaning upstairs when she heard Mrs. Sperling and the boys and went down to join them. She glanced past them to see if Jake accompanied them and scolded herself yet again.

"We went shopping," Luke announced in his wild hog-calling voice. "Gamma bought us new shirts. Can I show her mine, Gamma?"

Mrs. Sperling handed over a package wrapped in brown paper. The two boys tore at the paper and pulled out two store-bought blue shirts. Each held one up in front of him.

Hannah admired them. "Now why don't you sit down, and I'll get cookies and tea?"

Mrs. Sperling already sat at the table, her chin resting on her upturned hands. "That would be nice, dear."

The boys pulled out chairs. Sammy managed to upset his backward, and the two of them worked together to right it.

Chuckling, Hannah left them to sort themselves out as she headed for the kitchen to make tea. She put out a good number of cookies and carried a tray back to the lobby. She poured a little weak tea into cups of milk, passed them to the boys, and offered them cookies. They each took two. Then Hannah turned her attention to pouring tea for Mrs. Sperling.

"Thank you, my dear."

Hannah glanced at the older woman. Her cheeks were pale, her eyes glassy. "Are you feeling well?" she asked.

Mrs. Sperling closed her eyes. "I'm afraid I have a headache." She grimaced at Hannah. "A real one this time."

Sammy yelled something about the horses he'd seen on the street, and Mrs. Sperling flinched.

"Boys, talk like gentlemen," Hannah warned.

Mrs. Sperling shivered.

Hannah touched her hand. "It looks like you should go to bed."

Mrs. Sperling opened one eye and looked at the boys. "I can't take my eyes off them."

Hannah knew the older woman could barely keep her head up. "Why don't I take them for the afternoon?"

"I couldn't—" Mrs. Sperling began.

"It will be fun." She'd learned her lesson with the mattresses. Work could not be the shape of her life. She had to make room for fun as well. Besides, she had four rooms ready except for washing the bedding, and she intended to do that on Monday. "Why don't I take them out?" They'd been confined long enough. So had she. She wanted to see what lay beyond the streets and houses of town.

"I'd be so grateful," Mrs. Sperling whispered.

"Then it's settled." She touched Luke's chin to get his attention. "How would you two like to go exploring today?"

"Yeah!" they both yelled.

"Finish your cookies and tea." She shooed Mrs. Sperling upstairs, found Mort, and informed him of her plans, laughing when he looked as if she'd announced she intended to drive nails through her fingers. "We'll have fun."

"Yes, miss," he murmured, obviously not convinced.

≋

Jake didn't wait for the train to stop before he jumped to the platform. It had been a long day and a half, but he'd finally convinced Mr. Arnold to visit and assess for himself whether the rumors of sick cattle were founded. The man had promised to show up Monday morning. Two more days for Jake to cool his heels and chomp at the bit.

He waited for the conductor to push open the boxcar door where his horse rode. As soon as the animal stepped out, Jake threw on the saddle, took care of his bags, and arranged to have a message delivered to Riggs and Martin. Only then could he head for the hotel. He'd check on his mother and the boys before he checked on the animals.

Inside the lobby, he knew from the quiet the boys were not on the premises. He cocked his head toward the stairs, listening for sounds of Hannah hard at work. But there was only silence.

Mort shuffled in from the kitchen. "Your mother is upstairs resting. Had a headache. Not much wonder with all the racket."

Jake nodded. "Audrey hasn't come for the boys, then?"

"No, sir."

He tensed. That left the boys unsupervised. "Then where are they?"

"Miss took them."

"She say where?"

"Out of town, she said."

"Thanks." He decided to leave his mother in peace and headed outside. Out of town. . . That included a lot of territory. Where would she take them? She could manage the boys. She'd proved that time and again, but she didn't know the country. What were they doing? But instead of disaster, he pictured her chasing the boys, catching them, and tickling them, or perhaps playing beside a stream, throwing rocks into the water.

How long had it been since he'd done something for the sheer enjoyment of it? Too long to remember. Too long to matter. Seemed his whole life he'd been taking care of business. Trying to live up to his daddy's expectations.

"It's a big job," his father had warned him from his deathbed. "A man-sized job, but I've taught you well, boy. You can do it. Just don't be distracted by foolishness. You won't have time for it. Not even the things a boy your age would consider normal."

Jake rode to the herd. Zeke had managed to keep them fed and watered. The animals looked fine.

So how foolish would it be to ride out and find Hannah and the boys and maybe enjoy a few quiet hours? He chuckled at thinking there'd be anything quiet about an afternoon spent with his two nephews.

He rode as far as the feedstore. Lars stood on the step talking to a customer. He glanced up at Jake's approach. "You looking for Miss Williams and the two young 'uns?" Before Jake answered, the man pointed down the road. "She asked how far to the river. I told her to follow her nose."

"Thanks." Jake let the horse amble along the dusty trail. Occasionally he glimpsed three sets of footprints.

As he drew close to the river, he heard the boys' voices and turned aside. He tied the horse to a tree and edged forward to watch Hannah and the boys play. They stood on the edge of the river, throwing rocks. Sammy saw one he wanted just below the surface of the water.

"Take off your shoes and socks," Hannah said.

Jake slipped closer.

Both boys sat down, pulled off their shoes and socks, and rolled up their pants. They were soon knee deep, bent over, and up to their elbows in water as they tried to wrench rocks from the river.

Sammy tripped, fell to his bottom, and struggled against the current.

"Hang on. I'll get you." Hannah took a step forward then hesitated. She pulled off her own shoes and stockings, wadded her skirts up, and headed toward the boy.

Jake guessed she meant to help Sammy. He could have told her the boy was fine, but he preferred to enjoy the entertainment.

As she reached for the boy, she lost hold of her skirts and they swirled around her, sinking as they took on water. She paused, looking back as if wondering if she should retreat.

Jake found himself silently urging her on. Now was no time to play it safe.

Suddenly she laughed, grabbed water, and tossed it above her head. Then she splashed the boys. "No point in trying to keep dry now."

Jake leaned against a tree, smiling as the boys squealed then began to flail at the water. For a few minutes he could hardly see them through the spray.

He caught glimpses of Hannah as she retreated. Water beading on her skin caught the sun making her appear to be sprinkled with diamonds. Her hair fell from the coil she usually wore and hung in dark, thick ropes down her back. Her face glowed with laughter.

Suddenly Jake felt old and alone.

Hannah, tossing water into the air and laughing, didn't seem to notice the boys closing in on her.

Jake jumped forward. He knew what happened when Sammy tackled people around the knees. They fell like big old trees in a high wind. He reached the water's edge the same time Sammy reached his target. "Hannah," he yelled.

But she tipped backward, seemed to lie on top of the water for a heartbeat, then folded and disappeared under the surface.

His brain kicked into a gallop. She might be caught on the bottom, hampered by her clothing or unable to pull herself free from Sammy's clutches. He strode into the water, pushing through the resistance. He reached the place where she'd gone down just as she emerged blowing out water and scrubbing her hair out of her face.

"You trying to drown me, Sammy?" She laughed.

Jake grabbed her shoulders and dragged her to her feet. "You scared me."

She gasped and clutched his forearms to steady herself. "Where did you come from?"

He jerked his head in the direction of his horse but kept his gaze on Hannah, enjoying the way her eyes lit with recognition then shifted to confusion.

"How long have you been here?"

"Long enough to see you playing in the water."

She grinned. "I was being very responsible. Making sure the boys were safe."

"Such a wearisome task." He caught a strand of her wet hair and dragged it off her cold cheek and then felt her sharply indrawn breath. He paused, considered dropping his hand to his side, reconsidered, caught another strand of hair, and lifted it off her face.

Her eyes widened, reflecting the bouncing light off the running water and gentling it into something warm. She drew in a breath that seemed not quite steady to him. "No reason a person can't enjoy her responsibilities."

"First I heard about it." He again watched her emotions fill her eyes and shift through a range from amusement to surprise and then to mischief. He noticed the latter a second too late as two soaking bodies tackled him. "Uncle Jake, play with us."

He staggered under their assault and grabbed at Hannah to catch his balance. He knew immediately he'd made a mistake and pulled his hands away and let himself fall.

Unbalanced by his attempt to steady himself, Hannah splashed down beside him, sputtering as she took in a mouthful of water. She dragged herself upward until she sat swaying in the water.

Jake struggled against Sammy and Luke, who seemed intent on drowning him. "Boys," he yelled, "get off me."

Instead of obeying, Sammy sat on his chest and Luke on his legs.

"See my rock," Sammy yelled, shoving a small boulder in Jake's face.

"Nice rock," he grunted as he fought to a sitting position. "What're you going to do with it?"

"Keep it."

Why would he want to keep a rock? More specifically. . . "Where will you keep it?"

"On my pillow."

Hannah chuckled. "Nothing cute and cuddly about his pets."

"Audrey will probably let him, too."

Luke splashed his hands in the water. "I'm all wet," he announced.

Jake stated the obvious. "We all are." Suddenly it struck him what a picture they made sitting fully clothed in the middle of the river having an ordinary conversation. Something deep inside his gut started to rumble and build. It tickled at his insides and bubbled upward until he roared with laughter.

The boys grinned and started to giggle, and Hannah joined in with her musical laugh.

Jake laughed so hard his eyes teared. No one would ever know, though, as water trickled down his face from his wet hair. He laughed until he felt weak and his stomach hurt. He couldn't remember when he'd laughed so hard. It made him feel like his insides had been scrubbed.

Still chuckling, he pushed to his feet, pulled Hannah up, and then grabbed a boy in each hand. "Come on. Let's get out of the water." On the shore he worked off his boots and drained out the water, scrubbed his hands over his hair, and let his clothes drip. He watched as Hannah twisted and squeezed her long dark hair.

Seeing his gaze on her, she gave an uncertain little laugh. "I'm a mess."

He wanted to say he'd never seen anyone more beautiful, but his mouth had developed a temporary case of lockjaw. He could only manage a little grin and a shake of his head.

She must have read something in his expression that gave her a clue to his thoughts, because she lowered her head, hiding her face behind the curtain of hair.

Jake thought it was a good thing she didn't realize the gesture made him even more tongue-tied.

She stole a glance at him through the fringe of her moisture-beaded eyelashes.

He'd had girlfriends. He knew of the natural attraction between a man and a woman. Seen it in others. But what he felt with Hannah went far beyond that to something more personal, more special, more demanding, yet comforting. He felt as if their hearts had jumped from their chests and danced together in the bright sunshine.

He jerked his gaze away and pressed the heel of his hand to his forehead. The cold must be affecting him, making him fanciful. Downright foolish, in fact. "Good thing the sun is warm," he murmured as he turned to watch the boys racing up and down the bank of the river, collecting more rocks, leaves, and twigs.

"Uncle Jake," Luke called, "help me get this rock."

Glad of the diversion, he hurried to help Luke pull a rock from the grass. He could see nothing special about the rock. It was just black, mottled with white specks.

Luke, however, peered at it proudly. He grunted and tried to pick it up. "Uncle Jake, can you carry it for me, please?"

So Jake bore it back to the steadily growing mound.

Hannah met Jake's eyes. He thought he saw a questioning warmth in her eyes, as if she, too, had been aware of the moment of connection between them. If she had, did she know what it meant? He didn't.

Hannah turned to Sammy as he lugged another rock to the pile. She gave the boy the same gentle look he imagined he'd seen in her eyes when she looked at him. He'd been foolish in hoping—

He brought his thoughts to a halt. He hadn't been hoping for anything.

His life was already full to overflowing. Last thing he needed was someone else to take care of. He turned away and stared unseeingly at the river. Like Hannah needed taking care of. She'd made it plain she took care of herself.

Hannah laughed softly, making him forget who needed or wanted caring for. "What are you building?" she asked the boys.

"A mountain," Luke announced.

Jake resisted an urge to slap his forehead. Luke wasn't the only one building mountains. Jake had been doing so in his mind. Turning an innocent bit of play into something bigger and more important than it could ever be.

Chapter 6

Hannah shook the sand from her wet skirts, wishing she could as easily shake the confusion from her brain.

Why had Jake joined them? It didn't seem as if he'd come to check on her, which she would have understood. Instead, he seemed intent on having a good time.

She'd never heard such heartfelt laughter as Jake produced sitting in the middle of the river with two small boys crawling on him. It was a long laugh in the right direction and made her feel happy inside. Just remembering it brought a smile.

But thinking how he'd looked at her caused her smile to slide into something softer, less amused, more—she shook her skirts harder. More what? What did she think she saw in Jake's eyes? What did she want to see? She didn't know, but she felt achy inside. Like tears had built up somewhere behind her heart. She sensed if they escaped they would flood her insides. Her skin couldn't contain all she longed for.

She missed her dad. She missed her mom. She missed something she'd never had. She didn't even know what to call it.

Time to stop being silly. She swung her wet hair over her shoulder. No need to let a little jocularity affect her normal good sense. She longed for nothing more. She had her freedom and a hotel full of opportunities.

She turned back to the little boys piling up rocks. "It will take a lot of work to build a mountain. You're going to need some help."

She searched along the shore, found a rock, marched over to the "mountain" the boys were building, and added to it.

As she and Luke gathered rocks, Jake stood looking at the river. She paused to study him. Did he have troubling thoughts similar to hers? She snorted softly. He was probably thinking about his cows.

Sammy bounced up to Jake. "Uncle Jake, give me a piggyback ride."

Hannah waited to see Jake's response. Part of her saw him as the big, unapproachable, in-charge boss. She still had a hard time accepting his warmth toward his family. Warmth and caring and—something more. She searched for the right word. *Responsibility.* That was it. He wore his responsibility like a shirt covering every other emotion. Maybe it explained his attitude toward her. Her independence simply did not fit into his frame of mind.

He scooped up Sammy and hung the boy around his neck then raced up and down the shore, bouncing the boy until he screamed with laughter.

Hannah smiled. She liked this relaxed Jake much better than the one who seemed to think he had to be in charge of everyone in his sphere. But which one was the real Jake?

They had each dried to a wrinkled mat when Jake glanced at the sky. "It's time we got back."

"Aww," Sammy and Luke yelled together. They stood in front of their stone "mountain," now as high as Sammy's waist.

"Uncle Jake, what we going to do with our rocks?" Luke demanded.

"I wanna take them home," Sammy screamed.

"You can't haul rocks home," Jake protested.

Luke stuck his bottom lip out. "Why not?"

Hannah chuckled at Jake's quandary.

He shot her a helpless look. "Luke, there are lots of rocks at home."

"We want these ones, don't we, Sammy?"

The younger boy nodded vigorously.

Hannah giggled as the two small boys and one large man glowered at each other. The whole lot of them had stubborn streaks a mile wide and bright as polished gold. If someone didn't intervene, they could wrangle at this for a long time. She swallowed back her amusement and put on a serious face. "Boys, why don't you each pick out the rock you like the best and take it home. Leave the rest here. I'm sure you can come back and visit sometime."

Three pairs of eyes shifted toward her then toward the stack of rocks. Jake opened his mouth.

Fearing he might order the boys to obey her suggestion and likely trigger their stubbornness rather than their cooperation, Hannah went to the rocks. "Which one is your favorite, Sammy?"

The boy squatted down and studied the rocks with such concentration, Hannah had difficulty not smiling. "I like 'em all," he said. But he selected five and set them on the ground at his feet. "These are my favorites. Can't I take 'em all?"

"No," Jake muttered.

Hannah ignored him. "Can you carry them all?"

Sammy tried, but even with Hannah's help at balancing them in his cradled arms, he couldn't manage five and looked about ready to cry. "They're so nice."

"Maybe you can take three," she suggested.

So with much deliberation, he chose three. " 'Bye, rocks," he said sadly to those remaining.

Luke crossed his arms and refused to follow his brother's example.

Hannah rose and faced Jake. "I guess Luke doesn't want to take any. That's fine. His choice. Shall we be on our way?"

Jake grabbed the reins of his patient horse, muttering, "Why are you encouraging them? Who needs to carry home rocks?"

She chuckled. "I think they'll give them up without an argument after a few steps. On the other hand, if they want to pack them all the way, what difference does it make? Might keep them out of trouble."

Jake suddenly laughed. "If it does, I'll be surprised."

Luke waited until he realized they were indeed headed home then grabbed two good-sized rocks and followed.

For a moment they walked in relative silence. "Relative" meaning she and Jake didn't speak and the boys yelled endlessly about new treasures discovered along the trail. As she'd predicted, they soon ditched their rocks in order to pick up something more exciting.

The boys' clothes were spotted with mud and wrinkled. Her own blue cotton dress, one she normally thought rather attractive, was now bedraggled and dull with sand and dust. She glanced at Jake—his trousers stained, his blue shirt streaked from its dunking in the river. She chuckled. "We're a rumpled-looking crew."

He glanced down at himself, groaned, and then swept his gaze over her. "You've faired better than I."

Uncomfortable with his grinning assessment, she shifted her attention past him to the dusty haze along the trail. "How did your business go? Did you get everything settled?"

"I hope so. Mr. Arnold said he'd come out Monday morning and assess whether the cattle are healthy as we claim."

"Then you achieved what you intended. You must be pleased."

They strode on for several paces, the horse plodding along behind them, before Jake answered. "I'm happy enough that he's agreed to come, but this delay never should have happened. I should have foreseen the possibility of Murphy doing something and been a step ahead of him."

Hannah heard the frustration in his voice but wondered why be blamed himself. "How can you be responsible for something another man has done?"

"It's my job to be sure things go well."

"But Jake, you can only be responsible for what *you* do."

He made a noise she took to be disagreement before he spoke. "That's easy for you to say. You're set on proving just that. Responsible for no one but you, to no one but you, but I have others to think about, plan for, and make sure they're taken care of."

"You make my choices sound selfish. I don't see them that way. By becoming independent, I'm giving my mother and stepfather the chance to start a new life together without my being caught in the middle. And I'm honoring my father's memory by living up to his expectation of me."

She again heard that noise that seemed to come from deep inside him. Not a grunt. And yet definitely negative in tone. "I would think your father would want what's best for you."

Her vision narrowed as she regarded him through squinted eyes. "Of course he would."

"Then he would probably suggest you ask for help fixing the hotel."

She shook her head. "He'd expect me to figure out how to do it myself."

They stopped walking and faced each other.

A few days ago, Hannah would have erupted at Jake's interference, his continued insistence she couldn't manage on her own, but she began to suspect his problem stemmed from his own overgrown sense of responsibility. He seemed to think it was his job to take care of everyone. "Jake, it isn't like I'm entirely on my own."

He widened his eyes. "I thought—"

"I am God's child. He will never leave me nor forsake me. Hasn't He also promised to provide all our needs?"

"Well of course, but doesn't the scripture also say, 'If any provide not for his own, and specially for those of his own house, he hath denied the faith, and is worse than an infidel'? Doesn't that make our responsibility plain? It seems you have only yourself to think about, so I suppose that verse has no significance for you. For me, it's the guiding direction for my life."

Hannah knew the scripture he mentioned but had never heard it applied the way he did. "It seems to me you feel like you are personally responsible for things that are beyond your control. Aren't there times you have to let God do it? Trust Him?"

"I do trust Him. I trust Him to help me take care of the task set before me."

Hannah and Jake resumed walking side by side. She turned her attention to the two little boys hunkered down, examining something in the dusty tracks, before saying, "That's exactly how I feel. God has given me the desire for independence and now the means. I trust Him to help me take advantage of the opportunity He's provided."

Jake made that same sound of disagreement but didn't voice his feelings, for which Hannah was grateful. She had no desire to argue and ruin the enjoyment of the afternoon, though she suspected it would come to an end as soon as they were back in town. Jake would revert to the man in charge of everything. His ranch. His cows. His men. His family. Did he also feel responsible for friends and acquaintances?

That would explain why he felt he had to tell her she couldn't manage on her own. But she could. And she would. She'd prove it to Jake. Not that it would be her motivation. She wanted to live up to her father's expectations of her, prove worthy of his approval and thus honor his memory.

"Wagon coming," Jake said. "I'd better corral the boys." He lengthened his stride and caught up to Sammy and Luke, who were watching a caterpillar crawl through the dry grass at the side of the road.

Hannah hurried to them and held Sammy's hand as Jake held the reins on one side and Luke on the other.

The rattle and rumble of the wagon grew louder as the wagon approached and passed. The driver waved and called a greeting, and then Hannah turned aside to shield her face from the cloud of dust.

"Where's he going?" Luke demanded.

"He's taking supplies to settlements west of here beyond the railway," Jake answered.

"Can we go see?" Luke asked.

Hannah chuckled as the man and boys stared after the wagon as if accompanying it in their thoughts.

"We have to get back to town before Grandma starts to worry." Yet Jake didn't move.

Luke stood beside him. "Who lives out there?"

"Mostly miners, but I suppose farmers, ranchers, and townspeople, too." The wagon turned a corner and disappeared from sight, but still Jake and Luke stared down the road.

Sammy pulled away from Hannah's grasp and went in search of the caterpillar. She shifted so she could keep an eye on the younger boy yet watch the other two. It seemed they had both been mentally drawn away by the passing wagon.

"I heard there are big caves in the hills to the west," Jake said.

"I want to see them," Luke replied.

"It's too far." Jake led the horse and boy back to the road and waited for Hannah to fall in beside him. The caterpillar had disappeared, and the boys ran ahead in search of new discoveries. "I always wanted to see the caves," Jake said then sighed. "Don't suppose I ever will."

"Why not? Don't you deserve a holiday?"

"I'm the boss."

"Exactly. If you want to go see caves, you put someone else in charge and go."

He shook his head. "You've been boss of your business how long? A month? You'll soon find that being the boss doesn't mean you just sit around and give orders."

She laughed at his assessment. "I could shout orders all day long, but there's no one but Mort to hear me, and he does what suits him. But you have people who can help. I've seen some of your men. They appear very capable. So why don't you go see the caves?"

Luke had joined them. "Uncle Jake, can I see the caves, too?"

Jake laughed. "If I go, I promise to take you."

"Sammy, Sammy, we're going to see the caves," he screamed, racing toward his brother.

Jake caught Luke around the waist. "Hold up there, young man. I said *if* I go. Truth is, I don't plan to go, so you'll have to wait until someone else can take you."

Luke scowled at his uncle as he squirmed out of his grasp and stomped down the road, leaving little clouds of dust in his wake.

They soon arrived in town and turned the boys over to their grandmother, who had recovered from her headache.

Halfway across the dining room, Jake caught up to Hannah. "Let me take you out for dinner."

She ground to a halt. "Dinner?" They'd just spent the afternoon together and argued about the differences in how they viewed the world. They would always argue, because he would never accept her independence and she would accept nothing less. "Why?"

"You need a reason to consider an invitation from me?" He sounded shocked.

"I suppose you're accustomed to people seeing your invitations as orders?"

"Now that you mention it..." He chuckled. "Of course not. But I thought you might enjoy a nice dinner at the Regal."

She'd stolen glimpses through the window as she passed but knew she couldn't afford such luxuries. "I'm rather a mess."

"I am, too, but we could clean up."

Still she hesitated. She couldn't honorably accept an invitation just to get a free meal. Inside her, in a spot deep beneath her heart, something else urged her to say yes. Even though she knew they could never be more than friends, and not even good friends, not with his attitude toward her independence, something about this man appealed to her—his strength of character.

The very thing making it impossible to relax around him proved to be what she admired the most and the very reason she should refuse his invitation. But although she informed her brain of this fact, her mouth said, "I'd love to. Give me an hour to clean up."

❧

Jake held the chair as Hannah took her place in the Regal's dining room. She'd cleaned up really nice. She'd brushed her hair until it shone enough to make him think of a mink he'd once seen. He fought an urge to touch it to see if it were as smooth and soft as the animal's fur.

She wore a snowy white blouse with a narrow pin at the neck with some sort of clear stone that caught the light and shafted it into a rainbow of colors. Could it be a diamond? He hardly thought so. A woman who owned diamonds wouldn't be scrubbing smoke-damaged walls.

She nodded her thanks as he pushed the chair in for her. He took his place across from the table, hoping he'd cleaned up as nicely as she. He'd chosen a white shirt with a black string tie and his best black trousers. He'd even cleaned and polished his boots until they gleamed.

She leaned forward, smiling. "This is as nice as I imagined. All the white linen and sparkling white china." She took her time looking around the room. "Maybe someday my dining room will be as nice."

The waitress handed them menus, sparing him from speaking the words springing to his mind—that he doubted she would ever get her dining room usable, let alone fancied up like this one.

"Roast turkey. Sounds good." He hoped they provided large servings. He was starving.

"Sounds good to me, too," Hannah said.

The waitress filled the crystal water goblets and took their orders. Jake wished for something a little sturdier for his big hands but gingerly took the glass and sipped his water, unable to think of anything to say.

Hannah leaned forward. "See that old couple over there? He's so sweet. Look at the way he tries to please her." She watched them.

Jake kept his gaze on Hannah, wondering about her observation. "The old gentleman is taking care of his wife," he said. "Seems contrary to your stand on independence."

She slowly brought her gaze back to him. "Not at all. A person can be thoughtful and gentle and caring without robbing another of the right to make her own decisions. My father taught me that. There wasn't a more thoughtful man." She turned back to watching the older couple. "In fact, if he'd lived, I can imagine him and Mother like that."

He waited for their meals to be placed in front of them and inhaled the rich aroma of turkey and dressing, mashed potatoes and gravy, and a mound of peas and carrots. "A dead father, idealized, makes for stiff competition for any man." He knew he could never measure up to the standard her father set. Not that he wanted to. A woman like Hannah would be constantly challenging him. Life was complicated enough without asking for more trouble.

She concentrated on her meal for a moment. "I would never want anyone who didn't make me feel special like my father did."

Jake thought he saw sadness, regret even, in her eyes. "How did he do that?"

"He encouraged my independence. Told me I could do anything I set my mind to. At the same time, he—" She paused as if searching for the right word. "It's just that I knew I was special in his eyes." She turned back toward the older couple. "Just like that."

Seemed she had expectations no man could ever meet. It irked him. "You're the only child?"

"I am."

He recalled what she'd said about her mother. Seems the mother liked being taken care of. Hannah was less like her mother and more like— Jake narrowed his eyes. More like a son. "Did your father regret not having a son?"

She smiled. "If he did, he never said so."

To Jake, it seemed her father had tried to turn Hannah into the son he never had, despite the impossibility of disguising that she was a very pretty young woman. Those thoughts were best kept to himself.

She edged forward. "I thank God every day for allowing me to come west."

He studied her. She was a woman made to be cared for. She shouldn't be trying to clean up a burnt-out hotel that would challenge Zeke and half a dozen of his men. A man's job was to take care of such a woman, but determination blazed from her eyes. He stifled the argument building in his chest and fought the idea he wanted to take care of Hannah. He knew she wouldn't let him. Wouldn't even entertain the notion.

He filled his mouth with dressing, letting the sage flavor sift through his senses.

"Don't you find it awfully quiet?" Hannah whispered. "I seem to have gotten used to Sammy and Luke's volume of conversation."

He gave an expansive sigh. "It's bliss. Their noise is always a shock to my hearing. I don't know how Audrey and Harvey put up with it." He paused. "Or why. Seems they could have just as much fun without bringing down the roof."

"Your poor mother is about at the end of her patience with them."

"I know. Thank you for helping her as much as you have. It's a good thing we go home Monday. Even if Audrey isn't back, at least Sarie is there to help. She's our cook and also a good friend."

Hannah put her hands beside her plate and took a deep breath before she looked at him again. "So you will be leaving soon?"

"Monday. As soon as the cattle are sold." He wondered if she would miss him—them. He thought of his nephews' noise. If she missed them, it would no doubt be mixed with gratitude for the peace and quiet. "I hope Mother doesn't overtax herself in the meantime."

"It will be awfully quiet with you all gone." Her gaze held his. Went deep into his heart as if she sought something in him. Then her expression grew friendly but impersonal. "I'll miss the company."

His, too? Suddenly his brain flooded with wishes for things that could never be. Sharing more discoveries with this woman. Sharing laughter. Sharing enjoyment. Sharing each other's loads.

He turned to watch a young couple take their places at a table near the door.

Hannah did not want anyone to share her load. Nor did he need any more responsibilities.

The waitress took away their plates, replacing them with generous portions of apple crisp drowned in thick, farm-fresh cream.

He inhaled the scent of apples and cinnamon and prepared to enjoy the tasty dish when he heard Hannah suck in air like someone had hit her. He turned his attention back to her.

Eyes wide and glistening with tears, she choked out a whisper. "The last time we dined at a restaurant as a family, my father ordered this dessert."

He placed his hand over hers and squeezed. "I'm sorry. You must miss him a lot."

She nodded. "I thought I was over this. After all, it's been four years. But every once in a while something hits me and it's like it happened yesterday."

He wondered if she knew she'd turned her hand over into his palm. If they weren't in public, he'd have pulled her into his arms and held her. Despite her protestations, she needed holding and protecting.

"I guess I've been thinking of him more than usual because I feel like I'm finally living up to his expectations for me."

He couldn't fight her dead father. And she didn't seem to be able to let the man go.

She shuddered once, pulled her hand away, and then took a mouthful of the dessert and smiled. "It's good."

He had no reason to feel he'd been shoved out into the cold because she no longer reached for him. He watched the young couple, whispering together, flashing smiles as they spoke, and clasping hands across the table. He guessed they were fresh off the farm from some settlement to the west and thrilled by this new experience. He smiled at the way the girl's eyes widened at each new thing—the fine goblet, the steaming plate of food, and the silver teapot the waitress served from.

Hannah noticed his attention. She, too, smiled. "I bet they're newly wed," she murmured, "with eyes for no one else."

"They're noticing all the new things around them, though."

Jake pulled his gaze back to Hannah at the same time she looked toward him. His heart gave a peculiar leap he couldn't explain as if trying to escape his chest, as if stretching toward Hannah. A fleeting thought raced through his numb mind. *Will she ever consider giving up her freedom to become someone's wife?*

The waitress appeared at his side to ask if she could remove the dishes and inquired if they wanted anything more. He answered her without looking away from Hannah. "Are we done?" he asked but barely waited for her to answer before he shoved his chair back.

She nodded.

He hurried around to pull back her chair.

She paused to straighten her skirts.

They turned as the young man made a hoarse sound.

"I don't have enough money," he whispered to the girl across from him. "I must have left the rest in the hotel."

Hannah looked with shock-filled eyes toward Jake.

He took her elbow, steered her toward the exit, and left her waiting at the door as he went to pay the bill. He gave some extra money and spoke quietly to the waitress. "This is to pay for the young couple over there. Tell them God's best on their new life together."

As he and Hannah made their way out to the dusk, he took Hannah's hand and pulled it through his arm, telling himself he meant only to steady her in the darkening street. He felt rather pleased with himself when she didn't protest. "Do you want to go with me to check on the herd?" he asked.

"I'd love to."

They tramped along the sidewalk until they reached the end then crossed the street and made their way to the pens. Shorty had built a fire, filling the dusk with dancing shadows. Jake paused at the rail fence and breathed in the familiar, comforting smell of the animals. He expected Hannah to withdraw her hand.

Instead, she pulled him around to face her. "I saw what you did for that young couple. You were very kind." Exerting gentle pressure on his forearm, she leaned forward, raised her face, and kissed him on the cheek.

He couldn't believe it happened. Then a stampede of emotions raced through him. Emptiness finding its fullness, heart finding heart with a matching rhythm. He wanted nothing more than to hold this woman and keep her safe and protected. He slipped his arms around her shoulders and stared into her eyes, half hidden in the dim light. "Hannah," he whispered. Slowly, hesitantly, giving her plenty of opportunity to refuse, Jake lowered his head and kissed her.

The warmth of her lips went straight to his heart, where a gate exploded open, revealing yearning for a love of his own and loneliness he'd denied over and over. He slammed shut the gate. Dropped his arms to his side. Letting himself get too fond of Hannah presented major complications. Stubborn, independent, and determined to run a derelict hotel. He backed away. Time to pull his head together, or was it his heart that needed corralling?

"I better see if Mother is coping with the boys." He turned his steps toward the street and waited for Hannah to join him.

He'd been so busy with his own thoughts he hadn't given her any study. Now he did. She avoided looking at him as she pulled her arms around herself as if she felt suddenly cold. He half raised an arm to pull her close and protect her from the elements, dropping it again without touching her. No reason to think she might have had the same jolting reaction to his kiss. She likely had other things on her mind.

They murmured mindless comments about the weather and the town as they returned to the hotel. They barely made it through the door before he bolted for the stairs, claiming an urgency to make sure things were under control in the rooms his mother shared with his two nephews.

Chapter 7

Hannah's first waking thought had been to leap from bed and hurry out to the lobby. Jake checked the herd every morning. Maybe he'd ask her to join him. She wanted to spend every minute of the day with him. Tomorrow he'd be gone—along with his mother and nephews. She would be alone again except for Mort, who really didn't count as company.

She wanted to selfishly enjoy this, their last day. She had no illusions that once he got back to the ranch and his responsibilities he would give her another thought. They both knew they didn't fit into each other's worlds.

Her second thought kept her in bed staring at the white sheet blocking the early morning sun. It was Sunday—no reason to hurry out of bed. She wouldn't be doing any work. And after her foolish reaction to Jake's kiss last night, she'd be wise to avoid him.

She pressed her fingertips to her lips. Of course, she couldn't still feel his kiss. But she hadn't forgotten how she'd felt. She shifted her hand to a spot over her heart. She massaged gently, trying to ease the tightness, knowing the tension wasn't in her chest, nor in her muscles, but in her emotions. She felt safe in his arms. Felt a sudden urge to let go of all her burdens.

She blew out her lips. What burdens? The hotel was her ticket to independence and as such, a welcome challenge, not a burden.

She slipped from the bedcovers and prepared for church. If she took extra pains to look nice, it was only her self-respect as a businesswoman, not because she hoped Jake would notice.

She heard the boys yelling as they came down the stairs, heard Mrs. Sperling call to them, and then heard Jake's deeper voice ordering them to be quiet.

Hannah's heart broke into a breathless gallop, all her mental admonitions instantly forgotten. She had only to hear his voice for the tightness in her chest to return.

She remained in the kitchen, waiting for them to leave. She'd follow later, slip into the church unnoticed, and escape the same way. She couldn't face Jake, try and make ordinary conversation, when she had to keep fighting herself.

She went to the mirror over the cupboard and stared at herself. "Hannah Williams, you know what you really want. It's to open this hotel, become independent. Nothing less will ever satisfy you. No use in pretending you'd be happy being something you can't be. You can never be what Jake wants—a woman to take care of."

"What do *I* want from a man?" she asked her reflection. She recalled the words she'd spoken to Jake. *"A man who would treat her as her father had. Cherish her while allowing her independence."* She pointed her finger at her reflection. "And that, Hannah Williams, is not Jake."

"Hannah." The sound of Jake calling from the dining room caused her to spin away from the mirror. "Are you coming to church?"

Her heart soared. He wanted her to accompany them. She grabbed her Bible and hurried out to join him. "I'm ready."

Not until they were striding down the sidewalk toward the little white clapboard church at the north end of town did she realize she'd ignored her own advice to keep away from Jake.

They went inside the bright interior and slowly made their way down the aisle, pausing to speak to friends and neighbors—the Sperlings doing most of the greeting. Hannah knew only a handful of people yet.

Mrs. Sperling slipped into a pew with the two boys. Hannah started to follow, but Jake guided her into the bench behind them. She squeezed in beside Mrs. Johnson, and Jake lowered himself to her side. She shifted to give him more room, acutely aware of the pressure of his shoulder against hers. Though if he were three pews away, she would have been equally aware of him. She knew gratitude when the pastor stood and announced the first hymn.

She loved church. Loved singing with the others. Loved hearing God's Word. But as Jake's deep voice joined hers, she knew enjoyment she'd never felt before. They shared the same hymnal. She didn't look at him. Didn't need to in order to sense he shared the same pleasure in singing songs of the faith.

The preacher opened his Bible. "Our scripture for today is First Samuel, chapter seven, verse twelve. 'Then Samuel took a stone, and set it between Mizpeh and Shen, and called the name of it Ebenezer, saying, Hitherto hath the Lord helped us.' " He spoke of God's faithfulness to His people in the past and the assurance of His continued help and guidance in both the present and the future.

Peace filled Hannah's heart. She was here because God had given her the gift of a hotel, a way to leave the confines of her home with a new stepfather and a chance to become all that God intended.

She rose after the benediction, renewed by the message, and smiled at Jake. "I expect you'll have much to do today."

"Not really. Mother and the boys have been invited to visit friends for the afternoon."

"The cows?"

"All taken care of."

They exited the church and stood in the warm sun. "A quiet day for you then?"

"Would you care to have lunch with me?"

"But nothing is open."

He glanced after his mother. "I suppose we could go with Mother and the boys."

She laughed. "You sound excited about that."

"I'm not. Too much noise."

She hesitated. A whole Sunday afternoon alone held no appeal, but another day with Jake. . . Her emotions were already in enough turmoil. But telling herself she felt sorry for him, she said, "I could put together a few things and we could have a little picnic."

"Excellent."

He accompanied her back to the hotel and stood outside as she gathered up a few simple things for a lunch. "If I'd known about this yesterday I'd have baked a cake," she said softly so he wouldn't hear. No cake. Three-day-old cookies would have to do. And cheese sandwiches. An afternoon in the sun would surely make up for any lack in the food.

She wondered if they would go toward the river again, but he headed the other direction, past the church to a grove of trees. The sound of muted voices informed her it was a popular spot. They wouldn't be alone. *Good*, she told herself, stifling her sense of disappointment.

He spread the blanket she'd brought, and she passed him a sandwich.

"Did you enjoy the service?" she asked.

"I did, though I miss our little church out at the ranch."

"You have a church out there?"

He chuckled. "We're actually quite civilized."

"I didn't mean it like that. I just never thought. . . Well, I guess I thought it was isolated and. . .I don't know. I've never been to a ranch, so I'm not sure what it would be like."

"We'll have to remedy that, won't we?"

At the soft tone of his voice, she darted a look at him, intending only to steal a glance. But their eyes collided, and she couldn't pull away from his bottomless brown gaze. Did he mean his words as an invitation? Would she welcome it if he did? Wasn't it best to forget this unlikely attraction between them? "I've always lived in town," she murmured as if expecting him to see how far apart their worlds were.

"I guess you'd never be able to live on a ranch."

His doubts as to her adaptability forced her to say, "I could do just about anything I made up my mind to do."

He searched her gaze as if trying to determine exactly what she meant. She wondered herself. She couldn't define what she thought or how she felt, other than it gave her a sensation like swinging too high, her breath catching on the upward arc, holding there after she'd begun the downward flight, catching up with her body just in time for it to repeat. She sucked in air, heavy with the scent of leaves getting ready for autumn, and pulled her thoughts together. "Tell me about your church."

He chuckled again and turned away to pick a cookie from the tin. "It isn't *my* church even though it's on my land. Father built it as soon as he finished the house. Said they needed a place to worship. He wanted his outfit to have the option without traipsing off to town."

"What does it look like?"

"It's small. Constructed of logs like the house. Father made sure there was lots of light. The windows are clear so you look out on trees on one side and rolling hills on the other. I'd sooner worship outside, but the church isn't half bad, either."

"It sounds beautiful. What about a preacher?"

"Pastor Rawson, the preacher you heard earlier this morning, comes out in the afternoon."

Hannah fiddled with a leaf that had fallen by her knee. "Tell me about how you became a Christian."

Jake took two more cookies and leaned back against the nearest tree. "I can't remember not knowing God loved me. One Sunday when I was about seven, a warm spring day I recall, I simply decided I wanted to join God's family, and I went to the church after everyone had left from the service and knelt at the front."

Hannah's throat tightened with emotion as she pictured a young Jake making his choice all alone. Seems from an early age he stood alone and strong. "It sounds very special."

"It was. Still feels special."

Again they looked deep into each other's eyes. Hannah felt a connection beyond ordinary interest. This man had deep spiritual roots to accompany his strength of character. A person could safely lean on him. She sighed. His mother and sister were fortunate to have him.

"How about you?" he asked.

For a moment she thought he asked if she wanted to lean on him, too. But he didn't know she'd been thinking it. "Me?"

"How and when did you become part of God's family?"

Her breath gusted out. "I, too, always knew God loved me. But I had more of a struggle. I didn't want to give up my independence to belong to Him."

Jake laughed hard and earned himself a frown. He stopped laughing and looked suitably serious, though his eyes danced and the corners of his mouth twitched. "I can see that might be a problem. How did you resolve it?"

She grinned. "I didn't. God did. I'd been taught to read my Bible every day. I read some verses that made me willing to give up my ways because I knew I could trust God to do what was best for me. They're in Romans chapter eight. 'And we know that all things work together for good to them that love God, to them who are the called according to his purpose.' And 'He that spared not his own Son, but delivered him up for us all, how shall he not with him also freely give us all things?' " She smiled from the depths of her heart. "He loved me enough to give His Son to die for me. I guess He wouldn't do anything that wasn't for my good."

Jake took her hand. "Amen."

Hannah knew that more than their hands connected. They'd shared from their faith experience, and a bond of deeper understanding had been forged.

A zephyr blew through the treetops, rustling the leaves, sending a shower of them to the ground. Hannah shook her head to get them out of her hair.

"Hold still," Jake said, leaning close. "One's stuck in your hair." He gently eased the leaf from its perch. "It's like a golden crown." His voice seemed thick.

She felt his fingers working loose the leaf. Felt a thousand sensations race from her scalp to her heart.

He released the leaf and tossed it to the ground.

She didn't look up. She couldn't free herself from the longing in her heart—a longing to be held and cherished.

"Some gold dust left behind," he whispered, flicking his fingers through her hair.

She closed her eyes and thought of letting herself love this man.

She sucked her breath in and sat up straighter. "Thanks." She didn't belong in Jake's world where he dominated, controlled, took care of—gently touched her hair. No. No. He didn't belong in her world, where she expected to be cherished but also given freedom to make her own choices. She turned to put the lid on the cookie tin. She knew one subject that would pull them both back to reality. "I've got four rooms ready to open in the hotel, plus the suite will be available when you and your mother and the boys leave tomorrow."

He dropped his hand, picked up a twig, and broke it into inch-long pieces and tossed them aside. "What about the dining room?"

"I'll get Mort to board it off tomorrow."

"Seems you'll have to fix it sooner or later."

"It will have to be later. I think I'll be ready to put an open sign out by Tuesday."

"That's great." He stood, waited for her to put the picnic things in the bag, and folded up the blanket.

She felt him pulling away from her. She'd ruined the afternoon. But she had no choice. They both needed to stick to reality. Yet she regretted it ever so slightly. About as much as she would regret denying herself Christmas.

They returned to the hotel, and he handed her the blanket. "Thanks for the picnic. I have to check on the cows." He strode away without a backward glance.

She went inside, stared at the hole in the dining room floor, and wondered what it would be like to live on a ranch. She shook her head. She had no time for dreams of romance, especially with a man like Jake. She had a hotel to fix and run. It was her dream come true.

≋

The last animal jostled into the boxcar, and Shorty pushed the door shut.

Jake shook hands with Mr. Arnold. "Nice doing business with you."

"Sorry about the misunderstanding," the man said.

Martin and Riggs stood at Jake's side. He heard Martin's grunt, but thankfully, the man kept his opinion silent and avoided alienating the man they hoped to do business with again.

They shook hands all around.

Jake told the cowboys to head back to the ranch, and he swung to the back of his horse. At the livery barn he told Con to bring the wagon. Once the supplies were loaded, he could be on his way home. He couldn't wait.

He paused outside the hotel door. He didn't look forward to saying goodbye to Hannah, though in effect they'd said it yesterday. He didn't want to leave her here on her own, yet she'd made it clear as the sky above that she wanted nothing more from him. There wasn't room in her life or heart for a cowboy like him. Saying good-bye today would simply be a matter of paying the bill, shaking hands, and parting ways.

He pushed the door open and strode in. Mother sat in the lobby, the bags packed and ready. Looking after the boys for a few days had meant this stay in town turned out to be less of a holiday than he'd planned for her. She should have told Audrey to take her children with her, but Mother never could say no to Audrey. And to keep from upsetting his mother, he usually gave in, too.

Mother glanced past him. "What did you do with the boys?"

He checked the room. Saw no boys. "What do you mean?"

Mother grew pale. "I told them they could wait for you outside. Made them promise not to go past the corner."

"I didn't see them. The little rascals must have hidden." He threw the door open and bellowed, "Luke, Sammy, where are you?"

Mrs. Johnson, sweeping the steps in front of the store, paused to look at him.

"Have you seen the boys?" he asked.

"Not since earlier this morning when your mother took them out for breakfast."

"Thanks." He called them again. Nothing. He returned inside. "They're not out there. Maybe they're with Hannah." He strode into the dining room, noticing she'd removed the damaged tables and chairs and pulled the rest to one corner. The hole gaped like a cave, and he got down on his knees to look inside. No boys. "Hannah," he called again as she wasn't in the room. Jake continued his search.

He found her outside, stacking the chairs and tables for Mort to burn. "Are the boys with you?"

She jerked around to face him. "Haven't seen them since they came back from breakfast with your mother. Aren't they with her?"

"No." He wanted to brush the soot from her cheek and finger the strand of hair curling around her ear.

She looked toward the back door. "Are they playing a game?"

"I expect so." He hurried to the lobby, Hannah hard on his heels.

"I'll check the kitchen," she said.

"I'll look outside."

Mother sat up. "I'll—"

Jake held up his hand. "Wait here in case they come back. Then don't let them out of your sight."

He and Hannah returned in a few minutes. At the shake of her head and the worry in her eyes, he knew she'd had no more success in finding the pair than he.

The three adults turned toward the stairs. Jake took them in three bounds and searched their suite thoroughly. He didn't find his nephews.

Hannah stepped into the hall as he considered where to look next. "They aren't in any of the rooms up here," she said.

"They have to be hiding outside. I have to widen my search."

Hannah reached the bottom of the steps as quickly as he. "I'll help you look," she said. Her hard tone made it plain she wouldn't take no for an answer.

He chuckled. "Don't think you'll stop me from giving them a good bawling out."

She grinned then jerked her gaze away as together they headed for the door.

They searched and called. An hour later, Jake's frustration had given way to anger that dissolved into worry. "Where could they be?" He envisioned them sneaking into some little outbuilding and the door shutting on them, trapping them inside. But they'd gone up and down the alleys calling and listening and searched every conceivable hiding place.

"Maybe they're staying one step ahead of us," Hannah suggested. "If we split up we might catch them."

"We'll outsmart them. You go that way, I'll go this, and we'll meet back at the hotel."

But an hour later, back at the hotel there were no little boys. And Hannah hadn't returned.

He strode from one corner of the hotel to the other. He went outside again, jumped into the middle of the street, and glanced up and down the length. He started toward the railway tracks, stopped, and retraced his steps. He had no idea where to look for Hannah or the boys. But he couldn't simply wait.

He headed back down the street. He stopped in every store and asked if anyone had seen Hannah or the boys. He even stepped into the lawyer's office and asked. He knew Hannah wouldn't play games. But where was she? Why hadn't she come back? Was she hurt? Or worse? His stomach clenched into a twisted knot. How could the three of them disappear? How could he have let this happen?

~

Hannah searched every store, checked behind each counter. She knew how mischievous the boys could be. No doubt they thought this was a fine game. But it was no longer fun. She thought of all the things that might have happened to them. Maybe a runaway horse had struck them. But the whole community would have heard about it. Maybe they had fallen somewhere and been hurt. But unless they were both unconscious they could yell loudly enough to bring help from the far corners of this little town. It was almost impossible for them to get lost.

So where were they?

She stood in front of the general store and tried to figure out what they would have done. A dray rumbled to the store and stopped. Another wagon headed west. She'd heard one earlier in the day. A big shipment must have come in on the last train. The driver jumped down and went inside.

Wagons. West. Caves. She remembered how anxious Luke had been to see the caves. Could the boys have—

She raced into the store where the wagon driver purchased a handful of candy. "Mister, can I get a ride with you?" She tried not to think how big the man was.

"Ride to where, ma'am?"

"You're headed west, aren't you?" At his nod, she asked, "Are there caves out there?"

"Heard there was. Never seen 'em, though. I'm headed to Fall River. Little settlement."

"That will do. Do you mind a passenger?"

He studied her hard, openly. But thankfully, he didn't leer. "You running away?"

"No, sir. But I think two little boys might have stolen a ride on the last wagon. I have to find them."

"Sure thing. You come along with me. We'll find Frank and ask him if he seen the lads." He held out a hand as big as a mitt. "I'm Jud."

She gave her name, let him take her hand, and then quickly pulled away before he could squeeze the life out of it. "I need to write a note to Jake." The storekeeper slid a piece of paper and pencil toward her. She quickly wrote a note telling her plans. "Can you see that he gets it?" She handed it back to the man behind the counter.

He nodded. "I'll take care of it."

❦

The wagon proved rough and slow enough to make Hannah grind her teeth. And Jud was talkative. She soon discovered he pretty much carried the conversation on his own, which left her to her thoughts.

She prayed she wasn't on a foolish chase. She prayed the boys were safe. She prayed Jake would find her. If he didn't come, she and the boys—if she found them—would be stranded in Fall River.

"How long will this trip take?" she asked Jud.

"Two hours on a good day."

Hannah gasped. Two hours of rattling around on this hard wooden seat? Would the boys have stayed on the wagon that long? She couldn't imagine they would. Had they even hitched a ride on the other wagon? Somehow convinced they had, she strained to see any sign of little boot tracks in the trail. She scanned the surrounding landscape. *Please, God, if they're out here somewhere, help me find them.*

She thought of how frightened they must be by now. If they were here and not back at the hotel, laughing at the joke they'd played on everyone. In which case, she was on a silly chase. But either way, Jake would come and get her. She could count on his sense of responsibility. As soon as the storeowner delivered the note, she knew Jake would set out.

Two hours later, two relentless hours of having every bone in her body jarred continuously, Jud pointed toward a little cluster of buildings. "Fall River.

Hopeful little settlement. Everybody hoping to find gold or free land or maybe just freedom. And you be hoping to find two little boys. Sorry we saw no sign of them along the trail." Jud had soon realized she kept her eyes open for them and had grown as attentive as she to any indication the boys had been this way.

Her bones continued to rattle even after the horses stopped moving. Hannah felt certain she'd rattle for days. She wanted to jump down as easily as Jud had but discovered her limbs didn't share the same idea as her head.

Jud lifted her to the ground. "Frank's wagon's over by the saloon. You want me to go ask him?"

"Would you, please?" She didn't relish trying to get a man out of the saloon so she could talk to him. She followed Jud but waited several feet away while he went in to find Frank. Jud returned with a man as tall and thick as he was.

After introductions, Hannah asked, "Have you seen two little boys who might have been looking for some caves? Is there any chance they hitched a ride on your wagon?"

Frank scratched his head. "You know, it crossed my mind the boxes at the back had been shifted. I put it down to the trail, but now that you mention it, it could have been two boys. Thought I heard a strange noise a time or two." He roared with laughter. "Don't that beat all? Tough little tykes to head off on their own."

"But did you actually see them? Would you know where they might be now?"

Frank shook his head like a big bull. "Can't say's I do. You say they was looking for caves?" At Hannah's nod, he pointed toward the hills. "Guess I'd be looking over there." He pointed out a trail.

Hannah thanked both men, paused to get a long, cold drink at the pump, and then followed the trail. She shivered as a cool wind tugged at her hair. The sky darkened with a threatening storm. *God, help me find the boys.*

She bent to examine a print in the dust. The wind had obliterated much of it, but it seemed to be the right size for one of the boys. She stood, looked around, and saw nothing but trees and black clouds. "Luke, Sammy, are you there? Can you hear me?"

Chapter 8

Jake paced the sidewalk for fifteen minutes. It felt like three hours. With a muffled groan, he strode back into the hotel. "You're sure they didn't come back?"

Mother twisted her hankie into a rope. "Jake, don't you think I'd notice? I'm as worried about them as you. I never should have let those two out of my sight. But I thought, how much trouble could they get into in such a short time?"

Jake snorted. "A whole heap. And now Hannah seems to be missing. It's like there's a hole in the middle of the street swallowing them up." Thinking of a hole, he strode into the dining room and looked over the blackened edges. But no one lay on the dirt below. He returned to the lobby.

"I'm sure Hannah's fine," Mother said, her voice thin with worry. "She's a resourceful young woman used to managing on her own."

His mother's words did nothing to make him feel better. He stared out the window, ground around, crossed the dining room, and opened cupboards in the kitchen as if Hannah and the boys hid among the jars and dishes. He strode to Hannah's bedroom door but hesitated. He had no right to intrude into her privacy. But he had to assure himself the room was empty, so he pushed open the door.

He saw a room as neat and tidy as Hannah. A silver-handled brush and mirror lay on a white cloth on the tall dresser, a Bible on the little stand. A patchwork quilt covered the bed. He could feel the memory of Hannah's presence in the room, but neither Hannah nor the boys were there.

He checked the backyard again, called their names, and discouraged, returned to the hotel. "Mother, I can't wait here. If any of them show up, keep them here, even if you have to hog-tie them."

He plunked his hat on and hurried back out. He stood in the middle of the street and tried to think where to look that he hadn't already looked two or three times. His gaze touched the church at the far end of the street, and he hurried that direction. He quietly pulled the door open, stepped inside to the quiet, made his way to the front, and knelt at the prayer rail.

"God," he whispered, "I need help in finding Luke and Sammy and Hannah. You see them. Show me where they are. Protect them." He leaned his head against his forearms and let his heart open before God. How would he forgive himself if something happened to the little boys who were his responsibility?

And if he couldn't find Hannah? He'd known her such a short time, and yet he couldn't imagine life without her. He tried to think what that meant. Why was Hannah so important to him? It wasn't as if she wanted him to care. But his heart was too troubled to be able to sort out his feelings. He knew only that it was his responsibility to find the three of them and make sure nothing bad happened to them. Again he prayed for God's help.

He heard the door open and scrambled to his feet. But it was only a young boy waving a slip of paper. "Mr. Sperling, my father saw you go into the church and sent me to give you this."

Jake reached the boy in six long strides and snatched the paper and read:

Jake,
*   I think I know where the boys are. Remember how Luke wanted to see the caves. There are two wagons headed west today. I think they got on the first and I am getting on the second. I'll find them if they're out there, and we'll wait for you to come for us.*

*   Hannah*

Jake scrunched the paper and jammed it in his pocket. At the door he remembered his manners and called, "Thanks."

He ran all the way to the hotel to tell his mother where he was headed and then ran all the way to the corrals to saddle his horse and race through town. He'd gone half a mile when he realized he'd have to settle into a pace meant to last awhile.

Riding gave him time to think about what he'd do when he found Hannah. Once he made sure she was in one piece, he'd scold her for doing something so foolish. Then he'd kiss her and make her promise to give up the hotel and come out to the ranch where he could keep an eye on her and make sure she was safe.

A cold wind bit through his jacket. The sky twisted and churned like a mad bull. It seemed to take forever to get to Fall River. He jumped off his horse and hurried into the low-roofed store. "I'm looking for a woman and two little boys," he called. He didn't realize how loud his voice was until the other two people in the store stared at him, expressions startled. He lowered his voice. "They came in on the supply wagons."

A reed of a man nodded. "Woman came in. Asked about two boys. Seen her headed thatta way." He pointed to a trail.

"How long ago?" Jake demanded.

The man cocked his head as if looking for the answer someplace just above Jake's right ear. "Can't rightly say. Been busy unloading the wagon. But if I had to guess, I'd say an hour. Maybe two. You ask me, it's not a good day for a woman and young 'uns to be adventuring alone. Storm's a-brewin'."

Jake spun around and headed the direction the man pointed, aware the sky had grown even more ominous in the few minutes he'd been inside.

"Hannah, Sammy, Luke," he roared. The wind tore the words from his mouth.

❧

Hannah shivered against the cold and called the boys again. She didn't look at the sky. She already knew what she didn't want to acknowledge—they were in for a drenching. She pushed into the wind as she staggered up a hill. Her constant prayer had been reduced to a few words repeated over and over. *Help me find them. Help me find them.*

The wind increased. It moaned through the trees and screamed down the hills. The scream had a familiar sound. She stopped and stood motionless, listening hard. Could it be the boys?

She yelled at the top of her voice but knew they'd never hear her if they were yelling, too. She ducked her head into the wind, trying to determine what direction the screams came from. She shifted toward the right, shook her head, shifted left, and then continued another step and another. Were the voices getting clearer or did she only hope for it?

She shivered and took another step toward the sound. *Please, God, guide me to them.* The wind shifted, paused, and then renewed itself. But not before Hannah heard the screams. She knew for certain it was the boys and pinpointed the direction. She climbed a knoll and saw them a hundred feet away huddled in a hollow. She lifted her skirts and ran toward them.

Luke saw her first. "Hannah."

Sammy burst into tears.

Hannah reached them, fell on her knees, and pulled them both into her arms. "Thank God you're safe." They clung so tightly she could hardly breathe, but she wasn't about to complain.

Luke pulled away first. "It's my fault," he whispered. "I knew we shouldn't go away, but we wanted to see the caves before we went home."

Hannah backed into the almost-cave until she pressed against the cool earthen wall and pulled the boys to her lap. They were out of the wind and safe.

Sammy snuggled close. "We found this cave. Then we got scared 'cause we didn't know how we'd get home. And then we got cold."

Luke held his little brother's hand. "I prayed just like Mommy said I should.

I asked God to forgive me and send Uncle Jake to get us. 'Stead He sent you. I'm glad. Uncle Jake would be mad."

Hannah chuckled. "Uncle Jake is coming to get us."

Luke sat up. His bottom lip trembled. "He'll be mad at us."

"He's worried about you. So is Grandma. I was, too. We couldn't imagine what happened to you. You must promise never to do such a thing again."

"We won't," they chorused.

No doubt they'd learned their lesson. She couldn't imagine how frightened they were when they realized the significance of their little adventure. She held them close, enjoying the warmth of their little bodies.

In an effort to ease their worry about Uncle Jake's reaction, she told them stories of her own childhood. Living in town provided a stark contrast to their lives. She told about games she played with the neighborhood children—Auntie I Over, Kick the Can, and Cops and Robbers. "I loved running down the alleys, trying to keep out of sight of the others." Her father had built her a tall swing in the backyard and given her use of a little shed where she played house with her friends.

"I'm going to ask Daddy to build me a swing," Luke said.

Hannah watched the clouds grow darker and saw the first drops of rain. Where was Jake?

She felt neither fear nor worry. Jake would come. He would never let a person down. His conscience would not allow it. She just had to sit tight, out of the rain and wind, sheltered, and although not comfortably warm, at least not more than slightly cold.

Sammy's eyes drooped, and Luke seemed content to cuddle against her. She shifted to a more comfortable position. Jake might have taken shelter until the storm blew over.

She leaned her head back. It was nice to know she could count on Jake. In the few days she'd known him she'd been impressed with his strength of character and his sense of responsibility. She'd allowed herself to think it once before—she could love this man. She smiled widely. Who was she fooling? Not herself for sure. She'd fallen top over teakettle, flat out in love with him. She would even consider giving up the hotel if he asked her to marry him. The thought stunned her.

"Hannah?" Her name came to her on the wind. She heard it again and realized it wasn't just her gentle thoughts but a voice from outside in the rain.

She edged Sammy to the rocky ground, left Luke at his side, and scrambled to the opening. "Jake. We're here."

He rode into sight, waved, and galloped toward them. He reined in and jumped to the ground. "Hannah," he pulled her into his arms, pressing her cheek against his wet jacket. "Thank God you're safe. All of you." He released her and stepped back. "And here I am getting you all wet."

"I don't mind." She would ride through the storm if it meant being with him.

He ducked into the "cave." "Boys," he yelled, "what do you think you're doing running off like that?"

"Jake, they've learned their lesson."

"I'm sorry, Uncle Jake," Luke said at the same time.

And Sammy, startled awake, began to bawl at the top of his voice.

Jake took a step backward and scrubbed his hand over his wet face. "I kind of turned the peace upside down."

"Yes, you did."

"Aww. Luke, Sammy, I was so worried about you." He shrugged out of his wet jacket and held out his arms to the boys. They threw themselves into his embrace and hung on. Not releasing them, he scooted around and settled down. "We might as well sit this storm out. Room for you here." He tipped his head to one side. "We'll keep warm and dry together."

Hannah settled in beside him and took Sammy on her lap.

Jake spoke softly. "I was worried when I couldn't find you."

Hannah knew he meant her, and she smiled all the way to the bottom of her heart. "The wagon wouldn't wait. I felt I had to take advantage of the ride."

"Of course it never crossed your mind to come to me and ask for help."

She blinked. "I sent you a message. I knew you'd come." Her voice grew round with love for this man. He'd admitted his concern. But did it go any further?

"I would have preferred for you to come and inform me and let me be the one to go into the wilds to find them." He kept his voice soft because of the sleeping boys, but there was no disguising the iron behind his words.

"I did what I thought best. Surely you understand." She silently pleaded with him to see that she did what she had to. "I had to make a decision, and I did."

Luke's head tipped forward, and he snored softly. Jake shifted the child so his head rested on Jake's arm.

"You're far too independent."

She didn't know how to respond. Did he mean it as a compliment or a criticism? She hoped the former, but it was hard to tell as he kept his voice soft for the sake of the boys.

He shifted. "The rain is letting up. As soon as it quits, we'll walk back to Fall River. I'll see if I can borrow a wagon or buggy to get us back to Quinten. After I turn this pair over to my mother, you and I will have a talk."

That sounded just fine to her. There were so many things she wanted to tell him. Not that she planned to blurt out the truth about falling in love with him. But she was certainly open to any suggestion on his part. She sighed. Courtship and marriage sounded mighty appealing.

The rain stopped and the sun came out. Moisture sparkled on every surface. They wakened the boys. Jake put them on the horse, and he and Hannah led the way back to Fall River.

Hannah waited with the boys in the little store, gratefully accepting the offer of tea and sandwiches as Jake went to find a conveyance back. She hoped it wouldn't be one of the freight wagons. But in the end, that's exactly what they rode as Jud gave them a ride back to town. Jake sat on the hard seat beside Jud and listened to the man's stories while Hannah sat in the back with the boys.

Dark filled the sky long before they returned to the hotel. Mrs. Sperling broke into tears as she saw them all safe. "I've been beside myself with worry," she said.

Jake led his mother inside and settled her on the sofa. The little boys trailed in and climbed up on either side of her, and she held them close, tears flooding her eyes. "Thank you." She included Hannah in her look.

"I'm going to find something for us to eat." Jake hurried out the door.

Hannah sat and listened to the boys retelling their adventure. Luke again promised he would never be so naughty in the future.

Mrs. Sperling hugged the boys. "What you did was wrong, but I'm just glad you're both safe. And you, too, Hannah."

Jake returned bearing plates of food. A young man who worked in one of the restaurants carried more plates, and they settled in for a good feast.

Hannah didn't expect to be able to eat. Her insides felt jittery as she waited for the chance to talk to Jake alone. Yet her appetite took over. Even the little boys, so tired they could barely keep their faces out of their plates, ate with gusto.

Sammy finally caved in, and Jake pulled his plate away before the child's face hit the table. "I'll help you get them into bed," he told his mother. He scooped Sammy up and carried him up the stairs while Mrs. Sperling followed, half dragging Luke.

Hannah piled the plates and left them to be picked up. She wandered around the lobby. She paused to look out at the sleeping street.

When she heard Jake's footsteps on the stairs, she didn't immediately turn. Her heart felt like it had shrunk with trepidation and then ballooned with expectation. Would he say what she wanted him to? Give some indication that his feelings mirrored hers? Give her a reason to reconsider her need to fix this hotel?

"Can we talk now?" Jake asked, and she turned toward his gentle voice. She saw uncertain guardedness in his eyes. She smiled, hoping he'd see the longing and love she felt, then took the chair he indicated. He sat facing her and gave her a long look. She hoped to see her feelings reflected in his gaze, but what she saw didn't feel right. But then she understood his confusion. She hadn't even hinted at how she felt. She leaned forward in anticipation, encouraging him to reveal his feelings. "Yes?"

"Hannah, I've decided you should come to the ranch with us."

She blinked once and nodded. Was this Jake's idea of an invitation? He often chose the most direct way of saying something.

He continued. "I'll be able to keep an eye on you. It's the only way I can make sure you don't rush off and do something stupid and foolish like you did today."

"Stupid? Foolish? I found the boys. Kept them safe until you arrived."

"What you did was almost as irresponsible as the boys. No one knew where you were. And did you ever think what the wagon driver could have done?"

Her anticipation curled into anger. "It wasn't a thoughtless risk. I knew Jud wouldn't hurt me. I can read character pretty well, you know." Only she wondered if she could. She'd been expecting Jake to say something much different.

"I've made up my mind," he said. "You will accompany us to the ranch. You get along well with Mother. You can help her out, keep her company."

"You've made up your mind?" She could barely get the words past the disappointment clawing at her throat. "In case you've forgotten, I have a hotel to run."

"It's a dead horse. About time you put it out of its misery and forgot the whole thing. If you're concerned about money, I'll pay you to be Mother's companion."

She jumped to her feet, forcing him to tip his head back to look at her. "Jake Sperling, I will not be ordered around by anyone. I will not be sold or bought or controlled. I will only be accepted for what I am. I don't need taking care of, as you seem to think. And I will run this hotel." She raced across the dining room, barely avoiding the hole, and into her bedroom, slamming the door loudly enough to inform Jake the conversation was over.

She sank to the edge of the bed and moaned. How could she be so blind, so stupid? Jake didn't think of her with love in his heart; he saw her only as another responsibility. Someone to order about. She dashed away tears stinging her eyes and stared straight ahead, right at the chiffonier. She thought of her father's pocket watch and groaned. How could she have forgotten her goal—to honor her father's memory by living up to his expectations of her?

Chapter 9

Jake helped his mother into the buggy and ordered the boys to settle down. He'd had glimpses of Hannah in the kitchen as they prepared to leave, but she seemed determined to avoid him. Stubborn, headstrong, and far too independent, she'd made it plain he had no choice but to leave her here on her own. Even though it grated against his nature.

He wondered if she'd avoid him until they left, but she stepped out, her head high, smiling at the boys and his mother, avoiding his gaze. Yes, it annoyed him. Even hurt a little. He knew he'd made her angry last night. But sooner or later she would see he was right. She didn't belong here alone.

"I'll miss you," she told the boys, ruffling their hair. They each hugged her and promised to come see her again.

"I want you to come visit us at the ranch next Sunday," his mother said as she and Hannah hugged. "You will, won't you?"

"Yeah," the boys screamed.

Hannah hesitated. "I have no means of transportation."

"Jake will come and get you, won't you, Jake?"

Jake knew he was trapped. He couldn't refuse his mother. Besides, maybe Hannah refused to obey him because she had no idea what the ranch was like. He'd never thought of that. "Sure, I'll come and get you." She'd soon agree when she saw how beautiful it was.

"Why not make it Saturday so she can have a long visit?" Mother asked.

"Saturday, then? If you can tear yourself away from the hotel."

Hannah met his gaze then with her own silent challenge. "Saturday evening is fine."

He didn't miss the emphasis on *evening*.

"Mort will be here."

❧

It had been only five days, Jake reminded himself, as he drove into Quinten. Five days in which he thought of Hannah off and on. Like about a thousand times a day. He had no trouble picturing her waiting for him when he strode into the house, sitting across from him at the hand-hewn table, waving as he rode from the yard to check on the cows. She'd never been in his house or stood on his veranda or seen the hills of his ranch, yet in his thoughts she fit right in as though his world had been waiting all his life for her.

He pulled to a stop in front of the Sunshine Hotel and jumped off to go in search of Hannah. He found her in the lobby, her bag at her feet. He skidded to a halt and twisted his hat in his hands. She was even more beautiful than he remembered and didn't look any worse for wear, though he expected she had worked hard since he'd seen her, trying to prove she could do as well as a man. And although her eyes were guarded, he couldn't keep from grinning his pleasure.

She smiled uncertainly, answering his greeting softly.

"You're ready. Good." He crossed to her side, grabbed the bag, and held out his elbow to guide her. "Mother and the boys are eager to see you again, and Audrey is dying to meet you." He noticed the dining door had been boarded over with fresh lumber. He could smell the newness of it.

He waited until she sat beside him on the wagon before he asked her the questions burning in his mind. "Did you get the place open?"

"I have four rooms rented out already. No one has complained about the lack of a dining room." She gave a little laugh. "It feels good to finally be doing business."

He wanted to point out she didn't need to work. She could let someone else take care of her. She didn't have to prove anything. He stuffed back his arguments, knowing she wouldn't listen, moreover, would likely get angry if he voiced them and maybe refuse to accompany him. Then he'd have to face his mother's displeasure and Audrey's endless questions. Instead, he turned to the obvious. "Did you fix the floor in the dining room?"

"Not yet."

"Seems you'll have to do it one of these days. Wasn't it on the warning from the town council?"

"You know it was." Her voice sounded crisp, informing him she didn't care for his questions. "I'm waiting until I have enough money; then I'll hire some men to fix it."

He chuckled. "I kind of figured you'd be measuring and sawing it yourself."

"I probably could, but I prefer to get someone who knows how to fix the floor so it isn't a danger to my guests."

He didn't know how to respond. Her answers never satisfied him. He wanted her to admit defeat and give up the hotel. He believed she'd be singing another tune after visiting the ranch and experiencing a taste of life lived where a man was a man. He stopped himself before he finished the saying. *And a woman was a woman.*

He always thought of a woman as his father had taught him to see her. Someone to take care of. Weaker than a man. Hannah refused to fit into that description. She insisted she didn't need or want to be taken care of. What would it take to change her mind? His only answer—learning to love the ranch. Intent on making that happen, he turned to point out things along the trail. She seemed interested as he identified the trees and birds.

As they approached his land, he made sure she noticed its beauties. He drew to a halt near a copse of trees. "I remember finding a calf there, and when I got down to help the little guy, I found a baby rabbit." He flicked the reins and moved on, pointing out a tall tree. "Every year a pair of hawks nest there. Have you ever seen a young hawk try out its wings for the first time?"

"Can't say I have."

"It's a wondrous sight."

She chuckled. "You have a special connection to the land."

He grew quiet. His intention had been to make her see the beauties of the ranch, not how much he loved the place. But the visit had just begun. By the time she'd seen the sunset flare across the sky, felt the sun on her face in the morning, heard the coyotes singing at night, walked along the edge of a hill where she could see forever and a day. . .

Hannah had given herself a serious talk every day of the past week and a triple dose of caution today as she prepared for her trip to the ranch. This visit was a chance to see his mother and the two little boys and meet Audrey. Jake had fetched her to please his mother. She'd almost allowed herself to fall in love with him only to discover he saw her as yet another of his many responsibilities. It made her feel burdensome.

Yet as she listened to the love and pride in his voice as he extolled the beauties of his ranch, she didn't know whether to be envious of the land or angry he reserved his affection for nothing more than rock and dirt, plants and animals. But one thing she knew for sure—she wished he would look at her with half the love she saw glowing in his eyes as he pointed out things.

When he indicated a herd of antelope racing across a field, she had to sit on her hands to keep from grabbing his arm and pulling his attention to her. She wanted him to see her. Not as a responsibility but as a person equal to him with different strengths and abilities, just as capable of making choices and decisions.

She turned around to look away from him to the passing scenery. Why did she torture herself with impossible wishes especially when she had what she wanted back in Quinten? A hotel of her own. No one to tell her who she should be. So what if she was alone? It was better than being someone's responsibility.

Jake pulled the buggy to a halt and pointed. "There it is."

"So many buildings." A big hip-roofed barn, several scattered outbuildings she couldn't guess the use of, a long, low building that Jake said was the bunkhouse for the men, but the house dominated the scene. Two stories with balconies outside the upstairs windows and a veranda on the west side of the first floor. Made of weathered logs, large enough to be impressive, it looked solid enough to defy anything the elements might send.

"There's the church." He directed her gaze past the house, past the barn, past the clustered outbuildings to a narrow, steep-roofed log structure tucked against the trees on one side just as he'd said. "We'll worship there tomorrow."

"I look forward to it." More than she cared to admit. All her self-admonition, all her reminders of how proud her father would be were but whispers with this man at her side. Even though she knew he did not return her feelings, she could not deny her love for him. Spending time with him would be a pleasure laced with aching disappointment.

Jake groaned, "The boys have seen you."

Hannah chuckled. The pair bounced up and down on the veranda. Even from this distance she could hear them screaming her name.

Jake flicked the reins, and they made their way to the house. She waited for Jake to help her down. He remained at her side as the boys launched themselves at her. Only Jake's steadying arm across her back kept her on her feet.

She darted him a grateful look. She thought his gaze would be on the boys, but he stared at her, his eyes almost black and so bottomless she felt dizzy. She wanted to turn into his arms, but two bodies wrapped around her legs made it impossible. She pulled away, the world stopped spinning, and she bent to pull Sammy and Luke into a tight hug.

Mrs. Sperling joined them and waited for Hannah to untangle herself from the boys. Laughing at the joyous greeting, Hannah reached for Mrs. Sperling's outstretched hands.

"I'm so glad you're here, my dear," the older woman said. She then told the boys, "Better let her go so we can go inside." The boys raced ahead, and Mrs. Sperling took Hannah's hand and pulled it through her arm. "Audrey is eager to meet you."

Hannah glanced back and saw Jake still watching her, looking as if he wanted to say something. She hesitated. She couldn't keep from hoping he wanted to convince her things could be different between them. She'd accept anything as a starting spot. Anything but responsibility. But his expression changed, grew harder, determined even, and he swung back to the buggy seat and drove away.

Inside, a young woman bounced toward her and screamed. "You're Hannah. I've heard so much about you. I'm Audrey. I understand you rescued my two little imps. Thank you. I do my best to keep them out of trouble, but they still find it."

Hannah smiled and held her breath waiting for Audrey to run out of steam. It was obvious where the boys got their rambunctiousness.

Hannah looked around the room—she didn't know if she should call it a living room or a lobby. It rose two stories to the log ceiling. A balcony ran along three sides on the second level. Beyond the rails she saw doors she guessed opened to bedrooms.

She lowered her gaze to the huge windows at the far end of this room and gasped. Her heart felt ready to explode at the sweeping view of hills and trees. Slowly she brought her gaze back inside to the furnishings. A sideboard big enough to hide in. Three leather sofas formed a square with one open side. A bookcase eight feet high filled with books and collectibles—a globe of the world, a carving that looked to be from some Indian tribe, a perfectly round rock, and a china statue of a young woman with her skirts flared at her ankles.

As she looked around, the family slowly moved her across the floor to a large dining room featuring a long table of polished split logs. She brushed her fingers over it. Smooth as silk.

"Have a seat, dear," Mrs. Sperling said.

Hannah chose the closest chair. Sammy and Luke climbed up on either side of her. Mrs. Sperling sat at the end, and Audrey hurried around to sit opposite Hannah. A woman hustled in through the swinging door. Hannah caught a glimpse of a big kitchen; then Mrs. Sperling demanded her attention.

"Hannah, this is my dear friend and the one who keeps our household running, Sarie."

The big-framed woman with a mop of gray curls leaned over and hugged Hannah. "Any friend of this family's is a friend of mine."

A few minutes later, Hannah met Audrey's husband, Harvey, who had a bullhorn of a voice.

Sarie brought tea and a huge tray of cakes and cookies.

Hannah enjoyed meeting Audrey and Harvey and seeing again Mrs. Sperling and the boys, but she kept hoping Jake would join them. He finally did, and suddenly she felt awkward in his presence and wished he would leave.

She let the conversation flow around her, adding replies when required, but she felt like a spectator. Several times she felt Jake's gaze on her, but when she met his eyes, he jerked away. She almost sighed with relief when Audrey said it was time to put the boys to bed and took her family home. Mrs. Sperling turned to Hannah. "I'll show you to your room."

She rose to follow the older woman to the stairs then paused. "Good night, Jake."

He glanced up from his study of his teacup. "Good night, Hannah."

Their eyes locked. His burned through every argument, every reasonable defense she'd built. She felt its power right to the bottom of her heart and knew a moment of panic followed swiftly by shame. She was a strong, independent woman, but God forgive her, she knew if at that moment he'd asked her to give up everything she had and was and wanted, she gladly would have done it.

But he didn't ask. He wouldn't. Oh, he might order her to do certain things, but she would never allow herself to be ordered around. She had far too much spunk for that. She had an independent spirit.

She was the first to pull away from the fire of their gaze. With a nod she left the room and followed Mrs. Sperling to the second floor.

"I hope you'll be comfortable."

Hannah chuckled at the idea of anyone being anything but comfortable in this house. "It's a beautiful room."

"I put out a selection of books if you want to read. But don't feel you have to stay in your room. We rise early so I'm going to bed now, but if you want to go downstairs and sit by the fire, please do."

"I think I'll go to bed and read. Thank you." After Mrs. Sperling left, Hannah glanced through the titles of the books and chose one. But she didn't read. She went to the windows and looked out.

The ranch was beautiful. The house itself, spectacular, as big as her hotel with a warmer feel. It was a home, a home belonging to the ranch as much as to the family. She closed her eyes. She could almost feel the solidness of the place. She breathed deeply and opened her eyes.

The balcony outside her room looked so inviting, she slipped out. She shivered in the cool evening air and let the peace of her surroundings fill her. She could almost imagine belonging here. The sound of boots crunching on the ground below and the bulky shape she recognized as Jake sent her back against the wall.

How could she be so foolish to love a man who didn't love her back? She wondered if he knew how to love without being in charge. She slipped inside and prepared for bed then opened the book she'd chosen and forced herself to read the words.

≈

Hannah sat at the table with Jake, Mrs. Sperling, Audrey, her family, and Pastor Rawson. Last night she'd finally fallen asleep once she'd made her mind up to avoid being alone with Jake. How else was she to make it through Sunday without her emotions getting all knotted up?

So far she'd been successful. Jake hadn't joined them at breakfast. His mother said he'd gone to speak with some of the crew, so Hannah enjoyed a visit with Mrs. Sperling.

She managed to get Luke and Sammy on either side of her at the church. Audrey and Harvey had followed her into the pew, leaving no room for Jake. He sat behind them.

Hannah caught glimpses of him as they stood to sing. She continued to be aware of him and wondered if she would ever not feel his presence, whether he stood close or rode miles away.

It had been a beautiful service in a beautiful building, and she tried not to picture herself coming down the aisle with the light catching the threads of a shimmering veil. She'd had to close her eyes and pray for strength to keep herself from seeing Jake in a black suit waiting for her at the front.

She concentrated hard on the sermon. She knew it had been sent straight from God's heart to hers when Pastor Rawson read the text. "The spirit indeed is willing but the flesh is weak." As Pastor Rawson talked about how flesh warred against spirit, desiring things that were temporary, tempting the believer to settle for momentary pleasure, Hannah vowed to stick to her principles. She would keep the vow she'd made to her father, a vow given at his graveside. Even though he hadn't heard it, she had meant it. She'd promised to live up to his expectations. She would not compromise her independence. Not for the joy of living on this ranch. Not for the sight of Jake every day. Not for the hope his feelings would grow into love. Unless he accepted her as she wanted, there was no place for her here.

Pastor Rawson accompanied them home for supper, as apparently was his custom. Audrey, Harvey, and the boys joined them, too, so the conversation jumped from one topic to another. Audrey tried to keep the boys quiet, but after Sammy spilled his cake on the floor and Luke tipped over his third glass of milk, Audrey stood. "I think it's time to take this pair home and let them run off steam. Boys, say good-bye to Hannah."

Hannah hugged the pair, received two sticky kisses, and said good-bye to Audrey and Harvey.

As Sarie cleaned away the dishes, Mrs. Sperling glanced at Jake. "I'd like to speak to the pastor alone."

Hannah pushed back her chair. "I'll go up to my room and read."

"Nonsense," Mrs. Sperling said. "It's far too pleasant an evening to be cooped up indoors. Jake, take her for a walk."

"My pleasure." Jake slowly got to his feet, his gaze never leaving Hannah's face. She tried to look away, to pretend she didn't see the promise in his eyes. She couldn't any more than she could pull the stars from the sky or deflect the sun from its journey from east to west. Nor did she want to. She wanted the fulfillment of the promise in his rich brown eyes—a look, she felt certain, was full of love.

They walked side by side, talking of everything and nothing—the color of the sky, the sound of the breeze, the boys' mischief, the beauty of their surroundings. They passed the church and sat on a fallen tree.

"How do you like my ranch?" Jake asked.

"It's beautiful."

"Does it live up to your expectations?"

"It exceeds them. I never could have imagined a place could seem to be so much a part of the land, like one exists for the other." She ducked her head. "Now I'm being silly."

He took her hand. "I don't think so. In fact, you've perfectly expressed what I have always felt but didn't have words for. I'm glad you like it. It's important you do."

She kept her head down, but her heart had to know if his eyes would give a clue as to what he meant. Slowly, her breath clinging motionless to her ribs, she lifted her face and met his eyes. He looked uncertain as if he waited for her to indicate something. "Why?" she whispered.

He caught a strand of hair the breeze had pulled loose, tucked it behind her ear, and trailed his finger down her cheek. " 'Cause I want you to be happy here."

Happy? Knowing he was about to express his love, she knew happiness like she'd never known. Like the softness of rabbit fur, the scent of a perfect rose, and the sight of a newborn baby all rolled up into one and dropped into her heart. "I could be very happy here."

He dropped his hand to slap his thigh. "Then it's settled. You'll get rid of the hotel and move out here."

"Why?"

"Why what?"

"Why should I move out here?" If he would only hint he had some feelings toward her, but his expression grew hard, distant.

"Seems to me it's pretty clear. You need to be out here where I can make sure you're safe."

Her thoughts were dying butterflies falling to the ground. She rose and quietly headed back to the house.

He followed and grabbed her elbow, forcing her to stop and face him. "I thought you liked the ranch. Didn't you say you could be happy here?"

She nodded. "I could under the right circumstances. But being your servant is not one of them."

"You're far too independent."

She shook her head sadly. "I don't think so, but thank you for reminding me of what's important."

"I suppose you're going to say your independence is more important than your safety."

"I wasn't, because I would never put my personal safety at risk." But she'd put her emotions at risk by allowing herself to think Jake might actually care for her as more than a responsibility. "First, let me be very clear on one thing. You have no right or reason to feel responsible for me. And second, I would be dishonoring my father's memory if I sacrificed my independence in order to be taken care of as you suggest." Pulling herself from his grasp, she returned to the house, found Pastor Rawson preparing to return to town, and asked if she might ride with him.

Chapter 10

Next morning, Jake headed for the hills to check on his cows. He wanted space to think. And he didn't need to be around his family, inflicting his bad mood on them.

What was wrong with Hannah? She said she liked the ranch. She had no reason to lie, so it must be true. Yet she refused to do the sensible thing and move here.

His stomach knotted and twisted and turned sour as he thought of her remaining in town. Unless she could be persuaded to visit again, he'd have to go to town to see her, and how often could he do that? Not often enough to satisfy the emptiness inside him at the thought of not seeing her for weeks on end. He guessed every day wouldn't be enough. Something about that gal got under his skin and refused to let go. In a way he sort of liked. No, the idea of seeing her at most once a week, knowing she was in town trying to fix and run that hotel on her own, just sliced along his nerves like a sliver under his fingernail.

The hotel was the cause of this trouble between them. And it was all tied up to something she seemed to think her father expected of her. None of which made a lick of sense. He figured any man would see the predicament Hannah had gotten herself into and find a way to get her out. But Hannah was stuck with nothing but memories of what she thought her father wanted, and she couldn't seem to pull away from them. She'd said it often enough that he didn't have any trouble recalling what she thought her father expected of her—get the hotel fixed up and opened.

He sat on his horse, staring at the rolling hills he loved. The hotel kept Hannah from his side.

She would never admit defeat, because she somehow had it figured her father would be disappointed in her if she did. So the way to solve the problem was to help her get the hotel fixed up so she could walk away without feeling she'd disappointed her father.

And he knew exactly how to do it.

He reined his horse around and galloped back to the ranch. Only Zeke answered his call.

"The others are out checking the cows like you said," he replied in answer to Jake's demand to know where everyone had disappeared to.

"Go find half a dozen of them. I've got something in town needs doing."

Two hours later he sent Zeke and six of his outfit to town with instructions to fix the hole in the dining room floor of the hotel. "Get lumber at the hardware store. Do it right. I want it ready to use when you're done." He saw them on their way then rode over to the house to inform his mother he was on his way to town.

"Wait," she called, "I want you to pick up a few things."

"Mother, you were just in town." He wanted to see the look on Hannah's face when his crew showed up to fix the dining room. He could well imagine her surprise, her confusion, and then her delight at getting this job done before the deadline set by the mayor and his cronies.

"I need some more thread. Just wait while I get you a sample of cloth so Mrs. Johnson can match it."

He drummed his fingers on the banister as he waited for her to run upstairs. A few minutes later, she returned. "Audrey's just coming over the hill. Let me see if she needs anything."

"Mother, I'm in a hurry."

"What's a minute or two?" Ignoring his protests, she hurried out the back door to meet Audrey. Sammy and Luke screamed a greeting to their grandmother.

Jake twisted his hat and ground his teeth. He wanted to be there when the boys arrived with the load of lumber.

Mother returned. "She'd like you to pick up—never mind, I'll write it down."

Jake fumed as she found a piece of paper then had to sharpen the pencil, but finally he was on his way, galloping his mount to make up for lost time.

He didn't catch them by the time he slowed for Quinten's main street. As he approached the hotel, he saw the men still mounted, Zeke still seated in the wagon. Hannah stood on the sidewalk, her arms crossed over her chest. He'd missed seeing her surprise.

He reined in, dropped to the ground, wrapped the reins twice around the hitching post, and clattered to her side. "Are you surprised?" he asked.

She faced him. "Do I look surprised?"

His smile faded, his shoulders tensed as he took a good look at her. Her eyes flashed. Her mouth pulled down at the corners. He hoped he was mistaken, but she looked angry. He turned to his crew. "What are you waiting for? Let's get this done."

The men shifted and looked uncomfortable.

"What's going on here?"

"They might as well go back to the ranch. I've told them I don't need their help."

No one moved. Jake felt the heat of Hannah's gaze and saw the awkwardness of his men.

Hannah waved her hand dismissively. "You can leave now."

The men waited for his order.

"Jake." Her voice was deceptively soft. "Tell them to leave."

He scratched his neck. "I thought my crew could. . ."

She pushed her face closer to his. He felt her hot breath, caught a glimpse of hazel fire in her eyes before he shifted his gaze to avoid looking at her. "Jake, I will hire my own crew when I'm ready." She made an explosive sound, turned, and steamed into the hotel.

Jake sighed. "Boys, you might as well go on home. She's too stubborn to change her mind."

Looking relieved, they rode away.

Jake stood outside the door for a minute, trying to make sense of the whole thing, finally admitted there was no sense to be made, and pushed inside. "Hannah, you said you needed some men to fix the floor."

She spun around to face him.

He didn't need the sight in both eyes to see she was still angry.

"How dare you presume to take over my responsibilities!" Her voice could have cut steel.

"I—"

"What makes you so certain I can't manage on my own? How dare you treat me like you do your family!"

"I—" But whatever reason or argument he might have dredged up never got a chance.

"Why do you have to fix everyone?" She took a step closer. "Can't you see not everyone needs fixing or taking care of?" She took two more steps until her shoes were an inch from the tips of his boots.

He stifled an urge to back away from her anger.

"Have you ever tried just accepting people? Allowing them to make their own choices. Giving them the freedom to make mistakes. Why do you have to be responsible for everything? Why do you think if people make a mistake you've failed? Jake, did you ever think that people—your family—would like to be accepted as they are with their flaws and failings, dreams and expectations. And yes, even be allowed a little independence." She breathed so hard, he wondered if a person could get wind-broken.

Then she threw her arms in the air. "Oh, what's the use?" She stomped toward the dining room, apparently remembered the door had been boarded off, and with an angry mutter, shifted directions and headed for the stairs. "If you don't mind, I have work to do."

"Hannah, wait."

She paused and slowly turned. Her anger had calmed and was replaced with resignation. "What?"

"I—" How could he hope for her to understand his intention had been so much more honorable than she assessed it? Wasn't it? "I only wanted to help."

She shook her head. "No, you wanted to be responsible for me. You can't. I am responsible for me. It's not a job that requires two people." Slowly she climbed the stairs and disappeared down the hall.

Jake stared after her for a long time then rode away as fast as he'd made the trip into town.

Hannah sank to the edge of her bed and stared blindly across the room. She'd been holding on to a useless hope, thinking one day Jake would stop trying to control her and learn to love and accept her.

But he'd made it plain as household dust he didn't think she could manage on her own. He didn't see her as an equal, someone who could make decisions and handle challenges using her own resources.

He was right about one thing, though, she had to get the dining room floor fixed in less than a week in order to avoid further fines and run the chance of having the "safety inspector" shut her down. She'd been hoping for more money. But renting three or four rooms at a time, from which she had to pay Mort, buy wallpaper and paint, and purchase food for herself—it all ate away at the little bit of income she'd generated.

She picked up her Bible and opened it but didn't read. Instead, she prayed. *God, You have created me. You have given me opportunities. Long ago, when I first trusted You, it was because of Your promise to provide for my needs. I know You love me with an unsearchable love. Nothing is too hard for You. Show me how to meet this challenge.*

She sat quietly, waiting for God to reveal His will. Her gaze rested on the chiffonier. Her thoughts went to the black case inside the drawer and her father's pocket watch. She wondered what it was worth.

No, Lord. I can't sell it. It's the only thing I have left of my father's belongings.

What would her father want? For her to succeed at this venture? He certainly would. He would encourage her to sell the watch if necessary. She hated to part with it, but she needed the money.

Two tears dripped down her cheeks. She dashed them away. She would do whatever she had to do. Still she hesitated. Was she desperate enough to sell her most precious belonging?

It was that or face defeat. Her father would be disappointed if she didn't do her best.

She pushed to her feet, took the case from the drawer, and headed down the street. She'd never visited Stephen's Jewelers, but now she stepped into the shop filled with glass-fronted display shelves.

A few minutes later she emerged with more money than she'd anticipated and crossed the street to the hardware store, where she arranged for a man to measure the hole and supply materials to repair it.

A month later, Hannah wandered through the hotel. The dining room floor was finished—the new boards painted mahogany brown to match the old floor. She'd rescued a maroon rug from the storeroom and put it in the center of the room and placed tables and chairs around in a pleasing arrangement that left room for serving and provided a bit of privacy. White tablecloths and candlesticks provided the touch of elegance she wanted. She'd hired a cook and helpers to operate the dining room.

She paused in the lobby, pleased with the new green-apple paint on the wall beside the door and the new wallpaper behind the desk—decorated with cabbage roses. She climbed the stairs and checked each room. She now had a young girl to help clean. All eight rooms were usable and were often full.

The hotel had been successfully reopened. Not even Mayor Stokes or Mr. Bertch could find fault. She returned to the main floor.

Thelma, the cook, beckoned for her attention. "Did you want to serve biscuits tonight?"

Hannah reviewed the menu with her. She'd never realized how much work it involved to plan a selection of three meals a day, day after day.

She and Thelma managed to plan several days ahead. Hannah made notes of the supplies needed. "I'll order these this afternoon. But I want to do some mending first." It amazed her how much damage her guests did to the sheets and pillowcases. Every week the mending pile grew.

Betty, one of the girls who worked in the dining room, stopped her halfway across the kitchen. "Hannah, I can't work tonight. My mother's sick and needs help with the younger ones."

"Of course. I'll find someone else." She mentally added it to the list of things to be done this afternoon.

Thelma found her again a few minutes later to inform her the butcher hadn't delivered enough meat for their planned menu, and Hannah promised to take care of it.

She barely got settled in a corner of her bedroom and threaded a needle before several other things required her attention. By then the morning had fled away on invisible wings and she had to abandon plans for mending.

She spent the afternoon taking care of errands, managed to persuade Mr.

Mack to supply the promised meat, and had to make a few adjustments on her list because Johnson's was out of things. It would mean more planning in order to create the menu. She raced to the telegraph office to send an order for more supplies to be shipped on the train and remembered she didn't have anyone to take Betty's place. She stopped at several houses to ask for someone to work. No one was available, and finally, accepting defeat, she hurried back to the hotel. She had no choice but to help in the dining room and hope Mort would watch the front desk for her.

By the time she made her weary way to her bedroom, she ached from head to toe and a pain had developed in her left leg. She sank to the edge of the bed and buried her head in her hands. She had what she wanted—her business doing well and her independence. So why didn't it feel better?

It wasn't that she minded the work. It kept her from thinking of Jake too often. She hadn't seen him since he'd tried to fix the floor for her. But she missed him with an ache that never let up. It relented only momentarily when her mind was occupied with other things but grew worse at bedtime. How long would it take for her to be able to sit in the quiet of her own room without feeling so alone?

She thought of Mrs. Sperling and smiled. Had the woman learned not to fake headaches and faints? Did she realize her real ones seemed less dramatic when she faked such wonderful false ones?

And Sammy and Luke. Did they miss her? Would she ever again have the pleasure of exploring with them? She supposed the Sperlings would come to town again, and if Mrs. Sperling had her way, they'd stay in Hannah's hotel. But when would such an occasion arise? Probably not until Christmas or even next fall when the cattle were again driven to the rail yard.

Scattered visits were not what she wanted. And playing with Sammy and Luke, visiting Mrs. Sperling, and getting to know Audrey and Harvey better were not what she wanted, either.

What she wanted was Jake. Nothing more. Nothing less.

The hotel might have provided her with independence, but at what price? Why did it feel as if she'd sold herself to a hard taskmaster? Would it be any worse to let Jake order her around? Take care of her?

But she'd promised her father. He'd always valued her independence.

She sighed. What did she want?

The answer was easy. She'd said it to Jake several times. She wanted acceptance.

God accepted her just as she was. Jake's family accepted her.

She jerked up straight and stared ahead. "Oh, Daddy, how could I have been so blind?" she whispered. "It wasn't my independence you valued. It was me."

Perhaps, if she gave him another chance, Jake would learn to accept her as well. Not as a responsibility but as an equal. She chuckled softly. Now that was a goal worth working for.

She prayed for a long time, wanting to be sure the step she planned wasn't simply a reaction to a hard day. She searched the scriptures for guidance. When she read Ephesians, chapter two, verses eight and nine, " 'For by grace are ye saved through faith; and that not of yourselves: it is the gift of God: not of works, lest any man should boast,'" she knew she'd found her answer. God didn't need her to prove anything. Nor did she need to prove who she was to Jake.

She laughed. Maybe taking care of people was Jake's way of showing love. She could live with that as long as he could accept her as an equal.

She retrieved paper, pen, and ink from a drawer and wrote a letter to her grandparents. She'd mail it in the morning. And then wait to hear back.

Chapter 11

Jake picked himself off the ground and dusted his clothes.

"He's too much for you, huh, Boss?" Zeke kept all expression from his face and his voice flat, but Jake knew the men got a degree of pleasure out of seeing the wild horse toss him in the dirt. Probably figured it was fair payback for the way he'd driven them the last few weeks.

They'd ridden to the farthest corners of the ranch, searching every gully, every copse of trees, every bluff to make sure all the cows had been gathered in. They'd spent many a night camping out.

Usually a night under the stars mellowed Jake out like nothing else. But he rose early every morning, itching for something he couldn't scratch. He'd rouse the men and head out on another hard ride for some obscure reason.

Trouble was, no matter how hard he drove himself, it did nothing to ease his frustration. No matter how hard he worked, how fast he rode, how many nights he spent out under the stars, he couldn't escape the accusations Hannah had flung at him. Nor could he stop dreaming of her, thinking he saw her at odd moments, wishing she were close by.

Three days ago, he'd decided they'd buy a bunch of wild horses from a trader to the west. It had been a challenge to trail them home, and Jake had accepted no slacking from any of the men. "I paid good bucks for this bunch of knot heads, and every one of them is going to be driven into the corrals and broke."

"You hiring someone to break 'em?" Zeke asked.

"I'll do it."

"Yes, Boss."

But the first bronc proved to be difficult. It took all afternoon, but finally Jake managed to stay on the animal and prove who was boss.

He limped into the house for supper. He washed up and strode into the dining room. The table was set, but neither his mother nor Sarie was around. He followed the sound of their voices across the living room to the room his father had used as an office. Jake had never been able to persuade himself to use it. Instead, he'd put a desk in his bedroom where he kept the ranch records.

He ground to a halt and stared at his mother up a ladder holding a piece of fabric to the window. Sarie stood at the other side of the window holding the end of the fabric. "Mother, what do you think you're doing? Get off that ladder before you fall."

His mother shot him a startled look then turned back to Sarie. "It's perfect. What do you think?"

"Sure will freshen up the place."

"Mother." Jake strode across the room, intending to lift her from the ladder. She waved him away. "In a minute."

"Mother, I insist you get down before you fall."

She finally faced him. Not that he much cared for the gleam in her eye. "You insist? You think you can order me around like I'm one of the hands? Last time I checked, I'm a grown woman in charge of all my faculties. I will decide when I'm done here." And she turned back to pinning the fabric.

He backed off. "What are you doing in here? No one comes in this room."

"It's a lovely room. I'm tired of it being wasted. If you don't want to use it as an office, I'm going to fix it up as a small sitting room. I thought I'd put my sewing materials in one corner."

"Mother, I don't want this room changed."

"I intend to make new drapes and change it to suit my needs unless you want to use it as an office." She turned, waiting for his response.

He shook his head and backed away.

Mother lowered the fabric. "We'll finish later, Sarie."

Sarie nodded, sent some sort of secret message to Jake's mother, and then slipped out of the room.

Jake stood rooted to the floor. His father had spent his last days here, confined to a bed in a now bare corner. He could feel his father's presence, recall the combination of fear and determination he felt as his father prepared him to take over. The room made him feel trapped. With a muffled sound, he broke free of the spell and headed for the door.

His mother descended from her perch and caught his elbow. "Jake, sit down. I want to talk to you."

He blinked. It sounded like an order. He sat on the nearest leather chair, and his mother sat facing him in the matching chair.

"Son, I've been doing a lot of thinking lately, and I realize we need to make some changes around here."

The ranch was as successful as it had been when his father was alive, and his mother was well cared for. No one had a reason to complain. Nor to want to change things. "Everything is just fine."

"You've tried very hard to take your father's place. But you're not your father."

His gut twisted.

"Nor do any of us want you to be. Seth is dead. You are now owner of this place. Don't you have things you want to do differently?"

Jake hesitated. "I thought of buying a bull from a different breed. Bring in a new blood line."

"Why haven't you?"

His father's orders had kept him from doing so. *If you run the place just like I have, you won't have any problems.* But he didn't say it aloud.

"Jake, I'm as guilty as you are of trying to keep the past alive. Maybe more so." She ducked her head. "I've used you. Created headaches when I didn't have them in order to—" She fluttered her hands. "I'm not even sure why I did it. The headaches were real at first. Sometimes they still are. But they guaranteed I'd get your attention. Then I used them to get my own way." She shuddered. "I can't believe how shallow I was." She sat up straighter. "Hannah made me see how important it is to stand on my own two feet."

Hannah. Her independence had come between them. Now it had spilled over to his mother.

"Jake, I want you to understand that the promises your father exacted from you on his deathbed have been fulfilled. You have taken care of me and your sister better than he could have imagined. You have cared for the ranch as well as he did, if not better. I am hereby releasing you from your promises. I want to be free to move on with my life, and I want you to know you're free to do what you want, both with your life and this ranch." She took his hands. "You need to find someone to share your life with. Go find Hannah. Persuade her you love her and want to *share* your life with her."

"It's not that easy." He bolted from the room and raced for the barn to saddle his horse and ride from the yard. He bent low over his horse's neck and rode like fury until he reached the top of a distant hill and drew to a stop, staring out at the landscape, though in truth seeing nothing.

His mother had released him from his vow to his father. Said he'd completed it. But was it that easy? He groaned. Hannah was right. He was used to being in control. Could he suddenly let people around him make their own decisions while he stood back? What if they made mistakes? Wouldn't that be his responsibility? What had Hannah said? Just accept people as they are—flaws and all? He did that. Or did he? By wanting to take over their choices, was he saying he didn't accept their way of doing things?

He grunted. Everything he'd done had been to help those he loved. To be the man his father expected him to be. Was he just a shadow of his father? God forbid. "God," he groaned, "what do You expect of me?"

"I have loved thee with an everlasting love: therefore with lovingkindness have I drawn thee."

He let the words of scripture wash over him and through him until he felt cleansed and free. Yes, free. God loved him despite his failures or his successes. With an everlasting love. Could he do any less for his family? For Hannah? How wrong he'd been to try and force her to give up her dreams. She'd never be the sort of woman who contentedly let someone else make all her decisions. He chuckled. He didn't want her to be. He wanted to share his life with a woman who was his equal.

He could not ask her to give up the hotel. In fact—he reined his horse toward home—he'd go to town and give her a hand fixing up the place. If she'd give him a second chance, they'd find a way to work things out so she could keep her hotel.

❧

Hannah opened the letter from her grandparents in the post office, read it quickly, and laughed. She'd asked permission to sell the hotel, but they'd written saying they hadn't found what they wanted in California and would come back and take it over themselves. They were arriving tomorrow. She tucked the letter into her pocket and returned to the hotel.

Jake had once offered her a job as companion to his mother. She was prepared to go to the ranch and ask if the offer still stood. But she didn't have time to dwell on the future right now. The hotel demanded her complete and immediate attention.

❧

The next day she hurried to the train to meet her grandparents, laughing as her grandfather hugged her right off the ground. Her grandmother kissed her soundly on both cheeks.

"So you've decided you don't want to run a hotel," Grandfather said. "I expect you've found something else you would rather do."

She tucked an arm around each grandparent. "I think so."

Her grandfather squeezed her arm. "I hope he's worthy."

Grandmother and Hannah looked at each other and laughed.

"I want to give him a chance to prove it," Hannah said.

"Do I sense a problem, dear?" Grandmother asked.

"He thinks I'm too independent."

Grandfather snorted. "I guess it's up to you to prove him wrong."

"I hope I can." She hugged them both a little closer. "It's good to have you back."

She let them enter the hotel first and waited for their response to the changes. She'd told them about the fire but wondered if they'd approve of how she'd fixed up the place.

They glanced around. "The rug?" grandmother asked.

"Ruined."

The older woman nodded, went as far as the dining room for a look, and then returned. "It looks fine. We couldn't have done better ourselves."

Hannah gave them one of the bigger rooms upstairs until she could move out of the quarters on the main floor. She left them there to rest.

Partway down the stairs, she saw the door fly open. Jake stood silhouetted in the opening. Her heart finished descending without her then bounced back to her chest to shudder with surprise. She'd been planning to visit him, beg, if necessary, for the offered position. She hadn't expected him to show up in town, brandishing a paintbrush in one hand. Her brain had turned to stone, her tongue refused to work. Finally one thought surfaced. "What do you want?"

He waved the paintbrush. "I'll help you fix the hotel."

She took the rest of the steps. She couldn't stop staring at him. "It's all done." She waved her hand to indicate the surroundings.

His eager expression flattened, and he dropped his hand to his side. "Oh." He seemed to consider the facts. "Guess I'm too late."

"It's done," she repeated, unable to think what it meant that he'd come, offering to help.

"Well then. That's good. And the business is doing well?"

"Yes." She remembered she wanted to ask him about the position. "Jake, remember you asked me to be your mother's companion. Is the offer still open?"

"Huh? Oh. No. She doesn't need a companion."

"I see." She held her breath against the disappointment ripping through her chest.

"Hannah, I've changed my mind about a lot of things." He stepped aside as one of the guests came through the door. "Can we go someplace and talk?"

She hesitated. Could she stand any more announcements from him? And yet she followed him outside, allowing him to take her hand. He paused, glanced up and down the street, and then led her north to the church.

"We can talk privately here," he said.

They sat together on a pew. *Lord*, she prayed, *give me strength to accept this.*

He took her hand and turned to look into her face.

She kept her emotions buried. She would not reveal her pain, her weakness.

He studied her intensely. "Hannah, I've changed."

She nodded, though she had no idea what he meant.

"You were right," he continued. "I felt I was responsible for everyone. I couldn't let go for fear something would go wrong and I'd be to blame. You see, my father made me promise on his deathbed that I would take care of everything and do just as he would."

Again she nodded, still no closer to understanding.

"I realize I have fulfilled my vow to my father. I expect it will take a little practice to actually live what I decided, but from now on, I'm determined to let people make their own choices." He played with the collar of her dress. "If you want to run a hotel, that's up to you. I just want what's best for you." He sought her gaze, his eyes filled with longing and uncertainty. "I accept you, Hannah. Just as you are."

At her surprised blink, he hurried on, as if he felt he had to explain his whole plan, and she let him. She had to know exactly what he had in mind before she spoke.

"I don't want to run your life. I want to share it. You see, it was your independence that attracted me from the first. It challenged my idea that I had to be in control. You taught me how to let go of my overwhelming sense of responsibility. If you'll have me, we'll find a way to work things out so you can continue to run your hotel. I'll even help you."

Her whole being wanted to explode with joy. "I've let the hotel go."

"Go? Where?"

She giggled. "Nowhere, silly. I've turned the ownership back to my grandparents. They take over tomorrow."

His expression fell. "You're going back East?"

She smiled at his disappointment. "I had hoped I could still be your mother's companion, but you say the position is closed."

He chuckled. "Seems like you taught her the benefits of independence."

"That leaves me without a position." She lowered her head so he wouldn't see the longing, the hope, or the beginning of joy in her eyes.

He lifted her chin and waited until she met his look.

When she saw the way he studied her, his eyes dark with love and promise, tears stung the backs of her eyes.

"Hannah Williams, I love you. Do you care for me just a little? Do you think you could learn to love me?"

She whooped. "Jake Sperling, I love you so much now I can hardly think." She threw her arms around his neck and raised her face for a kiss.

Epilogue

Hannah adjusted her veil. It shimmered exactly as she had once dreamed it would.

"You're almost as beautiful as your grandmother was the day I married her," Grandfather said as he waited to escort her down the aisle.

She had decided to stay at the hotel until the wedding to help her grandparents get settled back in. Even though Hannah missed Jake when he had to be away, she appreciated the time spent with her grandparents. Their love for each other and support for her meant a lot. She kissed her grandfather's cheek. "I wish Mother would have come, but I'm awfully glad you and Grandmother are here."

Audrey peeked around the corner, giving them a commentary. "Mother and your grandmother have been seated." She turned to her sons. "You two are next. Now remember what I said. No running. No yelling. Walk quietly up to Uncle Jake and stand at his side."

"Yes, Momma," Luke said and took Sammy's hand.

Hannah kissed them both on their cheeks before they headed down the aisle. They made it halfway before they broke into a run.

Jake caught them as they reached the front and steadied them into position, their freshly scrubbed faces looking cherubic against the backdrop of a lovely floral arrangement.

Audrey went next, her pale pink dress swishing around her ankles as she walked. She took her place at the front and turned to wait for Hannah.

"It's our turn, little girl," Grandfather said.

She nodded and took her grandfather's arm. Even though she was glad her grandfather was there, she couldn't help but wish for a moment that it was her father escorting her down the aisle to her future.

She'd told Jake how she'd come to realize that it was acceptance she longed for more than independence. She'd confessed she'd sold her prized possession, her father's pocket watch. Jake had surprised her by presenting it as a wedding present. He had bought it back for her. Oh, how she loved this man.

She met Jake's eyes and forgot everything else as Grandfather escorted her to his side.

Pastor Rawson smiled at them and began the service by reading scriptures reminding them that marriage was a holy institution. "What therefore God hath joined together, let not man put asunder." He then began the vows. "Do you, Jake, take this woman—"

Jake squeezed Hannah's hand, silently assuring her of his intention to honor the till-death-do-us-part words.

Suddenly the vase of flowers at Pastor Rawson's side crashed to the floor, soaking the poor man.

A few splashes hit Hannah in the face, and she wiped them off.

Luke shoved Sammy to the floor. "It's your fault. You pushed me."

Sammy came up sputtering and flailing his arms. "Did not."

"Boys," Audrey warned.

Harvey, Jake's best man, grabbed for Luke, but the boy skidded out of reach and raced down the aisle, Sammy hot on his heels.

"They're your boys," Audrey muttered to Harvey. "You go get them."

Hannah giggled. She glanced over her shoulder and saw Jake's mother press the back of her wrist to her forehead.

Mrs. Sperling caught her watching and looked embarrassed before she sat up straight and ignored the screaming pair of boys.

Hannah glanced at her grandparents, who smiled widely and likewise ignored the commotion.

Jake drew her closer and leaned over to speak so the pastor could hear, "Let's get this done before they bring the place down around our ears."

Amid the sound of two rambunctious little boys, the embarrassment of a set of parents, and the obvious glee of her grandparents, Hannah and Jake promised to love and honor each other always.

LINDA FORD

Linda lives on a farm/ranch/acreage (depending on your point of view) in Alberta, Canada, where she can see the Rocky Mountains on a daily basis. A writer who is very much influenced by her surroundings, she recently had a huge window put in her office so she could see the great outdoors. She thinks growing up on the prairie and learning to notice the small details it hides has given her an appreciation for watching God at work in His creation. Her upbringing also included being taught to trust God in everything and through everything—a theme that resonates in her stories. Threads of another part of her life are found in her stories: her concern for children and their futures. She and her husband have raised 14 children—4 homemade, 10 adopted. She currently shares her home and life with her husband, a grown son, a live-in paraplegic client, and a continual stream of kids, kids-in-law, grandkids, and assorted friends and relatives.

LETTERS FROM THE ENEMY

by Susan May Warren

Dedication

To Pops and Grandma Niedringhaus. In my fondest recollections, I can see you sitting on the sofa, still holding hands after three decades of marriage. I miss you.

To Curt and MaryAnn Lund. It's your memories that make my own so sweet.

To the Lord Jesus Christ, for loving me first. Thank You for setting me free.

Chapter 1

Mobridge, South Dakota
June 1918

W e're going to miss the train!" Lilly Clark dashed across the South
Dakota prairie, trampling a clump of goldenrod with her dusty
boots. The withering grass shimmered under the noonday sun. A
humid wind skipped off the Missouri River, and clawed at her straw hat. She
clamped a hand over the back of her head and pumped her legs faster toward
the crumbling knoll that overlooked the town of Mobridge. Her heart beat out
a race against her feet; she could already hear the train thundering through the
valley.

Behind her, Marjorie Pratt strained to keep up. "Wait. . .for. . .me," she
gasped.

Lilly forced herself up the hill, gulping deep breaths. At the crest, she
yanked off her hat and wiped her brow. Squinting in the sunlight, she scanned
the horizon and spotted the iron snake threading its way between bluffs and
farmhouses toward the Mobridge depot.

"Is. . .it. . .here?" Marjorie staggered to the top.

"Almost," Lilly replied. "We have to hurry."

Marjorie shed her calico bonnet and patted her brow with it. "Just. . .let . . .
me rest." Shielding her eyes, she searched for the train.

"It's over there," Lilly said, pointing. Her other hand clutched a lavender
envelope, tinged with a thin layer of dust. She scowled and blew on the envelope,
assigning the soil to the greedy wind. For a brief second she regretted the extra
moments it had taken to saturate the precious letter in perfume and dry it, but
the thought of Reggie's smile as he smelled the fresh lilac erased her doubts. She
would just have to run faster.

She cast a look at her friend. Marjorie fanned herself, breathing heavily.

"Give me your letter, and I'll go on ahead," Lilly suggested.

Marjorie shook her head. "No. . .I'll make it."

Lilly nodded, then scrambled down the cliff, stepping on roots and boulders to slow her descent. There was an easier way into town, but taking that
route would sacrifice valuable minutes and probably her delivery of this week's

letter. She heard Marjorie hiss as she started down the cliff behind her, but Lilly knew her friend would make it. Marjorie came from sturdy English stock. She just didn't have the exercise of hoeing and weeding the kitchen garden in her favor. Instead, Marjorie devoted all her time to Red Cross work, assembling field kits.

"I'm going to fall!" Marjorie shrieked, sounding more angry than afraid. "It's your fault we're late! If we'd left on time, we wouldn't have had to scramble across the prairie like a couple of jackrabbits!"

Lilly laughed. "You're hardly a jackrabbit, Marj. Just be careful!" With Lilly's long brown hair quickly unfurling in the wind and her tanned face, she knew she was much more likely to be compared to a longhaired wild animal than her dainty friend. Thankfully, Reggie didn't seem to care that she didn't have Marjorie's sweetheart face, candy red lips, and blond hair.

Lilly reached flat land and sped toward town, picking up as much speed as her narrow gingham skirt would allow. At least it was wider than the dreadful hobble skirts that had been in fashion before the war. She'd ripped out two before her mother conceded defeat and allowed Lilly to sew her own styles.

The train's whistle let out an explosive shrill. Lilly glanced back at her friend, now a good fifty feet behind her.

"Lilly, hurry!" Marjorie waved her on.

Squinting into the sun, Lilly spotted the tiny depot, situated on the edge of town like a lighthouse to the outlying northern farms. As the train pulled in and belched black exhaust, Lilly ignored the fire in her lungs and forced her legs to move.

The exhaust settled, and Lilly caught sight of the doors of two livestock boxcars being opened and a ramp being propped up to each entry. Cowboys ascended the ramps, disappeared into the black hole of the boxcars, and emerged dragging angry bulls or frightened horses.

Suddenly, a scab of sagebrush caught the edge of her boot. Lilly screeched, stumbled, and directed her attention back to the jagged prairie.

The train whistle blared, emitting its first departure signal, and fear stabbed at Lilly's heart. She leaped over a railroad tie, used as a property divider and, grinning between gasps, glued her eyes to the station's platform steps.

If she'd been one step closer, Lilly would have been crushed under the hooves of a mustang, dancing in a frenzied escape from his handler. He blew by her like a tornado, his whiplike tail lashing her face and neck. Lilly screamed, stumbled, and plowed headfirst into the dirt, swallowing a mouthful of prairie in her vanished grin.

She sprawled there dazed, hurt, and dirty.

"Are you all right, *fraulein*?"

The words barely registered in her fog of confusion. Then a strong arm hooked her waist, pulling her to her feet. Lilly absently held on as she steadied herself. She ached everywhere, but nowhere more than in her pride.

"Fraulein, are you hurt?"

She looked up and gaped at a Nordic giant in a cream-colored ten-gallon cowboy hat. Dirt smudged his tanned face and dark sapphire eyes radiated concern under a furrowed brow.

"Sorry. That stallion is a rascal."

Lilly ran her trembling hand over her mouth, trying to gather in her scattered wits while she took in the man's apologetic smile. Her disobedient heart continued to gallop a rhythm of terror.

The cowboy squinted at her, as if assessing her ability to stand on her own, and Lilly realized she still clutched his muscled arm. She yanked her hand away, a blush streaming up her cheeks. When he bent over, she noticed how his curly blond hair scuffed the back of his red cotton shirt collar.

"This yours?" He held the lavender envelope, now dirty and crumpled between two grimy fingers.

"Oh!" Lilly cried in dismay. She reached for it, but the cowboy untied his handkerchief from his neck and used it to clean the envelope before handing it over.

Tears pricked Lilly's eyes. Her letter to Reggie, ruined. "Thank you," she whispered.

"Sorry," the cowboy muttered.

The train whistle screamed again. Lilly jumped, remembering her mission. She turned toward the depot but pain bunched at her ankle and shot up her leg. She cried out and began to crumple.

The cowboy gripped her elbow, steadying her. "You are hurt."

"Well, I would think so, after being almost run over by your horse," Lilly snapped, unable to hide her irritation.

"Can I help you inside?"

Lilly shook her head. "I can make it. Just go get that beast before it kills somebody." She yanked her elbow from his grasp and turned on her heel, biting her lip against the pain.

"I really am sorry," he offered again.

Ignoring the last apology, Lilly hobbled to the platform stairs and gripped the railing. She paused, then glanced over her shoulder at him.

The cowboy had taken off his hat and was crunching it in his hands. He gazed at her with eyes steeped in remorse. Her anger melted slightly. "Just go get that horse, sir. I'll be fine."

He nodded and shoved his hat on his head. Lilly blew out a frustrated breath and climbed the stairs, wincing. Reaching the top, she swept up wisps of her tangled hair and tucked them under her straw hat. She felt flushed and grimy, but at that moment she didn't care who saw her. Her letter had to make the mail train.

Lilly limped across the platform and entered the depot. The screen door squealed on its hinges. Two men looked up and stared at her.

She ignored the first, a grizzled Native American perched on a lonely bench by the window, and approached the second, a tall, pinched man who eyed her sternly.

"Hello, Mr. Carlson," Lilly said, noting her shaky voice and smiling. He took in her appearance and flared an eyebrow.

"Do you have some mail to send to France?"

Lilly held out the lavender envelope. He grabbed it and dropped it in a bulging canvas bag.

"Just in time." He bent to tie the bag.

"Wait, please." Lilly peered out the window, searching for Marjorie, just now hauling herself up the platform steps.

Mr. Carlson scowled. "Hurry up."

Lilly gave the station manager a pleading smile. "Please, it's for true love's sake."

Mr. Carlson sighed and shook his head. "This war has generated more true love. . ."

He waited, however, until Marjorie trudged through the door and handed him her own bulging envelope, before closing the bag and dragging it out to the hissing train.

Marjorie and Lilly watched in silence as the porters loaded the mailbag, hoping the letters would, indeed, find their recipients. Lilly realized it was a fragile link, this postal system across the Atlantic. She only hoped it was strong enough to sustain the covenant of love between her and Reggie Larsen.

Mr. Carlson returned, his brow dripping with perspiration. He leaned upon the tall stool behind his counter, glowering at the two girls. "So, what are ya waiting for?"

Lilly eyed him warily. "You don't suppose there is any chance you could look. . ."

"Be gone with ya!" Carlson bellowed, reaching for a glass of tepid water languishing next to his schedule book. "You'll get the mail in your boxes, like always."

Marjorie put a hand on Lilly's arm. "Let's go get a lemonade."

As they exited the depot, Marjorie noticed Lilly's limp. "What happened to you?" She stepped back and surveyed her friend. "Why, you're filthy!"

Lilly brushed herself off. "A wild mustang plowed me over."

Marjorie slid a hand around Lilly's waist. "Are you going to be all right?"

Lilly smiled wanly and nodded. Her ankle would be fine. What upset her more was the lingering image of a handsome young cowboy who had nearly derailed her well-laid plans.

Chapter 2

"Can we. . . rest. . .?" Lilly braced her arm on Marjorie's shoulder and gritted her teeth against the pain spearing her leg.

"You're really hurt, Lilly," Marjorie said. "Maybe I should take you home. I could ask Willard if he would drive you in his Packard."

"No!" Lilly snapped, then regretted her tone. "I want to wait for Reggie's letter. I haven't heard from him in two weeks."

Marjorie gave her a sympathetic smile. "Don't worry. I'm sure he's fine."

Fine? Lilly stamped down her bitterness, but it sprang back like a hardy thistle. Fine would be him here, planning their wedding, preparing to be a pastor. Fine would be him riding roundup or walking her home from church on Sundays. Fine had nothing to do with war or Germans or the fear that boiled in her chest.

She knew the truth. She read the newspapers, despite her father's ministrations to hide them, and knew how "fine" the doughboys were in France. Some were coming home with limbs missing, others in pine boxes. She bit her lip to ward off tears. How fine would she be if Reggie returned home in a flag-draped coffin? Then whom would she marry? Lilly winced at her selfish thought and shook her head to dismiss it.

A heated wind snared a strand of hair from her bun and sent it dancing about her face. Lilly caught it and wiped it back. "Yes, he'll be fine," she agreed, needing to hear the affirmation.

"You should be happy Reggie proposed before he left." Marjorie untied her bonnet and wiped the back of her neck.

How did Marjorie always manage to look beautiful, even under the blistering prairie heat? Her buttery hair turned golden in the blinding sun, and her creamy face never burned. Try as she might, Lilly couldn't control the mass of freckles that overran her face each summer; and her hair, well, she'd seen a prettier mane on her father's worn-out plow horse.

"He didn't formally propose, Marj." Lilly rotated her throbbing ankle, longing to unlace her high boots. "He just kissed me and told me we'd be married when he returned."

Marj sighed. "But that's enough." Her eyes glistened. "Harley didn't even do that much. Just waved with his floppy army cap as the train rolled out of the station."

Lilly smirked. "That's just because he refused to stand in line with all the other boys saying good-bye to the town sweetheart."

Marjorie blushed and had the decency to look chagrined.

"If I had half as many suitors as you—"

"You didn't need them. You have the most eligible bachelor of them all." Marjorie's eyes twinkled, and Lilly was instantly grateful for a friend who didn't point out the stark reality. Even when Reggie had been away at seminary and the town teemed with cowboys and railroad brakemen, not one had taken a shine to the poor Clark girl from the farm up the road.

Then Reggie reappeared on her front porch. Fresh out of seminary, he told her that life with him would be heaven and that he'd been waiting for her since she was in pigtails. His wide smile was like honey to her heart. He'd changed, of course, become refined, serious, exacting of himself and others, but that only inspired her respect. He never stepped over the line with her and treated her as if she was his own cherished possession. Reggie was her future, her security, the man God had chosen for her. Her feelings felt more along the lines of gratefulness, but then again, who wouldn't be grateful for the security of a husband and a family? Wasn't gratefulness a part of love? Reggie would protect her and give her a home. Reggie was God's steadfast reminder He had not forgotten her. After all the years of obeying the church and her parents and striving to be a woman of God, the good Lord had finally noticed and sent her Reggie.

And, if she did everything right, he would be hers forever.

"Let's go," Lilly said, pointing her gaze toward town. "Please drag me to Miller's, Marjie. If I don't get a lemonade soon, I might perish."

Marjorie laughed and shouldered Lilly's weight. They hobbled down the dusty road toward Mobridge.

They passed the shanties the Milwaukee Road had built for their brakemen and engineers who worked this end of the line and turned the corner onto Main Street.

"Billy Harper, you watch it!" Marjorie cried as a large hoop rolled in their direction. The barefoot ten year old deftly turned it, and a wide grin shone on his dusty face. As they shuffled along the boardwalks that edged the handful of false-front buildings, they dodged women in wilted bonnets scurrying from shop to shop, baskets of produce in one hand and unruly toddlers in the other. The clop of horses' hooves echoed on the hard-packed street.

Lilly spied Clive Torgesen parked in front of the armory, propped against his gleaming Model T, arms folded over his chest as he accepted the fawning of goggle-eyed teenage boys admiring his new toy. Clive spotted her and pulled a greeting on his black Stetson. Lilly turned away, not wanting to give the town troublemaker any encouragement.

The smell of baking bread drifted from Ernestine's Fresh Food Market, delicious enough to tempt Lilly to change her destination, but her parched throat won. She and Marjorie shuffled into Miller's Cafe.

Ed Miller had his hands full serving a row of thirsty cowboys and field hands who were downing lemonade or sipping coffee. Marjorie joined the line by the cashier as Lilly claimed a spot by the bookshelf near the windowsill. The shelf sported a yellowing pile of magazines from the East: *Vanity Fair*, *Ladies Home Journal*, and a thick stack of *American Railroad* journals. Lilly picked up a week-old *Milwaukee Journal*, flipped through it, and listened to the murmur of muddled conversation around her. Opinions of Wilson's latest political blunders, General Pershing's field maneuvers, skirmishes on the western front, and Hoover's wartime food regulations seemed to be the talk of the day.

"They're movin' the draft up ta age forty-five, I hear," said a weathered cowpoke.

"It don' matter, I'm gonna enlist anyway," replied his neighbor. "At least then we'll get ta eat some of the beef we've been tendin'. These ration days are gonna whittle me down ta bones."

"Yeah, but it might be better than having to face those Germans with nothin' more than a spear at the enda your gun. I hear Pershing has 'em runnin' straight into gunfire with no more than a yelp and a prayer."

"That ain't true, Ollie. I know that our doughboys have themselves real live ma-chan-i-cal rifles. Spit out bullets faster than rain from a black sky. I do think I'd like to get my hands on one a those."

"Well, you're gonna have to live through the boat ride across the ocean first. I heard Ed Miller's boy left a trail from New York to Paris."

Lilly smiled as she heard the cowboys' guffaw and Ed's growl in their direction. She wondered what the war really looked like, up close.

Marjorie nudged her, holding a fresh glass of lemonade.

"Thanks." Lilly took the cold drink and held it to her face, letting the cool glass refresh her skin. Then, she gulped it half down. Marjorie's shocked face stopped her from tilting it bottoms up.

"Sorry." Lilly licked her lips. "I was thirsty."

Marjorie scowled. "So it seems."

Lilly cringed, but caught sight of Rev. Larsen emerging from the alley between Ernestine's and Morrie's Barbershop. Lilly shoved her almost-empty drink into her friend's hand. "I'll meet you at the postal." She hopped toward the door, ignoring Marjorie's cry of protest.

Lilly limped across the street, dodging shouts of outrage from two cowboys on horseback and upsetting Billy Harper's hoop. "Rev. Larsen, sir!"

Rev. Larsen halted two paces from Morrie's front entrance. His angular face held no humor as he surveyed her disheveled appearance. "Lilly, what happened to you?"

Startled, she stared down at her dress. Grime embedded its folds and the sudden image of a cowboy with jeweled blue eyes glinting apology scattered her thoughts. Her mouth hung open, wordless.

"You ought to take better care of your appearance." Rev. Larsen's voice snapped her back to reality. "Just because Reggie is halfway around the world doesn't mean he doesn't care how you look. You have his reputation to uphold now." He cocked a spiny eyebrow.

Lilly bit back defensiveness and instead extracted a respectful tone. "Have you heard from Reggie?"

"Of course not. He has a war to fight. You just do your part and keep writing to him. I am sure he will write back when he can." He stabbed a skeletal finger into the air. "We all have a job to do in this great war, Lilly, and yours is to make sure our Reggie remembers what he has to come home to."

Lilly blew out a trickle of frustrated breath. "I have been writing, sir."

Rev. Larsen laid his bony hand on her shoulder, his gray eyes softening. "I'm sure you have. Mail's often slow at the front. Be patient and trust him to the Lord's hands. He'll write soon."

Lilly nodded. Rev. Larsen stepped into the barbershop, but his parting words lingered. Reggie was in God's hands, and God wouldn't let her down. She, her family, even the entire town knew she would become Mrs. Reginald Larsen, and she would trust the Lord to make it so. The alternative was simply unthinkable. Besides, she'd been so faithful to God, done everything right. She deserved God's cooperation, didn't she?

"Have you lost your senses?"

Lilly whirled and met a frowning Marjorie. "You look like you've wrestled a tornado, and you run up to Rev. Larsen like a lost puppy? What's he going to think about his son's fiancée?" Marjorie scowled. "You've got to learn to curb your recklessness if you're going to be a pastor's wife."

Lilly grimaced. Impulsiveness was her worst trait, constantly running before her to embroil her in a stew of awkward situations. If she weren't careful, Reggie would choose someone else to mother his flock.

"C'mon, let's check the mail." Marjorie tugged on Lilly's arm.

At the post office, they crowded in behind anxious women waiting for the mail.

"Is it here?" Marjorie whispered.

Lilly shrugged, but her heart skipped wildly. A letter from Reggie—something to remind her she was still his. *Please, O Lord.* Then she glimpsed Mrs. Tucker as the thin woman pushed through the crowd. She held a letter in her hands, raised high as if a trophy. Lilly's heart gave a loud inward cry, and Marjorie breathed the answer, "It's here."

Although the line moved faster than expected, an eternity passed before Lilly finally stood at the counter, biting her lower lip as they checked the Donald Clark family box.

They brought her a letter, postmarked from France, with tightly scrawled handwriting that could only belong to Reggie. Lilly clutched it to her chest and pushed her way to the door.

On the dusty street, Lilly paused, fighting the impulse to tear open Reggie's letter and know in seconds whether he was all right, unhurt, and missing her. But then it would be over, the news spilled out like sand on the Missouri River shore. Lilly gulped a breath and calmed her heart. No, it was better to wait, to savor each word and hear his voice as she read the letter slowly under the oak tree behind her house. Or perhaps she would go to the ridge, past the grove of maples that overlooked the river, and imagine him beside her as the sun slipped over to his side of the world. Lilly tucked the letter into her skirt pocket.

Marjorie's scream of delight preceded her from the post office. "It's from Harley!" She waved a wrinkled envelope at Lilly, her smile streaming across her face.

She ripped open her letter, and the envelope drifted to the ground. Lilly picked it up, watching Marjorie silently mouth Harley's words.

"He's okay," Marjorie mumbled absently.

Lilly breathed relief and gazed westward at the sun, now a jagged orange ball, low on the horizon. It had lost its fervor during the downward slide, and the air carried on it the cool scent of the Missouri. The field locusts began their twilight buzz, beckoning her homeward. Lilly limped away, leaving her friend standing in the street, a pebble among a beach of other women: sweethearts, mothers, and daughters who had paused to read the mail. But not just any mail. . .mail from France, Belgium, and all along the Western Allied front lines. Mail that gave them one more day to hope the madness and worry would soon end.

Reggie's letter burned a hole in Lilly's pocket, beseeching her to open it. She put her hand on the envelope, thankful for its presence. It was a shield against the unrelenting reminder of war and the horror that threatened to crash down upon her if Reggie never came home.

Chapter 3

The handwriting was bold and sturdy, the very essence of Reggie. Lilly clearly pictured him: his long fingers gripping a stubby pencil as he bent over the parchment, a shock of black hair flung over his chestnut brown eyes.

Lilly caught herself. Reggie's black hair had been shaved, kept short to ward off lice. And, the paper was smudged. Reality stabbed at her. Reggie would never willingly send her anything that was less than perfect. Her brow knit in worry as she devoured his words.

> *My Dearest Lilly,*
>
> *I would like to tell you it's quiet here, that Europe is beautiful and I'll return soon, but I know how you hate lies, and those would be falsehoods of great proportion. In truth, I sit now in a support trench, my back against a muddy dugout wall, hoping Harley and Chuck will help me stay warm tonight. It's not that it's cold; on the contrary, the blistering heat of June has been my greatest challenge yet. The urge to throw off my pack, my helmet, and this grating ammunition belt and scratch the sweat and slime from my body is nearly as great as my desire to gaze into your emerald eyes and see that you miss me, desperately, I hope. No, I'm not referring to the cold that comes with a gathering Dakota blizzard. I mean the cold fear that lurks in the silence between offensives. Alone, I cannot staunch the panic that floods my heart when I hear the command, "Over the top!" The charges are bloody and hopeless. We fling ourselves headlong toward the Germans, hoping to win their trench and thereby regain Europe, yard by yard. But I will never erase the sight of so many fellow soldiers, pale and lifeless in the mist at dawn, tangled in the lines of barbed wire that run through the no-man's-land between enemy lines. I stare at them and wonder if and when that will be me. It is then that I shiver.*
>
> *But Harley and Chuck help fend off the cold. Together we remember the things worth living for: you and Marjorie, little Christian and Olive and all the others we protect. We are our own fighting unit, and these brothers have become closer to me than blood. It is with them I hope to return to you, soon.*

Our troops are spread throughout Europe, providing the gaps left by Allied casualties in the French and British lines. I cannot tell you where I am stationed, but I serve with men such as Frances, Marc-Luc, Kenneth, and Simon.

As I reread this letter, I realize it's seems hopeless. But I am not hopeless. I have you and the vivid memory of your brown hair loosened and fingered by the wind as you waved me off that day, not quite a year ago, as our train pulled away from the platform. Your tears etched sorrow down your cheeks and spoke to me of your devotion to our plans. My thoughts are ever turned toward you, and if (I hate to write it, but I must) I should fall and perish on foreign soil, I pray you will remember me as yours, devoted until the end.

Faithfully,
Reggie

Lilly hugged the letter. Despite the horrors of war, the fear he fought by the hour, and the evident ache of loneliness, Reggie remained the perfect gentleman, honorable and devoted. Tears filled her eyes. Oh! God would just have to bring him back.

Lilly read the letter again, her tears blurring every word as night enfolded her. Lilly listened to the crickets hum and the melody of the grass as the breeze danced off the river. She wondered if Reggie was warm now. She ached to do something for him. . .but she could do nothing but pray. Reggie was in God's hands.

Wasn't that, however, what she feared the most? God was so unpredictable. What if Reggie wasn't a part of her future? What if he was to die in the war and she would never marry the boy she'd waited so long for?

But surely, God wouldn't do that to His faithful servant. Surely, she'd earned the right for Reggie to come home safely. She'd done everything right and proper, acting in perfect obedience. Wasn't that what religion was all about?

Lilly ground her nails into the palms of her hands as she looked past the dark fields toward the sparkling stars. She would not let panic leak into her letters. It would only spoil the pledge she and Reggie had made. Of course, God wanted them together. He was good and loving and blessed those who followed the church's teaching.

God could prove His love, however, by bringing Reggie safely home.

She picked a blade of grass and freed it to the wind. Reggie belonged to her. They had plans, a God-given future, and nothing, not even a war, could destroy it.

☙

Grateful to be out of the house, Lilly tightened her grip on her grocery basket's handle and picked up her pace along the dirt road. The heat pushed everyone to the edge of composure. It slithered into the house from the fields, soiling cotton blouses and melting patience. With three wild younger siblings, her sister Olive and her baby Christian living under the Clark roof, Lilly jumped at the scorching two-mile trek into town, hoping to find reprieve for her frazzled nerves.

Now, only the drone of buzzing grasshoppers accompanied her on the journey into Mobridge.

Daughters sent on last-minute errands packed Ernestine's Fresh Food Market. Lilly weaved past barrels of dill pickles, jars of sauerkraut, and burlap bags of dried corn and buckwheat kernels. The heady scent of peppermint and coffee encircled her as she slid into line, greeting Marjorie's sister Evelyn.

"What do you need today, Lilly?" Ernestine sighed, the sheen of perspiration glistening on her wide brow.

"Two pounds of flour, please."

Willard, Ernestine's balding husband, winked at Lilly as Ernestine dipped out the flour and poured it into Lilly's canvas bag.

"Get any letters from the front?" Willard's voice stayed low, but laughter sang in his eyes.

"Maybe," she replied, blushing.

His gray eyes twinkled. He winked again and turned away. Ernestine handed her the flour, and Lilly dropped a nickel into the shopkeeper's sweaty palm.

The basket groaned as Lilly dropped the bag of flour into it. She tucked it into the crook of her arm and pushed toward the door, where the late afternoon sun flooded over the threshold. As Lilly stepped out of the shop, it blinded her, and she plowed straight into a pair of thick, muscled arms.

"Oh, excuse me!" Lilly stumbled backward.

Wide hands clamped on her upper arms to steady her. Her victim's tall frame blocked the sun, and Lilly stared unblinking at a Viking with a crooked smile, golden blond hair, and eyes blue like the sky an hour before a prairie rainstorm. Lilly's heart thumped like a war drum in her chest.

"You again!" She pulled her arms from his grasp.

He fingered the brim of his battered ten-gallon hat in apology and salutation. "I keep running you over, fraulein." His grin teased, but his eyes spoke apology. "Pardon me."

Lilly felt a blush. "It's my fault this time." Her gaze skimmed his scuffed brown boots, then returned to his angular face. An attractive layer of blond whiskers outlined his rueful smile.

The cowboy's grin evaporated. For a moment, his brilliant blue eyes kneaded her with an obscure emotion. Then it morphed into pure mischievousness. He stepped aside and doffed his hat, sweeping low and indicating, like an Arthurian knight, that she should pass.

"Thank you," Lilly stammered. She swept past him, feeling his gaze on her back as she took off in a rapid clip.

Lilly was passing Miller's when she heard the ruckus start. Angry voices and a string of curses punctuated the air. Lilly whirled, horrified, wondering who would use such vile language in the middle of Main Street.

Brad, Gordy, and Allen Craffey, three burly brakemen and recent imports from Milwaukee, surrounded the man Lilly had bumped into. They pushed him with their offensive words to the middle of the street.

"What's the matter, can't ya read?" Brad brandished a long stick, poking at his victim.

Lilly's stomach clenched. The cowboy had his hands outstretched, as if trying to explain. Gibberish spewed from his mouth.

"I said, can't ya read?" Brad taunted.

The cowboy stilled, but his words hung like a foul odor. A crowd began to gather. Lilly could smell suspicion in the sizzling breeze. Then she saw the foreigner ball his fists.

"See this. . . ?" Gordy dashed up the steps to Ernestine's. An assembly of speechless women, Ernestine included, watched as he ripped a sign from her door. Lilly knew it well and hated it: No INDIANS ALLOWED.

Gordy scrambled down the steps and flung it at the man's feet. "No Injuns allowed!"

The stunned onlookers stared at him, awaiting his reply. The cowboy spoke in tight, clipped English, enunciating each word. "I. . .am. . .not. . .an. . .Indian."

Obviously. His fair skin and white-blond hair could hardly be compared to the crimson tan of the Oglala Sioux. But his accent alienated him. Lilly swallowed the hard lump in her throat. What was this young, strong foreigner doing here when the majority of Mobridge's male population was overseas fighting for their lives? An ugly murmur shifted through the crowd.

Lilly noticed Ed Miller, Roy Flanner, and Morrie from the barbershop clumped on the boardwalk, watching with stony eyes.

"Where ya from, blondie?" Brad said it, but it could have been anyone's voice.

"Deutschland." The cowboy lifted his chin slightly.

"Dutch land!" Gordy screamed. "Where's that?"

"I think it's near England!"

"It's next to Norway!"

"Isn't that where they make those wooden shoes?"

Lilly felt as if she'd been slugged. *No, it's our enemy, the people who are trying to kill your sons and husbands.* They had a German right here in their midst.

Brad took the confusion and turned it into violence. He cursed and shoved the German with his stick. Lilly held in a horrified scream as Gordy pounced on the German's back and Brad landed a blow into the man's chest. He sagged slightly, lost his hat. Brad trampled it and slammed his fist into the German's stomach. He grunted. Lilly winced. A broken bottle suddenly appeared in Allen's grip. The wiry Craffey sneered at the German and slashed wildly.

Lilly's breath caught when the German threw Gordy off his back then caught Brad's stick above his head. He wrenched it from Brad's grasp, while dodging Allen's jagged weapon.

Why didn't the German attack? Throw a punch to defend himself? Lilly teetered at the edge of the boardwalk, horrified yet transfixed. Craffeys came at him time and again, yet he stood his ground, no quarter given, but none taken.

Allen hurled the bottle at the German, and it ripped a gash down the side of his face.

Lilly bit her trembling lip and fought with herself. She should help him. No one had moved to his defense. Shame tasted like bile in her throat. What kind of town had Mobridge turned into when a group of Christians let a man be beaten? What had he done but be a foreigner in a suffering town?

Then again, he wasn't any foreigner; he was German. He deserved to be beaten.

Her sense of justice grabbed her and screamed logic. This German was not part of the Central Powers, the German/Austrian force that started the Great War. He might be an unwelcome presence in their town—but he hadn't caused the deaths of their South Dakota cowboys.

And Lilly could not let the Craffey boys cause his death.

She dropped the basket and ran headlong into the fight.

Chapter 4

Lilly didn't know what terrified her more, the venomous look on Gordy Craffey's face or her own bloodcurdling scream. The sound scattered the Craffey brothers with the effectiveness of three quick jabs.

Brad and Allen stared at her, eyes wide, backing away from her. Lilly halted in a strategic location between the Craffey brothers and the bleeding German. Balling her hands on her hips, she planted her feet and tried to appear fierce. Her pulse roared in her ears.

Gordy Craffey picked himself off the dirt. He stepped toward Lilly like a boxer, his fists high. "Get out of here, Lilly Clark."

Lilly shook her head, trying to summon her voice. She glanced at the German. His wide chest rose and fell in rapid rhythm; blood dripped off his chin.

"I said get, Lilly." Hatred animated Gordy's dark eyes.

Lilly held her breath. Would Gordy strike her? With his whitened fists and neck muscles bunched, he resembled a mad bull. Lilly battled the impulse to flee. *There are at least fifty people watching,* she reasoned. *Gordy wouldn't dare hit me.* Judging by the angry scowls from the onlookers, Lilly wasn't so sure they wouldn't join ranks with the Craffeys and drag her, kicking and screaming, from the fight.

She crossed her hands over her chest and fought a violent tremble. "Leave him alone, Gordy. Save your anger for the real enemy."

Apprehension rode through Mobridge on a smoldering breeze. Lilly smelled the foul odor of perspiration as she met Gordy's black eyes. They narrowed, raising gooseflesh over Lilly.

"Get him outta here," he growled.

Lilly freed a shuddering breath and glanced at the German. "Do you have a wagon?"

His gaze remained on Gordy as he jerked a nod.

"Good, you can drive me home."

Lilly dodged Gordy's searing gaze as she and the German back stepped. When they reached a graying buckboard parked in front of Bud Graham's pharmacy, the German untied the rig while Lilly scanned the faces of the townspeople. It wouldn't take long for news to race across the prairie. She briefly considered bandages for the German's wound, but when she saw the cold abhorrence in Bud's eyes, she snared her broken basket and climbed into the wagon.

"Where to?" the man asked without looking at her.

"North out of town, about two miles."

The acrid stares of the townspeople burned Lilly's neck as she rode tall and eyes forward on the bench. But her mind wrung out her impulsive actions. How many understood the German's words? Lilly bit a quivering lip.

They churned the dust into a thick cloud as they galloped out of the valley and into the yellowing bluffs. Horror throbbed behind Lilly's every thought, and only her grip on the bench kept her from covering her face with her hands and weeping. What had she just done?

Aside from the obvious foolishness of riding alone with a stranger, she'd just stuck her neck out, in full view of the entire Mobridge population, for a virtual enemy, for someone her own Reggie was trying to kill—and avoid being killed by! *Traitor*. Lilly went cold.

A mile out of town, the German slowed the horses to a walk. The road rippled as waves of heat skimmed it. Overhead, a stealthy red-tailed hawk hunted jackrabbits in an erratic pursuit. The field locusts hissed, interrupted only by the roar of an intermittent breeze. Perspiration layered Lilly's forehead and began a slow slide down her cheek.

She glanced at the man she'd saved. Blood continued to drip onto his work pants, but he seemed mindless of it. His eyes were trained upon the horses, the endless prairie, perhaps even a land far away across the ocean.

"Are you okay?" Lilly ventured. *No, obviously not!* Lilly grimaced at her question. *He is bleeding and was attacked by three men!* Lilly recalled the confusion, perhaps even panic, which twisted his foreign words. It had horrified her; now she only felt sorry for him. Her own countrymen sickened her.

Bigotry always incensed her. It only took her history with the never-ending problem of the prairie dogs to see that injustice eclipsed all rational thinking on her part. Her father was always inventing new ways to extinguish the pests, and it wasn't without a measure of sympathy for the furry creatures from the women in his family. For a time, Lilly headed up a smuggling ring, teaching Bonnie, DJ, and Frankie how to sleuth out and uncover the dammed-up dens. Then her father discovered their scheme and employed the thin end of a willow switch to help them see the error of their ways. Nevertheless, pity swept over Lilly every time she saw one dart through their carrot patch, and although she shooed them away, she still couldn't bring herself to alert the local posse. Perhaps, as Lilly watched the Craffey brothers pummel the hapless blond German, she'd been reminded of a prairie dog—hated and stalked. Perhaps that was why she flew into the middle of a street brawl, abandoning her common sense.

She was going to regret that act as soon as her father found out. And what if Reggie heard about it? Aiding and abetting the enemy in his own backyard. Lilly shuddered.

The horses snorted. Their coats were spotted with sweat, darkening their chocolate hides. The German clucked twice to them, encouraging their labors.

Out of the corner of her eye, Lilly scrutinized the blond, German cowboy. His eyes were hooded, and they squinted in the light. He'd left his hat in the dust back in Mobridge, and Lilly couldn't help notice his golden hair had dried into a curly, askew mop. He had a strong jaw, now clenched, as if reliving the fight.

Lilly cleared her throat and asked again, louder, "Are you okay?"

The German shrugged, deflecting her concern. Lilly frowned, annoyed. Didn't he know what her actions might cost her?

"You could at least thank me! You know, I'll never be welcome in town again because of you."

"I didn't ask for your help." His toneless reply sent fury into her veins.

"But you needed it. They could have killed you!"

The German turned, pinning on her an eternal, impenetrable gaze. Lilly raised her chin against it. Then the corner of his mouth upturned in a teasing grin.

"You think so, *ja*?"

Lilly's mouth sagged open, and she bit back a flood of hurt. *What an ego.* Lilly focused on the sharpening outline of the Clark farm.

Beside her, the German chuckled. She glared at him. He drove, eyes ahead, a loose smile playing on his lips. His powerful sunbaked forearms rested on the patched knees of his work pants as he fingered the reins, and he was so tall sitting beside her, she could hide inside his massive shadow. The absurdity of her protective act hit Lilly like a fist. This man was no prairie dog. No wonder he had laughed.

Lilly hung her head as a blush crept up her face.

Who was this man? Why was he here? Frustration blurted out her question. "What's your name?"

The German peeked at her and hesitated slightly before answering. "They call me Henry. Henry Zook."

"Henry Zook." Lilly twisted the name over her tongue.

"But my friends call me by my given name, Heinrick." He said it in a tone that made it sound like a request.

Lilly bit her lip. Friends? She wasn't, couldn't be his friend. A knot tightened in her stomach.

"Stop please!"

Heinrick yanked on the reins, and the horses skittered to a stop. They were still a stone's throw from the Clark lane, but common sense screamed at her to leave, immediately.

"What is it?"

Lilly gathered her skirt and hauled herself over the side. Heinrick watched her without a word as she retrieved her basket. When Lilly glanced at him, however, his jaw hardened and he swallowed. Lilly stepped away and waited for him to drive off.

Heinrick made to slap the horses, then paused. He turned and looked at her, and a palpable sadness filled his eyes. Lilly felt a small place in her heart tear apart.

"Thank you," Heinrick said in a soft tone. Then he flicked the reins and trotted away.

Chapter 5

"Mother, I'm back." Lilly swiped off her straw hat as the screen door slammed behind her.

Mother Clark entered the mudroom, wiping her hands on her patchwork apron. She scowled as she took the smashed basket from Lilly's hands.

"What happened to this?"

Lilly hung her hat on one of the pegs fastened to the wall. She steadied her voice, hoping it sounded close to normal. "I'm sorry, Mother. I dropped it."

Her mother first examined the basket, then she scrutinized Lilly's flushed face. Lilly offered a rueful smile and saw concern seep into her mother's brown eyes.

"Well," her mother said at last, "Go wash up. Dinner is almost prepared."

Lilly poured herself a bowl of water and washed off a sticky layer of prairie dust, as well as, she hoped, any indications of her outrageous behavior in town and the disturbing ride home. She freshly braided her hair and pronounced herself recovered, despite an odd soreness in her heart.

Dinner hour in the Clark home was as sacred as a church service. Lilly heard her father tramping about upstairs as he washed off the dirt from the fields and changed out of his grimy overalls. Her younger sister, Bonnie, hollered from the front door, and a moment later DJ and Frankie blew in from the yard like twisters. Lilly poured fresh milk into glasses while her mother removed a batch of biscuits from the wood-burning oven.

"Any news from town, Lilly?" Olive breezed in with a clean and chubby-faced Christian on her hip. Lilly's mouth went dry.

"Olive, could you please open a jar of pickles?" Mother Clark untied her headscarf and apron, hanging them on a hook near the mudroom door. Olive headed for the pantry, and Lilly licked her dry lips and felt her heartbeat restart. Maybe she could keep a lid on her latest reckless exploit.

Her father blew a feathery kiss across her mother's cheek, then took his position at the head of the table. The family gathered around him, leaving an opening where Olive's husband, Chuck, normally sat. Her mother set a bowl of gravy on the table and slid next to her husband on a long bench. Lilly noticed her father's face seemed drawn. After he asked the blessing, she discovered why.

242

"A drought is coming. I read it in the almanac, and I see it in the clear blue sky. No rain. The soil is drying up, and even the wheat I planted in last year's fallow field is withering."

Her mother slid a hand over her husband's clasped hands. Lilly noticed her father's green eyes seemed to age. "We need to find a way to lay up stores for the winter. I don't think we'll make enough on the wheat to hold us through."

Her father couldn't tend the crops alone, and without Chuck's help, the eighty acres he'd added two years ago would revert to the bank.

Despite the beckoning aroma of beef sauced in onion and dill gravy, dinner went nearly untouched. Only Frankie and DJ dove into their food. Lilly wished, just this once, she had their naive trust.

Olive adjusted Christian on her knee and handed him a biscuit scrap. "I volunteered to help out at the armory, with Red Cross packages, but maybe I can find a job, instead. I know they're advertising for cooks at Fannie's boardinghouse."

Her father, who had been examining his fork, glanced at her and smiled. But his eyes spoke regret.

Lilly played with the fraying edge of her cotton napkin. "Mrs. Torgesen asked me to make her something for the Independence Day picnic," she said. "That will help." She peeked at her mother, who flashed a reassuring grin.

"We'll all work together and put it into the Lord's hands," her father quietly summed up. The matter was dropped, but apprehension lingered as the shadows stretched out in dusty patterns along the kitchen floor.

❧

"Have you lost your senses, or are you *trying* to destroy your life?" Olive added a hiss to her furious whisper.

Lilly clasped her hands and sat still as stone on the straight-back chair. News traveled like a lightning bolt across the prairie and, as Olive marched out her fury on the clapboard floor of Lilly's second-story bedroom, Lilly knew her rash behavior in town had ignited.

Olive bounced little Christian over to her other hip. Christian giggled at the bumpy ride. The two year old loosened a strand of his mother's chestnut brown hair, unraveling the bun at the nape of her neck, to match Olive's demeanor. Her sister had stomped home an hour earlier, her after-dinner stroll with Elizabeth White destroyed by "a sordid tale that involved Lilly cavorting with a stranger in town."

"You have no idea who that man is, nor where he is from. He could have hurt you!" Olive's voice rose a pitch. Lilly winced. "You stepped into a fight that was none of your business! I heard the Craffeys caught him stealing—he had two apples in his coat pocket!"

"He wasn't wearing a coat, Olive."

"And he spoke a different language—like he was demon-possessed!"

Olive paused in her tirade to plunk Christian down on the double bed Lilly shared with Bonnie. Christian rolled across the quilt, drooling.

Lilly sucked a calming breath of air. "Olive, listen. I admit my foolishness." She held up her hands in surrender. "I won't do it again."

Olive bent down and glared into Lilly's face. "You bet you won't. Because if you do, I'll tell Chuck. . .and he'll tell Reggie!"

Lilly recoiled as if she'd been slapped. Her sister's threat hung in the air like an odor. Lilly willed her voice steady. "Don't worry, Olive. I don't even know who he is. I'll never talk to him again, I promise."

Olive clamped her hands onto her narrow hips. "You better not, or you'll be sorry." She scooped up Christian. "Reggie doesn't need distractions, Lilly. Do you want to get him killed?"

Lilly gasped. Olive stormed out, slamming the bedroom door behind her.

Lilly closed her eyes. "Please, God, no." She hadn't considered that perhaps God would punish her for helping the German. Perhaps He, too, considered her a traitor. But would He let Reggie die because she'd sinned?

Lilly fought the insidious idea and walked over to the window seat. The cushion in the alcove was one of her first sewing projects, a calico pillow in blue and yellow. Lilly climbed into the nook, pulled her knees to her chest, and rested her head on her crossed arms. The prairie stretched to the far horizon, forever past the hundred and twenty acres that belonged to the Clark family. The sun painted the wheat field hues of rose gold and the hay field to the north a jade green. Her father would begin haying soon, cutting the grass, letting it dry, and gathering it up into giant mounds for cattle feed during the winter.

Was it only two years ago she'd worked with Reggie, mowing the hay? She smiled at the image of his serious brown eyes, the sun baking his back and arms. Even then, he'd wanted to protect her. "Lilly-girl, you shouldn't be working here. This is men's work." She wanted to cry. After all he'd done for her, and she'd betrayed him.

Oh God, please send him home! If Reggie were here, perhaps he'd be working with Chuck, dragging in water from the Missouri to keep the crop alive.

The front door slammed, and she watched her father stride out to the barn, heading for the evening milking. The Clarks had two dozen Holstein her father used to run a fairly lucrative dairy route on the west side of the Missouri to the ranchers who didn't raise milkers.

But if the prairie dried up, so would their Holsteins. Lilly's eyes burned. The threat of drought made her escapade in town seem all the worse.

"I'm sorry, Reggie, I'm sorry." Had she really betrayed him? Lilly pressed her fists into her eyes, but she couldn't erase the clear image of Heinrick, hands up in surrender, backing away from the Craffey boys, jabbering incoherently. Nor could she forget the tone of longing in his voice when he'd offered his name in friendship. No, she hadn't done anything wrong; she'd merely performed a Christian duty of kindness. At least she hoped that was true. She hoped she hadn't somehow stepped over the line of faithfulness to Reggie or to her country and summoned punishment from the Almighty for her misbehavior. Dread seeped into her bones.

"Please forgive me, God," she moaned feebly.

She would never see the German again. Lilly resolved it in her heart, to herself, to Reggie, and finally to God.

Chapter 6

"Please, Mrs. Torgesen, just two more pins." Lilly snatched a straight pin from the corner of her mouth while she struggled with the flimsy newspaper pattern.

Mrs. Torgesen, wiggling about as if she were a two year old, held the latest edition of the *Ladies Home Journal* and flipped from page to page as if window-shopping in Boston.

"Oh, this eggshell blue chiffon is just breathtaking! How long did you say it would take to order?"

Lilly stifled a groan as another page tore across Mrs. Torgesen's ample backside. Doggedly, she pinned it together. "Two weeks, earliest."

Mrs. Torgesen sighed, then glanced down at Lilly. "Well, how's it coming?"

Lilly managed a smile. "Do you want pleats or gathers?"

Mrs. Torgesen hopped off the tiny stool, and Lilly heard the remainder of her pattern rip to shreds. She sighed and conceded defeat. Mrs. Torgesen would change it three or four times before completion, anyway. Lilly stuck the pins into her wrist cushion and collected the scraps of paper.

"How about this one?" Mrs. Torgesen held out the magazine, pointing to a picture of a two-tiered gown in muted lavender. The skirt slid to just below the knees, with wide pleated rows running hip to hip. An underskirt, in the same shade, continued to the ankles. The bodice was a simple white cotton blouse with puffed sleeves and a boat-style neck. What made the piece stunning was the sheer lace lavender overcoat that covered the blouse and flared out over the hips. The ensemble was then secured with a wide satin belt, accentuated on the side with a six-inch satin rosebud.

"How exquisite." Lilly passed back the magazine.

"Make it for me, Lilly. I know you can." Mrs. Torgesen rained a toothy grin down on her. Lilly smiled as if she couldn't wait, but she wanted to grimace. The woman would be a giant purple poppy.

Lilly stood up. "Let's see what you have for fabric. Maybe I can do it from scraps."

"You know where the fabric is, dear." Mrs. Torgesen patted her glistening brow with a lace-edged handkerchief. "I need a glass of lemonade." She waddled off toward the kitchen.

Lilly always thought Mrs. Torgesen could be described by one word: excessive. She was a woman who couldn't be contained—or contain anything, including her appetite for food and clothing. She lived with one foot dangling in the waters of lavishness and laughed away the criticism of brow-raising conservatives from the North Dakota border on down. Yet all tolerated Mrs. Torgesen, despite her fanciful ideas, and Lilly supposed it was for one very large reason—the breadth and strength of the Torgesen T cattle ranch.

Lilly slipped off her wrist cushion and tucked it inside her sewing box. She considered it a blessing to be employed by Mrs. Torgesen—not only did it allow her to work with feather-fine silk, transparent chambray, and filmy chiffon, but Mrs. Torgesen's dreams pushed Lilly's skills to new heights. And, despite Mrs. Torgesen's desire to dress like a French dame, her generosity had helped Lilly finance her wedding dress and prepare for the event she knew her father would struggle to provide. And now, the work could help keep the Clark family fed.

Lilly headed upstairs to the sewing room. Mrs. Torgesen couldn't even sew a straight stitch, but she owned a gleaming black Singer. Lilly preferred, however, to bring her work home and sew in the comfort of her bedroom, laying the pattern out on the hardwood floor or on the kitchen table. And, at home, her mother was always available for advice.

The high sun spilled through the yellow calico curtains, lighting the corner room in an array of cheery colors.

The remnant fabric was stuffed into a three-door oak wardrobe. The doors creaked as they opened, the wood split from years of dry prairie heat. Lilly wrinkled her nose against the pungent odor of mothballs and dove in, wading through a sea of jeweled fabrics from dyed wool in jade and mauve to calicos in every shade of blue.

Lilly finally unearthed five yards of plain, seafoam green cotton and a piece of white flowered lace large enough for the overcoat. Perhaps she could dye it. Tucked in the back, behind a piece of red calico, she pulled out a forest green satin, perhaps meant for a pillow edge. It would make a perfect sash. Mrs. Torgesen would be a flowing willow, drifting along Main Street on Independence Day. Lilly stifled a chuckle.

Lilly was piling the fabric pieces onto a small box table next to the Singer when movement in the yard below caught her eye.

The sight of a golden mustang, bucking and writhing beneath its rider in the sunbaked corral made her step toward the window. The animal's black eyes bulged with terror as the cowboy atop the bronc whooped, grabbed the saddle horn, and spurred the horse. The mustang reared, then threw himself forward and bucked, flaying out his hind legs. Sweat flicked off his body. Lilly stood transfixed at the desperate wrestle.

Suddenly, the cowboy dropped one of the split reins. Lilly winced as she watched him grab for the saddle horn. His whooping had stopped and only her thundering heart filled the silence as the horse bucked and kicked, twisting under its mount. Then, with a violent snap, the mustang pitched the cowboy into the air. Lilly watched him climb the sky in an airborne sprawl. He flew a good ten feet and landed with a poof of prairie smoke.

The mustang continued to twist, jump, and kick in a hysterical dance. His wide hooves landed closer to the hapless cowboy with each furious snort. All at once, the animal reared, pawing the air above the terrified rider. The man wrapped his arms around his head, curled into a ball, and waited to be trampled.

Lilly covered her eyes and peeked through her fingers.

Suddenly, a figure erupted from the barn door. A blond whirlwind, he burst right up to the furious animal. Holding out both hands as if to embrace the beast, he closed quickly and in a lightning motion snared the dangling reins and planted his feet. The downed cowboy scrambled toward the barn.

The mustang reared and snorted. The man extended his hand to catch the horse's line of vision. The horse jerked his head and pawed at the ground, but with each snort, the terror dissipated, his feet calming their erratic dance until, in one long exhale, he stopped prancing altogether. The man brought a steady hand close to the horse's eye. The mustang bobbed his head twice, then let his captor touch his velvet nose. After a moment, the man stepped close and rubbed the bronc between his eyes and over his jaw.

Lilly exhaled and realized she'd been holding her breath. Whoever he was, the cowboy had a way with animals that tugged at her heart and stole her breath. As she watched, the man turned and looked toward the house. The sun glinted in his blue eyes, and he wore an unmistakable half-smile. Lilly jumped away from the window. Her heart did an erratic tumble in her chest, and her skin turned to gooseflesh. Despite her vow, she'd somehow found Heinrick.

❧

Lilly heaped the fabric into a ball, scooped it into her arms, and scrambled downstairs. Her heart flopped like a freshly netted fish, dazed and horrified at the recent turn of events. The last thing she needed was a reminder of yesterday's scandalous incident. She would keep her head down and flee like a jackrabbit from the Torgesen T and its troublesome German.

"Ma, I don't think Buttercup is the right name for that mustang!" Clive Torgesen slammed the screen door and dragged a trail of prairie dust into the kitchen. Lilly skidded to a halt in the doorway, clutching the fabric to her chest. She didn't realize it had been Clive, Mrs. Torgesen's uncouth son, who had ridden the terrorized animal. At best, Clive was a roadblock to a speedy, unsuspicious escape; at worst, he would smear her with one of his crude remarks and recount yesterday's embarrassing tale in embellished detail. Lilly gritted her teeth and sidled out of view.

The fair-haired Torgesen boy was one of the lucky—he'd been granted a bye in the enlistment lottery. Some thought it was because he was Ed Torgesen's only son. Others believed it had something to do with a wad of George Washingtons in the county registrar's back pocket. Nevertheless, Clive Torgesen was now one of the few, and of them the most, eligible bachelors in the state.

To Lilly's way of thinking, that wasn't saying much. Underneath the ruggedly handsome exterior—his curly, sandy-blond hair, his earth-brown eyes, and his heavy-duty muscles—was a completely rotten core. As her father liked to say, "There was a foul smell to that bird's stuffin'." Lilly had the unfortunate experience of sitting next to Clive in school. She'd seen his pranks firsthand, from cutting off the braids of little girls to throwing youngsters into the Missouri River in October. Now older, he was downright dangerous. Lilly had heard the gossip, seen the faces of girls he'd "courted," and doubted the honor of the man in the wide-brimmed black Stetson.

Clive plopped down in a willow-backed chair next to his mother at the kitchen table. The housekeeper, Eleanor, served him a sweating glass of lemonade, and he guzzled it down.

Mrs. Torgesen dabbed at her forehead with her handkerchief. "Your father thinks the mustang will make a wonderful stallion. He is expecting two brood mares from Wyoming in a week or so."

"Well, he's impossible to ride. He ought to be hobbled."

"Hobbled!" Lilly cried and burst through the door. "What he needs is a gentle hand, Clive."

Clive sat back in his chair and tipped up his hat with one long, grimy finger. "Well, Lilly Clark. Since when are you the expert on wild horses?"

Lilly clamped her mouth shut. Her face burned, and she wanted to melt through the polished clapboard floor. Mrs. Torgesen leveled a curious frown at her. Lilly swallowed, and held out the fabric to Mrs. Torgesen. "I think I found something that might work," she croaked.

Mrs. Torgesen turned her attention back to Clive. "Give him a week or so, dear. He'll settle down. Pick a different horse."

Clive snuffed. "I almost had him broke, too, Ma. Until that stupid German interfered."

Mrs. Torgesen peeked at Eleanor, then drilled a sharp look into Clive. "He's not German, Clive. He's from Norway, just like us."

Clive's eyes narrowed, squeezing out something unpleasant. An eerie silence embedded the room while Clive and Mrs. Torgesen sipped their lemonade and glowered at each other. Lilly glanced at Eleanor, but she busily stirred a pot of bubbling jam on the stove. The sharp, sweet smell of strawberries saturated the humid air.

Clive gulped the last of his drink. He examined the glass, turning it in his hand. "Well, whatever he is, he's a troublemaker, and I'd keep my eye on him if I was you, Ma."

Mrs. Torgesen slid a dimpled hand onto Clive's arm. "That's why you're the foreman."

Clive emitted a loud "humph." He set the glass on the table and ran a finger around the edge. "So that means I can do what I want with him, right?"

"It's your crew, dear."

Clive smiled, but evil prowled about his dark eyes. He stood and tipped his hat to Lilly. "See ya 'round." He winked at her as he turned away.

The bile rose in the back of Lilly's throat.

Mrs. Torgesen sighed. "Let me see the fabric, Lilly."

The next two hours crawled by as Lilly fashioned a makeshift pattern from a remnant piece of muslin. The costume would require a mile of fabric, it seemed, and Mrs. Torgesen would bake in it under the hot summer sun, but she obviously had no regard for such discomforts.

"I want it ready by the Fourth of July."

Lilly pushed a rebel strand of brown hair behind her ear. One week. "Yes, ma'am."

The low sun tinged the clouds with gold and amber as Lilly plodded home. Three miles to go and her arms screamed from the weight of the small mountain of fabric. But the wind was fresh on her face and not only had she avoided another perilous run-in with the German, but neither Mrs. Torgesen nor Clive hinted Lilly might know him. Either they hadn't heard or they were hoping she'd keep their secrets if they kept hers.

A hawk circled above, and Lilly heard Reggie's voice, strong and wise, in her head. *"Watch the hawk, Lilly, it will lead you to dinner."* She didn't do much hunting, but somehow his words stuck in her memory. Just like his firm hand upon the small of her back, or nimble fingers playing with her hair. She could never forget his kiss—just one, on an eve such as this, as the sun slid behind the bluffs beyond the river. She and Reggie had strolled to her favorite refuge, a tiny retreat nestled in a grove of maples. There, he told her he would marry her. He didn't have anything to give her, he said, "but his promise." Then he cupped her face in his strong hands and kissed her.

He'd left for the war the next day, yet she could still feel his thumb caressing her cheek, feel his lips upon hers. *Oh Reggie, please come home soon.*

The creak of a buckboard scattered her memories. At a hot breath over her shoulder, Lilly gasped and sprang into the weeds lining the dirt road. Laughter, rich, deep, and unpretentious, filled the air. Lilly whirled, squinting into the sunlight.

"Hello. We meet again." Heinrick greeted her with a sweeping white smile and twinkling blue eyes.

Lilly's heart raced like a jackrabbit eluding prey.

"Want a ride?"

Lilly shook her head.

"C'mon. I can repay you for saving me." His grin seemed mischievous.

"I thought you said you didn't need saving." Lilly shut her impulsive mouth and squeezed the fabric to her chest.

He raised his eyebrows. "Did I say that?"

Lilly frowned. Had he? It didn't matter. She wasn't getting into a buckboard with an enemy of the community. She'd vowed it to Reggie and to God, and she wasn't going to break her promise.

"I don't want a ride." Lilly stepped into the road and started walking, her legs moving in crisp, quick rhythm. "Thank you, anyway."

Heinrick followed her, the horses meandering down the road.

"Go away, Mr. Zook!" Lilly called over her shoulder, annoyance pricking her.

"My friends call me Heinrick!"

"I'm not your friend."

He did not immediately reply, and Lilly felt the sting of her words. The locusts hissed from the surrounding fields, their disapproval snared and carried to her by an unrelenting prairie wind. Lilly pounded out her steps in silence, her knuckles white as she clutched the fabric.

"Why not?"

Lilly stopped and whirled on her heels. "Because you are German! And if you haven't noticed, America is in a war against Germany! My fiancé, Reggie, is over there," she flung her arm out eastward, "trying not to get killed by your countrymen. I can hardly accept a ride from a man who may have relatives shooting my future husband at this very moment!" She sucked a breath of dry, searing air and willed her heart to calm. "That, Mr. Zook, is why I can't be your friend."

She saw a glimmer of hope die in his eyes with her painful words, and Heinrick's misshapen grin slowly vanished. A shard of regret sliced through her. She wasn't a rude person, but she had no choice but to be brutally frank. They were at war, America and Germany, she and Heinrick. And war was ruthless.

"Please, just leave me alone," Lilly pleaded.

Heinrick nodded slowly. "I understand." His eyes hardened. "But that's going to be a bit hard, seeing we both work for the Torgesens."

"Try, please, or you're going to get us both into a mess of trouble."

He leveled an even, piercing gaze on her. "I am sorry, fraulein. Trouble is the last thing I hope to bring you. I'd much prefer to bring you flowers." Then he slapped the horses and took off in a fast trot.

Lilly gaped as she watched him ride away, his muscular back strong and proud against a withering prairie backdrop. Then her throat began to burn, and by the time she neared her house, she was wiping away a sheet of tears.

Chapter 7

An early afternoon sun cast ringlets of light through Lilly's eyelet curtains and across her vanity. Her brown hair was swept up into a neat braided bun, and a slight breeze, tinged with the smell of fresh lily of the valley, played with the tendrils of hair curling around her ears. Lilly bent over her parchment, scribing her words.

June 28, 1918

My Dearest Reggie,

My thoughts were with you this morning as we walked to church. DJ, who'd lingered behind us, startled a ring-necked pheasant into flight, and I recalled the year when you found an entire nest and gave us three for Thanksgiving dinner. I also remember Harley's envy that year when you brought in two bucks to his doe. I am counting on your aim to protect you and Chuck and can't help but shiver with you when I think of you huddling in the foxholes. I haven't said a word to Olive, who, I fear, believes you all within the safety of a fortified Paris. Perhaps it's for the best; she and little Chris prefer the cheerful reports from the censored Milwaukee Journal.

On to glad news. The city fathers have agreed to preserve tradition and host the Mobridge rodeo on Independence Day. In the absence of many regular participants, they have extended an invitation to the children, allowing them to compete in the center ring. Frankie is hilarious with joy. He commandeered Father's plow and spent the last week practicing his steer roping. As Father won't let him near the cows, Sherlock became his unfortunate victim. Frank stood upon the plow, flung about him the lasso you constructed, and then wrestled the hapless spaniel to the dirt. After three days of tireless practice, Sherlock finally crawled behind the lattice under the back porch, and since Friday has refused to reappear. Twice I saw Mother slide a bowl of scraps under the steps; I believe she has more than an ounce of empathy for the old pup!

The prairie is already beginning to wilt; the black-eyed Susans and goldenrod, which were so vibrant only a month ago, have joined the fraying weeds. The heat this year is insufferable, and I know if you were here,

I'd find you in the Missouri, fighting the catfish for space. Do you miss the river and the song of the crickets at dusk? I can't imagine what France must be like—does it have coyotes or prairie dogs or cottonwoods to remind you of home?

Marjorie is distraught over Harley's cold. I hope he is recovering and has rejoined you in the trenches, not that I wish any of you there; rather I would have you all here. But I know how you must miss him, and I can't bear to imagine you alone during an offensive. May God watch over you.

Mother and Father send their love. I talked to your father in town two weeks ago, and he looked fit and calm, as is his nature. His courageous, faithful prayers continually inspire me; my own petitions seem so feeble in comparison. Nevertheless, my thoughts are constantly upon you and the pledge we made in the shadow of the maples near the bluff. Please come home to me.

Faithfully,
Lillian

Lilly folded the page, slid it into a creamy white envelope, and propped it against her round mirror. She hadn't mentioned Heinrick, and a sliver of deceit pierced her heart. But, why should she? She'd hardly mentioned the drought, either, for Reggie's own good. She didn't want him to worry, and neither did she want him to imagine a scenario that had never existed, would never exist, between her and Heinrick. Better to let the matter die in the dust. If he ever did ask, she would tell him she'd merely saved a man from a good pummeling.

She heard the screen door slam, then voices drift toward her room. Her heart skipped. The Larsens, and perhaps they had news from Reggie!

Or, and her smile fell at the thought, maybe they had news about her. So far, no one other than Olive had hinted a word about the event in Mobridge, already almost a week past. But, then again, her parents were busy people and didn't cotton to gossip. Unless, of course, it involved their daughter.

Lilly gulped a last bit of peaceful air, painted a smile on her face, and bounced down the stairs.

Rev. and Mrs. Larsen sat in two padded green Queen Anne chairs in the parlor, glasses of lemonade sweating in their hands. Rev. Larsen rose and greeted her. Lilly smoothed her white cotton dress, glad she hadn't changed after church, and sat next to her mother on a faded blue divan.

"So, news from Reggie?" she asked and tried to ignore the tremor in her voice.

Mrs. Alice Larsen shook her head. "Simply a social call to our future daughter-in-law and her parents."

Lilly grinned. The coast was clear, no storms brewing on the horizon. Olive sauntered into the room, little Chris on her hip, still in his Buster Brown church uniform. She waggled his pudgy arm at the small crowd. "Going for a nap," she said in a baby voice, then backed out of the room. She glanced at Lilly, who caught the scorching look, as if in reprimand, from her older sister.

"Reggie wrote and told us that you're planning to join the Red Cross?" Rev. Larsen asked Lilly.

Lilly shrugged. "Oh, that was just talk. I'm not sure right now."

"Well, I heard they need volunteers. It sounds like the work is endless." It seemed Rev. Larsen knew everyone's needs, business, and talents. At least those of his congregation. "I am sure Reggie would be proud."

Lilly blushed.

"Lilly's been doing a lot of sewing, especially for the Torgesen family." Her mother winked at Lilly.

Mrs. Larsen dabbed a lace-trimmed kerchief on her neck. "It's so nice that you can help out your family, and sewing is such a needed talent in the church. It will serve you well as a pastor's wife."

"Lilly has much to offer to help Reggie get a firm hold on a nice flourishing congregation when he returns."

Lilly shot a glance at her father. She suddenly felt like a prize milking cow, up on the auction block.

"That is, until she starts filling the house with babies." Mrs. Larsen cocked her head and slathered Lilly with soupy eyes. "I can't wait to be a grandmother."

"So Reggie is going into the ministry after the war?" Lilly's mother rose to refill the half-empty glasses.

Rev. Larsen nodded. "He's all ready to follow in his father's footsteps." He held out his glass. "But I won't be handing over the pulpit too quickly. He'll have to tuck some experience under his belt first. Maybe take on a smaller church, perhaps up north in Eureka, or plant a missionary church over in Java, that new Russian community."

Lilly stared past them at the patterned floral wallpaper her mother had lugged west from her home in Illinois. Her mother had been a banker's daughter, brought up on fine linens and satin draperies. Life on the prairie had toughened her hands and character, but her refined, padded childhood still lingered in her choice of home decor. Lace curtains blew at the open window, and a portrait of Lilly's stately maternal grandparents hung on the wall over the rolltop desk. Lilly often wondered who her mother had been before she'd met Donald Clark, before he'd moved her to the prairie, and before life with blizzards, drought, and birthing five children etched crow's-feet into her creamy face.

"Lilly, are you listening?" Her mother's voice pierced her musings.

"What?"

"Mrs. Larsen asked you if you'd started your wedding dress yet."

Mrs. Larsen leaned forward in her chair. A thick silence swelled through the room. The tick of the clock chipped out eternal seconds.

"Uh, well, no, actually. I felt I should wait."

With her words, the fear about Reggie's future ignited. The questions, the fears, the unknowns. With one bullet, one misstep in the no-man's-land between battle lines, their hopes would die. Mrs. Larsen gasped, her eyes filled, and she held a shaking hand to her lips.

Lilly hung her head. "I'm sorry."

Maybe she should start on her wedding dress, as much for her own sake as Mrs. Larsen's. Maybe that was just what she needed to get her focus back on the plan and erase the memory of her traitorous encounter with Heinrick. The fact that she easily conjured up his crooked smile or those dancing blue eyes bothered her more than she wanted to admit.

"Thank you for the lovely sermon today, Reverend." Mrs. Clark filled the silence. Rev. Larsen leaned back into the molded chair. It creaked. "Thank you, Ruth. The passage about Abraham and Isaac is such a difficult one to interpret."

Her father threw in his chip as if to reassure the preacher. "You did well, helping us to remember it was Abraham's obedience that won Isaac back to him. He obeyed God, regardless of the cost; that's what is important."

Rev. Larsen nodded. "That's what I continue to tell our young people," and he fastened steel eyes on Lilly, adopting his preaching tone, "Obedience to God and to the church is the only sure path in this world. If they want to find peace, they will walk it without faltering."

Lilly smiled meekly and noticed he'd balled his free hand on his lap, most likely a reflex action. Unfortunately, the Clark parlor had no pulpit to pound.

"Take Ruth, for example," he continued, his voice adopting a singing quality. "She, without a husband, obeyed her vows, despite the fact that it would mean a life without children, and followed Naomi to a foreign land. And God gave her Boaz and blessed her for her obedience."

" 'To obey is better than sacrifice,' Samuel told Saul," added Mrs. Larsen.

"That's right, dear." The reverend tightened his lips and nodded.

Bonnie entered the room with a plate of shortbread. Her mother took it from her and served the guests. "But what about faith? Wasn't it because of Abraham's faith that God counted him righteous?"

Lilly shot a quizzical look at her mother.

"Of course!" Rev. Larsen stabbed his finger in the air as if her mother had made his point. "Obedience is faith. It's faith in action. If we want to show God that we love Him, we will obey. And then, He will bless us—reward us for our faithfulness. Our obedience assures us of God's blessings and of His love."

Rev. Larsen shifted his gaze to Lilly's father. "That is why so many of our youth have problems today. They abandon the teachings of their church and parents. Without guidance, their lives simply run amuck."

Her father nodded soberly.

"But not your Lilly, here." Every eye turned toward Lilly. "I always told Reggie that Lilly would make a fine wife. I've watched her since her childhood, especially while Reggie was at school, and decided she would have no problem being a submissive, obedient wife. I told Reggie so when he returned from college." He leaned forward, balancing his elbows on both knees, and pinned her with a sincere look. "I'm glad he listened to me."

Lilly forced a smile. Had Reggie chosen her because of his father? No, Reggie said he'd been chasing her since her bloomer days. She couldn't believe the look in Reggie's eyes was anything but true love. Besides, she *would* be a good wife. She would see to that herself. She had no intention of falling off the path of the straight and narrow and landing "amuck," as Rev. Larsen so delicately stated it. She knew her path in life, and when God brought Reggie home, she would start walking down it.

Lilly saw Mrs. Larsen dab at her forehead. She suddenly became conscious of her own glistening brow and the oppressive heat that filtered through the lace from the prairie. It oozed into her pores, flowed under her skin, and bubbled in a place inside her body. The pictures of her grandparents spun at odd angles.

"Will you excuse me, please?" Lilly rose to her feet, reaching out her hand to grasp the back of her chair.

"Lilly, are you ill?" Her mother put down the tray.

Lilly shook her head. "I just feel a bit hot and dizzy."

"By all means, go lie down." Mrs. Larsen had also risen, concern on her pale face. Somehow, the woman managed to avoid the sun despite living in a virtual oven.

"Thank you for coming, Rev. Larsen, Mrs. Larsen." Lilly fingered her temple, as if her head were throbbing. But as she exited the parlor and felt a cool breeze filter in from the kitchen, she realized it wasn't dizziness that had attacked her in the parlor. . .it felt more like the numbing grasp of suffocation.

Chapter 8

The week before Independence Day passed in a flurry of fabric, needles, and fittings. Lilly hiked out to the Torgesen ranch three times during the week to fit the skirt, then the bodice, and finally the end product.

She couldn't help but look for Heinrick. His presence at the Torgesen T was a magnet, and despite the warnings in her heart, Lilly couldn't stop herself from scanning the horizon as she left the ranch, certain she would see him and strangely disappointed when she didn't. Of course, if she had, she would have ignored him, but still, the fact that he seemed to be avoiding her registered an odd despondency in her heart.

Mrs. Torgesen did resemble a willow tree. Lilly's mother dug up a half-bottle of Christmas dye, and Lilly colored the lace overcoat a rose-leaf green. The three shades of green blended into a pleasing harmony, and Mrs. Torgesen bubbled with delight as she sashayed around the kitchen during the final fitting.

"Lilly, dear, fetch the millinery box from the parlor, will you? I want you to see the new hat I ordered from Chicago. It came on yesterday's train."

Yesterday's train! Lilly had been so busy, she'd forgotten about the mail train the day before. Her heart pounded as she retrieved the hatbox. There might be a letter from Reggie waiting in her mailbox right now.

Lilly set the box down on the kitchen table. Mrs. Torgesen opened it and wiggled out a wide-brimmed, purposely misshapen hat. It was long and oval, meant to be propped low and sideways on Mrs. Torgesen's head. The brim curled like an upturned lip in the back and sported three layers of transparent white lace wound around the bowl. A flurry of leftover lace dangled from the back like a tail. The crowning feature of Mrs. Torgesen's new hat was a molded bluebird, nestled in the lacey layers and snuggled up to the shallow bowl of the hat in the front. Lilly swallowed a laugh—a bird in the willow! Mrs. Torgesen plopped the hat on her blond head and tied the mauve satin sash under her chin.

"Well?"

Lilly shook her head slowly. "Amazing."

Mrs. Torgesen glowed. "Well, just because one lives in the middle of a wasteland doesn't mean one has to blend!" She let out a hearty laugh, as did Lilly. The one thing Erica Torgesen *didn't* do was "blend."

The sun was still a high brilliant orb as Lilly stepped out into the Torgesen yard. Mrs. Torgesen had paid her well, and Lilly headed for town to pick up more sugar for her mother's currant jam, also planning a quick stop at the post office.

Lilly tugged on the brim of her straw hat and tucked her basket into the crook of her arm. A hot breeze whipped past her and brought with it a horse's whinny. Lilly shot a glance toward the corral just in time to sight a cowboy riding in astride a magnificent bay. The man didn't notice her. His shoulders sagged as if from exhaustion, and dust layered him like a second skin. But, as he dismounted, Lilly plainly recognized Heinrick. She gasped and reined in her traitorous heart. Her feet seemed rooted to the ground. Heinrick looped the horse's reins over the fence and turned toward the house.

In a breathless moment, Heinrick's eyes fastened upon her, and a wave of shock washed over his face. It seemed as though, in that instant, some film fell away from him and she could see him clearly, unfettered by prejudice and stereotypes. He was a man etching out a life on the prairie, building simple hopes, maybe a home and a family, just like every pioneer before him. The sense of it overwhelmed her, shredding her resolve to turn a hard eye to him. Trembling, Lilly bit her lower lip and blinked back tears.

A smile nipped at the corners of Heinrick's mouth. She waited for it to materialize into fullness, but he abruptly extinguished it and offered a curt nod instead, tugging on the brim of his hat. He didn't move, however. They stood there, fifteen feet apart, staring at each other, and Lilly felt the gulf of an entire ocean between them. The desire to tell him she was sorry and ask how he was doing pulsed inside her. But she stayed mute.

Heinrick finally pulled off his leather gloves, tucked them into his chaps, and turned away from her. She watched him lumber toward the bunkhouse, feeling in his wake the weight of his loneliness.

She carried it all the way into Mobridge.

Independence Day preparations had sparked the town into activity. Westward, near the Missouri, Lilly spied the makings of the Fourth of July fair: unfamiliar rigs, buckboards, tents, and various prize livestock. On the other end of town, stood makeshift cattle pens and a large corral. In two days, cowboys from all over South Dakota would gather to duke it out with untamed beasts in the Mobridge rodeo. Lilly loved the exotic, recaptured display of bygone days from a now-tamed West. Reggie always participated as a hazer for his authentic cowboy buddies. A rugged memory hit her like a warm gust of wind. In his nut-brown leather cowboy hat, the one with the Indian braid dangling down the back, and his fringed sandy-colored chaps, Reggie easily passed for a ranch hand, and a dashing one, besides.

Despite the fresh ache of Reggie's absence, Lilly knew Mobridge desperately needed the rodeo and the mind-numbing gaiety of Independence Day. They needed to celebrate with gusto, to remind themselves why they sacrificed, all of them—mothers, sons, wives, and husbands. They were at war to make the world safe for freedom, for independence.

Lilly jumped at the *hee-haw* of a late model Packard. She skittered to the side of the street and watched a mustard yellow Roadster roll by, the *oohs* and *aahs* of admiring farmers rolling out like a red carpet before it. Lilly smirked. Clive's Model T wouldn't be the only attraction in town over the holiday.

Ernestine's burst with shoppers, most of whom had unfamiliar tanned faces. A handful of Russian women, their wide, red faces glistening under colorfully dyed headscarves, haggled with Willard over a batch of home-canned sauerkraut and pickles. Their jumbled words stirred a memory within Lilly, and at once, Heinrick's sharp, strange mother tongue filled her mind. She fought the image of his tired eyes and sagging shoulders.

"What do you want today, Lilly?" Ernestine barked.

"Two pounds of sugar, please?"

Ernestine pinched her lips and searched under the wooden countertop for an extra burlap bag. She filled it with sugar and passed it over to Lilly. "Bring the bag back."

Lilly paid Ernestine, turned, and plowed straight into Marjorie's mother, Jennifer Pratt.

"Be careful, girl!" Mrs. Pratt exclaimed.

Lilly blushed. "Excuse me, Mrs. Pratt."

Mrs. Pratt's voice softened. "How are you, Lilly?"

"Fine, thank you. How is Marjorie?"

"She's at the armory. Why don't you stop in and ask her yourself?"

Lilly tried not to notice the stares of three other women who had turned curious eyes upon her as soon as Mrs. Pratt announced her name. Shame swept through her bones.

"I'll do that," she mumbled. "Good day, ma'am."

Mrs. Pratt nodded and moved past her. Lilly made for the door.

She stopped next at the post office. Lilly's heart did a small skip when the clerk handed her not only a letter from Reggie, but also one for Olive, from Chuck. Her sister would be ecstatic. She tucked both into the pocket of her apron as she crossed the street and headed to the armory.

The former one-room tavern swam with the odor of mothballs, cotton fibers, and antiseptic. A handful of uniformed girls ripped long strips of cloth.

Marjorie appeared every inch a Red Cross volunteer as she cut and wound long sheets of muslin and assembled first aid kits to send to the front. Over her calico prairie dress, she wore a standard-issue Red Cross white cotton pinafore, with two enormous pockets sewn into the skirt. Pinned on her head was a fabric-covered pillbox hat emblazoned with a bright red cross on the upturned crown.

"Lilly!" Marjorie dropped her fabric onto a long table and embraced her friend. "Did you hear the news?"

"What news?"

Marjorie's eyes twinkled. "Harley proposed."

"What?"

Marjorie grinned. "His last letter said he couldn't keep fighting without knowing I was pledged to him and our future. We'll be married as soon as he returns."

"But Marj, what if he doesn't come back?" Lilly instantly clamped a hand over her mouth, wishing her words back.

Marjorie gaped at her. "How can you say that? Of course he'll be back."

"I'm so sorry. Please forgive me."

Marjorie's anger dissolved, and she gathered Lilly into a forgiving hug. "No harm done. I know you're worried, too."

Tears pooled like a flash flood, spilling from Lilly's eyes. "I keep telling myself Reggie will be all right," she whispered. "I just wish I knew for sure that he would come home."

Marjorie looped her arm through Lilly's. She led her away from curious ears. "Let's not think about it. There is nothing we can do anyway. We just have to wait."

Lilly wiped the tears with her fingertips, already feeling her composure returning. But they had left their mark. Obviously, she missed Reggie more than she realized. She hadn't cried over him since receiving his last letter.

The pair stared out of a grimy window onto the street, at women lugging loaded baskets and dirt-streaked children running with hoops. Morrie stood in his doorway, his apron stained with shaving cream and strands of hair. A pack of cowboys emerged from Flanner's Cafe. Some straddled their horses while another group surrounded the Packard, wishing for a more sophisticated form of transportation.

"By the way, are you all right?"

"What?" Lilly glanced at Marjorie and frowned.

"You can tell me, Lilly. Did he force you to help him?"

Lilly peeled her arm from Marjorie's grasp. "What are you talking about?"

Marjorie's eyes darted away, then back to Lilly. She lowered her voice. "The foreigner. I heard all about it from my sister. She said he grabbed you and forced you to drive him home."

So that was the local story. Or, at least one version of it. She shook her head. "That's not how it happened, Marj."

Marjorie paled. "What do you mean, Lilly? Did something else happen?"

Lilly held her friend's hands. "Listen, I will only say this once because, frankly, I am trying to forget it happened. The Craffey boys attacked Heinrick. It was unprovoked, no matter what anyone says, and entirely mismatched. I felt sorry for him, so I butted in."

Marjorie's eyes widened. "Heinrick?"

Lilly's face heated. "Forget I told you. I've already forgotten it and him."

Marjorie peered at her friend, as if seeing into her soul. "You don't look like you've forgotten it, Lilly. You're blushing."

"Am I?" Lilly's mouth went dry, and she dropped Marjorie's hands as if they were ice. "I'm just embarrassed, that's all."

Marjorie stepped away from her, her eyes skimming her in one quick sweep. "Right."

Marjorie's mistrust felt like a slap. She winced and wanted to argue, but for a moment, in her friend's suspicious eyes, she saw the truth. Despite the fact she'd rejected the enemy and turned her back on Heinrick, his sapphire eyes glimmered steadily in her mind. He was far from forgotten.

Chapter 9

Lilly headed to a bluff overlooking the Missouri, a nook nestled in the shade of a few now withering maples, to read Reggie's letter. The sun, a salmon-colored ball, bled out along the horizon. As the wind loosened her unkempt braid, a meadowlark sang a tune from the fallow field nearby. The smell of dust and drying leaves urged feelings of fall, although the summer heat spilled perspiration down the back of her cotton dress.

This letter was longer, the writing blocked and smudged in places. Lilly determined to analyze each agonizing detail and truly know the cold he'd described in his last letter. More than that, she hoped to sense they were together somehow, that they could bridge this awful, growing chasm between them.

My Dearest Lilly,

I hope this letter finds you well. It's been two weeks since my last batch of mail, and I have concluded that the mail service has fallen into the hands of ineptitude, as has much of this man's army. Although I am proud to be serving the Red, White, and Blue and can say I know it my Christian duty to protect the ideals of democracy, I am sometimes weakened by the lack of supplies and the ever-worsening conditions. I know, in principle, this is not a result of Pershing's leadership or even of President Wilson. Rather, it is the result of too much war, too little sleep, too few supplies, and, worse yet, too many casualties.

I sit now in a reserve trench. Dawn approaches, long shadows licking the edges of the gully where I sleep, eat, and spend my off days. Others head for a nearby village, where they take refuge in French cafes, taverns, and, I fear, boardinghouses within the arms of French women. But of this I do not know firsthand, of course. I will sit here today and try and sleep on my helmet or on one of the many lice-covered bunks left in the shallow dugouts. Oh, how I loathe lice! I feel them move over me as if my skin is somehow unhappy on my bones and seeks to find new habitation. I have been without a bath for so long, I have forgotten the sense of water upon my body. How I long for the Missouri.

I spent the last week on the front lines, in the firing trench, curled in a dugout while the cover trench lobbed shells over my sleepless head. We are awake at night, searching the darkness for foreign bodies that attempt to cut the barbed wire and murder us in our gopher holes. God has preserved me thus far so I know He must be hearing your prayers. One morning, as the dawn revealed the unlucky, I saw that two of my compatriots had been struck. One was a Brit named Martin and the other a fellow Dakotan from Yankton, who had received so much mail here we dubbed him Lucky Joe. I remembered then a moment of agonized cries and frenzied shelling, like lightning in the sky, and knew a firefight had been waged a mere hundred yards from me. And where was I in that desperate moment? Blinking through the darkness, holding at bay the erratic, armed shadows. I know, Lilly, if I blink too long, one of those shadows will emerge, and then I will be the one to sleep forever, slain in this muddy dugout.

Poor Lucky Joe. He often told me of his parents' small wheat plot and worried about their fate with their crops this year without him. He was their only son.

I will not think about it. I will come home to you and our future. It is for you I fight, you and our God-ordained dreams.

Mother, in her last letter, told me you were among those to help house and feed a group of Wyoming doughboys, headed east in May. My heart was both envious to think of those boys having the advantage of seeing your lovely face and pleased my future bride is so faithful in her outpouring of love and concern. I am proud of you, Lilly-girl, and wrote my mother precisely that in a recent letter.

Is it warm there? Did your lilies bloom this year? I remember how tediously you tended them in years past. How are Bonnie and DJ? Chuck tells me all is well with Olive, and I am glad for him. He carries her picture in his helmet.

The sunlight is upon us, and I hear the clang of the kitchen bell. This morning, perhaps, I will get a hot meal. Please hold on to the promises we made and write to your soldier doing his part at the front.

Yours,
Reggie

Lilly smoothed the letter on her lap, and her throat burned. Fixing her eyes on the streak of orange that scraped against the far bluffs, she fought the image of Reggie lying in a dugout hole, a lone man holding back the German lines. On Sunday, she would say an extra-fervent prayer for his safety. Lilly closed her eyes and searched her heart for any sins that might somehow, through Divine justice, send a bullet into Reggie's hideout. She didn't have to dig far to unearth one. It was painfully clear she must fight every errant, impulsive thought of Heinrick, his jeweled eyes and the way she felt embraced by his smile. She must purge the German from her mind and instead cling to the future Reggie had planned. She must do her part to help Reggie come home alive—tend to her letters and never think of anyone but Reggie again. Ever.

A hawk screamed and soared into the horizon, where it melted into the sunset. Behind her, the wind rustled the drying leaves of the maples. They seemed to sizzle as they shattered and fell. The prairie was drying up. The world was at war. And Lilly's future seemed as fragile as the maple leaves.

≈

Lilly held the reins to a dozing Lucy and patted the horse's soft velvet nose. The Appaloosa's eyes were glassy mirrors, glinting the barely risen sun. She gazed at Lilly and seemed to ask, "What am I doing here?"

Lilly rubbed her hand along the forelock of the twenty-year-old mare. "I don't think this is a great idea, either, old girl. Just be careful and don't go too fast."

Not far off, Lilly caught a different set of instructions delivered by her father to his antsy ten-year-old son. "Ride like the wind, Frankie. Don't let those other cowboys nose in front of you. Keep your eyes straight ahead and remember you're a Clark!" He clamped the boy on the shoulder, and Lilly stifled a giggle as Frankie nearly landed in the dirt.

"I don't know, Donald. . . ." Mrs. Clark pinned her husband with a worried look.

"He'll be fine," he assured her.

Lilly tugged on Frankie's beat-up hat as he swung into the saddle. "Behave yourself." She knew he had other plans in mind—another route for the race that might indeed place the youngster at the head of the pack. A piercing gunshot ripped through the morning air. Frankie urged Lucy to the starting line. From Lilly's point of view, Frankie would have a time just getting the horse up the hill out of Mobridge, let alone all the way to the Torgesen T and back. Frankie grinned like a hyena, oblivious to the fact he was the youngest contender. Lucy fought sleep. Then the next shot rang out and the pack exploded. Frankie kicked Lucy, wiggled in his saddle, and plowed his way through the dust churned up by the other horses. The horde had long vanished by the time Frankie disappeared behind the bluffs.

Lilly plopped down on the picnic blanket and watched the sun stretch golden fingers into the first hours of the Independence Day picnic. Two hours later, every rider had returned but Frankie. Mrs. Clark sent her husband furious glances as she squinted toward the north. Lilly fought the urge to betray Frankie's plan to cheat and cut a shortcut across the Clark farm to the Torgesen T. Just when she'd decided to turn him in, he and Lucy appeared on the horizon. As they plodded closer, she noticed two things: He and old Luce were covered to their hips in Missouri mud, and he wasn't alone.

Frankie rode in sporting a sheepish grin, bursting with an obvious story to tell. An exuberant crowd greeted him as if he were a doughboy returning from war. But Lilly's eyes were glued to the cowboy in the wide milky ten-gallon hat and muddy black chaps, who beamed like he'd caught the canary. His blue eyes twinkled, and he pinned them straight on Lilly.

Lilly crossed her arms against her chest, turned to Frankie, and ignored the man she couldn't seem to get rid of.

His father helped Frankie down from Lucy, and his mother wrapped him in a fierce hug. Ed Miller, the race official, pushed through the crowd. He glared at Frankie, and demanded an explanation.

Commanding the crowd like a well-seasoned preacher, Frankie spun a tale of adventure and peril. He glossed over the part where he cheated and focused on the usually free-flowing Missouri tributary he'd attempted to cross during his shortcut to win the race.

"Good Ole Luce fought like a rattler caught by the tail, but the mud sucked her down!" All grins, Frankie described Lucy's battle with the clay only the Missouri could produce. Lilly grimaced as she pictured Lucy slogging about in panic, gluing herself and Frankie to the riverbed.

"I tried to break her free, but finally gave up. There weren't anything I could do but holler," Frankie said. To illustrate, he bellowed loudly over the crowd, which elicited riotous laughter from the other competitors.

"I was just plain lucky this here cowboy was near enough to hear me." Frankie gestured to his hero and grinned in glowing admiration. Heinrick, who had moved with his mount to the fringes of the crowd, kept his head down and tugged on his hat. Lilly's heart moved in pity for him. Obviously, he didn't want to revive any previous memories of his appearance in town. But if any of the folks recognized him, they stayed mute. Frankie continued his saga by describing how Heinrick had wrestled Lucy and Frankie from the grip of the mud with an old bald cottonwood.

When Frankie finished his tale, Ed dressed him down, then clamped him on the shoulder. "I do believe, son, you win the award for most daring contestant." The crowd erupted in good-natured cheering. Even Lilly's father, who had listened with a frown and pursed lips, gave in to forgiveness and tugged on his son's grimy hat.

The crowd dispersed, and Frankie pulled his father over to meet his hero.

"Thank you," Mr. Clark said to Heinrick as he pumped the German's hand.

Heinrick shrugged. "Glad to help." Lilly noticed the proud, triumphant smile had vanished, and in his eyes lurked that lonely, desperate look she'd seen earlier.

"Would you like to stick around for some breakfast? My wife's fixed up some hotcakes and has some homemade peach preserves in her basket."

Lilly's heart jumped. She heard Olive's quick intake of breath behind her. Heinrick looked past her father to Lilly, reaching out to her with his blue eyes and holding her in their magical grip. His tanned face was clean-shaven this morning, although his hair was longer, curling around his ears and brushing the collar of his red cotton shirt. He shifted in his saddle, considering her father's request, all the time staring at Lilly, who felt herself blush. She forced herself to close her eyes and look away.

When she opened them, Heinrick was shaking his head and extending his hand again to her father.

"Thank you, sir. But I'm afraid I need to prepare for the rodeo this evening, and I don't have time."

Mr. Clark nodded. "I can understand that well enough, son. Maybe another time."

"Sounds good," Heinrick returned, a smile pushing at his mouth. He tossed a last glance at Lilly, one eyebrow cocked, and an inscrutable, almost teasing look, pulsed in his eyes. Lilly gasped, and the blood simmered in her veins. The nerve of him, suggesting she was wrong and he could be accepted as a friend into their family! Well, her father didn't know he was shaking hands with a German in front of the entire town. Lilly shot Heinrick a halfhearted glare. To her chagrin, Heinrick only gave her a delighted smile. Then he pulled on his hat again, spurred his quarter horse, and trotted toward the Torgesen T.

"Who was that?" gasped Bonnie, her eyes saucers.

Lilly produced an exaggerated shrug, turned away, and pulled Chris from Olive's arms. Olive's dark eyes smoldered. Lilly offered an innocent smile. She'd done nothing to encourage their father's offer, and could she help it if Heinrick had been the only cowboy willing to lend a hand to a scared ten-year-old boy?

Heinrick's comment puzzled her, however. He couldn't possibly be riding in the rodeo, could he? Certainly, Mrs. Torgesen and Clive wouldn't allow him off the ranch to share their little secret. She still hadn't figured out how he'd come to work for them in the first place. But she would never know, because she would never ask.

The blistering sun was on its downward slide, and the heat was dissipating. Still, sheltered in a merciful trace of shade next to the Clark wagon, little Chris's downy curls were plastered to his head in a cap of sweat as he nestled against Lilly. She'd spent the last hour watching her nephew sleep and harnessing her relentless obsession with the mysterious German. Thankfully, thinking upon the events of the fair gave her some respite.

Practically overnight, their little town had become a metropolis, including a fine display of motorized vehicles and parasol-toting French prairie ladies. Their stylish outfits seemed outlandish, however, among the handful of sensible farm wives who wouldn't be caught dead at a picnic in spike-heeled boots and a suit coat. Even so, Lilly and her sisters wore their Sunday best: high-necked blouses, puffy sleeves with lace-trimmed cuffs, and empire-waist cotton skirts. Her mother had even dusted off her wide-brim fedora, saying, "It will keep my face out of the sun."

The picnic started shortly after the race with a weight-guessing contest. Someone suggested they guess the weight of Erica Torgesen, who wasn't there, fortunately, and the townspeople erupted in good-humored laughter. They resorted to guessing the weight of Hans Sheffield's prize burnt-red duroc, and Lilly cheered when Frankie nabbed the prize with a guess of 942 pounds.

Since no one had a scale, they took the word of Hans, who was delighted to hand over the city's prize—free lemonade at Miller's. Frankie and a flock of boys migrated into town and started a stampede that lasted most of the day, until Miller announced he'd run out of juice.

The rest of the picnic continued with an array of harmless amusements from prairie dog chasing to pie eating to rock skipping in the shallow, muddy Missouri. Lilly stayed glued to Olive, watching little Chris and avoiding curious looks from Mobridgites who, she supposed, toyed with the idea she might have been kidnapped. Gratefully, she heard not a scandalous word, and, by the end of the day, Lilly decided the entire event had succumbed to a quiet, merciful death.

"I'm going home now." Olive's lanky shadow loomed over Lilly. "Are you coming with me?"

Lilly considered Chris's sleeping form. His eyes were so gently closed they looked like film. Not a worry lined his face. A small spot of drool moistened her blouse where his lips were propped open and askew. Oh, to be so young, naive, be gathered inside safe arms and believe the world was in control.

"No," Lilly said. "I'm going to the rodeo."

Lilly ignored Olive's vicious glare. She climbed to her feet, eased Chris from her arms, and gently handed him to Olive. Olive marched away, his head bouncing against her bony shoulder.

Lilly beat back the hope of seeing Heinrick and ambled toward the rodeo grounds.

Chapter 10

The rodeo grounds teemed with spectators, animals, and anxious cowboys. A pungent brew of dust, animal sweat, hay, and manure hung in the air. The familiarity of it moved a memory in Lilly and she couldn't stop the twinge of guilt. Last year, it had been Reggie she'd come to watch.

Lilly spotted Erica Torgesen perched in all her green finery on the seat of her covered surrey and went to greet her.

"You're looking wonderful tonight, Mrs. Torgesen," Lilly said, grinning.

Mrs. Torgesen winked at her. "You're an angel, Lilly. Already Alpha Booth from Eureka and Eve Whiting have asked for your name. And I gave it to them!" She clasped her hands together, beaming as if she'd just published her best apple pie recipe.

"Thank you," Lilly replied before blending into the swelling crowd. Mrs. Torgesen's reference could mean more business for her, which would in turn help her family. Glancing over her shoulder, she giggled, deciding the eccentric Norwegian resembled a queen upon her throne, peering over her subjects with her little bird in a nest.

Lilly threaded through the crowd to the makeshift bleachers, constructed from dead cottonwood and oak trees dragged from the drying riverbed. Those who didn't want to sit on the skeletons of old trees found stumps or stood on the backs of wagons.

Marjorie had commandeered for them a place on the upper branch of a wide peeled cottonwood at the south end of the corral. Lilly climbed aboard next to her friend just in time for the first event. Somehow, the town officials had rounded up more than a smattering of eager cowboys. A group of cowpunchers lined up at the animal pens, adjusting their spurs, straightening their fur chaps, and wiping the sweat from the lining of their Stetsons.

Ed Miller mounted the announcer's platform and yelled over the audience. He read the names of the contestants for the steer wrestling competition. Twenty brave cowboys lined up, and, one by one, young steers were loosed. Lilly's heart beat a race with the hazers as they kept the animals on course. She winced when the bulldoggers ran a steer down on horseback, tackled it, and wrestled the hapless animal to the ground. But the animals pounced to their feet, unscathed.

Occasionally, she broke her attention to search the stands for Heinrick. He was nowhere to be found.

The bulldoggers worked quickly, and a cowpoke named Lou out of Pierre took first prize. Calf roping was next, and another set of unlucky creatures ran through the gamut. Two cowboys from Rapid City won the ten-dollar prize. Sandwiched between events, a clown, Ernestine's Willard, entertained the crowd with cornball antics. His real job was to protect the cowboys from dangerous, enraged animals. Lilly decided he was the perfect clown.

Frankie claimed fifth place in the youth barrel racing event on an exhausted Lucy.

The grand finale was bronco riding, and Lilly was shocked to hear Clive Torgesen's name announced as a contender.

"I saw him bucked off a mustang just last week," she whispered into Marjorie's ear. Marjorie arched her brows in astonishment. Lilly knew Clive's bragging often left an entirely different impression, so she nodded and returned a grim look.

From Ed Miller's introduction, Lilly found out that Clive's bronc, dubbed Jester, had a habit of slamming his body into the fence, squashing his rider's legs. Lilly leaned forward on the branch and held her breath, suddenly thankful for Willard.

The bronc tore out of its pen like a frenzied bee, furious and craving blood. Clive made a valiant show and stayed on for five entire seconds. When Jester finally threw him, he hung in the air, as if taking flight upon a hot gust of wind, and the crowd held their breath in a collective gasp. When he hit the ground, Lilly heard his breath whoosh out as clearly as if he'd landed in her lap. The stands quieted while Willard raced after the bronco and quickly succeeded in snaring his loose reins. He pulled the skittering beast through the exit gate, then rushed to Clive.

Clive rose feebly to his elbows, and it seemed all of South Dakota erupted in a massive cheer. Even Lilly clapped, wondering how he'd managed to stay on that bronco.

The prize went to a fresh young cowpoke from Minnesota, Patrick Hanson. A congregational murmur of appreciation ascended from the stands. The rodeo had managed a decent showing.

Disappointment flickered briefly in Lilly's heart. She doused it quickly, disgusted that she'd wanted to see Heinrick at all, let alone see him perform in a rodeo. But why had he lied to her father?

Ed Miller shot a rifle in the air, the sound creating a cascade of unhappy responses from nearby livestock, as well as mothers with sleeping babes. He held up his arms, and the crowd settled into expectant silence.

"Stick around, folks, we have a new event this evening! Fresh from Wyoming, where cowboys know how to ride the wind, comes—bull riding! This Brahma bull will make your blood curdle! One look at this beast will remind you why cowboys don't ride bulls. We've even found three courageous cowpokes who will give it a go! Please welcome Lou Whitmore from Pierre, Arnie Black from the Double U, and Henry Zook from the Torgesen T!"

Lilly's heart went dead in her chest. It couldn't be. "Heinrick," she whispered.

Marjorie shot Lilly a quizzical look.

Lilly sought out Erica Torgesen's face in the crowd. The woman smiled and chatted with her neighbors, unaffected. Something wasn't quite right. Maybe it wasn't Heinrick. . . .

Then, there he was, on the platform, next to Lou and Arnie, waving his hand to the crowd, his crooked grin flavoring his face with amusement.

What was Heinrick thinking? Those bulls had horns—sharp ones!

"Is that *your* Heinrick?" Marjorie breathed into her ear.

"He's not my Heinrick," Lilly hissed.

"Of course he's not," Marjorie said indignantly. "You know what I mean."

Lilly bit her lip and nodded slowly.

"He's got spunk," said Marjorie in amazement.

"He's going to kill himself," Lilly replied, horrified.

≈

Lou from Pierre sailed through the air. He landed with a grunt and scrambled to his feet. The bull raced after him like a dog to a bone. He swung his massive head, slashing the air, and missed skewering Lou by a hair as the bull rider dove under the fence. The Brahma's bulky frame thudded against the corral. The wood cracked, the sound like a whip, stinging the crowd and extracting a chorus of gasps from terrified women and children. Marjorie covered her mouth with her hands and went ashen. Lilly clenched her fists in her lap.

Having dispatched Lou, the bull turned and memorized the horror-struck crowd, as if searching for his next victim. His black eyes bulged, furious. He breathed in great hot gusts. Fear took control of Lilly's heartbeat. Heinrick was a greenhorn, a laborer from Europe, big but inexperienced. He would be, in a word, sausage. He was either a fool or the bravest man she'd ever met.

Arnie Black from the Double U fared worse than Lou. He escaped the bull's razor-sharp horns only because Willard the Clown rolled a tall rain barrel in his direction. Arnie dove in a second before the bull grazed the backside of his britches. The Brahma rammed the barrel around the corral until it lodged under the bottom of a flimsy fence rail. Arnie scrambled out, breathing hard.

Willard, turning out to be a braver man than Lilly assumed, opened the exit gate and flagged the bull through where three cowpunchers herded him into the starting pen.

Heinrick straddled the pen, one leg on each side of the narrow stall. When ready, he would wind his hand under the rope that encircled the bull's massive body and jump aboard. Lilly held her breath. Heinrick rolled up his sleeve, worked his ten-gallon down on his head, and tugged on his leather glove. His face was grim, his mouth set, and he didn't spare a glance at the crowd. After an eternal moment, he slipped his hand under the belt and nodded. Lilly's heart skidded to a stop.

The bull shot out of the pen, snorting, heaving his body as if possessed. His powerful back legs kicked; he threw himself forward, jerked his head from side to side, whirled and twisted. The stunned crowd was so silent, Lilly could hear Heinrick grunt as the bull jolted him. But he hung on. Five seconds, six. The disbelieving crowd began to murmur. Then the Brahma started to spin, a frenzied cyclone of fury. Lilly covered her mouth to seal her horror. How would Heinrick stay on for the required eight seconds? He would whistle off like a piece of lint, and the bull's horns would spear him on takeoff. Lilly squeezed her eyes shut, then forced them open.

Willard grabbed a red handkerchief and readied himself to dash into the ring.

Suddenly, Heinrick freed a war whoop that sounded like a forgotten echo from the valley of the Little Bighorn. He flung his hand up over his head and rode the bull, melding into the whirlwind spin. Man and beast seemed to flow and dance as if they were one.

A nervous titter rippled through the audience.

Round and round the pair twirled. Lilly lost count of the turns and only watched, mesmerized. Heinrick's powerful legs gripped the sides of the bull and his hat flew off, his blond hair a tangled mass flopping about his head. Lilly could see the muscles ripple through his wide forearm, steady and taut as he clung to the belt. The violence of the event made her reel, yet the raw courage that it took to wrestle a two-ton beast awed her.

A shot fired, and Lilly nearly bolted from her skin. The eight-second mark! Heinrick spurred the bull, and the Brahma burst out of his erratic dance into a headlong stampede for the fence, bucking forward and back. A dusty hazer on a quarter horse shot up to the animal. Heinrick let go of the bull's belt, wrapped an arm around the waist of the cowboy, and slid off his perch. The bull snorted and bolted toward Heinrick. Heinrick hit the ground running and dove under the corral fence. The barrier stopped the Brahma, but as he pawed the dirt, his furious snorts pursued the escaping bulldogger. Willard whooped and sprang into the middle of the ring. The bull turned, considered, and then launched himself toward the next available prey. Willard's quick dash to the exit fence drew the animal like a magnet, and in a moment, he'd dispatched the bewildered bull into a safe holding paddock.

The crowd paused for a well-earned sigh of relief, then exploded in triumph. Henry Zook, whoever he was, was some sort of cowpuncher to last over eight agonizing seconds on a raging bull! Lilly's heart restarted in her chest. She trembled, blew out long breaths, and smoothed the wrinkles from her skirt. Heinrick was a strange brew of interesting surprises, at the very least.

Lilly watched the handsome blond German dust off his coal black chaps and climb the announcer's platform, embedded in riotous applause. Clive Torgesen followed him, waving to the crowd as if he himself had ridden the bull. Lilly's eyes narrowed. What was Clive up to?

Heinrick accepted the handshake and congratulations of a flabbergasted, but beaming Ed Miller. Clive Torgesen stood beside his hired hand, grinning like a Cheshire cat. Ed Miller raised his arms and calmed the crowd.

"Ladies and gentlemen, I am pleased to announce the winner of the first annual Mobridge bull riding contest—Henry Zook, from the Torgesen T!" The crowd burst into another chorus of applause that could have been mistaken for thunder roaring across the prairie. Then, as Ed handed the envelope containing the fifty-dollar prize money to Heinrick, Clive reached over and plucked it from Heinrick's grasp. The clapping died to a spattering.

"And, on behalf of Henry, who represented the Torgesen T in this momentous event, the Torgesen family accepts this award!" Clive waved the envelope above his head, and Lilly noticed Heinrick inhale deeply, his barrel chest rising. But the ever-present white smile never lost its brightness. The crowd offered a modicum of confused applause which quickly died into a raucous murmuring as Clive thumped down the platform steps.

Lilly gaped in bewilderment. Why would Heinrick risk his life, then hand over the prize money—a half-year's salary for a cowhand—? It didn't make sense at all. Heinrick Zook was a confusing tangle of secrets, and he intrigued her more than she wanted to admit.

Chapter 11

Long shadows crawled over the rodeo grounds. Lilly threaded through small clumps of townspeople absorbed in conversation. A sense of reluctance to abandon the illusive normalcy the rodeo, picnic, and fair provided hung heavy in the air.

Lilly was oblivious to the cheerful conversation. Heinrick and his perplexing behavior consumed her mind to the point of distraction. She meandered toward the cattle pens and stopped at the bullpen, where the Brahma raised its head and considered her. A thick rope was tightly knotted around his nose ring, and his wide sides moved in and out in largo rhythm. His eyes were fathomless black orbs, as if he, too, was trying to comprehend the evening's events.

Why did Heinrick give up his painfully-earned prize money for a family who loathed him? She turned over the question in her head, examining it from every angle, discovering nothing.

Gooseflesh prickled her skin a second before clammy breath lathered the back of her neck. Lilly whirled. The pithy odor of whiskey hit her like a fist.

"Well, Miss Lilly. What are you doing over here, staring at the cattle?"

Lilly reeled as Clive Torgesen grabbed the rail behind her. His eyes were dark and swam with trouble.

Fear pounded an erratic beat in Lilly's heart. "Get away from me, Clive." She started to slide away.

Clive snaked out a hand and grabbed her by her slender arm. "Where are you going, Lilly?"

Lilly trembled, and her pulse roared like a waterfall in her ears. Her voice seemed but a trickle behind it. "Let go of me."

"You're such a pretty thing, Lilly. Don't think I haven't noticed over the years."

Lilly twisted and pulled her arm, but his grip tightened. A cold fist closed over her heart.

"Why, Lilly, it seems to me you should show your boss a little respect."

"You're not my boss," she bit out.

Clive laughed at her. "Sure I am, honey. You work for the Torgesen T."

He leaned close, his unshaven chin scraping her cheek. "And that means you work for me."

Lilly bit her lip. Her knees went weak. "Let me go, Clive."

The smell of dust and sweat enclosed her, and dread pooled in Lilly's throat. She felt a scream gathering, but for some reason couldn't force it out.

Clive's whiskey breath was in her ear. "You know, Lilly, your boy Reggie ain't comin' back. Those Germans are going to kill him like a dog in the dirt, and then you'll need somebody to turn to." He loosed a savage chuckle. "I'm here for you, darling."

He raised his gloved hand, as if to stroke her cheek. Lilly glimpsed something odious prowling in his dark eyes. Fear shot through her; she lashed out, kicking him hard on the shin.

He swore, caught her other arm, and shook her. "Be nice!"

Lilly glanced over Clive's shoulder. *Please, God, anyone!* But the shadows had widened, and darkness layered the rodeo grounds. Along the bluff, campfires teased her with their safe glow.

"I'm going to scream, Clive."

"Go ahead, Lilly," Clive mocked her. "Who's gonna hear you?"

Lilly trembled as her courage fled. Tears blinded her.

"I will, Clive."

The voice came out of the darkness, with just enough accent for Lilly to recognize it at once.

"Let her go."

A smile curved up Clive's cheek. His eyes narrowed. "I'll be back," he promised as he shoved Lilly against the fence. He whirled. "Get outta here. This ain't none of your business." The curse that followed made Lilly sick. She shrank back, rubbing her arms, poised to bolt as soon as Clive was out of reach.

"What's wrong with you?" Heinrick's disgust thickened his voice, even through the haze of a German accent.

He stepped up to Lilly and held out his hand. "C'mon, miss."

Clive slapped it down. "I said get outta here! Or you'll spend two more years hauling manure on the Torgesen T!"

Heinrick's voice was low, but Lilly detected a warning edge. "I paid you six months' worth tonight, Clive. Christmas, then I'm free. No longer than Christmas."

"We'll see about that." Clive shuffled closer and balled up his fist. The pungent odor of whiskey sauced the air.

Lilly knew she should run, but she couldn't move past the fear that had her rooted.

Heinrick sucked in a deep breath, and his voice escaped with a sigh. "You're drunk, Clive. Go home."

"I'm going to skin you like a piece of Missouri driftwood," Clive sneered, undaunted.

A muscle tensed in Heinrick's jaw, but he blinked not an eye as he batted away Clive's fist. Clive roared and charged, throwing his arms around Heinrick's waist. The German stepped back and easily tossed Clive to the ground. Clive wobbled to his knees and wheezed.

Lilly's fingers bit into her arms as she waited for Heinrick to resign Clive, face first, to the dirt. Instead, Heinrick swiped Clive's fallen Stetson from the ground and held it out. "Go home, Mr. Torgesen. It's late, and you're tired."

Clive cranked his head upward and glared at Heinrick, his brown hair matted, a line of drool dangling from his lips. He leaned back on his haunches and lunged for his hat, snaring, instead, Heinrick's forearm. He yanked hard and landed a blow on the German's cheek. It echoed like the snap of an old cottonwood.

Heinrick jerked back. He set his jaw, and his eyes hardened to ice. His fists balled, but he held them to his sides. "Okay, that's enough. Go home, Boss."

The exertion of that one punch had emptied Clive. He gaped at Heinrick, his mouth askew, confusion glazing his eyes.

Heinrick stepped toward Lilly and again extended his hand. She hesitated, then slid hers into it. His hand was warm and firm and held hers with gentleness. Lilly scooted around Clive like a jittery cat.

Lilly and Heinrick marched ten quick, solid paces before he released her hand. It continued to tingle, and she felt the absence well. Heinrick had saved her. The significance of that hit her hard, and she squinted at the man she'd considered her enemy.

"I never did get your name," Heinrick said, his eyes ahead.

Lilly fought a war of emotions. He was still a foreigner, the enemy. But as she walked next to him, hearing only the crunch of prairie grass and the beating of her heart, she knew that wasn't a fair assessment. He deserved courtesy, if not her friendship. "Lillian," she whispered. "But my friends call me Lilly."

"Lilly it is, then." A smile tugged at his lips.

They walked through the velvet darkness, the field grass crunching under their steps, the crickets singing from the riverbed not far off, and a lazy ballad humming over the bluffs from distant campfires. The wind skimmed the aroma from a pot of stew and carried it across the prairie. Lilly's stomach flopped, but not from hunger.

"I guess I owe you." She peeked at Heinrick and saw his smile widen.

"How's that?"

"You're one up on me. You saved Frankie and now me."

Heinrick chuckled, and Lilly was oddly delighted.

"Well, let me see. How can you save me?"

Lilly walked along and pondered that question, wondering what she could offer a man who seemed to carry the world in his wide palms, wondering even if she should. Curiosity swelled inside her. Who was this man, and why did he risk everything for the Torgesen T? The confusion stopped her short.

Heinrick walked out before her.

"Heinrick?"

He turned. "I haven't heard anyone use my name for nearly five years. It sounds like a song coming from your lips."

Lilly's delight was like a strong gust of warm wind. She felt an impending blush and bit her lip. But the endearing twinkle in his eyes mustered her courage. "Why did you give Clive your prize money?"

His expression darkened.

"What is it?" Lilly's heart fell, afraid she'd offended him after he'd been so kind to her. "I'm sorry."

Heinrick held up a hand to stave off her apology. He gazed into the protective obscurity of night. "I gave Clive the money because," he cleared his throat but couldn't dislodge a distinct hoarseness, "they own me."

"What? How can they own you?"

Heinrick freed a sigh of pure frustration. "It's a long story, Lilly."

She crossed her arms. "I like stories."

Heinrick winced as if his words brought pain. "I don't think that is a good idea."

He turned away, running a hand through his thick, curly hair. "Don't you remember? I'm the enemy. Your fiancé, Reggie, is being killed by my relatives." He blew out another breath, then turned back to her. "I'm dangerous."

A brief, melancholy smile flickered over his face, but his eyes betrayed ache. "Or did you forget?"

Shame poured over Lilly. He was right, and the truth of it distanced them as if he was a coyote and she a long-eared jackrabbit. They were enemies.

Somehow, however, Lilly just couldn't muster up the feelings of loathing one ought to feel for an enemy. Today had changed all that. He'd gone out of his way to save Frankie and had toed up to Clive for her. Heinrick was too kind, too forgiving, too, well, downright honorable, to be the enemy. And therein lay the paradox. She didn't want him to be an enemy. She wanted him to be Heinrick, her friend. It would mean nothing. Reggie was still her fiancé. She wasn't stepping past the boundaries of their covenant.

Heinrick wasn't part of the massacre. He was, in fact, a casualty himself, imprisoned and wounded by Clive and the Torgesen T. And he needed a friend.

If Reggie were caught behind German lines, hurt and friendless, wouldn't she want some kind German fraulein to watch over him? The answer sealed her decision.

"You're not my enemy, Heinrick. I was wrong to call you that. Please forgive me."

His radiant smile nearly knocked her off her feet. "You're forgiven." His reply lit a glow of peace in Lilly's heart.

"Please," she said softly, "tell me your story."

Heinrick's eyes crinkled with delight. They turned and began to stroll across a prairie lit only by the windows of heaven and an unblemished full moon.

"Well, the Lord sure does bless a man when he is patient. To think my first friend in this new country is a pretty little lady named after a flower."

Lilly caught her breath, ignored the trembling of her heart, and slowly relaxed into the gentle rhythm of his step.

Chapter 12

Heinrick unfurled his story as they strolled into the black expanse of prairie. With each step, Lilly sensed that the telling was a catharsis, a long healing sigh after years of silence. The soft strength of his voice soon erased her haunting encounter with Clive.

"I was born in Germany, but my mother, Anna, was Norwegian. She came to Germany to study and lived in Hullhorst. My father worked as a farm hand in Neidring-hausen, a nearby village." Heinrick swiped off his hat and rubbed the rim as he walked.

"As love stories go, Papa met her at a church social and they were married a few months later. My best memory of Mama is watching her roll out the *kuchen* in our tiny kitchen. She always gave me the first piece, sprinkled with sugar." He hummed. "I love the taste of a freshly fried roll kuchen." He paused, and she felt memory in his tone. "Mama was laughter and sunshine, sugar, kisses, and the smell of fresh bread." He paused again, this time longer. "I was eight when she died of typhoid fever."

Lilly bowed her head. "I'm sorry."

"My father never recovered," he said hoarsely. "To an eight year old, a father's despair can be felt as your own. I suppose I was really a...what do you call a person without parents?"

"An orphan."

"Ja, an orphan. My mother had family in Norway and distant cousins in America. They arranged passage when I was seventeen, five years ago. I've spent one year working for each family, paying off my passage." Heinrick's voice turned hard. "And then some."

The wind fingered the disobedient strands of Lilly's hair, tickling her neck. "So, the Torgesens *do* own you."

Heinrick sighed. He stopped and turned, his face a defined shadow in the darkness. "No, I was wrong to say that. The Torgesens don't own me. I came to America of my own will, and I chose to honor my promise, or rather my family's promise, to them. Perhaps they consider me their servant, but I serve them because I serve my Lord."

"Your Lord?"

"God Almighty, the Maker of the heavens and the earth."

Lilly nodded. "Of course. I am a Christian."

Joy glittered in Heinrick's eyes. "So am I!"

Lilly frowned. "How can you be—?"

"Just because I am German doesn't mean I don't love and worship the same Jesus you do. Not all German Christians agree with Kaiser Bill. But we do agree the Lord Jesus is God and our hope for eternal life."

Lilly frowned. She hadn't considered that a foreigner, especially a German, would know the same God she did. She felt a strange kinship with this foreigner. "What will you do when your debt is paid?"

They began to walk again, bumping now and then when the prairie knocked them off balance.

"I don't know. Whatever God tells me to do, I suppose."

"Don't you have a plan? A dream?"

The breeze juggled Heinrick's laughter. "I have many dreams, Lilly. A family, a home, a good job, but most of all I dream of serving the Lord, wherever He desires to put me."

"How will you know? Who will tell you where that is?"

"God will, of course." Heinrick stopped, turned to her. "Doesn't God tell you what He wants you to do?"

Lilly stared past him, out into the sky, into the eternity where her God lived. "He doesn't have to. I already know."

Heinrick arched his brows.

"I'm going to marry Reggie when he comes home and be a pastor's wife. We have it all planned out."

"Who has it planned?" Heinrick said softly.

Lilly shivered. He wasn't just looking at her, he looked *into* her, examining her soul. The prairie was suddenly small, the night sky enclosing, the breeze cold, his presence invasive, and their walk, reckless.

The whinny of a horse shot through Lilly like an arrow. She whirled, squinted through the darkness, and recognized her father astride old Lucy. Frankie snoozed on Lucy's neck.

"I have to go," Lilly said quietly.

Heinrick nodded. He crossed his hands over his chest. Lilly stepped away, a tentative, grateful smile pushing at the corners of her mouth.

"Thank you for saving me, Heinrick."

Something in his eyes made her hesitate and halt her dash to intercept Frankie and her father. Standing there, with his shoulders sagging and with the wind shifting his golden mass of hair, Heinrick appeared every inch the orphan he'd described earlier. His eyes reached out to her with an almost tangible longing.

"Lilly, wait." Heinrick cupped a hand behind his neck and examined his scuffed boots. "You *can* save me back."

Lilly's eyes widened. "How?" She could hear Lucy scuffing closer.

"Teach me to read."

"What?"

"Teach me to read English. I never learned, and I'd like to be able to read and write."

Lilly glanced at her father. He hadn't seen them yet. Teach Heinrick to read? That would mean spending time with him, getting to know him.

It was a bad idea. She knew it in her heart. Her father may have been friendly this morning, extending the hand of fellowship to Heinrick when he thought him a ranch hand and Frankie's hero. But eventually he would find out he was German. . .then what? And what about Reggie? He could never know.

But Heinrick had called her a blessing. And he'd risked his freedom for her, standing up to Clive Torgesen. She owed him.

"Okay, one lesson, to teach you the alphabet. Agreed?"

He resembled a schoolboy with his churlish grin. "When?"

Her father was nearly within earshot. "Tomorrow, in the maple grove on the bluff near our property. Do you know where?"

Heinrick nodded.

"After church."

"I'll be there."

Lilly slipped into the envelope of darkness, heading toward Frankie and her father. The wind stirred the prairie grass, and Lilly thought she heard Heinrick call after her, "*Auf wiedersehen*, Lilly."

Chapter 13

The condemnation that simmered in her chest during the morning worship service, under the glare of Rev. Larsen's stern sermon, threatened to turn her away from her promise. Then her mother had to ask her where she was off to when she breezed past her on the way to the maple glen.

"Going down to the river," Lilly answered, but shame settled upon her and deceit felt like a scarlet letter around her neck, even if based on the best of intentions. If Reggie found out, he would be cut to the core. At best, it would be hard to explain. At worst, he would leave her at the altar, resigning her to spinsterhood. She could be annihilating her dreams by this one simple meeting.

But the mystery of her German friend was just too puzzling to ignore. Since the day his mustang had almost plowed over her, Heinrick had been chipping his way into her thoughts. Her mind kept returning to a moon-basked prairie and the memory of a tall, muscled German disappearing into the folds of darkness. Heinrick's low, gentle voice, the syllables of foreign words, and his heart-filling laughter dulled her pangs of guilt. Moreover, Heinrick was a walking contradiction. There was something about him that seemed peaceful, unencumbered, even free. Yet he wasn't free. He was, for all practical purposes, an indentured servant, paying off a bill that seemed way too high. And he counted it as serving the Lord. He seemed even joyous about the task, and Lilly couldn't unravel the paradox in that. Bondage was not joyous. It was suffocating.

In the end, this riddle drove her to the river.

❦

The maple glade had skimmed an adequate supply of cool air from the morning, and gooseflesh rose on Lilly's arms as she entered the shaded glen. A ripe river scent, rich in catfish and mud, rode in on the breeze and threaded through the trees. Lilly shoved a few rebellious, damp strands of hair under her hat, rubbed her arms, and hunted for her pupil.

He wasn't there. Lilly listened to the wind hiss through the leaves, feeling uneasy. Maybe it was for the best. She half-turned, poised to fly back to the farm and blot Heinrick from her memory, when he emerged from the shadows.

He peered at her with curious eyes and a crooked smile. "*Guten tag.*"

He'd dressed for the occasion: a clean pair of black trousers, polished ebony cowboy boots, a fire-red cotton shirt, and a buckskin vest. His blond hair may have been neatly combed, but the wind had laughed at his efforts and mussed it into wild curls. A hint of blond stubble peeked from tanned cheeks.

"You're here." Lilly gulped.

"Of course," he said. "I wouldn't miss it."

"Ready for school?" Lilly's voice sounded steadier than she felt. She shuffled toward him, dead leaves crunching beneath her boots.

He cocked his head, and a hint of mischief glinted in his blue eyes. "I'm not a very good student."

Nervousness rippled up Lilly's spine and spread out in a tingle over her body. Then Heinrick grinned wide and white, and his smile encircled her like an embrace. She had to admit he was just plain charming. She bit her lip and looked away, lest he see something he ought not to in her eyes.

His smile dimmed. "What is it, Lilly? Do you still think I'm the enemy?"

Lilly hid her eyes, staring at her shoes. "No, it's not that." Her mind raced. "I just don't know if I can help you. . . ."

Heinrick slid a hand under her elbow, and Lilly almost flew out of her skin. "I think you can help me more than you know."

The soft tone of his voice brought her gaze to his face. His eyes pleaded with her, and the longing in them took her breath away. "Please?" he whispered.

Since her mouth was dry and wordless, Lilly nodded.

"Let's sit by the river."

Heinrick led her into the sunshine, down the bluff, and they sat on a piece of bald cottonwood. Lilly pulled out her Bible, and passed it to him.

He held it in his large, rough hands and caressed the smooth leather with his thumbs. "A Bible," he murmured.

"Do you have one?"

"Of course, although mine is in German."

She nodded, letting that information digest. Then she flipped the Bible to Genesis and read the first verse. "Reading is just a matter of decoding the letters, sounding them out to form words your ear already knows."

"My ear doesn't know many words."

"Heinrick, I've heard enough to know that you will read just fine. You have a wonderful vocabulary. And what words you don't know, I'll explain."

He nodded, and she continued the lesson. "Our English alphabet is made up of twenty-six letters. From these letters, you form words, using a few basic rules, which I will teach you. First, let's learn the letters."

She pointed out each letter from the text in Genesis. He was a good student, despite his warning, turning each one over his tongue with little accent. Recognition came more quickly than she expected, and by the time the bluff swathed them in shadow, he'd read all the words in the first and second verses.

Lilly beamed at him. "You're a good student."

"Thanks," he said, his gaze buried in the Bible. He was running his finger over the third verse when she pulled the book from his grasp and folded it on her lap.

"Enough school," she declared. "Tell me why I've never met you before. I've been working for Erica Torgesen for almost a year."

"I only just arrived to the Torgesens. I've lived many places in America: New York City, Ohio, Milwaukee, Iowa, and now Dakota."

He acted as if it was normal to live so many places, like a homeless stray.

"I see," Lilly said, realizing how lonely his life must be. "Do you miss your home?"

He was silent, and when he turned to her, a thousand images gathered in his eyes. He blinked as if trying to get a fix on just one. Then the images dissolved, leaving a residue of pain in their wake. "Yes."

Lilly noticed how his hands curled over his knees, completely encasing them.

"But Germany isn't home anymore."

Lilly's eyebrows gathered her confusion.

"Dakota is home now. I am home wherever God puts me, because I am in God's hands."

Lilly shook her head. "Home is family. Home is friends. God gives us those, but you certainly can't say that Reggie, or Chuck, or Harley are home."

"Perhaps. But to spend your entire life yearning for something else, instead of surrendering to God's plans seems like a foreign land to me. Home is peace. And peace is being where God puts you."

"And God has put you here, in bondage to the Torgesens?"

"For now. But I know He has a plan, just like He had a plan for Joseph in the book of Genesis. I just have to trust Him and wait."

"But what if. . . ?" The words lodged in her throat. She looked downstream, away from Heinrick.

"What if what, Lilly?"

"What if things get messed up; what if life doesn't go according to plan?" Lilly felt Heinrick's gaze on her neck and bit her lip. She knew she'd just opened her heart for his scrutiny.

"Whose plan?" he asked softly. His knee bumped hers as he turned toward her.

Lilly swallowed her leaden heart. "Well, our plan, of course. The plan of life, the one we spend our entire lives creating."

"Whose plan is it, though? Don't you think Joseph struggled over the death of his dreams, while trudging behind a caravan of camels on his way to Egypt?

But he trusted God's plans, even while sitting in a prison, accused of a crime he didn't commit. God delivered him and a nation. Shouldn't all our plans belong to God?"

Lilly studied her fingernails, acutely aware of his gaze on her. "But God's plans are what the church and your parents say they are, aren't they? Isn't that God's voice?"

"It could be. God does speak through our church and family." He nodded slowly. "That's one way."

"How else, then, do you know what God wants you to do?"

Heinrick tapped her Bible. "God's Word. You have to read. God's plans are revealed one day at a time, through His Word and the Holy Spirit working in our lives."

Lilly rubbed the leather. "Listen, Heinrick. This is all very interesting, and I am sure, where you come from, it is part of your religion. But here, God leads me through my pastor, through my parents, and through Reggie. I just have to obey them to do what God wants."

Heinrick stared out over the water and beyond. "Lilly, do you know the difference between faith and obedience?"

Lilly's eyes narrowed and she shook her head warily. Whose lesson was this, anyway?

"Why wasn't Cain's sacrifice acceptable to God?"

Lilly frowned, confused. Heinrick's eyes gleamed, so intent was he on his sermon. He tucked a hand over hers on the Bible.

"Because it was a fruit offering?" she stammered, her gaze on his warm hand.

"No. It wasn't about the offering; it was about his heart. God looked at Cain and Abel first, then upon their offerings. He looked at their hearts and their faith. Cain's offering was all about fulfilling the law, about serving himself, about doing what was necessary to secure his forgiveness. But Abel's heart belonged to God, and he offered his lamb out of worship and faith in God's salvation. Abel's sacrifice was accepted because of his faith."

"Lilly, faith is an action. Obedience is a reaction. We obey God because we love Him, not because we want God to love us or want to earn a place in heaven."

Lilly lifted her chin. "Show me your faith, and I will show you my faith with actions."

Heinrick pulled the Bible from her hands and flipped through it. Silently he scanned the pages, then, blowing out a breath, he handed it back to her. "Could you read Hebrews 11:1 for me, please?"

She scowled at him, but found it and read aloud, " 'Now faith is the substance of things hoped for, the evidence of things not seen.' " Lilly closed the Bible.

" 'If you love me you will obey my commands,' " she countered. She hadn't spent years softening a pew for nothing.

Heinrick sighed and again pulled God's Word from her lap. He flipped, wearing his determination like a mask. But, in time, his resonant tenor voice stammered out the verse. " 'For by grace are ye saved through faith; and that not of yourselves: it is the gift of God: Not of works, lest any man should boast.' " He paused. Lilly listened to the hammering of her heart.

When he at last spoke, the words seemed to unroll from his very soul, passionate, authentic, and nearly desperate.

"Lilly, God loves us so much that when we were still sinners, before we obeyed even His slightest desire, He died for us. We don't have to earn His love or His salvation. He has good things waiting for us, even if sometimes it doesn't seem like it. We have to be like Joseph. He put his life into God's hands on a daily, moment-by-moment basis. But to put your life into God's hands and to surrender to His plans, you need to know Him. You have to read the Bible to know what He wants you to do."

"I know the Bible. It says that faith is obedience."

"Obedience is evidence of faith, Lilly. It isn't faith itself. Faith is unwavering trust in God to lead and to guide, wherever He wants. And it is knowing, in the pit of your soul, that He loves you and knows best."

His eyes glowed with their intensity. She wanted to flinch, but his gaze drew her in, like a warm fire on a cold night. Heinrick passed her the Bible. "Hebrews 11:6."

No one had ever spoken to her this way, not Rev. Larsen and certainly not Reggie. It seemed edging near impropriety to be talking about God so openly, so intimately with anyone, let alone Heinrick. Yet she was drawn to the mystery of his God, and when she read the words, something seemed to ignite deep inside her.

" 'But without faith it is impossible to please him: for he that cometh to God must believe that he is, and that he is a rewarder of them that diligently seek him.' "

Lilly closed the Bible and rubbed the smooth leather.

"Lilly," Heinrick whispered, "do you have faith in God? Do you trust Him to plan and manage your life on His terms? Do you know He loves you?"

Lilly bit the inside of her lip to keep tears at bay. "I'm confused. I don't know God that well, maybe."

Heinrick's voice was soft, like a caress on her skin, yet his words still bruised. "Lilly, perhaps you're afraid. Do you think that if you knew God and heard His voice, He might tell you something you don't want to hear?"

Lilly swiped away a tear.

The sun polished the surface of the river platinum. "I need to get home," Lilly mumbled.

"And I have chores," Heinrick agreed, but his voice betrayed disappointment. He pushed himself from the driftwood, then turned and offered her his hand. Lilly deliberated, then slipped her hand into his.

"Tomorrow?" he asked. "I promise I'll be a good student."

"You were a good student today," she replied, lifting her chin. She stood almost to his shoulder and noticed how the buttons to his shirt pulled slightly across his wide chest. He put an arm around her waist and hauled her to the top of the bluff. They stood there for a moment, the wake of their conversation shifting between them like a fragrance neither could acknowledge.

"Tomorrow, after supper," Lilly blurted. Then she yanked her hand from his and ran toward home.

Chapter 14

Lilly sat on the bald cottonwood by the river watching the amber sky melt into the mud, listening to the crickets scold her for her naiveté. Why had Heinrick stood her up? After four days, she'd learned to count on his punctuality. He read with remarkable precision, and although she hated to admit it, his accented voice made warm syrup run through her veins. Her heart began to long for that moment when he turned his blue eyes into hers and asked for another lesson.

Where was Heinrick? Tears bit her eyes. How rude! Didn't he know that she dodged suspicion every time she raced down to the river to meet him? It was becoming harder to weave tales that only skimmed the definition of lies.

But she ached to see him. Heinrick was no longer a mystery, an enigma, to her. He'd ended each lesson with a story, something from his childhood. He wanted to own land. To travel. To have a family. And he longed for, more than anything, to find a niche for himself in this new world. He'd left it unspoken, but Lilly guessed that Heinrick's deepest fear was his harsh reality—being forever a foreigner in his adopted homeland. She couldn't help feel as if he had handed her the delicate pieces of his heart.

And now that she'd seen it, she was drawn even more to the mysterious German, to his gentle character, his passionate love for God, his simple yet noble dreams.

Was this the end? Was it the end of his infectious laughter, his enthralling stories of an unruly boyhood in the Black Forest? Lilly dug her nails into her bare arms and steeled herself against the ripple of sorrow. How could she expunge the flame that he had ignited in her heart? The warmth of their friendship drew her to the bluff every evening like the glow of a beckoning campfire on a brisk autumn night. Somehow, even the July twilight would seem cold without Heinrick's smile.

Was Heinrick playing games? Maybe all he really wanted from her was language lessons. Had she imagined the warmth in his eyes and the softness of his touch on the small of her back?

A sour brew of fury and hurt burned in her throat. She jumped to her feet and scrambled up the bluff. It was all for the best, anyway. Heinrick was nothing but trouble, and she should have seen that when his horse almost trampled her.

Lilly marched through the grove, her feet pounding out a rhythm with her heart. Tears dripped down her cheek, and she violently whisked them away. She'd been a fool to trust him, to let him into her heart. At least she would be free of his endless probing questions about her faith. His God was simply different from hers. . .closer somehow, but perhaps that wasn't a good thing. She hardly wanted to trust a God who might cast her into the hands of a person like Clive Torgesen. Heinrick must have fallen out of God's favor, somehow, although she questioned the idea of such an honorable man offending God. Still, surely, God blessed those more who obeyed Him best. It just made sense that God balanced things out, and if she managed her side correctly, He would keep things even.

Lilly skidded to a halt in the middle of a withered clump of goldenrod. Maybe this was God's way of punishing her! She'd betrayed Reggie and deserved to have her heart ripped out, even by another man. Shame wound into her soul.

She'd made a terrible mistake. The only thing left to do was to forget. Thankfully, Reggie would be home soon, and the entire horrid experience could be safely tucked inside a secret chapter of her life, never to be read.

Lilly tightened her jaw as she climbed up the porch steps. She tiptoed into the house, noting her mother knitting at the kitchen table, lost in conversation with her father. Lilly ducked her head, scampered up the stairs, and threw herself across the bed. There, in the privacy of her folded arms, she cried herself to sleep.

⬧

Her subconscious put a picture to her fears. She found herself on a battlefield, searching among wide-eyed, lifeless soldiers. Some clutched pictures of sweethearts; others embraced their weapons like teddy bears. Lilly whimpered as she peered into faces, finally uncovering the one she feared to find. She cried out when she saw him, his dark hair hanging over his closed eyes, lying upon a pile of erupted earth as if he was sleeping. She crawled to him, gasping, and removed his helmet. His face was covered in a layer of black stubble, and he seemed warm. But she knew, as she curled a hand under his filthy neck, Reggie was dead.

In the background, she heard the *rat-a-tat-tat* of machine gun fire. A voice, crisp and clean and accented in German, rose over the clatter. "Trust me."

Lilly shuddered, for in its wake came a knowledge that if she surrendered, it would cost her everything she held dear, her dreams, her will, her very life.

Lilly woke herself up screaming.

Chapter 15

Five days crawled by, and the dream, instead of dissolving into the hazy folds of memory, invaded like a virus, multiplying in strength and repeating itself in crisp, horrifying detail every night. Lilly awoke each time gasping, tears rushing down her cheeks, hands clenching the snarled bedclothes. Twice she woke up Bonnie, who frowned with worry in the streams of dawn. Perhaps her sister had even mentioned it, because once, while Lilly and her mother gathered in the sun-dried laundry, her mother questioned Lilly about not sleeping well. Her mother hesitated when Lilly brushed off the matter, but didn't pursue the truth.

Lilly clawed through the days, trying to drown the German-accented voice in her ears. She pulled weeds, the only things that seemed to be thriving in the kitchen garden, canned cucumbers, and stirred jam on the potbellied stove. Not once did she wander down to the river after dinner hour.

On Thursday, Olive returned from Mobridge with two letters, one for herself and the other for Lilly. Olive tucked the letter from Reggie into Lilly's apron pocket while Lilly was wrist deep in a bowl of bread dough. The kitchen smelled of dill weed and onions, and jars of pickles cooled on the washboard. Lilly, shocked at the addition to her apron pocket, glanced at Olive. Her sister returned a glower.

"Did you forget the mail train came today?" Olive balled her hands on her hips.

Lilly's mouth dropped open, not only at Olive's loaded accusation, but also at the knowledge that she did, indeed, forget about the train and for the briefest of moments, Reggie.

"What is wrong with you?" Olive's screeching voice summoned their mother to the kitchen. "You're stumbling around the house like a drunkard, not paying attention to anyone! Why, yesterday, Alice Larsen came by, and you didn't even come out of your room to greet her." Olive's lip curled and she nearly snarled. "What sort of daughter-in-law are you?"

"That's enough, Olive," her mother said sharply. "Please leave us."

Olive shot an exasperated scowl at her mother, then stormed out of the room.

As Mrs. Clark sat on a straight-backed chair, Lilly dove into her bread dough and kneaded with vigor.

"You *have* been acting strangely, Lilly. I'd call it snippy, and that's not you." She paused and touched Lilly's forearm. "Bonnie told me about the nightmares. Sit, child, and talk to me."

Dread multiplied through her bones as Lilly met her mother's gaze. But her eyes beheld a tenderness that reached out and enfolded her, and Lilly's fear ebbed. She wiped her hands on her apron and drew up a chair, wondering what to reveal, opting for the truth.

"I taught that cowboy who saved Frankie how to read."

The shock Lilly expected was strangely absent. The older woman folded her hands together on the table. "Hmm, so that's what you were doing."

"You knew?"

Her mother's eyes twinkled. "I know a lot more than you think, Lilly. I watched you every night clean up, fix your hair, and change your dress. I knew it wasn't for the prairie dogs. And, when you finally floated home, I knew something other than the sunset had touched your heart."

"Why didn't you stop me?"

Mrs. Clark studied her clasped hands. "Because I trust you. Obviously more than Olive does. And I know that in your heart is a seed of goodness and wisdom."

Lilly blew out a ragged breath. "Does Father know?"

Her mother shook her head. "He's too worried about the wheat and the drought to be caught into the tangled mystery of his daughter's heart." She reached for Lilly's hand. "Darling, this nightmare. Does it have to do with the cowboy?"

Lilly closed her eyes, seeing Heinrick's heart-catching smile and his mesmerizing blue eyes. "Mother, do you pray?"

"Of course."

"No, I mean pray, when you aren't in church. By yourself, without Pastor Larsen leading you."

Her mother smiled. "I pray when I hang laundry, when I see the sunshine spray the grass with tiny gold sparkles. I pray when I kiss DJ and Frankie in their sleep and see the peace of innocence written upon their faces. I pray when I see your father, dozing in his rocking chair, his spectacles dripping down over his nose and the Bible open on his lap. I pray for Olive and Christian and especially Chuck every night when I read the paper. And I pray when I notice you, Lilly, standing at the edge of the yard, your long hair taken by a prairie gust. I thank God and pray for His protection and His will to be done in all our lives."

Her mother's speech enraptured her. For the first time, Lilly considered her mother had thoughts beyond cooking, and canning, and hanging laundry. She saw her mother young, dreaming of a family and a home, and most of all trusting in a God who reigned over her life. In that instant, Lilly was jealous. Jealous her mother knew where she was planted and was already reaping the harvest in the garden of life God had given her.

Somehow, during the past week, Lilly's own surety about the life she thought God had planted for her had been swept up like dry prairie soil into a whirlwind of doubt. Heinrick's suggestion that God would do what He wanted, regardless of her prayers and her sacrificial obedience to everyone's plans for her, scared her more than she would admit. Was Heinrick right? Were she and Reggie like Joseph, helpless and at the mercy of an unpredictable God?

"Mother, did you always know it was God's plan for you to marry Father?"

Mrs. Clark gave a slight frown. "Have I never told you how I met your father?"

"You met him at a social at your church."

Her mother shook her head. "It wasn't at my church. Your father was from a church in the country, a different denomination. And, Lilly, I had promised to marry another man."

Lilly froze.

Her mother nodded. "He was a rich man, had been married before, and his wife died giving birth to their son. But he was still young and a friend of your grandfather's. He wanted a wife, and my father wanted a secure future for his only daughter. So Timothy began to court me. He was a very nice man. Good humored and kind. He treated me with respect, and my family and friends told me it was a good match. And, I agreed. So he proposed to Father, then to me, and the plans were laid."

Lilly's chin drifted downward.

"Then I met your father." A playful smile lit on her mother's face. "He was a hired hand on a farm outside town. I went to the social with my friend, Marcie, whom I was visiting for the weekend. We were studying together at a finishing school in Chicago. Donald was at the social, and the day I met him, I knew."

"You knew?" Lilly breathed.

Her mother's eyes sparkled with an unfamiliar passion. "I knew I couldn't do what was expected, that I couldn't live a life committed to a man I did not wildly love."

"Mother!"

Mrs. Clark sat back in her chair, folding her hands across her chest. "It's true, Lilly. Marriage is difficult and not a place for lukewarm commitment. I knew if I married Timothy, it would be for many good reasons, but not the one that mattered."

"But what about your family, your parents?"

"Your father was patient. He courted me for three years and proved to my parents that he was committed and a hard worker. Finally your grandfather relented."

"But weren't you afraid?"

"I was more afraid of not surrendering to God's plans for my life and missing out, perhaps, on the fullness of joy He wanted for me."

"How did you know that was what God wanted. . .I mean, your father and all your friends said you should marry Timothy. Why wasn't that God's plan?"

"Because I never felt it was right. I knew I didn't truly love Timothy, although he would have been a wonderful husband, I am sure. When I prayed, it seemed as though God wrote your father into my heart. He was the answer."

"So, in answer to your question, yes, marrying your father was always the plan. But I didn't know it until I asked, then listened to God."

Lilly blew out a troubled breath. "Well, I know it is God's plan for me to marry Reggie."

Her mother's chair creaked as she leaned forward. "God always has a plan for our lives, Lilly. But it may not be the one we think it is. We have to ask Him, then listen."

Lilly sloped back in her chair and crossed her arms, not sure she'd recognize God's voice if she heard it.

Dinner was a quiet, contemplative event. Lilly's father informed the family that haying season had arrived, and Olive read portions of Chuck's letter aloud.

> We rotate through the line of trenches by week; next week Harley and Reggie and I will move forward to the supply trench, running ammunition to the support trench. I feel most sorry for the Sammies stuck in their bunkers on the front, knowing it's wet and cold and they are eating out of tin cans. But, in two weeks, I will be there, and they will feel sorry for me. Don't worry, Olive, for our good Lord protects us, and in a few short months I'll return, victory in hand. Kiss my Christian for me.
>
> Corporal Charles Wyse

Reggie's letter burned a hole in Lilly's pocket and suddenly she wanted to tear it open, clutch it to her chest, and remind herself of the sanity of their commitment.

Olive's tears streaked down her cheeks, and next to Lilly, Bonnie hiccupped a sob. Melancholy bound them together in silent meditation.

"He'll be back, Olive," Lilly reassured in a solemn tone. Olive lifted red-rimmed eyes, attempting an acquiescing grin. It dissolved into the trembling of her chin. She buried her face in Christian's neck.

Guilt pierced Lilly's heart and twisted. How could she have forgotten Reggie?

Olive wiped her stained cheeks with a free hand. "Lilly, I saw Erica Torgesen at Ernestine's. She asked if you could come to the ranch tomorrow."

Despite the wild dance of her disobedient heart, Lilly bit her lip and nonchalantly nodded.

❧

Lilly stretched across her bed and read Reggie's letter.

Dear Lilly,

I gladly received your letter of June 23, and your tender words greatly encouraged me. I cannot express to you adequately the happiness your promise brings me; it is a beacon of hope during this chaotic and unforgiving war. When the enemy is upon us, shells exploding in our bunkers, I clutch my helmet and think only of you, your emerald eyes, and the future we have laid out. I am not the only doughboy to cling to dreams of home; this hope is the veritable fuel that drives all us good Sammies over the top in a desperate attempt to chase those Germans back into the hole from which they crawled and thereby return to our shores that much sooner.

I am sure you have heard of Harley's proposal to Marjorie. I advised him toward it, he being the shy one. I assured him that Marjorie's promise would give him the courage he needs to survive this horrendous war. Just as you give to me. He is happy, and, although he has not received her reply, he is assured in his heart of her affirmation.

As I write this, the sun is disappearing behind our lines, giving relief to the relentless view of the unburied dead, destroyed machinery, and shattered earth. Tonight I am in a cover trench, my job to fire over the heads of those in the firing trench as they move along the front. Hopefully we will not hear, "Over the top!" this evening, as most of us are tired and ready for a night to merely avoid the German star shells and lob an occasional barrage over to their side. Last night, the Germans decided to focus on our sector and shelled us for three solid hours. I spent much of the night in cover, wearing my gas mask and dodging the bombs, but we did manage to pitch a few shells and, I think, send a few Germans to their unholy eternity. We are fighting like the coyote, desperate and unrelenting and hopeful that soon, very soon, we will save the world for democracy.

I am hesitant to address this next topic, but, as your future husband, it is my duty to direct you toward righteousness. My mother wrote me about a rather unpleasant altercation in town where she mentioned you had placed yourself in grave danger between two fighting men. Then she

*suggested, and I pray in error, you may have ridden off with one of them!
I am grieved by these words, Lilly. I hope it is either an erroneous report
by my mother or a miscalculation in judgment on your part. Whatever the
case, I admonish you to choose carefully your behavior. As my wife, you must
set an example for the community on proper and modest behavior and not
be fodder for gossip.*

*Of course, I know you are aware of this, and I trust you to conduct
yourself as the Christian lady I know you to be.*

*One other thing, Lilly. Mother mentioned your employment by the
Torgesens as a dressmaker. Please, I beg of you, be ready to cease this activity. It is not befitting a Christian wife and mother to have an occupation.
You will be busy enough taking care of our children and home. I know
perhaps this is a hobby for now, while you wait for my return, and because
of this, I will permit it. But when we are married, and I pray soon, you
will have enough to occupy yourself—taking care of me!*

*I think of you always and commit you in good faith to our God in
heaven to honor our plans and reunite us once again.*

*Love,
Reggie*

Chapter 16

Perhaps it was exhaustion from the sun sucking every ounce of energy as she trudged toward the Torgesen T. Maybe it was fresh guilt, churned up at the reading of Reggie's letter. Or, it could have been the hope of seeing Heinrick. Lilly couldn't put her hands around the exact reason, but regardless, knots twisted her stomach by the time she reached the Torgesen ranch.

"I need a new dress!" Mrs. Torgesen exclaimed after she'd piled Lilly's lap full of new editions of *Ladies Home Journal* and *Butterick Fashions*.

Something nouveau and fabulous." Mrs. Torgesen's eyes twinkled as she wiggled her pudgy fingers at her. "Get to work."

Lilly flipped through the pages, determined to make Mrs. Torgesen look better than a willow tree this time around. Mrs. Torgesen headed for the kitchen.

After examining fashions from velvet empire skirts to long-neck prairie blouses with poet sleeves and French cuffs, she decided upon a two-piece suit, ankle length, with a double-breasted jacket. She showed it to Mrs. Torgesen, who drooled over the page, then Lilly buried herself in the fabric wardrobe for over an hour measuring scraps. She finally settled on brown and beige twill for the jacket and a skirt of brown wool.

She spent the rest of the morning piecing together a muslin pattern from scraps until she'd produced a pinned-together likeness of the skirt and jacket.

"When will I have my first fitting, Lilly?"

"Next week, perhaps. I think I can have the skirt ready to fit by then."

Mrs. Torgesen sat at the kitchen table, eating a fresh peach like an apple. Juice pooled at the corners of her mouth and dripped off her wrist. The humid kitchen absorbed the rich aroma and spiced the air. At the stove, Eleanor was steaming jars and parboiling a pot of peaches for canning. Stacked near the door were three wooden crates of fresh peaches, wrapped in green paper. Lilly couldn't help but to stare longingly at Mrs. Torgesen's peach. The Clark family would have no peach preserves this winter.

"Would you like a peach, Lilly?" Mrs. Torgesen gestured toward the crates.

Lilly shook her head. "Oh, no thank you, Mrs. Torgesen." She didn't know why, but suddenly she felt as if accepting the peach would be traitorous to the entire Clark family. She already felt like Benedict Arnold.

Mrs. Torgesen shrugged. Lilly gathered up the fabric and folded it into a canvas bag.

The noon sun burned the prairie until even the crickets hissed in protest. Lilly noticed a clump of Holsteins on the horizon as she left the Torgesen T. She hadn't seen Heinrick, and an errant thought escaped, *Where is he?* Seeing Heinrick would only open the crusty scar upon her heart. Yet, she couldn't ignore the shard of disappointment that seemed to wedge deeper with each step away from the ranch.

A sharp whinny caught her ears. Lilly stiffened. She hadn't seen Clive at the Torgesen T either, but he was never far off. She quickened her pace, not looking back, but the thunder of hoofbeats beat down upon her. Lilly gritted her teeth and whirled, intending to meet the brute head on.

"You look angry, Lilly." Heinrick reined his mount, pushed up his hat, and leaned on his saddle horn.

Lilly gaped, then clamped her mouth closed. A thousand words rushed to mind, but not one could be formed upon her lips. Instead, Lilly balled her fists, fixing them onto her hips.

"You *are* mad." Heinrick's crooked white grin faded. "I'm sorry I didn't show up, I. . ." He glanced away, across the golden-brown prairie. "I just couldn't make it, that's all."

Lilly's bottled fury erupted. "I guess it didn't matter that I put my reputation, not to mention my future, on the line for you! You don't feel like it, so you don't show up? Do you think I was bored and needed some cheering up? Or did you just determine to pester me with all that talk about God and my religion?" Lilly crossed her arms across her chest, squeezing hard to smother her anger. "Well, it just so happens, Mr. Zook, that I was planning on telling you that you know enough English and you can learn to read just fine on your own." Lilly turned on her heel, shaking. He would have to ride away now, and she wouldn't have to worry about him one day longer, him or his probing spiritual questions.

Her knees shook when she heard him dismount and felt his presence edge in on her, ushered in by the smell of soap and a tinge of masculine perspiration. He placed a hand on her shoulder and gently turned her around. She glued her eyes to his scuffed boots, refusing to betray what might be hidden in her eyes.

"I'm sorry, Lilly. I *am* grateful for all you did for me. Please forgive me."

Lilly squinted at him. He looked stricken.

His pitiful posture turned Lilly's heart. "Okay. I forgive you."

His crooked grin reappeared. "Thank you. Now, come riding with me."

"When, right now?"

Heinrick nodded "I have to ride fence this afternoon down near your place. Come with me."

Lilly's jaw dropped. "Are you sick, Heinrick? Have you heard one thing I've said to you? I can't be seen with you anymore. I'm going to marry another man!"

Heinrick raised his blond eyebrows and peered at her as if she was the one with the sickness. "I'm not courting you, Lilly. I just miss your company." His mouth flattened into a line. "But of course, I understand. I don't want to force you into anything; I just thought it might be, well, fun." Heinrick pulled on the brim of his hat. "It sure was good seeing you again, though."

Regret boiled in her chest as she watched him ride away. She felt as if she'd been offered the priceless pearl, turned it down, and would never be the same for it. A compelling urge told her to call him back, to ride with him under the full view of the sun, and not be afraid.

"Heinrick!"

He reined his horse, turned, and smiled.

Chapter 17

Heinrick didn't allow Lilly time to change her mind. "Stay here, I'll be right back." With a whoop, he galloped back to the Torgesen T to saddle another mount. Lilly shrank into the shade of an aging ash and fought her swelling emotions. She kept telling herself he was just a friend, her student, and they were only taking a ride through the fields on a sunny day. But her stomach fluttered, and she couldn't deny the music in her heart.

Heinrick returned with a gray speckled mare tethered by her reins to his saddle horn.

"Do you know how to ride?"

"I've ridden Lucy a few times." She tied her bag to the mare's saddle.

Heinrick helped her place her foot in the stirrup, and she slid on, sidesaddle. "We won't go fast."

It felt awkward and unsteady to be halfway on a horse, and Lilly struggled to find the rhythm. "I wish I was wearing my riding skirt," she muttered. Beside her, Heinrick erupted in honeyed laughter.

They meandered through Torgesen grazing land, which rolled like giant waves toward the Missouri riverbed.

"Someone once told me the Dakota prairie was like the ocean, endless and constantly moving," Lilly commented. The sun overhead winked at her. Prairie grass crunched under the horses' sturdy hooves, and a lonely meadowlark called to them, hidden in a clump of goldenrod. Lilly pushed her straw hat off her head, letting it dangle down her back by a long loop of ribbon. The wind fingered her braided hair. Beside her, Heinrick hummed softly.

"Perhaps," he finally agreed. "The prairie does seem to be constantly moving, and the wind is louder here than on the ocean, more fierce. It roars." Heinrick followed the movement of a circling hawk. "Look, Lilly," he said, "watch the hawk. Where it is, you will always find food."

Lilly's mouth went dry. "What did you say?"

Heinrick's voice was an ocean away. "My father and I used to hunt in Germany when I was young. He told me that, and I've never forgotten it."

Lilly nodded slowly, her heart thundering. The sun began to glare. The hot wind stung her face. "It's not a thing you forget, I suppose," she said weakly.

Heinrick continued, as if lost in a memory. "The hawk reminds me of the seagulls, soaring above the seascape. The sea seemed endless, like the prairie, but much more unforgiving. I was sick for fourteen days."

Heinrick reined his horse to a stop on a small bluff. Lilly took in an unmarred view of the Clark homestead and, farther on, the Pratt farm. Heinrick pointed to a *V* in the horizon. "That's the end of Torgesen land, and the little black line running along the hills is the railroad. See how it disappears behind that bluff?"

Shading her eyes, Lilly nodded. She hardened herself to the guilt that nipped at her, reborn by Heinrick's words—Reggie's words!—and focused on Heinrick's voice.

Heinrick now pointed past her own home. "The train reappears there and runs all the way into Mobridge." He shook his head. "I hear the railroad connects one end of the country to the other. Amazing."

Lilly wasn't examining the railroad tracks. She saw only Heinrick and his blue eyes. They were almost transparent, as if she could see inside him to his optimist's heart. He wore a faded bronze shirt, untied at the neck, and had pushed his brown bandana around so that the knot seemed a little bow tie at the base of his thick, tanned neck. He wore leather gloves, but his sleeves were rolled past the elbow to reveal muscled forearms. Weathered tan chaps covered his strong legs, and he seemed to be almost one with his mount. But Lilly was especially drawn in by his voice and an accent that betrayed a man who had surmounted fear, climbed aboard a ship, ridden over an angry sea, and was forging out a life in a hostile land.

"I want to work on the railroad someday, Lilly," he said softly. "I want to ride those black rails from shore to shore and see America. Discover why my relatives left Norway for America."

"Heinrick, why did you stand me up?"

Heinrick's gaze fell away from her, and a shadow crossed his face. "Clive needed the barn mucked out."

Lilly's heart twisted and shame eclipsed the anger she'd felt. "I'm sorry."

He lifted his gaze to hers, and she saw in his eyes a passionate blaze that betrayed his frustration. "Christmas, Lilly," he said. "By Christmas, I'll be free!" He suddenly whooped and spurred his horse, which shot off into a gallop along the ridgeline. Lilly clucked to her mare, and the horse cantered after him. She clutched the saddle horn and tried to swallow her terror.

"Move with her, Lilly. Don't be afraid." The wind brought his voice to her. "Give her some rein!"

"That's easy for you to say, you're not riding in a dress!"

Heinrick's laughter formed a vivid trail, one she could have followed with her eyes closed. He slowed his mount to a walk.

"Give your horse some freedom to move, Lilly. She wants to obey you, but if you choke her, she has no choice but to fight. Your horse has to be controlled by you, but you have to give her room to trust you. A horse that is afraid and choking on the bit is a horse that can't be ridden."

Lilly fingered the leather reins, loosening her hold. Her mare fell into a graceful walk next to Heinrick.

"It's like faith in God, Lilly. You are like that horse. You have to trust God, who loves you. No matter what He does, it is for your eternal good. You can't make God do what you want, just like your horse can't make you obey. The rider is the master of the horse, but the horse can make things a lot harder by grabbing the bit in her mouth and running off with it. A horse that won't surrender freely can't be used and is no good." Heinrick leaned over and put a hand on her reins. A crooked smile creased his face. "We shoot horses like that."

Lilly grimaced. Heinrick winked at her, his eyes twinkling in the sunlight. Then his smile vanished.

"You have to trust in God's love to fully surrender to His leading. Without that trust, you'll constantly be trying to grab the bit."

Lilly ran her eyes along the horizon. The fence line hurtled the next ridge and ran beyond that to the Clark farm. The joy had evaporated from the afternoon ride. First the reminder of Reggie and now Heinrick's spiritual invasion. Couldn't he just leave her religion alone? Why did he have to rattle her beliefs every time they were together?

"Lilly, do you trust that God loves you?"

Lilly shrugged and turned away. Tears edged her eyes.

"What's wrong?" His soft voice caressed her fraying emotions.

His saddle creaked as he dismounted. He stood next to her, holding her reins, searching her eyes. Lilly bit her lip and turned her face away. Heinrick pulled off his glove and took her hand.

"Did I say something wrong?"

She shook her head but couldn't form words. How could she explain something she couldn't even understand herself? Of course, God loved her; the Bible said so, right? And Rev. Larsen had spelled it out so many times, she didn't have room for doubt. Believe and obey. She did both.

Then why did Heinrick's religion seem so different from hers? She was envious of Heinrick's absolute confidence of God's love. God's love to her had always meant tangible blessings, life in control. If Reggie died, did that mean God didn't love her? Lilly frowned at the turquoise, cloudless sky.

Why did Heinrick have to challenge everything? He'd practically accused her of not being a Christian! He'd ripped apart her religion until it was shredded. Now she didn't know what she believed.

Two betraying tears sneaked down her cheeks. Heinrick wiped one away with his wide thumb. "What is it, Lilly?"

Lilly grabbed his wrist and pulled his hand away. She shook her head, until, abruptly, the fear shuddered out of her. "No, I don't know God loves me, and I'm afraid! I'm afraid I can't be everything He wants me to be, that I will somehow destroy my chance at happiness, maybe even my salvation! And I'm afraid He's going to let something bad happen, maybe even because of something I've done, and it'll ruin everything." The truth thinned her voice to sobs.

Heinrick's brows puckered. "Lilly, God does love you. He wants to give you salvation *and* a happy future. You just have to trust Him."

Lilly shook her head. "How do I trust Him if I don't know what He's going to do?"

"You trust Him because He's already shown you His love. And you can count on that."

Lilly frowned and bit her lip. How had God shown her His love? She dared to look at Heinrick. Compassion swam in his blue eyes, and, in that moment, all she wanted to do was slide off the mare and into his strong arms. And that frightened her almost as much as surrendering to an uncontrollable God.

"Heinrick, I have to go home. This is no good. I can't be here with you. I'm going to ruin everything."

Lilly leaned on his shoulders and slid off the horse. Then she stepped away. "Thank you for the ride."

"Lilly, you aren't going to cause Reggie to be killed by going for a ride with me."

Lilly's heart lodged in her chest. She stared at him, horrified. He'd summed up, in his statement, every nightmare she'd ever imagined.

"Do you think you can earn God's favor or His love by following all the rules? By doing all Reggie, your parents, and your church tell you to?"

Heinrick pulled off his hat. The wind picked through his matted hair. "Your salvation is not based on anything you do, Lilly. No one can be good enough to be saved. That's why Jesus came and allowed Himself to be crucified. No one can live up to the Jewish law. It only serves to point out our sins. But Jesus sets us free from death by paying the price for our sins. All we can do is ask for forgiveness and receive salvation! We cannot earn it. Salvation isn't a bargain with God, it's a gift from Him."

Lilly saw him through watery eyes.

Heinrick wrapped his massive hands around her upper arms. "I don't know much, Lilly, but I know this. It is by grace you are saved through faith. Grace, Lilly. Something unearned, undeserved, and without rules." His voice was like the wind, refreshing and tugging at the bonds of her soul. "If you truly want to follow God and to know Him, then you have to understand this. If there is nothing we can do to earn salvation, if Jesus paid for our sins before we knew Him, when we were the *worst* of sinners, then there is also nothing we can do to lose it. His sacrifice is enough to pay for *all* of our sins. You cannot ruin your salvation because it is not in your power to ruin it! He loves you, and there is nothing you can do about it."

Lilly gasped as the truth hit her heart. She felt the first inklings of a freedom she'd been searching for all her life. "Not in my power to ruin it?"

Heinrick lifted her chin with his forefinger, and his gaze held hers. "God loves you, Lilly. You can trust His plans; for you, for Reggie, for your life."

She nodded, then slipped under his arms and started toward home. Halfway across the Clark hayfield, she began to laugh, joy bubbling from some broken vault in her soul. Lilly opened her arms, embracing the sky, twirled twice, and broke into a run. The canvas bag bumped against her back as she went leaping across the fallow field, laughing, crying, and most of all singing, as her soul, for the first time, found freedom.

That night, after Bonnie's breath deepened in sleep beside her, Lilly slipped out of her bed and onto her knees. Embedded in the glow of moonlight, Lilly prayed and, for the first time in her life, fully surrendered to the One who loved her.

Chapter 18

The melody of an early rising bluebird floated in on a cool dawn breeze. Lilly awakened slowly, bathed in the peace of a new morning, and realized she'd slept straight through. No nightmare. The terrifying dream had vanished, as had the fear that seemed to dog her since Reggie's departure. Worry still throbbed on one side of her heart, but it wasn't the same frantic panic that had boiled in her soul.

The second thing that impressed her as she sat up and gazed at her light-dappled walls, was the unfamiliar, remarkable lightness of soul, as if the day was hers and nothing could pin her down. It was the intoxicating breath of unconditional love, giving her hope wings. It made her gasp.

Bonnie sat up next to her, rubbing her eyes. "What?"

Lilly whirled and embraced her sister. They fell together on the stuffed mattress and giggled.

Lilly threw off the sheet, skipped to the window, and pulled back the curtains. The shadow of the house loomed long across the yard, but the sun lit the field rose gold. "With each sunrise, there is new hope."

Bonnie stared at her as if she'd grown another leg.

Lilly pulled off her cotton nightgown. She needed something refreshing, something sunny. She chose a one-piece cornflower blue calico with minute yellow daisies. It had a fitted bodice, with a lace-trimmed boat neck and turned-up cap sleeves. Lilly slid it over her head, then loosely braided her hair down her back.

"You going somewhere?" Bonnie asked, her knees drawn up to her chest under the sheet.

"Going out to greet the dawn."

Lilly reckoned, from Bonnie's look, she must have turned purple. But she didn't care. On impulse, she grabbed her Bible and tucked it under her arm. Then she left her bewildered sister to flop back onto the feather pillow and tiptoed down the stairs.

Lilly's mother was in the kitchen whipping pancake batter. She glanced up, spied Lilly, and her brow knit into a frown. Lilly shot her a wide smile and stepped out onto the porch. Across the yard, the barn doors were open, her father inside, milking. Lilly headed toward her maple grove.

The wind whispered in the branches, and the glade was cool and shadowed. Lilly strolled to the bluff and stared out at the endless prairie. A hazy residue of platinum, rose, and lavender simmered along the eastern horizon. From the opposing shore, a startled pheasant took flight from a clump of sage. Hope rode the air, tinged in the fragrance of columbine and jasmine, which continued to bloom in hardy defiance of the drought.

Lilly sat on a piece of driftwood to read her Bible. She had no idea what she was doing, but it seemed the right thing to do. Like Heinrick said, if she was to trust God, she ought to know Him. And Heinrick seemed to think knowing God meant more than just attending services. She randomly flipped open the thick Bible and determined to give it a try.

She landed somewhere in the Old Testament. Jeremiah. She hardly recalled the book, but ran her finger down the page. Then, to her profound surprise, she noticed someone had marked a verse. Verse eleven of chapter twenty-nine was underlined ever so slightly in pencil, and she heard her heart thump as she read. " 'For I know the thoughts that I think toward you, saith the Lord, thoughts of peace, and not of evil, to give you an expected end. Then shall ye call upon me, and ye shall go and pray unto me, and I will hearken unto you. And ye shall seek me, and find me, when ye shall search for me with all your heart.'"

A shiver rippled up Lilly's spine. *Ye shall seek me, and find me, when ye shall search for me with all your heart.* Lilly bit her lip and looked up at the pale, jeweled sky. Could the Maker of the heavens really be talking to her, calling out to her? *The Living Word,* Heinrick had said. God talking through the Bible. The thought was terrifying and exhilarating and beyond her comprehension.

Lilly bowed her head. *Yes, God. I want to seek You. I want to find You. I know You love me, and I want to surrender to You and Your plans for me.*

As she lifted her eyes, the fragrance of peace swept through her heart. She drew in a long breath, and the feeling seeped into her bones. But would it linger when the heat of day battered it, when fear reared its head in the form of news from Europe? Would she be able to trust?

This surrender would have to be a daily, moment-by-moment thing. *God, please, help me to know You so I am not afraid, so I see Your love. Help me to trust You.*

It was the briefest of moments after the prayer left her lips that she realized she must tell Reggie. Everything. The half-truths of her letters were, simply put, sin. She had to be honest. Most of all, she had to share with him the joy of grace. Maybe it would give him the one thing he so desperately needed—release from the cold knot of fear.

She would write to him on lavender paper, send a pressed lily, and hope he would truly understand her newfound joy.

Most of all, she would pray somehow the news of her spiritual awakening would cushion the tale about Heinrick. To tell Reggie the truth, she would have to tell him about her German friend. She would put her surrender, that peace, to the test and trust the Lord for the outcome.

Lilly stood, flung out her arms as if to welcome the day, and then picked her way through the grove of maples and back to the Clark farm for breakfast.

Lilly spent the morning laying out and cutting the skirt for Mrs. Torgesen's suit on the kitchen table. Lilly's mother peeked over her shoulder, offered a few hints, and finally admitted to Lilly that she'd surpassed her mother as a seamstress.

"I don't know how you can just look at a picture and make it come alive." Her mother shook her head in parental admiration.

After a lunch of warm milk, bread, and jam, Lilly escaped to her room and wrote to Reggie. The story was more difficult in the telling than she'd anticipated, and it took her two full hours to fill two evenly scrawled pages. She started over twice and finally resigned herself to the reality that regardless how she wrote it, she'd betrayed him. She'd spent a week in the company of a man not her fiancé, despite its innocence, and she would have to hope Reggie trusted her. She slipped a sprig of lily of the valley into the envelope. Its tiny white bells were withering, but the fragrance lingered. She hoped Reggie would be encouraged by it. She sealed the letter and propped it on her vanity. She couldn't mail it until Monday's train, but she felt that much the cleaner for having revealed the truth.

"Lilly, could you run into Ernestine's for flour and molasses?" her mother called from the bottom steps. Lilly grabbed her basket and her straw hat and set off for Mobridge.

A buzz of tension, beyond the hum of the riverbed grasshoppers, drifted through the town. Horses were packed into tight rows, tethered to hitching posts. Buckboards stood at a standstill, filled with goods. Women in bonnets and men chewing on straw milled about on the clapboard sidewalk. Curious, Lilly quickened her pace toward Ernestine's.

The news met her there.

"Did you hear about the battle?" Ernestine's fat sweaty hands worked quickly, filling the flour sacks. Lilly handed her the empty burlap bag she'd borrowed. Ernestine took it and continued her monologue. "We just got the news in the *Milwaukee Journal*. A big battle over a river in France someplace." She gave Lilly the flour. Her probing eyes seemed to soften. "They say our boys are in the fray."

Lilly bit her lip and nodded. "Can I have some molasses, also?"

Ernestine turned and searched the shelves for a bottle. Lilly was glad for the moment to compose herself. Her heartbeat throbbed in her ears, and she fought a tremble. Ernestine returned with the molasses. Lilly dropped it into her basket and paid her.

"God be with you and Reggie." Ernestine offered a smile that felt too much like a condolence.

"Thank you," Lilly managed. She darted for the door.

At Miller's, Ed shrugged. "Sorry, Lilly, we're fresh out of newspapers. Try the postal."

Lilly hustled to the post office and discovered they, too, were sold out. Heart sinking, she headed for the door.

"Lilly, you have a letter." Mildred Baxter, the postmistress, handed her a small envelope.

Lilly frowned. "Did I miss the train?"

Mildred shook her head. "I don't know who it's from."

Lilly stepped out into the sunshine, confusion distracting her disappointment over the shortage of newspapers. The letter *was* for her. Her name was spelled out in small, bold capitals on the bleached parchment envelope. And there was no postage.

Lilly examined it for a moment, then decided to open it on the road home, away from any prying eyes on the street. She slipped the letter into her basket.

Her last stop was the armory. She found Marjorie red-eyed and folding bandages with unequalled passion. Lilly pulled her friend into an embrace.

"Don't worry, Marj. God will watch over them."

Tears flooded Marjorie's eyes. "That doesn't mean Harley will come back home. It doesn't mean everything will be okay."

Lilly peered into her friend's anguished face, her heart reciting everything she'd embraced over the past day. "Yes, it does. God loves us, and because of that, everything will be okay."

Marjorie studied her a long moment, as if absorbing her words. Then she laid her head on Lilly's shoulder. Lilly held her, briefly bearing her friend's burden. Then Lilly left Marjorie to assemble soon-to-be needed action kits and headed home.

A half-mile out of Mobridge, Lilly remembered the letter. She retrieved it from the basket and worked the envelope open.

It was from Heinrick.

Dear Lilly,

I never thanked you for the lessons. Please meet me at our "school" tomorrow night at sunset.

Your friend,
Heinrick

Lilly's mouth dried, and she nearly allowed the wind to snatch the letter from her grip. In some strange, awkward way, his invitation was a soothing balm on the worry tearing at her heart; as if time with Heinrick could actually help her believe the words she'd so confidently spoken to Marjorie—that God would make everything okay.

She ambled home, attempting to unsnarl the paradox in her heart.

Chapter 19

With the news of the ongoing battle in France, worry moved into the Clark home. It brought with it a foul mood. Olive did nothing but clutch Christian and sit on the porch in the wide willow rocker, staring with glassy eyes out over the dead wheat field. Her father and Frankie rose long before dawn to cut prairie grass. Her mother canned three dozen jars of gooseberry jam, her lips moving in constant prayer. Lilly basted together, in wide stitches, Erica Torgesen's skirt and hoped she would have a happy occasion to wear it, instead of a funeral.

Lilly had greeted the dawn by the river, praying and watching the sun creep over the horizon from Reggie's side of the world. Her morning reading, from Psalm 56, seemed a shield against the barrage of the day. " 'What time I am afraid, I will trust in thee. In God I will praise his word, in God I have put my trust; I will not fear what flesh can do unto me.' " God certainly knew how to meet the need of the moment. Lilly memorized the verse and recited it often, especially when worry curled around her heart like a stinging nettle.

The day drew out like old honey. Although anxiety strummed in her heart, Lilly couldn't deny that time crawled in response to the anticipation of seeing Heinrick. Curiosity ran like wildfire through her thoughts. More than that, however, she longed for his calming presence to remind her of God's love. Somehow, Heinrick could see into her soul, unearth her deepest fears, and scatter them with a word of wisdom.

Dinner was sober and simple: new potatoes, hot bread, and gravy. Lilly made a salad from carrots and dandelion greens. Olive excused herself to her room, and Bonnie cleared the table. Lilly washed the dishes in silence, but her heart thundered with the ticks of the mantle clock. Finally, the last dish sparkled, and she dashed upstairs. She changed into a jade green skirt and white blouse with a Buster Brown collar and puffy short sleeves.

Lilly noticed her mother glance up from her knitting and raise her thin brows as Lilly flew past her on the porch.

Heinrick was waiting, embedded in the shadows of a great maple. He'd spiffed up for the occasion, a pair of clean black trousers, polished boots, a brown cotton button-down shirt, albeit frayed at the elbows, and a fringed dark chocolate leather vest. He'd even slicked back his golden hair. He gave her a wide grin and stepped from the arms of the tree.

"*Guten abend*, Lilly." His voice was warm, and he offered her his arm.

"Hello, Heinrick," Lilly returned, suddenly gripped with shyness. She lowered her eyes, but wrapped her arm around the crook of his elbow. He led her out onto the bluff, then down to their cottonwood bench. The sun melted along the horizon, and the air smelled faintly of drying hay.

He didn't look at her, but instead chose a family of prairie dogs, darting along the other shore, for his attention. "I wanted to thank you, Lilly," he started in a halting voice. "You've given me my future. If I can read, I can do anything. I know it cost you to meet me, and I will never forget your sacrifice."

Lilly considered him, her gaze running along his wide-set jaw and his blond hair curling behind his ears. His shirtsleeves tightened around the base of his muscled arms, and he had his hands folded in his lap. She remembered the way those hands had caught the blows of the Craffey brothers, tamed a wild stallion, batted away Clive's anger, and tenderly wiped a tear from her cheek. So powerful, yet profoundly gentle. She may have taught him how to read, but he'd taught her how to live.

"I have to thank you, also." Lilly gazed toward the melting sunset. "I did it, Heinrick. I prayed and surrendered to God's love." She glanced at him. His eyes drew her in and held her. They were filled with a vivid, tangible joy, and in that moment, she saw herself as he saw her. Not as Reggie's fiancée, or as a farm girl, or even as his teacher, but as a lady he admired. She knew, as long as she lived, she would never forget the way Heinrick made her believe she was special. . .and loved. Then he smiled, and she could have danced in the music of it. Heinrick reached into his vest pocket. "I have a gift for you." He pulled out a wad of cotton and held it out to her.

Lilly unwrapped it carefully and gasped. Inside lay a long-toothed, hand-painted, brass butterfly comb, with an emerald-colored glass stone in the center. Wide wings, painted a ginger brown, flared from the center stone body. At the bottom, a brass tail was fashioned into a row of delicate loops. It was antique, exquisite, and doubtlessly expensive.

"It's breathtaking," Lilly whispered.

"It belonged to my mother."

Lilly's eyes teared. "I don't know what to say. I can't accept it."

Heinrick frowned. "Why not?"

Lilly bit her lip. Why not? It was just a gift from a friend, a sort of payment for her kind deed. She felt herself shrugging. "I. . .I don't know."

"Please take it, Lilly. I want you to have it."

With trembling hands, she folded the comb carefully back into the cotton. "Thank you. I'll treasure it."

Heinrick smiled, and delight glimmered in his blue eyes. "Now, tell me about the dress you are making Erica Torgesen that has her waltzing around the ranch."

Lilly laughed, and together they sat on the cottonwood bench, knees touching, while she told him about Mrs. Torgesen, the willow tree dress, and her fashion dreams. Heinrick laughed and listened, resting his head on his hands as he watched her.

Twilight hued the Missouri copper. Lilly heard a voice threading through the maple grove, calling her name. A voice edged in panic.

Lilly jumped to her feet. "Over here, Bonnie." She cast a frown at Heinrick. "I have to go."

He nodded and scrambled up the bluff, then reached down for Lilly. Lilly climbed over the ridge just as Bonnie burst from the shadows. She skidded to a halt and stared at the pair, eyes bulging, mouth agape. She found her senses quickly, however, and turned her attention to Lilly. Her eyes were troubled and her voice shook. "Come home, Lilly."

"Bonnie, you're scaring me." Lilly wound her arms around herself.

Bonnie's eyes flooded and her chin quivered, but she managed an explanation. "Olive got a telegram. Chuck's been killed."

Lilly covered her mouth with her hand, stifling a cry of anguish. She felt Heinrick's arm wind around her waist.

"Lilly, that's not all." Bonnie paused and took a step toward Lilly, a hand extended as if to steady the news. "Rev. and Mrs. Larsen are up at the house."

The blood drained from Lilly's face.

"Reggie's missing."

Chapter 20

Lilly leaned back on her heels and rubbed a grimy wrist across her sweaty brow. Her body felt dry and dusty, and her hands were cracked and sore from pulling weeds. But the sting in her palms felt easier to bear than the searing wounds in her heart. Each member of her family dodged the specter of grief in their own way. While Lilly tediously weeded the dying garden, her father worked from dawn till dusk in the hay field, dragging an exhausted Frankie with him. Her mother canned thirty-six jars of dills and twelve of relish, DJ chased the kittens around the dry yellowing yard and played with Christian, and Olive stopped living. She was a wasteland, crushed in spirit and hope, withering by the hour. She ceased eating and, after the first day, stopped dressing. By Sunday, she wouldn't even rise from her double bed. Lilly brought her meals, stroked her sister's waist-long chestnut hair, and tried to comfort her. But for Olive, there was no solace. To Lilly, she was a frightening prophecy of what might come if Reggie was confirmed dead. Lilly clung to the hope, should that dark hour transpire, her newfound peace would carry her above the grave and keep her from being, in essence, Olive, a woman who believed she had no tomorrows.

Lilly buried herself in the Psalms. It seemed a desperate escape at first, and Lilly doubted that the Bible would offer her any sort of encouragement. She was infinitely mistaken. The never-before-read passages became nearly tangible in their spiritual embrace and, as she wound herself inside the sorrows and joys of the Jewish king, David, she reaped the one thing Olive lacked—faith. David praised God in the midst of sorrow, and she would as well, clutching the belief that God loved her.

※

"It's addressed to Lillian Clark." Bonnie's face was ashen as she handed Lilly the telegram. Lilly took the envelope with shaking hands. Two weeks without a word and finally the army had sent news. It must have taken them that long to sift through the bodies.

Her mother crept up beside Lilly and wound an arm around her waist. "Open it, honey."

As the last embers of hope died within her, Lilly worked the telegram open. Brutally short, it was from the person she least expected to hear from.

Dear Lilly,

Alive. In Paris hospital. Harley KIA. Chuck KIA. Coming home.

Reggie

Lilly gasped, covered her mouth, and sank into a kitchen chair. She handed the telegram to her mother, who read it aloud and wept.

Hot tears ran down Lilly's cheeks. God had saved Reggie. He was coming home. She wrapped her arms around herself and pushed back a tremble.

"Oh, Lilly! It's so wonderful!" Bonnie squealed and embraced her, and Lilly's father squeezed Lilly's shoulder as he passed by. Only Olive was speechless. She stood at the end of the table, looking brutal in her bathrobe and wadded, greasy hair. Lilly glanced at her and, in that instant, felt her sister's jealousy as if it were a right-handed blow.

Lilly offered a sympathetic smile, but Olive's disbelieving eyes tightened into a glare. She whirled and ran to her room.

The only thing left to do was to tell Marjorie. Dread weighted Lilly's footsteps all the way to the Pratt farm. When she rapped on the peeling screen door, Mrs. Pratt opened it and greeted her cheerfully. When she saw Lilly's face, however, she ushered her to the kitchen, then sent Evelyn into town to fetch Marjorie.

Why it had been ordained for Lilly to inform her best friend her fiancé had been killed, she would never understand. It seemed utterly unfair to be shouldered with the job. And yet, she knew the hope she'd just discovered and so desperately clung to was the only hope she could offer her friend. She longed to tell Marjorie that God could not only comfort her, He could create a future for her despite the destruction of her well-laid plans.

Marjorie read the telegram twice and handed it back to Lilly. Her hands shook. "Maybe he's mistaken."

"Maybe." But doubt filled Lilly's reply. Marjorie heard it, and her mourning wail shredded Lilly's heart. Marjorie crumpled into Lilly's arms and sobs shuddered through her. Lilly rubbed her hair and mourned with her as the horror of war shattered their hearts.

Lilly finally tucked a spent Marjorie into bed. Wandering home under a starlit sky, she listened to the breeze moan in her ears and wondered what tomorrow would bring.

Chuck and Harley were gone, but Reggie was coming home. It was a sign. God wanted them together. She would obey, even though she only saw Heinrick each night in her dreams.

❧

Alice Larsen visited a few days later, recovered from her grief and unfurling dramatic plans for Lilly's wedding. She was aghast to discover Lilly hadn't started on her wedding dress.

"I would think, with your love of sewing, you would have it cut out and basted, at least."

Lilly smiled and mentioned she was helping Erica Torgesen with a dress. Mrs. Larsen waved the thought away with the back of her hand. "You'll just have to tell Erica Torgesen you are much too busy now to dress her up like a doll. She's too concerned with frills, anyway." Mrs. Larsen laid a hand on Mrs. Clark's arm and, looking at Lilly, breathed into her mother's corner of the table, "It's as if she thinks life is a fashion show!"

Lilly and her mother exchanged looks and smiled. That was exactly what Erica Torgesen thought.

"Even so, Mrs. Larsen, I promised her an outfit, and I intend to finish it," Lilly said.

Mrs. Larsen recoiled as if Lilly had slapped her. "Well, I know you like to sew, Lilly, but really, your priorities are with Reggie, now that he is coming home. I thought he'd written to you as much."

Lilly gaped. Was Reggie duplicating his letters to her to his mother? She quickly clamped her mouth shut and folded her hands on the table. "Reggie and I will discuss it when he returns."

Mrs. Larsen gave her a disapproving look. "You shouldn't have to *discuss* anything with Reggie. He's your husband, and your job is to obey."

"He's not my husband yet, Mrs. Larsen."

Mrs. Larsen gasped, but recovered in lightning speed. "And he may not be with that attitude!" She shot a glance at Lilly's mother, who'd planted a smile on her face.

"Well." Mrs. Larsen pounced to her feet. She seemed to search for words. "Good day, then."

Lilly stood. "Good day, Mrs. Larsen." She smiled, but Mrs. Larsen did not.

"I hope to see some progress on that dress and the wedding plans when I return."

Lilly nodded as if that was exactly what Mrs. Larsen could expect. The woman let the screen door bang behind her.

Mother Clark's smile faded as she eyed her daughter. "Is there something you want to tell me?"

"Of course not, Mother," Lilly replied in a thin voice.

❧

She was just confused. Things were happening too fast—Reggie's telegram, Chuck's death, the elaborate Alice Larsen–created wedding plans. Lilly lay on her bed, staring at the ceiling. Confusion was the only reasonable explanation for the heaviness that settled over her when she thought about life with Reggie. She was just feeling rushed, all her dreams cascading upon her. Even her prayers seemed to be hitting the ceiling and bouncing back.

She determined to count her blessings and make Reggie's homecoming everything he and Mrs. Larsen hoped it would be.

August slid by without a word from Reggie, or Heinrick, for that matter. The cessation of Reggie's letters lit worry in Lilly's heart. She wondered if perhaps Reggie had been mistaken about his homeward destination. September rode in, carrying with it the crisp, expectant fall air. Lilly finished Erica Torgesen's suit, but turned her down when Mrs. Torgesen asked for a Thanksgiving outfit.

Mrs. Torgesen frowned her disappointment. "Why, dear?"

Lilly forced a smile. "Because I plan to be getting married right about then."

A delighted Mrs. Torgesen clasped both hands to her mouth, then embraced Lilly.

Lilly tarried as she left the Torgesen T the final time. She leaned on the corral and watched Buttercup run among the group of stock horses, obviously the master of the herd. The mustang trotted near, stopping five feet away to examine her. His glassy brown eyes seemed to search hers, and she extended a hand to him. He sputtered and backed away.

Lilly withdrew her hand. Well, she understood. Her heart seemed just as skittish, afraid to step forward and be caught.

And yet, that was what she'd been waiting for her entire life.

She dragged home. The prairie grass had turned golden. The leaves were tarnished, the maples blushing red and orange. The smell of wood fires spiced the air. A skein of Canadian geese overhead honked their way south. Winter would soon shroud the prairie, with its endless whiteness and wind that seemed to scream in one eternal blast. Winter was for family, and quiet times, and embracing all hibernation had to offer. By then, she hoped, Reggie would be home, they would be married, and she would finally again know the sweet fragrance of peace.

Chapter 21

"May I walk home alone?" Lilly gathered her shawl over her shoulders and glanced up at her mother, who was tucking DJ into his woolen coat. Her mother met her gaze, compassion written on her face. She nodded.

Lilly let a sigh of relief escape her lips. The cool starlit night would be a refreshing change to Rev. Larsen's heated sermon.

The reverend's territory-wide announcement for all members of the congregation to meet and pray for the safety of their soldiers was a gathering meant to heal and extend hope to the hurting. The entire community, tired of harvesting a dying crop and weary of leaning on faith, mustered to the call, and the little church nearly burst to overflowing, yearning for fresh hope. Rev. Larsen, recognizing an opportune moment, preached a pointed sermon about obedience. It seemed to Lilly every word was meant for her ears.

Over the past month, Alice Larsen had been dutiful in her visits, inspecting Lilly's progress on her wedding dress, as if Lilly was sewing together the older woman's hopes and dreams.

Lilly exited the church cloakroom. The cool autumn breeze nipped at her ears as she watched Dakotans scatter in all directions, walking or riding buckboards. Her parents, Frankie, DJ, and Bonnie in tow, hustled past her.

"Don't tarry too long," her mother whispered.

Main Street was lonely and deeply shadowed. As she meandered down the dirt street, early stars winked at her. Dying leaves hissed, stirred by the breeze. Lilly stared into the night sky, and emptiness panged in her heart. Despite her prayers and growing faith in God's love, her spirit seemed to be dying within her, and she'd never felt so despondent. "God, what's wrong with me? Why do I feel as though I am walking through a tunnel that's only getting darker? Why am I not rejoicing? Reggie is coming home. This is a gift from You!" She wrapped her arms around her waist and moaned. The sound was snagged by the wind and amplified. "Help me, Lord." The words seemed a catharsis, and, with them, she realized she needed God more than she ever had before. She needed Him to remind her He had it all worked out, that He was still in charge—that marrying Reggie was right and His ordained will. "Please, God, give me peace in my heart." Her words ended in muffled sobs as she buried her face in her hands.

"Lilly?"

Heinrick approached her dressed in a muddy ankle-length duster, and holding the reins to his stomping bay. He smiled, but his eyes betrayed worry.

"Where have you been?" She clamped a hand over her mouth, ashamed at the desperation in her voice.

"Roundup."

Lilly felt like a fool. All this time she thought he'd been ignoring her, hiding somewhere in a clump of Holsteins.

"I'm sorry, Heinrick. I just, well, missed you." There, she'd said it. And it was the truth. She could have used his kind words, his wisdom, and his nudges to trust in the Lord.

Heinrick looked stricken. He grabbed her by the arm. "I need to talk to you." Flinging his reins over a hitching post, he led her to the alley between Graham's Pharmacy and the armory. Lilly frowned as he stepped into the shadows, but followed. Camouflaged in the semidarkness, Heinrick blew out a heavy breath, turning her to face him. His hat was pushed back on his head, and his hair was an inch longer, caught in the collar of his coat. Thick, white-blond stubble layered his cheeks, and something disturbing darkened his eyes.

"Lilly, I'm sorry. I didn't tell you the whole truth."

Her brow knotted in confusion.

"I saw you when you came out to the Torgesen T the last time. But. . .well, I didn't want to see you, so I rode out, away from you."

Lilly's frown deepened, and she crossed her arms under her wool cape.

"I didn't want to hurt you, Lilly, or confuse us."

Us? "What are you talking about, Heinrick?"

He swept off his hat, rubbed the brim with his hands, and stared at the ground.

"I'm talking about you belonging to another man, Lilly. I'm talking about the fact you are pledged to marry someone else, and. . .I'm in love with you."

Her jaw dropped and a tremor rippled up her spine.

"But I can't have you." Heinrick's voice was hoarse, and he avoided her eyes. "And every time I see you, it feels like a knife turning in my chest."

Shock rocked Lilly to her toes. Then, like a fragrant breeze, the joy swept through her heart. Heinrick *loved* her. That was why his eyes twinkled with delight when she was with him, why his voice always turned tender, and why he now looked more afraid than she'd ever seen him, even when facing the Craffey brothers. And she knew why her own heart now felt suddenly, wonderfully, alive.

"Oh, Heinrick," Lilly blurted, unable to stop herself. "I love you, too."

Heinrick's blue eyes probed hers, searching for the truth.

Lilly smiled broadly, love coursing through her veins with every beat of her heart. "Ja, Heinrick, I do!"

His eyes shone as a lopsided grin appeared on his face. He closed the gap between them in one smooth step. Then he slid a gloved hand around her neck. She jumped, then leaned into his strong grip.

Heinrick studied her for a moment, as if imprinting her face on his memory, examining her eyes, her hair, her nose, finally her lips. The expression in his eyes betrayed his intentions.

He wanted to kiss her.

Lilly's breath caught in her throat and she tingled from head to toe. She felt frightened and hopeful all at once. She wanted to be inside his powerful arms, to feel the tenderness of his touch. But it was wrong. Despite her feelings and his, so vividly written on his face, she couldn't allow him to kiss her. Lilly touched his chest, intending to push him away.

"Lillian Clark, what are you doing?"

The voice ripped them apart. Heinrick stepped away from her as Lilly whirled. Marjorie Pratt stood on the street, next to the armory, staring at them as if they had planted a bomb on Main Street. "What are you doing?" she repeated, her voice rising in horror.

Lilly felt sick. "Marjorie, please."

"You are engaged to Reggie! And this man," Marjorie pointed wildly at Heinrick, "is a *German!* His kind *murdered* Harley and *Chuck* and almost killed Reggie, and you are *kissing* him?" Her voice reached a shrill pitch, and Lilly stepped toward her.

"Marjorie, I'm not kissing him. We're just talking."

"That's not what it looked like to me!"

Lilly shook her head, "Marj, please listen. . . ."

"I will *not* listen, you. . .you. . .*traitor!*" Marjorie glared at her, shaking with fury. Lilly saw Marjorie's rage and realized her friend was beyond reason. Then Marjorie bolted, plunging into the darkness. Lilly started after her, groaned, and let her go.

She turned and shot a helpless look at Heinrick. His defeated expression terrified her more than Marjorie's fury. Heinrick replaced his hat, his mouth set in a muted line. His eyes were distant. "I'll take you home."

Lilly wanted to scream, weep, throw herself into his arms, and make him affirm his love for her. But his emotions were locked safely behind the same tortured, lonely expression she'd seen back at the Torgesen T. This time, however, instead of reaching out to her, pulling her into his world, he pushed her away. Her eyes filled.

Heinrick helped her into the saddle, then mounted his horse behind her.

His arms wrapped around her, and she let herself enjoy the strong, safe place inside his forced embrace. He said nothing the entire ride home, but Lilly felt his chest move in heavy sighs as she leaned against him. When she glanced up into his shadowed face, hoping to find a glimmer of the love he'd unveiled in the alley, she saw only stone blue eyes peering into the darkness.

The wind moaned, along with her heart. The smell of wood fires lingered in the air, and perhaps the smoke singed her eyes, for tears edged down her cheeks.

When they reached her road, Heinrick reined the bay. "Should I take you to the house?" His voice seemed pinched, as if pushed through a vice.

Lilly's throat burned. "No. I'd better get off here."

Heinrick nodded and dismounted. Lilly let herself slide into his arms. He held her one moment longer than necessary, or maybe she imagined it. Then he released her, and she stepped away. She lifted her chin, waiting for him to remount his horse. A thousand words formed, but she couldn't get them past the sorrow flooding her heart.

Heinrick grabbed his saddle horn and stared out across the prairie. "You were right, Lilly. I should have listened to you from the beginning. I seem to bring you nothing but trouble. I'm sorry."

Lilly longed to refute his words. *Oh no, Heinrick, you've brought me nothing but joy.* But she saw in his eyes the futility of argument.

"I think, for your sake," Heinrick's voice turned stiff, "and for mine, this is good-bye."

Lilly bit her lip and nodded woodenly.

"Lilly, don't forget God loves you." He kept the rest unspoken, but oh, how she wanted to hear it: *And so do I.*

She shivered as she watched him climb into the saddle. He spurred his horse and, in violent abruptness, was gone in a full gallop toward the Torgesen T.

Then there was just the terrible roaring of emptiness in her heart.

By Lilly's estimation, the shelling started shortly after midnight. The first rock shattered one of the glass windows on the front of the house and landed in the living room, next to her mother's willow rocker. The second volley destroyed the other window and smashed a stack of fine china her mother had carted west from Chicago.

By the time the third rock hurtled through the parlor window and crushed the mantle clock, her father was in the living room, pulling on his cotton work-pants and flipping suspenders over his shoulders. Lilly watched from the door-way of her bedroom as her mother flew down the stairs, despite orders to stay put. Lilly realized her mother's intentions were not to save her collection of china teacups from the old country nor the freshly caned straight-back chairs. No, she headed straight for Olive and Christian's room, located in the lean-to on the main floor.

Olive appeared, clutching a screaming Christian, her face the color of chalk. "What's going on?" she shrieked.

Mother Clark slung her arm around them. "Upstairs!" she commanded.

From the landing, Lilly clutched Bonnie's hand and watched them race for the stairway. A rock blew through the kitchen window, scattering glass at their heels. Olive's terrified scream shook the house.

"Hurry!" Lilly yelled.

Olive and her mother scampered up the stairs two at a time. Her older sister dove past Lilly and flew into her parents' room. Lilly saw her throw Christian on the bed and cover him with her body. Mrs. Clark grabbed Bonnie by the arm, meaning to pull both her girls along with her, but Lilly broke away from Bonnie's grasp and scrambled down the stairs.

"Lilly, come back here!" her mother called, racing down the hall to retrieve the boys.

Lilly skidded to a halt in the parlor. Her father was crouched below a window. He shot her a frown. "Get down."

She dropped to all fours and crawled across the floor. "Who's doing this?"

He put a finger to his lips.

Outside, Lilly heard slurred, enraged voices.

"That's Clive Torgesen!" Her chest tightened. A rock ripped through an unbroken pane and glass sprayed the room. Lilly cried out as her father shielded her with his body. The rock thudded into a Queen Anne armchair.

"I'm going out there," he said.

Lilly grabbed his arm. "No, Father, they'll kill you!"

He jerked his arm away. "I've got to stop them before they do real damage, like set fire to the house."

Lilly's heart froze in her chest.

Jumping up, she scuttled behind her father.

"Lilly, get upstairs!" He opened the front door.

She backed away and hid behind the parlor doorframe.

Her father stepped onto the porch. Lilly tiptoed to the front door, sidled to one side, and peeked out. In the moonlight, she could make out four men: Clive Torgesen, two of his cattle hands, and an older man. Lilly gasped. The last was Harry Bishop, Marjorie's cousin, and from latest accounts, an outlaw. Marjorie had obviously raced straight home and informed her family what she'd seen in Mobridge.

Mr. Clark held up a steady hand and spoke in a loud voice. "Howdy, boys.

What seems to be the problem?"

Guilt edged Lilly onto the porch. This was her doing, and she had to face it.

Clive balled his hands on his hips and swayed. "Your daughter's a Benedict Arnold, Clark!"

"I have three daughters, boys, and all of them are loyal to the Red, White, and Blue." Her father's calm voice mustered Lilly's courage.

Harry pointed a quivering finger at him. "That ain't true! Marjorie caught her kissing a German right here in this very town!"

Lilly's breath caught, but she propelled her legs forward and darted behind her father, clutching his arm. The wind whipped through her cotton nightgown and even from five feet away, the pungent odor of whiskey hit her with a stinging force. Lilly's eyes watered from the stench. Her father didn't spare her a glance.

"My daughter is engaged to Reggie Larsen, boys. She wouldn't go near another man." His voice sounded so sure, Lilly was sickened to think he was about to be made a fool.

"You need to keep a shorter leash on her!" Clive stumbled forward and threw a bottle onto the porch. It smashed at her father's feet. He didn't even flinch.

"This here is a warnin'—you keep that girl of yours under lock and key and away from the enemy, or we'll teach her and your whole family a lesson in patriotism!" Clive curled his lip and spat on the ground. He waved at Lilly, who shrank behind her father. "I see you there, missy. And I know what ya done. Your friend Henry is gonna git a reminder about keepin' his paws off American girls!"

Lilly went cold. Heinrick against Clive and three drunken brutes? She closed her eyes and buried her face in her father's back.

"Get outta here, boys." Her father's voice carried on the wind and must have seemed like thunder to the inebriated men because they spooked and backed up.

"You remember what we said, missy! You stay home!"

As her father stood there, Lilly saw him as a lone wall of protection between a prejudiced world and his family. She was horrified to know she'd brought it on, but profoundly thankful for her father's courage. He was stoic as the four men rode off. Then he whirled, grabbed Lilly by her thin cotton-clothed arm, and marched her back into the house.

That's when she began to tremble.

Chapter 22

W e'll clean up, then we'll talk." Her father's voice was tight.
Lilly instantly discovered untapped energy. She swept the broken glass and fastened the shutters. Her mother, Olive, and Bonnie worked silently beside her. Lilly shed noiseless tears as she watched her mother pile the broken china on the kitchen table. Bonnie occasionally frowned in her direction, but it was Olive's unmasked glare that made Lilly want to crawl under her bed and hide.

Finally, the house was put in order. Their mother sent Bonnie, DJ, and Frankie to their rooms. Olive stomped upstairs and slammed the door to her parents' bedroom. Lilly's mother sank into the willow rocker and folded her hands on her lap, her mouth a muted line. Her father ran his hand through his brown hair and paced in a circle near the sofa. Lilly knew he fought a swelling anger.

"What's this all about, Lilly?"

"I know what it's about!" Olive snarled from the top landing. A scarecrow in her white nightgown, fury blazed in Olive's dark eyes, and her face twisted in rage. She stormed down the stairs, waving a parchment envelope.

Lilly went numb. "Where did you get that?"

Olive ignored her. "It's a letter from him. From that German spy she met in town!"

Lilly clenched her teeth and glanced at her father. A muscle tensed in his jaw as he looked between his two daughters. He frowned at Lilly, and she shrank into a hard-backed chair.

Olive wore a crazed look. "You've been getting letters from him, haven't you? Letters from the enemy! You're a traitor! You've betrayed us all." She threw the letter at Lilly. It spiraled to the floor. Lilly ducked her head.

"Go to bed, Olive."

Olive recoiled from her father's command as if she'd been slapped. She stabbed a finger at Lilly. "She doesn't deserve Reggie."

Silence threw a thousand accusing jabs as Lilly weighed those words. Then Olive's wretched sobs broke the stunned quiet. She covered her face with her hands, and her body shook. Her father held her.

Lilly's heart twisted and tears flowed as she watched her sister suffer. She'd never meant to bring this kind of grief to her family.

Olive finally disentangled herself from her father's grasp. Without a glance at Lilly, she turned and climbed the stairs, every thump echoing through the house. Lilly heard her parents' bedroom door close.

Her father turned to her. His lips were pinched in suppressed fury. She sucked in a deep breath and glanced at her mother, who offered her a slightly pitying look. Mr. Clark sat on the edge of the sofa, clasped his hands together, and raised his brows.

Lilly gulped. Then, working her fingers into knots, she spilled out the story. She started with the fight on the street, included the English lessons, the horse-back ride, the butterfly comb, and her confrontation with Marjorie.

"But I didn't kiss him," Lilly insisted.

Her father shook his head. "You didn't have to—you already gave him your heart. That's betrayal enough."

Lilly caught her breath. He was right. She *had* given Heinrick her heart. And in doing so, she'd been unfaithful to Reggie. But they were all missing the most important part of her story.

"Father, Heinrick opened a door to God. Somehow, through his words, I saw that I feared God, as if He was a wolf waiting to eat me if I did something wrong. But Heinrick showed me that isn't true. God loves me and has a good plan for my life. And when I make mistakes or don't do everything right, I am still loved. Heinrick taught me how to trust God, no matter what happens. He showed me the keys to freedom, to joy, and God unlocked my prison."

Her father's face softened, and Lilly was relieved to see his anger dissolve. "Lilly," he said in his controlled bass, "you've cost this family a great deal this evening by your impulsiveness. You've shown bad judgment—"

"But what about—"

He held up a hand and silenced his daughter with a piercing look. "You're engaged to another man, Lilly. You've made a commitment to him, and you owe him your promise."

Lilly glanced at her mother. Her mother's eyes were wide, and she leaned forward in the rocker.

"I forbid you ever to see this Heinrick again, Lilly. You will stay home, and if you leave the house, you will be with Bonnie, Olive, or your parents." Her father lowered his voice. "When Reggie gets home, you will plead his forgiveness. And we will all hope and pray he forgives you and decides to marry you anyway."

Lilly felt as if he had slugged her. "Father, you can't want me to marry someone I don't love!"

He leaned back into the fraying sofa and put his wide weathered hands on his knees. "You do love Reggie, Lilly. You haven't seen him for over a year. You were lonely, and we can understand your vulnerability. But that's over. Reggie is coming home, and you'll see I'm right." His eyes kneaded her with a sudden tenderness, and Lilly's eyes filled with new tears. "Honey, I am doing this for you. For your own good." He glanced at his wife. "She'll thank me later."

Lilly couldn't look at her mother. Tears dripped off her chin, and she felt as if she'd just been dressed down like a six year old. She had less freedom than Frankie did. And her father was going to give her to a man she didn't love.

The realization hit her like a winter blast. She didn't love Reggie. How could that be? She'd grown up with him, practically worshiped him from the day he started teasing her at school. She thought he'd made her dreams come true when he asked her to marry him. Reggie was her life. How could she think she didn't love him?

But it was true. Somehow, she'd denied it, for how long she couldn't guess. Her feelings for Reggie were wrapped in a package of expectations, respect, and gratefulness. But Reggie couldn't make her heart soar. Only Heinrick could do that. Only Heinrick knew the real, unmasked Lilly, the afraid Lilly, the impulsive and even brave Lilly. He unearthed her innermost thoughts and embraced them with a touch of unconditional and breathtaking love. Lilly choked, feeling as if her father had tightened a noose around her neck. She had no choices. Trusting God, consulting Him, surrendering to His plans, whatever they were, were not a part of the equation. She had others to obey—her parents, Reggie.

Despair snuffed out the ember of hope that had burst into flame only earlier that evening.

Lilly hung her head. "Yes, Father."

❧

Darkness hovered like a fog over the wheat field. Lilly sat in the window seat, her head in her folded arms, her eyes swollen. Her father had dismissed her to her room an hour prior, but sleep was forgotten in the mourning of her heart. She slouched in the windowsill and felt a numbing cold creep over her.

Lilly rose and tiptoed toward her closet. Maybe her father would allow her a brief trip to the river to watch the sunrise. She needed the fingers of light to weave into her soul; and the maple grove, despite the memories it stored of Heinrick, was also the place God had spoken to her and reminded her to seek Him. He promised she would find Him when she looked for Him. Even when she'd been bereft over the loss of Reggie, God had carried her. He could carry her now.

She changed into a brown wool dress and long stockings and grabbed her knit gray shawl as she padded from her room.

Lilly approached the landing and heard her parents' muffled voices from the family room below. They had not gone to bed, either. Guilt burned in her chest, but she couldn't keep her curiosity from planting herself on the top step. Their conversation became distinct as she held her breath and ignored her pounding heart.

"My father felt the same way," her mother was saying. "Don't you remember the night you asked him for my hand? He nearly broke his arm throwing you out of the house."

Lilly's heart lightened to hear her father's soft chuckle. Then his voice turned solemn. "This is different, Ruth. I wasn't a foreigner. The world wasn't at war."

"No, you were from a different church. And you were poor. To my parents, that was worse."

Lilly wrapped her arms around her knees and concentrated to catch every word.

"And what about her new faith, Donald? You can't say Reggie brought her that."

"Reggie is a good man. He loves God and will guide her spiritually."

Her mother's harrumph ricocheted up the stairs. "If Reggie's belief in God is anything like Pastor Larsen's, I think it is Lilly who will teach him."

"Now, Ruth, Pastor Larsen is a wise man."

"Wise and firm. But is he kind? And what about Reggie? Will he treat Lilly with gentleness and love?"

"Of course he will. And he has a sound future in front of him. What kind of life can some German immigrant give her? Is that what we want for Lilly?"

"I don't think it's up to us, Donald. Lilly trusts us, but we need to let her make her own decisions."

"I'm her father. I have to look out for her."

Lilly sensed the texture of her mother's voice soften. She imagined her touching her husband softly on the arm, as was her habit. "Just like my father looked out for me and gave you a chance to prove your love. He knew I loved you, and he knew I thought God wanted me to marry you. So he waited in giving my hand until he was sure of the one God had chosen. God's given me a good life with you, dear. It may not have been an easy life, but it's been a joyful one."

Tears edged Lilly's eyes. She shouldn't be listening to their intimate conversation. She gathered herself to creep back to her room. But her father's last words burned in her ears.

"Ruth, you're a persuasive woman. If this fella can prove to me he loves her more than Reggie, I'll give him a chance."

Lilly stumbled to her room, stifling a cry. Her father would have let Heinrick prove himself! But it was too late. Heinrick had told her good-bye, and right now, he was probably lying in a pool of his own blood. Lilly threw herself on the bed next to Bonnie, curled into a ball, and wept.

Chapter 23

Get your paws off Christian," Olive snarled and turned her dark eyes on Lilly. Lilly slowly put the toddler back on the floor, where he'd been playing with a wooden spoon, and backed away from him. She avoided Olive's glare, but shuddered as she heard Olive slam a plate down at her place on the table. Olive acted as if Lilly's betrayal had singularly led to Chuck's death. It was more than a cold, aloof snubbing. Olive sizzled with hatred and was directing the blaze at Lilly.

Lilly felt like the apostle Paul, under Roman house arrest. She even envied the birds, the lark and crow, who scolded her, then lifted in flight over the prairie. What did their eyes see when they flew over the Torgesen T? Did they see Heinrick, well and hustling cattle? Or was he lying in a bunkhouse, bleeding, broken, near death? The horror of it assaulted her at odd times; while she hung laundry, when she dipped out water from the rain barrel, once when she milked the cows. And, despite her attempts to push the memory aside, she couldn't seem to escape the look of joy in his eyes when she told him she loved him.

Lilly mourned Heinrick in private, pouring out her tears late at night under cover of her quilt and praying for release from the grip of heartache. His magnetic blue eyes and tireless smile pressed against her, and there were times she felt crushed and thought she would break from the pain. Other times, the load seemed to lighten, as if some hand had lifted it from her heart. Lilly fought to put him out of her mind. From dawn to dusk, she buried herself in her chores, read her Bible, and hoped for dreamless, exhausted sleep. She relentlessly tried to believe her father's words—she'd simply been lonely and her feelings for Heinrick were built upon boredom. But, as the days turned over into weeks and October blew the fire-lit leaves of ash and maples into the yard, she realized a part of Heinrick would always be hers. He'd left her his legacy, the imprint of the force that defined his life—a personal relationship with the Lord of the universe. The key to joy incarnate was Heinrick's gift to her. For that freedom, she would always be grateful she'd met him.

❧

Lilly altered her wedding dress, finishing it the first week of November. She embroidered, white upon the white satin, a floral pattern designed from her own drying lilies of the valley, with oversized bells that cascaded down the skirt from the sculptured empire waistline. She removed the sheer lace overskirt and added the lace instead to the elbow-length sleeves. The wide, wispy cuffs were contrary to popular styles, but they were exactly what she wanted. She hung the dress over the door of her wardrobe.

"Lilly, it's breathtaking." Her mother folded her arms and leaned against the doorframe.

Grateful, Lilly smiled.

Her mother drew Lilly into her arms. "You'll be a beautiful bride."

Lilly nodded into her mother's shoulder.

Her mother pulled away and held her at arm's length. "I know you had hoped for something different. . . ."

She forced a smile. "No, Mother. I'm ready to marry Reggie."

Mother Clark's brows arched.

"I know it's the right thing to do."

Her mother flattened her smile and nodded, as if understanding. She laid a hand on Lilly's shoulder and squeezed gently, and Lilly wished she'd spoken the truth.

$\approx$

Lilly tucked her hair into a knit bonnet, pulled on a wool duster, and hustled out the door. Her family, minus Olive and Christian, were already headed into town.

Minutes ago, a rider on horseback had galloped through their yard, leaving in his wake the triumphant announcement—the Germans had surrendered to the Allied Forces somewhere in the middle of the French wilds. The war was over. Lilly watched the messenger tear north, toward the Torgesen T, and wondered how the news would greet Heinrick. He was no longer the enemy. She shoved the thought aside and caught up to her family. It didn't matter, anyway. Reggie would surely be home soon.

In town, forgiveness drifted on the crisp winter air. Mrs. Larsen, who had heretofore regarded Lilly with frigid eyes and an acid tongue, wrapped her in a two-armed hug and squeezed. "Now we can all get back to our lives," she whispered.

Main Street was packed, and Miller's did a thriving coffee and tea business while selling copies of the Armistice telegram that had sped across the country. Bonnie skipped down the steps of the pharmacy, waving the surrender details. Huddling next to her mother and listening as her father read the account, Lilly spied Marjorie standing in a clump of ecstatic women. Lilly tightened her jaw and ignored the stab in her heart.

The train whistle blew. Lilly took a deep breath and wondered if today, finally, she would receive word from Reggie. She had no address for him, had no idea where to send her own half-written scripts. But she didn't know what to say, either. They would have to sort it out when he came home, if he came home.

The train pulled into the station and coughed. The echo of it carried across town. Lilly made a mental note to check her box later.

She leaned forward and listened to her father finish the newspaper story. Her mother patted her hand. "Praise God, it's over."

Lilly could only nod. Finally, Mobridge could regroup, collectively mourn its losses, and rebuild. The community could patch the wounds, lay to rest the fears and the horror, and stumble forward into the future. Lilly knew they would find a way to hold onto the land, their legacies, and their love. They would survive.

A gasp washed like a wave through the clusters of gossiping townspeople. Lilly bristled, and an odd sensation rippled up her spine. She looked up and went weak.

"Hello, Lilly." Reggie stood in the middle of the street, his khaki uniform wrinkled under an open overcoat, his dress cap tilted crazily over his head, and a sprig of short black hair sticking out like a flagpole over his eyes. He smiled a smooth milky grin. He leaned forward, as if she hadn't heard him, and repeated himself. "Lilly?"

Lilly cried out and rushed toward his open arms.

Mrs. Larsen beat her to him. She clung to her son and wept. Reggie buried his head in his mother's neck and held her.

Lilly stood paralyzed. She waited, watching the wind toy with his hat, then knock it aloft. It fingered his short hair, lifted the collar of his coat, and carried to her the smell of wool and perspiration, confidence and strength. The smell of Reggie. She breathed in deeply.

Reggie finally extracted himself from his sobbing mother and stepped toward Lilly. She met his eyes and saw buried in them a thousand battles, not all with guns and bombs. Reggie reached out and slipped his hand around her neck. He paused, then in a desperate moment, drew her against him, burying his face in her hair. "Lilly," he groaned. "I feared I would never see you again."

She encircled his waist with her arms and pulled him close. They embraced while a hundred eyes watched them, measuring, considering. Lilly knew this was probably their last untarnished moment. Once his mother had him alone, she could reveal to him the indiscretions of his disobedient fiancée. If not her, then Marjorie, Ernestine, or even Olive. Somehow, the tale would emerge, and the unwavering trust between them that had been theirs before the war and now, in this magical moment, would be forever scarred. She clutched him tighter.

"You missed me," he said, his voice husky.

Lilly pulled back and stared into his wounded brown eyes. She felt the pricking of tears and nodded. A grin tugged at his mouth. "And I missed you."

Then he lowered his face and kissed her. It felt familiar and warm.

Reggie finally released her, pinned on her one last meaningful look, and then stepped into the multitude. Lilly let free a shuddering, cleansing breath. Hope had returned to the prairie in vivid intensity.

Mrs. Larsen pulled at Lilly's arm, her face close. "We'll be up tomorrow to discuss wedding plans."

Lilly nodded and saw Reggie disappear into the crowd.

❧

That night, as she and Bonnie were undressing for bed, Bonnie stole up behind her and placed a small parchment envelope on her vanity. Lilly stared at it and blanched. "Where did you get it?"

Bonnie looked at her, curiosity in her youthful eyes. "I picked it up at the post office today."

Lilly fingered the envelope and examined the bold, block letters. Her skin prickled.

"Is it from him?"

Lilly shot her sister a glance.

Bonnie shrugged and smiled mysteriously. "Sometimes you talk in your sleep."

Lilly swallowed hard.

Bonnie giggled. "Don't worry. Your secret is safe with me."

What secret? Lilly turned over the envelope in her hands and cautiously worked it open.

Short and dated the first week of October, the note made her tremble.

Dear Lilly,

I heard about your home, and I am sorry for the trouble I caused you. The Torgesens have released me from my contract, and I am leaving Mobridge. Thank you for your friendship; you are written upon my heart. The words from Ruth 2:12 speak my hope for you. May the good Lord repay you for your kindness. May He protect you and reward you. Go with God, Lilly.

Yours,
Heinrick

Lilly moaned and clutched the letter to her chest. He was gone, and somehow, with him, went the last shred of a love that had seemed so intoxicating, so breathtaking, so encompassing. And so right.

Lilly fell to her knees, buried her head into the crazy quilt, and sobbed. Bonnie knelt beside her and rubbed her back.

Why, on the day of Reggie's return, when peace should finally be hers, did she feel as though she were back in battle?

Chapter 24

I think we'll have a Thanksgiving wedding." Reggie tucked his hands in the pocket of his woolen gray duster and peered into Lilly's eyes. Sheltered in the grove of maples, the howl of the unrelenting wind didn't seem as loud and menacing. Lilly folded her mittened hands together and nodded, an acquiescing smile on her face. Two weeks seemed a mere blink away, but she'd been waiting for two years. The sooner it happened, the better.

Reggie studied her. "You've changed, Lilly. You seem, oh, I don't know, more serious. I expected my bubbly, carefree Lilly." His eyes clouded. "You seem pensive."

Lilly bit her lip.

Reggie turned away and propped up his collar. "You aren't even happy to see me."

Lilly's heart twisted. She put a hand on his arm. "Of course I am."

He turned and considered her a long moment. It seemed to Lilly he seemed shorter, not quite as towering as he'd been. And his dark eyes were sharper, older. His face was lean, his angled jaw cleanly shaven. She'd observed him all week, especially today at morning service, and noted he carried an unfamiliar air of wariness that could only be reaped by war. And once, when she'd slid her hand onto his arm while he gazed across the frost-covered fields, he'd nearly jumped out of his skin. His eyes brimmed with anger, and it took him a full painful five seconds to tuck some horrific moment into the folds of memory. But the residue of hatred frightened her.

Reggie pulled away from her touch and stalked out to the bluff. The breeze blew through his short hair. He stared across the river. "In France, this view was all I could think of. Home. Being with you. It seemed the only reason worth fighting. Whenever the commander yelled for us to attack and the blood froze in my veins, the thought of you waiting for me gave me the courage to climb over the barricades. One step at time, one shot at a time, I figured I was headed home."

Tears welled in Lilly's eyes. She edged toward him. "Why didn't you write? It's been three months since your telegram." Her voice cracked. "What happened?"

Reggie's voice hardened. "I couldn't write because I couldn't see. Some nurse sent the telegram for me." Rawness, as though the incident had happened yesterday, entered his tone. "I was hit by mustard gas the day Harley and Chuck were killed." He paused and drew in a deep breath. "Luckily, I shoved on my mask right after it hit, so I didn't get the worst of it. Instead, I saw my best buddies killed." Grief twisted his face. Lilly tugged on his arm and led him to a bleached cottonwood. He sat and hung his head in his hands.

Lilly tucked herself beside him.

"It was horrible. I couldn't breathe. After the fighting stopped, we crawled out of our bunkers and took off our masks. Then the torture began. My eyes felt as if they had been seared with a branding torch. They glued together, and my throat closed. It swelled up, and I couldn't swallow. I was choking."

Tears chilled Lilly's cheeks.

Reggie's voice dropped. "They had to strap me down."

Lilly gazed across the ice-edged river and conjured up a ghastly image of Reggie tied to a hospital bed. She felt ill and longed to close her ears to his words.

"All I could think of the entire time was you, Lilly. You and our future."

Lilly wrapped her arms around herself, pushing against physical pain.

Reggie turned to her. "I don't want to wait until Thanksgiving. I would marry you tomorrow if I could. I just want to get back to some kind of normalcy, the life I always dreamed of." He wrapped her upper arms in an iron grip and turned her to face him. "Please, say you will marry me, Lilly."

His brown eyes probed hers, and Lilly saw in them desperation and longing so intense, she knew she couldn't deny him. She couldn't cause him more pain. "Of course I will, Reggie."

He pulled her to himself and kissed her, powerfully, winding his arm around her neck and holding her tight.

❧

Lilly fled into her wedding plans. Somehow, tucked inside Reggie's grins and Mrs. Larsen's babbling, Lilly felt a measure of calm, as if she'd negotiated a cease-fire in her heart. She marched forward, toward the inevitable conclusion, and told herself this was right.

But tiny sputters of doubt began to explode deep inside her heart.

"I saw Erica Torgesen in town today," commented Reggie as they sat together on the porch steps, bundled and staring at the hazy sputter of the sun.

Lilly peered at him sideways.

"She asked if you had time to sew her something for the New Year's social." He gave her a stern eye, his mouth a firm line. "I took the liberty of telling her you wouldn't be doing that sort of thing anymore."

Lilly looked past him, north toward the Torgesen T, and said nothing.

Sunday, after church, Reggie closed in during the walk home. "Mother told me you haven't been attending the Ladies Aid meetings." His hand seemed rough on her arm. "I thought we agreed you would help with tea, Lilly."

She shot him a frown. Did she agree to help? Or had Reggie and Mrs. Larsen consented for her?

Lilly beat back the flames of doubt, however, with prayer and a patient spirit. She was just nervous, as any bride would be. She clung to the faith that God had her future in His hands and would lead her to a lifetime of joy. God would give her peace as she walked forward in faith. She just had to be patient.

❧

Snow peeled from the clouds in soft translucent layers and melted on the hard-packed road. Lilly meandered toward Mobridge, her hands tucked in a beaver skin muff, occasionally catching a few flakes on her tongue and nose. The sun was a glittering pumpkin, brilliant against a silver gray sky and frosting the bluffs orange.

Lilly sighed and picked up her pace. She was already late, expected by Mrs. Larsen and the others on the Ladies Aid committee to help decorate the church. Her family would join her in an hour or so, Olive and her mother each toting the Clark family's contribution to the Thanksgiving pie social—pumpkin and apple pies.

Next year she would be appearing with Mrs. Larsen, toting her own pie, as Reggie's wife. Reggie had already prepared a room for them at the Larsen home while he readied himself to take on a congregation of his own. He mentioned a year of preparation while he worked with his father and learned the "trade." Lilly had considered, with the anger that bubbled out occasionally when he mentioned Chuck, Harley, the Germans, or anything that had to do with the Great War, it might take him longer to find the peace to minister to others. But she'd clamped her mouth shut after he told her it was none of her business and asked how she could possibly understand his nightmares. So, she determined to find a way to live in the Larsen household until she could create one of her own.

Mrs. Larsen was thrilled at the thought of having another helping hand around the house and told her so.

The town was barren; the shops closed, customary on the day before Thanksgiving. Lilly heard the train whistle skip along the frozen prairie in the distance and recalled the days when she would race the wind to greet the mail train with a letter. It was a time of innocence and naive hopes, a lifetime apart from what she knew now—the reality, and cost, of love.

She rounded the armory and was passing Miller's when she spotted him. She almost didn't recognize the man, dressed in a pair of forest green woolen pants and a knee-length matching wool coat—standard issue brakeman's uniform for the Milwaukee Road. He could have been any other railroad man, toting a lead lantern, headed for work. But he wasn't. She knew him the minute her gaze traveled upward and took in the long blond hair trickling out in curls from his wool railroad cap.

"Heinrick," she breathed into the wind. He whirled and saw her.

He paused, as if determining the distance between them, in so many ways, then turned and strode toward her. As he drew closer, she reached out her hand. He caught it in his and purposefully led her to the small alley between Bud's and the armory, where they had nearly kissed and been discovered. Where her heart had entwined hopelessly and forever with his.

Heinrick set down his lantern and glanced into the empty street. He released her hand, gripped her upper arms, and pinned his eyes to hers. "Lilly."

Lilly's breath caught. She heard in his raw tone and saw in his eyes what she hoped for—a longing for her, a missing so intense it was etched into his heart.

"Are you all right?" she whispered.

He cracked a crooked grin, and Lilly's heart thumped.

"I'm all right."

Three words, and yet with them, fear broke free and relief crested over her. Her voice shook. "I've been so worried, Heinrick. Clive said he was going to hurt you, teach you a lesson."

Heinrick closed his eyes and nodded. "Well, he tried, that's for sure." Then he opened his eyes and they twinkled with a familiar mischief. "But, those boys never fought a man who worked shoveling sand ten hours a day. Besides, Erica Torgesen doesn't like roughhousing, and she put it to Clive to either let me go or leave me be."

Lilly squinted at him, noting an unfamiliar scar above his left eye. She wondered what he wasn't telling her. Lilly arched her brows. "So Clive let you go?"

"Ja. Did you get my note?"

Lilly nodded.

"I wrote it after I got my job on the line. I was passing through here and dropped it off."

Heinrick looked away. "I have bad timing."

Lilly frowned, then remembered the day she'd received his letter. The day Reggie came home.

"You saw Reggie."

Heinrick's mouth was pinched, and when he looked at her, hurt ringed his eyes. "I'm very happy for you, Lilly."

Lilly's eyes misted.

"I'm stationed in Sioux Falls, now. I just stopped in today to pick up some gear I had in storage." He nodded to a rucksack on his back.

He bent to grab his lantern, as if intending to say good-bye and walk out of her life forever.

"Heinrick, wait." Lilly stepped toward him, not really knowing what she wanted to say, but realizing she had to say something, anything to keep him there long enough for her to know. . . .

Heinrick paused and looked down at her, almost wincing. He reached for a rebellious strand of hair that had loosened from her bonnet and rubbed its softness between his fingers.

"Lilly, I can't take you away from Reggie. You have to choose, on your own. You have to come to me freely. Because if you don't, you'll be exchanging one prison for another."

He dropped her hair, ran his finger along her jaw, then lifted her chin. "More than that, you must do what God wants you to do."

Lilly opened her mouth, and her thoughts spilled out. "But I don't know what that is."

Heinrick considered her a long moment. "Have you asked Him and really listened for the answer?"

Lilly gave him a blank look while her mind sifted through his question. He was right. She'd never seriously listened to God's answer, never considered any reply but the one she already knew.

But it was too late to change course. Her wedding was two days away. She shook her head.

Heinrick's jaw stiffened. "Then I can't make your decision for you." The train whistle screamed as it pulled into the station. "I have to go, Lilly. May God bless your marriage." He turned away.

Lilly put a hand on his arm and folded her fingers into the wool. "I have to know, Heinrick." Her tone betrayed her heart.

He frowned.

"Do you love me?"

His mouth curved wryly, and she thought she saw a flicker of sadness in his stormy blue eyes. He covered her hand with his own. "I've loved you since the day you saved me on the street."

"I thought you said you didn't need any help."

His voice turned raw. "I needed help, Lilly. I needed, more than anything, for someone to walk beside me, to be my friend and encourage me to fight for a place in this country." He touched her cheek. "God sent you to do that for me. And now, because of you, I have a future here." His gaze lingered on her, and she felt the strength of his feelings sweep through her.

Then, he snatched the lantern and strode away. And, with each long step, Lilly knew he was taking with him her heart.

Chapter 25

Lilly headed for the cloakroom and pulled off her coat. Mechanical. Steadfast. Resolute. She walked into the sanctuary and presented herself for service. Alice Larsen shot her a scowl. Lilly ignored it.

The pews in the small sanctuary were pushed back against the walls, creating a large square gap in the center. Two cloth-covered tables lined the center of the room, a throne for the pies.

Ernestine put her to work lighting candles. Lilly glanced out a window. Pellet-sized snowflakes fell from the darkening sky and covered the fields in a thick blanket. Families began to stream in, pies gathering on the two tables. Lilly smiled, nodded, and greeted.

Her mother and Olive arrived and added their pies to the table. Bonnie peeled layers of wraps off DJ and Frankie. Her father came in, a film of crystalline snow on his wool jacket. "We're in for it, folks," he commented wryly.

Rev. Larsen offered Mr. Clark his hand. "Nothing like the winter of 1910, though. It started snowing in June that year and didn't let up till the following July!"

Lilly's father guffawed and pumped the preacher's arm.

Lilly slid up to the two men. "Excuse me, Reverend. Do you know where Reggie is?"

Rev. Larsen raised his eyebrows. "Lost track of him already, Lilly? And you aren't even married yet!" He eyed her father, who smirked.

Lilly blushed. Rev. Larsen put a hand on her shoulder. "He rode out earlier with Clive Torgesen and some of the other boys, hunting pheasants. He'll be here."

The crowd thickened quickly. The Thanksgiving pie feast was akin to the fair in terms of pie competition. Everyone had a favorite. Lilly favored Jennifer Pratt's vanilla crème. She surveyed the crowd but didn't find either Marjorie or the Pratt family.

Rev. Larsen led them in a time of Thanks-sharing, then the pies were attacked. DJ and Frankie grabbed their favorites, a tart crabapple from the Ed Miller family and a fresh peach from Ernestine's, which Willard admitted he'd made. Lilly accepted a bite of each, but wasn't hungry for her own. Her thoughts were occupied with a still missing Reggie, and Heinrick.

The crowd began to scatter, the adults bundling up the children for the ride home.

"Coming with us, Lilly?" Her mother's voice carried over the room as she tugged DJ's cap over his ears.

Lilly shook her head. "No. I'll wait for Reggie."

Her father looked worried. "Don't stay out too long, Lilly. That storm is whippin' up."

Lilly helped clear tables with the Ladies Aid, but avoided the women when they clumped in gossip. The wind outside began to moan, but it drew her to the church entrance. Perhaps a blast of cold air could untangle the knot in her heart. Pulling on her coat, she cracked the door open and slipped outside. The wind encircled her, groaning in her ears, and pawing at her coat. She stuck her hands in the pockets and wrapped it around her.

Instinctively, her hand closed around an object in the well of her pocket. She pulled it out and her heart tumbled. Heinrick's butterfly comb. She turned over the exquisite gift, and the dull, throbbing wound in her heart ripped open.

How had it landed in her pocket? She shifted through memory and found the day when she'd pulled it from her drawer and tried it on. The ginger-colored wings illuminated the few gold threads in her hair, and Lilly had left it in as she read her Bible that morning. She'd lost herself in the Beatitudes and completely forgotten the butterfly comb until she made ready to run into town with Bonnie for supplies. The comb had tangled in her wool bonnet. She'd pulled it off and slipped it into her coat pocket.

Tears welled in her eyes. Heinrick had given her a gift of his heritage. To complement her gift to him—his future.

"What are you doing out here, Lillian?" Mrs. Larsen's crisp tone scattered Lilly's thoughts. Mrs. Larsen yanked Lilly inside and shut the door behind her. "What's the matter with you, are you trying to make yourself sick?" The older woman pushed her toward the sanctuary.

Lilly bit the inside of her mouth and tried in vain to conceal her tears. But they spilled out. Mrs. Larsen looked at her, her brow puckered. "Reggie will be fine, dear."

Lilly watched her pinched, soon-to-be mother-in-law join a group of cackling women and suddenly knew only one thing: She couldn't marry Reggie. She couldn't spend the rest of her life living a halfhearted love. She whirled and made for the door.

The door shuddered open just as she laid a hand on the latch. Reggie caught her as she stumbled forward.

"Where're you goin'?"

Her breath left her, and words locked in her mouth.

"You weren't going to wait for me?" Reggie's dark brows folded together. "What's this?" He snatched the comb from her hand. Turning it over, he examined it. His face darkened. "Where did you get this?"

Lilly balled her hands in her coat pockets. He looked at her, read her face. Then gave a sharp intake of breath, as if he'd been stabbed. He stared at her, shaking. "So it's true, then."

Her eyes widened.

"I know all about it, Lilly." His face tightened into a glare. "I know all about how you disgraced me, how you *kissed* another man, a German."

She saw the hate pulsing in his eyes, and her mouth went dry. She shuffled back into the church foyer. *Help me, Lord.*

"No, Reggie. You don't understand—"

Reggie hurled the comb out into the darkness. Then he stepped inside and pulled the door shut. The world seemed suddenly, intensely, still.

Lilly's pulse roared in her ears.

Reggie sucked in a deep breath. He spoke quietly, through clenched teeth. "I can't believe you betrayed me with a German! If you were going to be unfaithful, couldn't you have chosen an American?"

Lilly's knees shook. "I'm sorry, Reggie."

Reggie must have detected her fear, for his glower softened, leaving only cool, stony eyes. He backed Lilly into the wall, put a hand over her shoulder, and leaned close. She felt his hot breath on her face and couldn't move. He seemed to be making an effort to keep his voice calm. "Listen, Lilly, I'm willing to marry you anyway. Because you're mine and all I've ever wanted."

She fixed her eyes at the snow melting on his shoes, not wanting to speak the truth. But she owed him honesty. She'd never sent the letter she'd written explaining everything, so he didn't know. Didn't know the painful news about Heinrick, yes, but he also didn't know about the joy and life she'd found. He didn't know that God could change the plans, and everything could still turn out all right, even better, for both of them.

She summoned her courage. "But I don't know if that's what God wants," she said softly.

He took it like a blow and recoiled. "What?"

"I don't know if I am supposed to marry you, Reggie. I don't know if that is what God wants. I, we've, never really asked Him."

Reggie frowned at her. "Of course not! We don't have to ask God whom we're to marry. We just decide what we want, and if we do it right, He blesses us. God doesn't care whom we marry. He just wants us to go to church, to obey His commandments, to do what is right."

"I think He does care. I think He cares so much that if we don't ask Him, it's a sin."

Reggie blew out an exasperated breath. "Lilly, what do you know? I'm the one who is going to be a pastor." He looked at her steadily. "I want you. That's enough for me. Even though you betrayed me. Doesn't that prove my love for you?"

Confusion rocked her. Reggie's love felt constricting, suffocating—so different from Heinrick's.

"I don't need God's blessing to marry you."

Lilly raised wide eyes, thunderstruck. Embedded in Reggie's words, she discovered what was missing from their future, their plans, and her heart. She realized why her soul had never been, could never be, at peace about her marriage to Reggie. She didn't feel God's blessing.

"I. . .I can't marry you right now," Lilly stated in a faltering voice. "I have to wait on God. I have to know what He wants. Because I know He loves me, I want His plans for my life."

Reggie pounded his chest and stared at her, desperation punctuating his voice. "*I'm* His plan for your life!" He raked a hand through his snow-crusted hair. "Maybe Mother was right. I should have picked Marjorie." His expression darkened. "At least she would have been faithful."

Lilly felt a cold fist squeeze her heart.

Reggie's voice turned wretched. "But I chose you. You were the one I wanted. I've been planning this for years." He punched the wall behind her. Lilly trembled. "It isn't fair, Lilly. I've been through hell itself, and I return to find that someone's stolen my girl?"

Reggie's voice curdled in pain. Lilly closed her eyes, feeling ill. He was right. This wasn't what he deserved. But they couldn't base their marriage, the rest of their lives, on pity.

"It wasn't like that," Lilly said evenly. She opened her eyes. "Heinrick didn't steal me. But you're right. It isn't fair. Not to you—or me!" She thumped her own chest. "I found something, Reggie. I found God. I found freedom and joy." Her voice slowed. "And maybe that's how God wanted it. Maybe He wanted to give us some distance so we could see He had something better for us. That's how it's supposed to be, I think. His will and not ours, and that's better, even when it doesn't make sense."

Reggie buried his head in his forearm. "This can't be God's will. God wouldn't take you away from me. Don't throw our lives, my life, away."

He drew back and fixed her with a desperate intensity, as if, by his gaze, he could control her bizarre thinking. "Lilly, listen, you belong to me. You don't have a choice."

Lilly put a hand on her chest and pushed back an odd panic. "I do have a choice. You can't force me to love you. If you make me marry you, it still doesn't mean I'll love you. Love can't be forced or, for that matter, earned. It has to be a free gift. Like God's love for us, and ours for Him."

Reggie looked away. "He doesn't deserve our love."

Lilly winced at his words. She understood all too well. He believed God had let him down in leading him somewhere dark and painful.

"He *does* deserve our love, Reg, because He loved us first. He saved us when we didn't deserve it—still don't! But He loves us anyway. And we have to trust Him. We count on His love and His strength, and we surrender to His will. Because if we don't, I think we can never have peace."

"We get peace by obeying. By doing what we know is right. We don't have to ask; it's all written out for us."

Lilly leaned her head against the wall and sighed.

Reggie looked at her, his eyes narrowing. "I don't know what you think God wants, but I know this, Lilly. If you don't tell me right now you will marry me, then I don't want you."

She gaped at him and saw years of careful planning melt in the heat of his fury.

"I can't say yes," she whispered. "Not until I'm sure we have God's blessing, and right now, I don't know."

Reggie crossed his arms over his chest and stepped back. His face was granite, and he said nothing.

Lilly muffled a small cry as the reality of her words hit her. She ran past him, threw open the door, and flung herself into the swelling blizzard. Scrambling away from the church, she ran everywhere and nowhere and straight into the blindness and pain of her surrender. Though faint and swallowed by the moan of the wind, Lilly thought she heard a voice trail her. "Lilllyyyy!"

Chapter 26

Lilly hugged her body and ducked her head against the snarling wind. Under the coal black sky, Lilly couldn't even discern her feet. She shivered as snow gathered on her neck.

She had no idea how far she'd run. But her feet were numb, and she shivered violently. She felt the fool. She'd plunged not only into the blizzard, but also into a life without Reggie, without the plans of her family or her church.

"What am I doing, Lord?"

The wind roared and spun her. She stumbled, then pitched forward. The snow climbed into her sleeves, layered her chin. She realized over a foot had accumulated. Lost and in the middle of a Dakota blizzard, she felt panic crest over her. "O God, help me!"

Climbing to her feet, she whacked the snow out of her sleeves. She tucked her hands into her pockets, wiggled her chin into her coat, and struggled forward. Her hair felt crusty and the wind whined in her ears. Lilly heaved one foot in front of the other, no longer able to feel the swells and ruts of the prairie landscape.

The bodily struggle felt easier than the war she waged against the angry voices in her head. She fought to filter through them, to hear only one. *What is Your will, Lord?*

If she'd asked earlier and had the courage to listen and obey, maybe she wouldn't be stumbling in the cold darkness.

She could no longer feel her legs. They seemed like sticks, and, at times, she wondered if she were truly moving or merely standing still. She was so tired; she just wanted to close her eyes. Couldn't she just rest a moment? Her ears burned, her hair was frozen, and her head throbbed.

She hit something head on, and it knocked her on her backside. *Lord, is this it? Will I die because of my impulsiveness?* She rolled to all fours, gritted her teeth, and reached through the darkness. Her hand banged against something solid. She traced it upward and discovered metal at head height. A handle. Sliding her wrist around it, she heaved it open.

The smell of hay and manure had never been so sweet. Lilly crawled inside, feeling the heat of barn animals warm her face and filter through her clothing. She heard the snuffing of hay, the low of a cow. Fumbling forward, she bumped into a bucket of water, tipping it over. The water doused her hands and knees and felt like fire against her skin. Lilly pulled herself to her feet, knees quaking. Her head spun multi-colors. Groaning, she shuffled the length of the barn, clasping the stalls with her stinging hands until she discovered a mound of hay stacked in an empty paddock. Collapsing into it, she clawed out a hole. Then she climbed inside and curled into a ball. She knew she shouldn't sleep, but, oh, how sleep called her name, moving over her slowly, laying like a blanket upon her eyelids.

Lilly blew on her hands. *Thank You, Lord, for this place.* She tucked her legs under her coat. She must stay awake. She recalled stories of victims who had succumbed to sleep and frozen under a mound of crusted snow. Sleep was her enemy.

If she could stay awake, she was safe for the moment. But a much larger storm lurked outside the barn doors. Eventually they would find her, discover what she'd done, how she'd hurt Reggie. Then what? Heinrick was gone. Even if she could somehow find him and declare her love, what kind of life would that be? Outcasts, shunned by her family, her community. Living life as strangers in some foreign town. Lilly shook her head as if to exorcise the images. Besides, was Heinrick God's choice for her?

She kept returning to the lack of the blessing for which her soul seemed to scream. And what had her mother said so long ago? Marriage was too difficult for halfhearted commitment. And something else about missing out on the fullness of joy God had planned for her.

Lilly buried her face in her hands. *Lord, what should I do? What do You want for me?* She closed her eyes and listened, aching to discern an audible voice. But the only things she heard were echoes, impressions from things she'd read, illustrations from Matthew about Jesus, the way He reached out in love, extreme in His pursuing of the people who rejected Him. They clung instead to the law, to an old way that would lead to death, most certainly beyond the grave, but in large part to death in life, also. A death of joy, a death of an exhilarating relationship with Christ.

Reggie was that death. That thought became the one clear beacon in her sleep-fogged mind. Reggie was the law. He clung to a religion that created laws that led to salvation rather than a salvation that led to obedience. It was a stagnant, suffocating, demoralizing religion. And it had been hers as well.

Until Heinrick introduced her to a God who loved her enough to die for her, when she was the most wretched of sinners, then gave her the choice to respond to Him in love. It was the ultimate love affair. Love given, not demanded. Love offered unconditionally.

Suddenly she knew she could never be trapped inside the circle of suffocation again. Better to fling herself out into an unknown dark blizzard and into the arms of her Savior than cling to a life that threatened to choke her.

Even if she could never see Heinrick again, even if he wasn't God's choice for her, she knew she could never return to the law, to Reggie. The resolve deepened with every warming heartbeat.

The straw crunched as she settled deeper into her well. She took a cleansing breath. She'd asked God and listened, and the Almighty had answered clearly.

She would wait for His choice, His blessing. One day at a time, she would surrender to His plans. She would ask, seek, and find. And she would live in the fullness of joy.

The door at the end of the barn rattled, groaned, and then pushed inward. The snow screamed as it entered, rolled around the startled animals, and ushered in a figure wrapped in wool. Lilly bolted upright. Her heart hammered as she peered through the padding of darkness.

The hooded figure raised a massive lead lantern, glowing blue from one of its brilliant orbs. It cast eerie gray shadows off the haystacks and caught the cows wide-eyed. "Lilly?"

Perhaps she was already asleep, and this was a dream. "Heinrick?"

He swung the lamp toward her voice, his feet crunching cold, stiff hay. From his muffler dripped a layer of snowy diamonds, and his eyebrows stuck out in frosty spikes. His blue eyes, however, blazed.

"Over here." Lilly's heart thundered as she fought to believe her eyes.

Heinrick closed the gap in two giant steps. "Oh, thank You, Lord." He set the lantern down, dropped to his knees, and reached out his frosted arms. He pulled her to his chest and tucked her head under his chin. His heart banged in his strong chest, and she felt relief shudder out of him. He held her long enough to betray the depth of his worry.

When he released her, he pulled off his gloves and clutched her face with his icy hands. "Are you all right?" He looked her over, head to toe.

Lilly closed her eyes and nodded.

"Ja, but you are freezing!" Heinrick peeled off his coat.

"How did you find me?"

He tucked the coat around her. "By the grace of God, Lilly." He dusted the last snow off the collar and avoided her eyes.

Lilly squinted at him. "I thought you left town. What happened?"

"The train got snowed in." He began to knock down hay. "I was headed toward Fannie's when I saw you run out into the storm." The hay fell in quiet rustles around her. He worked steadily, mutely, and she knew something was amiss. Had he heard her fight with Reggie? Heinrick didn't stay quiet unless he was fighting a battle. Then he was a man of few words and a set jaw.

She watched him build a tiny castle of insulation. The heat from Heinrick's coat was warming her with the effect of a roaring fire. But the fact he'd found her in the middle of a whiteout heated her from the inside out. This had to be her answer, her audible voice. Just like the voice calling through the mists of the battlefield in her dream, Heinrick had searched through a blizzard for her. Loving him would cost her everything, but as she embraced the idea, the fragrance of peace was so intense, she gasped.

Heinrick was God's answer. He'd been trying to tell her for months. From the moment Heinrick had nearly run her over with a mustang, to the day he sent her the note committing her to the Lord, God had written Heinrick on her heart and filled her mind with his voice. Only Heinrick loved her the way God wanted a husband to love—unconditionally, fully, and sacrificially. Only Heinrick pointed her to the Savior.

Heinrick crawled inside his fortress, then threaded an arm around her and pulled her against his muscled chest. "We'll stay here until the storm breaks. Then I'll take you home."

"I am home." Lilly tilted her head to look at him.

Heinrick considered her, his arched brows like a drift of fine snow. "Lilly, you're cold and confused. I saw you run from the church, and I saw Reggie standing in the door. You had a fight, that's all. Things will look better after the storm blows over."

"I am home, Heinrick," Lilly repeated emphatically. "Home is where God puts you. It's being with those you love. It's where you have peace, remember?"

Heinrick gave her a slow nod.

"I have peace with you. I think *you* are my home."

A rueful grin slid onto Heinrick's face. "But I am the enemy, Lilly. A foreigner."

Lilly put a hand on his cold, whiskered face. "Do you remember your last note? You quoted Ruth, when she made the ultimate act of commitment. Let me finish it for us." Lilly closed her eyes and paraphrased, "Don't urge me to leave you or turn back from you. Your people will be my people, and your God my God."

Heinrick placed his hand over hers. It belonged there. "And you will be blessed because you left your home and traveled to a foreign land."

"Ja," Lilly said.

Heinrick winced at her terrible German impression. Then, growing serious, his intentions pooled in his eyes for a second time. He ran a finger under her chin; she lifted her face to his and let him kiss her. It was gentle, lingering, and full of promise.

Lilly pulled away, her eyes wide, and saw that his own were dancing. "You do love me."

"Ja, my Lilly, I love you." He kissed her again, and she knew she had never loved Reggie like she loved this man.

Suddenly, she pulled away and groaned. "Heinrick, what about my parents? I told Reggie I didn't want to marry him. I told him I had to wait until I knew what God wanted, until I had His blessing. But I can't get married without my parents' blessings, either."

Heinrick caressed her face. "And do you know what God wants? Do you have His blessing?"

"Yes."

His eyes glowed with an unmistakable passion. "Jacob worked fourteen years for the woman he loved, and it seemed to him but a moment for his love for her. I am a patient man. I will wait until I am no longer the enemy."

Then he leaned back, the straw protesting, and nestled her against his chest. She warmed and eventually slept. He held her until the sun rose and chased away the irate wind and kissed the fields with tiny golden sparkles.

"See, the prairie is the ocean," said Lilly as Heinrick helped her through waves of crested snow.

Heinrick laughed. "I crossed it, my sweet Lilly, to find you."

Epilogue

They had planned a Thanksgiving Day wedding, and when Lilly awoke that morning and saw the pink beads of dawn glinting off the snow-blanketed fields in heavenly magnificence, she knew Heinrick was right. Thanksgiving was the perfect day to commit their lives to one another; after all, it was a celebration of God's grace and salvation after a season of struggle. Lilly counted it as a miracle that it had taken only a year for her father to consent to their marriage.

"Are you ready?" Bonnie asked. Lilly glanced at her sister, whose joy was evident in her teenage smile and dancing eyes. Lilly nodded. She cast one last look at the prairie from the window seat in her bedroom. Giant waves of snow, halted in mid crest, leaped across the fields, the sun's rays glancing off them like a golden mist. It was glorious, the aftermath of a Dakotan blizzard. The contrast between the fury and the calm never ceased to amaze her, just like peace that filled her heart after a difficult surrender.

Lilly felt a warm hand on her shoulder. She turned, and her mother's gentle eyes were on her. "He's waiting," she said softly, a smile tugging at her lips.

Lilly stood, brushed off her slip, and stepped into the wedding gown her sister held. A twinge of regret stabbed her; she wished Marjorie were here. But her friend's wounds were deep, and Lilly knew healing would be long in coming. Lilly's prayers for Marjorie were constant, as were her prayers for Reggie. She hadn't seen him since the night of the fateful blizzard a year ago and heard he'd left to find his fortune in the Black Hills gold mines. It hurt her to know she'd caused his flight, and she prayed he would find peace, as would her sister Olive. Olive continued to live in the shadow of grief, crawling through each day without words or hope. Although her sister's form was present downstairs, her spirit was still locked inside a prison of despair. Lilly knew only Christ held the keys to her freedom.

Bonnie buttoned up the dress in back while Lilly fiddled with the veil.

"You're beautiful," her mother said, and Lilly caught a glistening in her eye. "I'm so glad you waited for the Lord's choice."

Lilly nodded and bit her lip to keep her own eyes from filling.

Her sister and mother left her alone, then, to sort out her last moments. Lilly listened to shuffling below, then the sound of Willard, plunking out a hymn on the piano. The stairs creaked, and Lilly recognized the footfalls of her father. She pulled a calming breath and felt a wave of peace fill her just as a rap sounded on the door.

Lilly opened the door. Her father looked dapper in a black woolen suit. A smile creased his face, but tears in his eyes choked his voice. "This would be more difficult if Heinrick wasn't such a good man."

His words left her speechless, so she wound her arm through his and nodded.

Her father patted her hand and escorted her down the stairs. The parlor overflowed with guests, a smaller crowd than would have been at the church, but even so, a solid, well-wishing crew. At the end of the room, next to the fireplace, which glowed, waited Heinrick. He appeared every inch the hero she knew him to be. His blond hair was clipped short, but the curly locks refused to lie flat. She noticed his clean-shaven chin and the outline of thick muscles over his tailored navy blue suit. His job as brakeman on the Milwaukee Road and part-time hand on the Clark farm kept him in good shape and had cultivated in him an aura of confidence. He'd become a man who made others feel safe and comfortable.

Lilly's heart fluttered as Heinrick's blue eyes locked on hers. Then his mouth gaped in an open smile, and written on his face was a tangible delight. She wanted to sing. He was a hard man to unsettle, but obviously the sight of his bride had unraveled his stalwart composure. She floated toward Heinrick and the new preacher from Java, noting the happiness glinting in her mother's eyes and others who thought, a year earlier, Heinrick was the enemy.

Even Erica Torgesen was radiant, grinning uncontrollably in her new sky blue wool suit. Lilly slid her hand into Heinrick's gentle grip and felt embraced by the love shimmering in his eyes. In a trembling voice, Heinrick pledged to love and care for her as long as they lived. Then, he cradled her face between his wide hands and kissed her. At that moment, Lilly knew she would be forever thankful to God for bringing the enemy into her midst.

Rose gold sunshine flooded the room as they marched down the aisle. And, as Lilly glanced up at her young, handsome husband, she knew, one step at a time, she was walking in the fullness of joy.

Susan May Warren

Susan is the award-winning, best-selling novelist of over twenty novels, many of which have won Inspirational Readers Choice awards and ACFW Book of the Year awards in addition to qualifying as Christy and Rita finalists. Her compelling plots and unforgettable characters have won her acclaim with readers and reviewers alike. She and her husband of twenty years live in a small town with their four children on Minnesota's beautiful Lake Superior shore where they are active in their local church.

A Letter to Our Readers

Dear Readers:

In order that we might better contribute to your reading enjoyment, we would appreciate your taking a few minutes to respond to the following questions. When completed, please return to the following: Fiction Editor, Barbour Publishing, Inc., P.O. Box 719, Uhrichsville, OH 44683.

1. Did you enjoy reading *Prairie Hills*?
   ❏ Very much—I would like to see more books like this.
   ❏ Moderately—I would have enjoyed it more if _____
   _____
   _____

2. What influenced your decision to purchase this book?
   (Check those that apply.)
   ❏ Cover   ❏ Back cover copy   ❏ Title   ❏ Price
   ❏ Friends   ❏ Publicity   ❏ Other

3. Which story was your favorite?
   ❏ *Treasure in the Hills*   ❏ *Letters from the Enemy*
   ❏ *The Dreams of Hannah Williams*

4. Please check your age range:
   ❏ Under 18   ❏ 18–24   ❏ 25–34
   ❏ 35–45   ❏ 46–55   ❏ Over 55

5. How many hours per week do you read? _____

Name _____

Occupation _____

Address _____

City_____ State_____ Zip _____

E-mail_____

♡

HEARTSONG
PRESENTS

If you love Christian romance...

$10.⁹⁹

You'll love Heartsong Presents' inspiring and faith-filled romances by today's very best Christian authors. . .Wanda E. Brunstetter, Mary Connealy, Susan Page Davis, Cathy Marie Hake, and Joyce Livingston, to mention a few!

When you join Heartsong Presents, you'll enjoy four brand-new, mass market, 176-page books—two contemporary and two historical—that will build you up in your faith when you discover God's role in every relationship you read about!

Mass Market, 176 Pages

Imagine. . .four new romances every four weeks—with men and women like you who long to meet the one God has chosen as the love of their lives—all for the low price of $10.99 postpaid.

To join, simply visit www.heartsongpresents.com or complete the coupon below and mail it to the address provided.

✂- -

YES! Sign me up for Heart♥ng!

NEW MEMBERSHIPS WILL BE SHIPPED IMMEDIATELY!
Send no money now. We'll bill you only $10.99 postpaid with your first shipment of four books. Or for faster action, call 1-740-922-7280.

NAME_____

ADDRESS_____

CITY_____ STATE _____ ZIP _____

**MAIL TO: HEARTSONG PRESENTS, P.O. Box 721, Uhrichsville, Ohio 44683
or sign up at WWW.HEARTSONGPRESENTS.COM**